About the Author

Born in Winchester in 1991, William grew up in Hong Kong before returning to England where he graduated from Durham University with a degree in Natural Sciences. William first started work on the Ragnarok Saga while studying Mandarin in Beijing. Currently working in London, William splits his spare time between writing and rugby.

To Emily, Oliver and Alice, for your help and encouragement, and with huge thanks to everyone at Austin Macauley for all their hard work in getting *The Rusted Crown* to print.

W H H Baker

THE RAGNAROK SAGA: THE RUSTED CROWN

AUSTIN MACAULEY
PUBLISHERS LTD.

A CIP catalogue record for this title is available from the British Library.

ISBN 9781785543876 (Paperback)
ISBN 9781785543883 (Hardback)
ISBN 9781785543890 (E-Book)

www.austinmacauley.com

First Published (2016)
Austin Macauley Publishers Ltd.
25 Canada Square
Canary Wharf
London
E14 5LQ

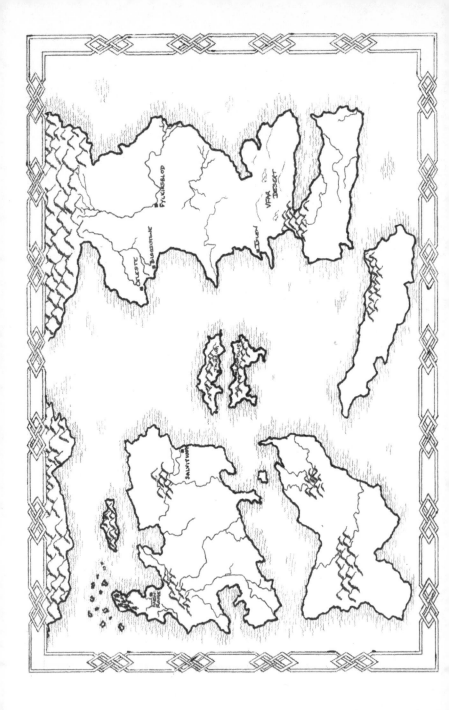

Chapter 1

Skjarla cheered as the two bearded Einherjar to her left slammed their drinking horns to the table. She roared again as they reached for another, resolute in their quest to match the consumption of Thor. It never ceased to make her smile; every night Bjalfi and Bryn would do their best to keep pace with the Thunder God. They would always fall short, wake the next morning with pounding hangovers, and then try again the next evening. Such was the raucous life of the people of Valhalla, fighting all day and feasting all night, preparing for Ragnarok in the immortal halls of Odin One-Eye. The dark, weathered timbers of the mead hall stretched for nearly a mile, packed with Gods, Ljosalfar and Einherjar, all banging the table as they guzzled horn after horn of honeyed mead. Fires separating the tables of warriors roared with the revellers, the flames crackling and spitting as fat from the slowly turning carcasses dripped into the bright orange flames.

She smiled across at Reginlief, one of her Valkyrie Shield sisters. Her friend's straw blond hair and ice white skin mirrored her own yet the Reginlief's eyes were unique in that they shifted colours like the rainbow bridge Bifrost. Skjarla's were more human, the dark green of Ygdrassil's leaves. The two of them were the first amongst the Valkyries. They were the finest warriors and Odin's favourites, both fearless leaders and beautiful beyond measure. Skjarla grinned as she stood, raising the brimmed mead horn, feeling some of the amber liquid within slosh over onto her hand. In one breath she poured the rich mead down her throat, belching loudly to the uproarious cheers when she slammed the now empty horn back onto the bench. The revelry in Valhalla had been unusually loud recently, the death of Baldr and the imminent advent of Ragnarok had put everyone on edge, driving the residents of Valhalla to savour every moment of their immortal existence. Even the Aesir, the Gods themselves, seemed to feel their mortality more keenly these days.

Skjarla glanced along the length of the wooden hall to the high table, and saw Odin feeding chunks of steaming beef to his two ravens, Hugin and Munin. The All-father had a weathered, craggy face, dominated by the dark and twisted scar of his missing eye, given up in return for the gift of prophecy. He and half a dozen Aesir were still sat at the top table, draining mead horn after mead horn. The other Aesir were scattered about the great hall of Valhalla, drinking and cavorting with those who shared that crazed paradise. Skjarla felt a chill as Skadi, the icy goddess of hunting, came up beside her. Skjarla always felt as if Skadi was looking straight into her soul. The goddess's frozen blue skin and penetrating white eyes always set her on edge.

"A battle going on below Valkyrie, I would gather your sisters for the ride," Skadi sounded mournful and resigned. Every being within Valhalla knew of the inevitable outcome of Ragnarok, yet it was agreed that the more heroes they had then the greater the chance of them carving the legacy of Asgard into the stones of Midgard. For that they would need Einherjar, warriors brought to Valhalla by the Valkyries. "You know as well as I do," she continued as she rubbed her hands along the worn limbs of her thick bow, "We need every warrior we can get for the day when Ygdrassil shakes and our world is rent and sundered."

Skjarla nodded to the cold faced goddess, all levity from the evenings feasting evaporating in an instant, and turned to stalk out through the great doors of the hall.

The sounds of revelry chased her outside as she made her way across the packed earth of the courtyard, her breath steaming in the cool night air. The trees that were scattered around the space were in full flush of life, green leaves whispering in the gentle breeze, as they always did in the endless summer of Asgard. Skjarla strode across to her chambers, pulling on her armour and strapping the two blades she used across her back, no Valkyrie went to harvest souls unarmed. The last thing she did before stepping out beneath the starry sky was to grab her twin headed spear, Dreyrispa, Prophecy of Blood. Although most Valkyries carried a shield, Skjarla much preferred the graceful motions of spinning Dreyrispa about her, moving like water as she danced through the endless battles of Valhalla.

Her shield sisters were waiting for her at the great stables, their horses tacked and ready to go, some pawing anxiously at the ground as they sensed the ride to come. Skjarla took her time though, leaving the other Valkyries to stand and wait as she plucked an apple from one of the trees which stood in the centre of the stable yard. She wandered over to the plain wooden stable where Sleipnir stood, leaning on the door as she offered the eight legged bay the apple. The great horse's eyes lit up and the ruby red apple was soon plucked from her gauntleted hand. She smiled as she listened to the horse crunch the apple, chunks of flesh and red skin bursting from the horse's mouth to fall among the straw below. Skjarla had always wanted to ride Sleipnir, but had never yet managed to pluck up the courage to ask Odin All-father for permission to ride his mount. Instead, all she could do was walk down towards where the other Valkyries were clustered by the door to her mount's stable. Vedr, the giant black she rode, tossed his head impatiently as she heaved the heavy saddle across his back. Tightening the girth she led him out into the stable yard. Skjarla pushed down against the horns of the high saddle, springing into position and kicking to horse into a canter in one easy motion.

Her fellow Valkyries screeched with joy as they set their mounts behind Vedr, chasing Skjarla across Valhalla and out onto Bifrost, the rainbow bridge which linked the home of the Aesir to the lands of Midgard. As they passed his dwelling at the top of the Bifrost Skjarla tossed a wave to her lover, Heimdall, the watchman God who stood ready to alert Asgard to the coming of Ragnarok. She had no time to stop though, as their horses pounded into the night sky above Midgard, invisible to all below them as they sought out the battle where they were to harvest souls for the All-Father's armies. They rode beneath the stars, over grasslands, forest and tundra, no trace of their passing left as their mounts strode silently through the air. One of the Valkyries passed around a skin of ale, the mood was light as they finally heard the din of battle.

Skjarla raised her arm and her shield sisters fell in behind her, waiting, watching the battle raging beneath them. On a beach, close to a dozen longships were drawn up on the shingle, their Viking occupants drawn up before them and holding off a milling crowd of woad painted savages. The Valkyries sat above the carnage, watching and waiting to see who would catch their eyes from the army below them. There had been a time when they would go to skirmishes such as this and return empty handed, but with Ragnarok getting nearer they could ill afford to be as picky. "Cowards," spat Bryna, a hatchet faced Valkyrie, as she pointed at a dozen Vikings being led away in the darkness, following a bear of a warrior. Skjarla mentally tuned out Bryna's rant, watching as the men made their way up onto the hill tops beyond the beach.

She smiled to herself as she saw Bryna's cowards turn on the top of the hill and run, roaring as if Hel herself was at their backs, straight into the rear ranks of the painted savages. The Woads were instantly on the back foot, looking out for a reinforcing army, bracing themselves for hundreds to follow this vanguard into their backs. The Vikings on the beach used this momentary relief to drive forwards, further crushing the savages' morale, seeing those on the fringes of the fight drift away into the darkness. It made her heart hammer with pride as the Norsemen below her raised a roar and pressed home their advantage, turning a bloody stalemate into a crushing victory.

"Those ones," Skjarla said, pointing to the bodies of the dozen who had attacked the rear of the painted lines, dead to a man. The Valkyries rode down to the field of death, unseen by all who still dwelt in the land of the living, extending arms to the dead warriors who lay upon that field of corpses to pluck their chosen few from the arms of death. The souls of those chosen by the Valkyries gratefully took the offered hands and swung themselves up behind the women. Vedr was such a powerful mount that he barely seemed to notice the large Viking who had led the mad charge hop lithely up onto his back. Once all of the Valkyries had a man up behind them Skjarla nodded to them and kicked her heels into Vedr, sending the black horse climbing into the night sky, riding towards the rising sun in the east. They galloped back to Valhalla, charging up the Bifrost, myriads of rainbow sparks exploding upwards with every strike of their horses' steel shoes.

As they passed the gates of Valhalla, Skjarla couldn't help but think of Heimdall, and with a girlish smile beneath her helm she called one of her shield sisters over. The large Viking climbed on beside the other Valkyrie, clinging onto her saddle with one foot in the stirrup, her horse snorting indignantly as it took the extra weight. Unencumbered,

Vedr ran like his namesake, galloping to Heimdall's humble dwelling. The rugged God stood outside with a wry smile playing across his lips as he saw Skjarla charging straight at him. The smile split into a deep, booming laugh as she threw herself from the galloping Vedr and rolled to her feet in one smooth motion, standing barely outside his arm's reach. "Girl, your horsemanship never ceases to amaze me. Come inside, there is ale and a joint of goat on the fire."

She followed him into the small hut, the rough-hewn stone walls providing protection from the wind, the door positioned to give him a clear view of Bifrost and the large, open plains at its foot. A simple wooden bed, covered over with furs, was the only piece of furniture in the earth floored dwelling, a far cry from the opulence and grandeur of Odin's mead hall. The two of them simply sat down around the fire blazing in the centre of the one room, the occasional crack coming as drips of fat splattered into the embers. They danced around it for a time, talking about friends, the food, ale, anything at all, but with Ragnarok imminent it was not long before both of them had shed their metal skins and leapt atop the rough bed. Skjarla could feel the soothing embrace as the soft, worn furs rubbed gently against her skin, enjoying the moment until her Valkyrie nature came to the fore and she became wilder, shifting atop Heimdall and controlling their movements. She led them in the increasingly frenetic dance until, with a harsh shout, their mingled voices both reached a crescendo, and she collapsed forward onto him, her chest heaving and every inch of her skin dripping with sweat.

They lay together until morning, Skjarla asleep with her head on Heimdall's chest, the hairs gently tickling her face as it rose and fell with his every breath. They parted company before the dawn sun had completely risen above the horizon, Heimdall to continue his lonely vigil over Bifrost and Skjarla to the day's battle. She knew how mad the life in Valhalla would seem to those she and the others had brought in last night would seem. Fighting all day, feasting all night, with wounds healed almost instantly, eternal preparation for Ragnarok. She walked in the direction of the fields of Asgard, the sound of blades and armour meeting already ringing loudly across the home of the Aesir. She joined the fighting, gleefully moving amongst the melee with Dreyrispa sowing chaos all around her, the sound of horns and the oaths of men ringing in her ears.

Suddenly a wave passed through the packed warriors, a horn's call rose high above the noise of the battle, every man and woman there knew exactly what that call meant. The Gjallarhorn was being blown, Ragnarok had come. Strangely there was no panic, the Gods and their servants had been preparing for this moment since Ygdrassil had barely been a sapling and the world had been young. The armies of Valhalla marched towards the Bifrost, gone were the songs and cheers of their daily battles, only the grim determination of men going to their doom hung over the column. In menacing silence they marched down the Bifrost, taking position at the base of the bridge, watching as the ominous cloud of fire and smoke inched its way towards them. The Ljosalfar, light elves, stood with the Einherjar, their graceful limbs holding equally graceful weapons. There was little order to the Aesir lines, Valkyrie, man and elf all stood intermingled behind the Gods, waiting for the first furious clash of blades.

Skjarla glanced down the lines either side of here, waiting for the earth to open up and spew forth legions of Dokkalfar, the dark elves, and their Dwarven fellows, both of whom lived deep beneath the surface of Midgard. There was no sound of collapsing earth though, only the ominous, low rumble as the forces of Hel and Loki continued their inexorable march towards the host of Valhalla. Anxious murmurs rippled the length of the line as Man, Elf and God alike wondered when and if their allies would appear, or if courage had failed those who dwelt beneath the earth. As the endless tide closed to within a mile of each other Skjarla could begin to pick out the great Giants and Jotunn who stood amongst the slathering throng. The red flames which chased the horde glinted menacingly from the polished steel scales worn by the giants, who strode alongside the shambling corpses released from Hel's clammy embrace for the final battle.

She was going to die, Skjarla knew that that was her fate, alongside everyone else who stood before Valhalla that day, but it still raised her spirits to see Heimdall take his place in the line in front of her. Still, the heavy plate of steel she wore, and the scales which hung around her waist felt heavier today than they ever had before, her helmet felt claustrophobic as panic gnawed at her; to calm herself she forced herself to focus on Heimdall. The god looked magnificent in his golden scale armour, shining like the dying rays of the sun against the glow of the flames inching ever closer. Odin One-Eye strode before the battle line, calling on those present, "Fight with me, and we shall carve such an end that the fires of our glory shall yet burn when all the world is nought but dust and frozen ashes!" Roars from the lines of Valhalla chased his speech up and down the lines, and without any word they began to creep forward, moving into a charge against the creatures of Hel.

***

Skjarla swore at her men to reform their shield wall, holding their oaken shields braced against the shambling throng even as the men behind jabbed their few remaining spears into exposed, rotting flesh. They were steadily being driven back up the Bifrost, killing dozens for every Einherjar who fell, but still the horde drove them back towards Valhalla. Beneath the silver metal of her helmet tears streaked white paths across her ash stained face, even as she continued to weave a shroud of blood around herself with Dreyrispa. She had seen so much death and misery that day that her mind could barely comprehend it, she had seen her beloved Heimdall and Loki fight one another to a bloody standstill, both collapsing from loss of blood. She felt a heavy weight pressing against her leg, the Gjallarhorn, the one relic of her Heimdall that she had been able to recover from the battlefield before she had been driven back from his body. Mighty Thor had finally struck down the world serpent Jormungand, managing to walk nine paces before the toxins in the foul monster's breath had finally brought him low. The great wolf Fenris, who had bitten off Tyr's right hand all those years ago, had swallowed the All-Father in one bite, before being struck down in turn. Glancing up into the sky Skjarla could see Fenris's father, Skoll gaining on the sun, the time when he was fated to devour that burning orb and plunge the world into darkness was finally upon them.

Skjarla and her ever shrinking band of warriors were driven back into the centre of Valhalla, it tore at her heart to see those mighty buildings licked by flames and hear the terrified whinnying of the horses as the fire crept closer to their stables. There were loud crashes as the ancient wooden roofs crashed down to earth in an explosion of sparks, flames stretching high into the sky as the day grew old. As they were driven back towards the trunk of Ygdrassil, Freyr, one of the few Gods who was still standing was torn apart in front of their eyes by the fire Jotunn Surtr. Pushing her way to the front of the shambling horde the few remaining Einherjar could see the half youth, half corpse goddess Hel. Even the Goddess's clothes were split, half seemed to be made of the finest wools and silks while the dead half was falling apart, held closed with a rusted iron brooch. There, thought Skjarla, there is a chance for me to make my mark upon this day, if I can kill Hel then maybe this day of carnage and misery will not have been for nought. With that thought in her head, and the hope of joining her beloved Heimdall wherever those who had fallen had gone, she thrust Dreyrispa into the air and called on her tired and battered survivors for one last push forward.

They set their shoulders to their chipped and splintered shields, straining tired leg muscles as they fought to clear a path for the last surviving Valkyrie towards the last of Loki's children. The men wielded dulled blades and blunted spears but the will in their hearts kept them fighting, even though blood dripped from every one of them, staining the hallowed stones of Valhalla a dull red. Even though their bravery thinned the ranks between Skjarla and Hel they were still pushed back by the sheer weight of numbers arrayed against them. Skjarla ground her teeth in frustration within the sweaty confines of her helmet as the men around her died, even as the dark goddess drew slowly nearer to her and Ygdrassil. With a vicious, animalistic snarl she threw herself forward, out of the shield wall in a desperate attempt to cut a path to Hel and she managed to thin the gap between them dramatically, but she was still slowly being forced backwards.

Finally the angry Goddess waved her arm and a path between the two women was cleared. Skjarla took a deep breath to prepare for the coming struggle and glanced about her. Her heart almost ceased to beat as she saw the last of the Einherjar strewn about the stones amidst growing pools of blood. The realisation that she was most likely the last of the Aesir in Valhalla, in all of Midgard, crushing her spirit like a blow from Mjolnir. Her chest heaved heavily, pressing up against the Aesir steel of her armour as she sucked in lung-fulls of burning air, heavy with the taste of soot. It was strange, in this moment of her imminent, certain death, she felt more alive than she had ever done.

Maybe this is what we have all missed, she thought in the silence as Hel drifted towards her, immortality means we have no pressure to savour every moment we have.

"Look around you Valkyrie," hissed Hel malevolently, her arm sweeping across the field of corpses around her, "Lay down your arms and I will grant you a quick death, more than you deserve, Aesir slut." Her dead eye in the rotted half of her face seemed to look right through Skjarla, who hung her head as if considering the offer.

She did the only thing which a true child of Valhalla could and roared out, "Odin," with every ounce of breath she had in her as she drove Dreyrispa towards the Goddess's heart. With inhuman speed Hel swayed to the right, the hardened point of Dreyrispa piercing her dead shoulder and stinking green rot erupting from the wound. Hel merely looked at the blade as if it were a minor irritant, reached up and pulled it from her grey, cold flesh, pulling Skjarla close before backhanding her across the face, sending the Valkyrie flying through the air to crash against the trunk of Ygdrassil. Hel drifted closer to where Skjarla was trying to push herself back to her feet, bending close to the prone Valkyrie and whispering softly to her. As both of them locked eyes and for the first time Skjarla felt the cold fingers of fear caress her heart and shuddered.

"Look upon me, Valkyrie, and know that you will suffer for daring to strike me. You will live past the coming fire, you will live with the knowledge that you have failed, you will carry the souls of all those who fell today with you, and know that you can never go where they are. Now witness my triumph, and despair." She spoke with a cruel stare, her voice dripping with cold venom and her dead hand punched against the hard steel of Skjarla's breastplate. Hel stood up and shot the Valkyrie a triumphant yet wicked smile. "Watch me find my destiny; yours will pass you by forever." With that she raised her dead hand to the trunk of Ygdrassil and the moment that the rotting flesh came into contact with the worn bark flames jumped up the tree. Skjarla shuddered as the land jerked underneath her and the tree seemed to shriek as it twisted and contorted, struggling to get away from the clammy embrace of Hel. Flames exploded around them and Skjarla looked down to see her silvery armour lose its shine and turn black as if stained by the soot already billowing forth from the wound in the flank of the World Tree. As she pulled her helmet from her head she felt her hair spill down across her face, no longer blond it was now dark as a raven's wing.

All she could do as Ygdrassil swiftly turned into a tower of flame, as Hel appeared to be consumed by the fires was flee as fast as she could, still clinging tightly to Dreyrispa. Around her the enemy vanished from existence, taken with their mistress to somewhere beyond her kind, the threads of their fate run to the end, their destiny fulfilled. She ran to the burning stables, hoping that there was still some animal able to carry her as far from this world of fire and pain as was possible. She heard the cracks as the great beams exploded from the heat; she felt the heat as cinders settled on her armour and singed her hair where it now spilled across her brow. The stables were completely consumed by fire and there was not a sound from within, save for the hiss and crackle as the fire ate the corpses of the horses. Then she saw the unmistakeable silhouette within the smoke, Sleipnir was tethered outside the burning stables, waiting for her. Her heart soared with bittersweet happiness as she saw the mighty eight-legged creature, she had always wanted to ride the beast, but never in circumstances like this, never to flee from her home and the bodies of all those she held dear. Nonetheless she swung her tired frame onto the horses back, dug her heels into the frightened animal's flanks and gave the beast its head. As Sleipnir climbed high above Valhalla she felt her eyes blinded by tears at what she left behind her, at all that had been lost on that day of blood and fire. As Sleipnir carried her far away from the ruin and into the darkness she could swear that she could hear Hel's mocking laughter chasing her from the home of the Gods.

Through the veil of her tears she could see the ground beneath her shift like a wounded beast, lands divided and new seas springing up in the void. The people far below scattered like panicked ants as what they saw as the end of days fell upon them. For many it would be the end of days, but many would survive, some twisted by the power unleashed by Hel. Others would live on only marked by the memories which would fade into fable with the passing of the ages. For all who survived though, the death of Ygdrassil meant that nothing would be the same again.

Chapter 2

The small town of Lonely Barrow nestled into the fringes of the great north forest, and was bounded to the south by one of the many tributaries of the river Scath. The autumn evening fog twined around the thick pines of the forest, moisture already starting to collect on the carpet of browned and drying needles which formed the forest floor. The town got its name from the single grassy burial mound which lurked ominously at its north eastern edge, the worn grave of a single, nameless warrior from years before. It was early evening, and the windows of the town twinkled with the orange glow of the fires within, the lights appearing uncomfortably bright against the dark of the walls and the thatched rooves. The centre of the town was dominated by the two large storehouses, both of which were used to dry the timbers which were cut from the surrounding forests before they were sent south to be used by their masters. Lonely Barrow came under the authority of the Haemocracy, and in return for the valuable wood they sent south their high born, pure blood masters sent shipments of grain north to feed the town. The Haemocracy was governed by local lords, all struggling to improve the standing of their families by marrying into supposedly purer bloodlines. All of the lords answered to the High Council, a select group representing the purest families in the lands, although what made one man's blood better than another's was almost impossible to tell. Beneath their petty squabbles were the ordinary people, like those of Lonely Barrow, simply hoping to enjoy a quiet life.

The only other building of note in the town was the inn, on the south western edge where the town gave way to the forest and the single track leading into the depths of the fog stretched off into what seemed like eternity. Inside there were only a few men and women, the majority of the town being at home with their families, those who liked to spend their excess coin, of which there was precious little, would be along to the inn later. Lonely Barrow was unusual for the time, in that it had very few of those who had become known as Abhorrens, those who had been left malformed by the power of Ragnarok nearly five hundred years ago. There were others who had been changed by that great day of upheaval, but none to the extent of the Abhorrens, many of who carried extra limbs of grossly swollen proportions. From what the people had been told by travellers most of these creatures had been wiped out in other lands centuries ago, but the Haemocracy had spared them, seeing other possibilities for their mangled forms.

The fat innkeeper looked around the smoky room, seeing his few customers hunched over mugs of ale or steaming plates of stew. That was one good thing about living in this blasted forest, he thought to himself, at least there were people able to supplement their tables with meat from the woods and fish from the streams here. Notionally, all of the animals in the forest were the property of the local Haemocratic lord, but out here no one paid any attention to such rules. The man rubbed his greasy hands on the stained apron which was pulled tight around his bulging middle and cocked his head to one side; he could have sworn he heard screams from the other side of town. He shook his head, for all of the lone strange beasts which lurked within the twisted shadows cast by the pines there was never any fear of those creatures venturing into Lonely Barrow.

Then he stiffened as he heard screams again, more clearly this time, and nearer, too, from the sounds of things. Anxiously he glanced around the room before his gaze finally settled on one cloaked figure, their back pressed up against the wall with the cloak's hood still shadowing thier face as they slowly spooned steaming hunks of meat from the bowl into thier mouth. Normally he wouldn't have given the person a second glance, but the sight of the twin headed spear balanced across the customer's legs and the lumps on their shoulders of what could only be the hafts of other weapons meant that they were his first choice. Nervously he crossed the room, clearing his throat as he reached the table; he expected the stranger to look up, but they just kept eating in absolute silence.

"It sounds like there is some fighting going on further up the town, you look like a warrior so would you be able to see what is going on, we only have a few militia men and they aren't up to much?" the innkeeper said as politely as he could, nervously wringing his hands in his apron.

Without moving, a voice emerged from the black maw of the hood. "How much?"

"What? What do you mean?"

"I mean how much coin you will give me to go and look." The voice had a much harder edge to it this time, like the sound of steel being rasped across a whetstone. The innkeeper looked more closely at the traveller once he had recovered himself, and he cursed silently. He had missed the small, yet obvious mark on the breast of the cloak that gave this person away. They were a Reaver, one of a small group who all operated under the insignia of a sword and a skull, monster hunters and swords for hire. There were very few of them, but they were renowned for two things, first was their skill with blades and all manner of weapons. It was said that to stop just anyone operating under the

Reaver badge any two Reavers who crossed paths must duel. Unless they were similarly matched in skill then the stronger would kill the weaker for sullying their company. They were best known though for their avarice. The running joke, although never told to a Reaver's face, was that they would not pass water unless someone was paying them to do so.

The screams were getting nearer still and the innkeeper thought that he could smell burning wafting its way across the thatched roofs which softened him a little. "Fifty gold Sanguines and not an Orich more."

Still without the least hint of emotion the voice hidden within the cloak shot back, "Two hundred Sanguines, I have no idea what I am going up against and that makes it more expensive."

"One hundred, you thief," spat the innkeeper, furious that this person would try to profit from the threat to the town.

"One hundred and fifty and you have a deal, friend," said the voice without a hint of irony in the use of the word friend.

A loud scream outside made up the innkeeper's mind for him, "Very well. One hundred and fifty Sanguines to protect the townsfolk from whatever is out there, you will be paid when you return, but for the love of mercy go and see what is causing those screams." The man was getting increasingly agitated, even more so when, with almost serpentine grace, a gauntleted hand emerged from beneath the folds of the cloak.

"Deal," said the voice flatly as they shook hands, "I shall leave my cloak here, but if it is gone then I add an extra fifty Sanguines to my due." With that the figure unfolded itself gracefully from behind the worn table, leaving the food and mug of ale waiting as they shrugged off their thick travelling cloak. The innkeeper could barely control his shock as he discovered that the person he had been arguing with was a woman. He could not believe that one would choose the hard life on the road of a Reaver. However, the jet black armour and the feline grace with which she moved and handled the vicious, twin-headed spear kept his tongue firmly behind his teeth. His eye briefly caught on the worn, curled horn tied tightly to the baldric at her hip, but the spear in her hand and the swords on her back were more important for the fate of the village. Without a word Skjarla marched towards the door, opening it with a long creak, and bracing herself against the cool night air which was sucked past her into the inn, she strode out to find the source of the evening's chaos.

She strode through the town, loosening muscles as she had been taught by her tutor in the land of Leske, far to the east. It had been a strange time, she reflected, since the death of Valhalla. In those early days she had tried and failed in several attempts to kill herself. Her own weapons had refused to pierce her skin, and normal iron forged ones had bent and blunted on contact with her. Other attempts proved equally fruitless, and more curious still she had found that she could be wounded when fighting, but the moment she let the blade through to strike her down, she was once more invulnerable. It seemed that the harder she had sought death, the further away from her it was. She had been saddened as Sleipnir, without the magic of the All-father to sustain him, had succumbed to the slow march of time. Others had survived, but Sleipnir had been fighting against his fate, he had never been supposed to outlast the Gods.

After several years of wandering the face of Midgard, watching as society began to rebuild itself, alien cultures thrust together by the cataclysmic changes of Ragnarok, and she had found purpose. She had come up with the idea of hunting monsters, which had flourished since Ragnarok, mainly as a way of passing time thanks to Hel's curse of immortality. Over time other souls had followed in her footsteps, operating under the mark of the Reaver, Skjarla still wasn't sure how she felt about those who tried to imitate her, and trade on her fame. She had been the one to introduce the duels which had swiftly thinned the numbers and driven off any who had hoped to make quick coin by wearing the Skull and Blade.

She wasn't sure what had brought her to this small town on the edge of the world, in four centuries she had crossed the globe several times over. She had studied and trained with warriors from far flung cultures, men whose knowledge had survived Ragnarok, but her agelessness meant she could never settle, condemned to wander forever. Skjarla had seen many strange and wondrous things, but so far she had never once ventured into the polar mountains, a wasteland of the bones of the world. Occasionally one of the many monstrosities created by Hel's touch upon the world tree would come lumbering out of the earth, or crawl down from the mountains. She had seen cultures rise and fall in the days since Ragnarok, as peoples once separated by oceans were suddenly thrown together, the small kingdom of Leske swallowed beneath the tide of the Red Father's teachings. New beings had been created by the cataclysm, and some ancient cultures had been lost beneath the face of Midgard.

She could smell burning and the light from the fires licking across the thatched roofs cast an ominous, flickering glow across the face of her black steel armour, which seemed to gleefully drink in the light. The screams were getting louder and townsfolk were streaming in the other direction, parting around her like water around a rock as she strode towards the source of the chaos, swinging Dreyrispa in menacing circles. The small wattle and daub cottages of the town thinned out on the northern edge, and amongst those wide, dusty alleyways Skjarla could start to pick out scenes of battle, where the few men of the militia were struggling against some alien beasts. She could hear the sounds of fighting further off as the villagers grappled with yet more of the creatures using whatever they had to hand.

One of the monsters turned towards her, its face caught in the glow of a fallen roof beam. The face was covered in reptilian scales, small eyes on the side of its long, horned and beaked head; the most striking feature, though, was the large bony crest which sat like a shield at the back and top of the monster's head. The creature's scrawny torso was covered in rough leathers and the odd piece of rusted iron while its clawed fingers held a crude club, studded with volcanic glass shards.

The creature gave a piercing shriek and leapt towards her, swinging its club wildly. Skjarla waited patiently, before contemptuously stepping aside and thrusting Dreyrispa into the Wyrmling's chest, she rolled the stinking carcass to the side where it collapsed against the side of a hut, leaving a shining smear of blood against the wall. She reached the edge of the town then crouched down as she heard a hissing voice; a much more heavily muscled creature with a horned crest was giving orders to half a dozen of its subordinates. "It is … here. I can ... feel it; the master ... will be whole again. Find it … burn the village." The voice hissed, the words struggling to escape from the bony beak. Skjarla wondered what in all of the lands this village could have that would be worth taking.

Then the crowd of Wyrmlings intoned one word which sent icy fingers up her spine, "Fafnir," the dragon who had been slain over three hundred years ago. Her mind remembered fragments of a legend, but not the whole thing, but a shard of that memory told her that if children of the Dragon were abroad in the land then all was far from well. With a ragged battle cry she ran around the corner, striking down the nearest Wyrmling before the others had even recovered their shock. They then converged on her, and she swung Dreyrispa in wide arcs to keep the six of them at bay. The leader swung his sword, which was closer to an iron bar than a blade and drove her to her knees. A bolt of rage flashed through her, but before she could take advantage of the adrenaline, she heard a man's voice and a figure clad in shining golden armour leapt in swinging a gigantic sword and taking two heads clean off. She used the moment of shock to swing Dreyrispa in a low arc, opening the bellies of the four Wyrmlings still standing, all of whom collapsed to the ground, trying desperately to press the rope of purple guts back into the crimson holes.

The figure, encased from head to toe in shining golden metal which gleamed like the sun even in the dark of night, offered her a hand. It may have seemed petulant, but Skjarla hated being offered help by anyone, she had built herself into an island and wanted nothing from the rest of the world. As such she studiously ignored the gauntleted hand and pressed herself to her feet. She ignored the gilded warrior and instead walked over to the muscular leader of the Wyrmlings, bending down near to the creature, moving back as the vicious beak cracked together where her face had been moments before. She put her foot on top of the monster's guts, eliciting a shriek of pain, before saying softly, "What are you here for? Tell I and I grant you a swift death, silence and I hang you with your own guts." Her cruel smile was exposed by her helmet, which covered the top and sides of her head, but aside from two thick rings around the eyes left the rest of her face clear. The blood fury written across that terrifying, yet flawless face left the creature in no doubt as to the seriousness of her threat.

"Fafnir ... will be whole ... again, the Children of the Dragon will ... burn the world. More of us will come ... you all will die." The creature shrieked at her with the fervour of a zealot. Behind her, she could hear the soft thumps as the man's broadsword thudded into the flesh of the remaining Children, finishing them. Skjarla reached down to the wound, grabbing a handful of the creature's guts and pulled them further out of the wound, eliciting a shriek of pain.

"Again. What are you her for?" Skjarla's voice dripped with malice and her blue eye's shone with icy menace.

"The Fangs ... A Fang is here." Shrieked the creature before its agony drove it into the dark recesses of unconsciousness. Skjarla straightened up with shock, the word Fang had completed the memory of the legend she had been searching for. Hundreds of years ago, barely a century after Ragnarok, the great warrior king Sigurd led a chosen group of men north to slay the dragon Fafnir after it had burnt his lands. Sigurd had never returned to his lands in the south, he had been usurped while he was on his quest. His vassals had fallen to fighting among one another for control of the kingdom which had subsequently fallen apart, and the most prized part of that kingdom had been the great, now ruined, fortress of Castle Dour. No one knew what had happened to Sigurd, but the legend held that the fangs of the dragon had been stripped from its corpse and brought back across the mountains, along with the blade which had formed its nose horn. The legend warned that if any Fang were sown into the ring formed by the aging skeleton then a steel Jotunn would rise from the earth to find the other fangs, and if all of the missing Fangs and the horn were returned then the Dragon would rise once more.

She almost laughed at the thought that something as powerful as a Fang of Fafnir could be held in a place such as this. Then she thought of the name of the town, Lonely Barrow, the tradition of building barrows for the dead was only still practiced in the southern peninsula of the continent, what if this was where one of Sigurd's warriors had fallen. The townsfolk were getting the fires under control, but the sounds of fighting were now coming from the mill where the river and the forest met the town. Skjarla picked up Dreyrispa, slashing the throat of the unconscious Wyrmling, running towards the remaining sounds of combat, the tall warrior falling silently into step next to her as she ran across the town. There was a niggling feeling of irritation at this warrior alongside her, she was capable of dealing with this alone, and more importantly she wanted to do this alone.

There were two dozen of the Children gathered around the water driven mill, even now the wheel turned slowly, creaking on its axle as the water drove it round. There were few of them left alive in the town, she could tell as the screams had died on the air, the only sounds she could hear came from the group in front of her. There was a small knot of men defending the mill, all wildly swinging lengths of wood as they desperately tried to fend off the crested Wyrmlings around them. One of the creatures stepped back a few paces and grabbed a slender tube from its belt, which it then put to its beaked mouth. One of the defenders collapsed in a twitching heap as the dart struck as the poisons acted on his body. Skjarla struck their line like a blow from Mjolnir, Dreyrispa sending arcs of blood drops flying through the air. The large, golden warrior followed her in, cutting a bloody swathe through the enemy and scattering limbs in every direction. The gangly, scale covered creatures broke and ran for the trees, leaving their dead upon the well-trod earth around the mill.

Skjarla tore her helmet from her head, her raven-black hair spilling across the still pale skin, sweat chilling her skin as it poured down her brow. Her mind clicked through various thoughts, before asking the question, why were there so many of the monsters attacking the mill instead of any other building in the village. She walked purposefully up to the small knot of men still clutching their bloodied lengths of timber around the front of the mill. They were looking down with pale faces at the body of the eldest of them, a man in his fifties who had been struck down by the vicious dart of the Children. The three men standing were either mill workers or the man's sons, either way they all stood there like a collection of lost sheep. Skjarla looked at each one of them, before beckoning the youngest one of them forward; he had a leather thong tied around his neck and a bulge in the front of his rough wool shirt.

"What is on the end of that?" she asked softly, trying to keep the sharpness out of her voice.

The young man looked at her blankly, he was well built, with hair the colour of straw and his large expressive eyes, which were almost lost in the wide and solid face, were a lustrous brown which seemed to shine even in the poor light of the stars. Finally, slowly he reached up and drew his hand tight around the item, still hidden beneath the shirt. "It was my father's, and his father's before him, been in our family for who only knows how long." And with that he reached down and withdrew a worn but still wickedly sharp tooth, set into a plain iron mount.

Skjarla could scarcely believe her eyes, one of the Fangs in a place like this, it defied belief. She was disturbed from her amazement by a gentle tap on her shoulder. She whipped round, ripping a dagger from the leather baldric wrapped across her body, pointing it unwaveringly at the gap in the front of the great helmet which sat proudly atop the sculpted plate armour of her new companion. The man acted as if he did not notice the knife, which Skjarla cautiously returned to its sheath, as he bowed low and removed his helmet. "That was well fought, my lady," his voice had the richness of honey, but lacked the oiliness of sarcasm she had expected, "I had heard tell of the Reavers' skills but I am indeed fortunate to see them in the flesh." Skjarla had to give it to the man, he had a fine smile, long white-blond locks spilled to his shoulder, twisted together and held in dark strands by the sweat of his brow. The eyes were flickering between the white of snow and the pale blue of a cloudless sky, full of life and light.

Skjarla swallowed a petulant reply before saying, "Thanks, your help was appreciated." She offered her hand, noting the firm grip as he shook hers. She saw his eyes flick over her shoulder and alight on the young man, whose fang pendant now rested on the outside of his shirt.

He stepped closer and whispered softly and excitedly to her, "Is that what I think it is?"

"If by that you mean one of the Fangs, then yes, I believe so."

A wide grin split the thin face, the smile giving him a boyish look which clashed with the blood-stained warrior before her, and as he tossed his head back she caught sight of the pointed ear tips. This drew her attention, as fair skin and elvish ears were rare these days, the Ljosalfar had been wiped out on the field before Valhalla, and the Dokkalfar had skin the colour of ebony. Before she could question him he shouted excitedly, "Praise the Goddess, I've found it. At last I have found it." The man was grinning like a lunatic and seemed about to dance for joy. Skjarla backed away a little, suddenly worried as to the mental state of the warrior before her.

She didn't have time to worry about that though, as the knowledge that more of the Children of the Dragon would be coming for the Fang meant that she had to get it out of here as far as possible. The likelihood was that the Children would tear the town to pieces in their search for it, but it was far too dangerous to fall into their hands. She turned to the young man behind her, "I need that tooth, and it needs to be taken as far from here as possible."

The young man shook his head, "It's the only thing I have left from my father, and my family has had it for generations. I can't give it up."

"Look, those beasts will be back, that thing round your neck is what they were looking for, and if they get it then the world will become a far more dangerous place." She hissed at the youth, part of her mind screaming at her to cut the Fang from his neck and leave with it.

"Well, what are you going to do to protect the town if more of those things are coming back?" This came from the gilded warrior, and Skjarla was about to tell him that it wasn't her problem, then she cursed silently as she saw the fat innkeeper standing at the armoured man's shoulder

"I paid you to protect this town from that threat, if they are coming back you are still under contract." The innkeeper tried to sound forceful, but his sweating face and clammy hands which he continually rubbed on his apron gave lie to that fact – he was terrified.

Skjarla was tempted to take the Fang and leave the people to their fate, but at the same time she knew the truth of the innkeeper's words. Also, she knew that her word was the only thing that she had left, and if she broke it and forfeited her honour then the last shards of the Valkyrie were gone and she was merely a Reaver. Her mind was made up as the golden warrior leant close and said, "Lady Reaver, I place myself under your command, whatever aid I can offer in saving the people of the town is yours."

Skjarla spat on the ground, unladylike maybe, but it was how she felt; she couldn't help but find that the golden man's manner of speaking was overly formal and grating on her. She didn't want to take command of a town full of useless mouths but it seemed she was stuck playing mother to the lot of them. She took a deep breath, the bellow of command taking her back to the painful memories of her centuries as a Valkyrie. "Very well. You ask me to protect you, I cannot do it here. More of the Children of the Dragon will come, to kill and burn every living thing in this town. Go to your homes, gather everything you can carry, bring food for the long walk south. The nearest city is the port of Celeste, I will escort you all there, and then my service is done." She turned and whispered harshly to the young man with the Fang, "You do not leave my side for an instant."

The people milled around looking at one another, starting to murmur protest, before the Gilded man took charge, gently pushing the people apart, sending them to their own homes. "We leave in one hour, tell your friends and neighbours, everyone must be ready at the inn within the hour."

While he sent the people about their jobs Skjarla turned to the young man next to her and said softly, seeing that he was still standing there like a lost puppy, "Where do you need to go?"

He responded miserably, "My home was one of those consumed by fire, I was lucky in that it was my night to watch the mill, otherwise I'd just be another corpse tonight. The only place I want to go is there," he pointed into the darkness, to where the dark hump of the barrow lurked ominously, "my family have been here since the beginning and I want to say goodbye."

Skjarla nodded and fell into step behind the young man as he stepped listlessly off in the direction of the barrow. Skjarla felt strange, destiny should have been sundered when the Norn's tapestry was consumed by fire during Ragnarok, but this seemed far too convenient to be coincidence.

"What do I call you, Reaver? Lady?" her companion asked, trying to make conversation and to put himself at ease with his new guardian.

"Skjarla will do fine. How about you?" she asked with a sigh, resigned to having to protect this man.

"Sigmund, Sigmund Olafsson." He stopped short in front of the stone lintel of the Barrow, the aged oak door covered in moss and mould. "This is where the founder of the town was buried. He was the first of my family to be buried here, or so my mother said, although most everyone here claims blood ties to whoever lies in there." He stood in silence, not knowing what to do now that he was standing here.

Skjarla knew what to do though, and before Sigmund could stop her, she had strode up to the door and kicked it off its rotten hinges, leaving the solid steel lock still dug into the stone frame. "What are doing?" Sigmund exclaimed incredulously.

As if it were the simplest thing in the world, she replied, "Well I'm damned if I am going to give you one of my weapons, so I need to find you a blade somewhere, and as I would guess that you are similar in shape to your ancestor then this would seem the sensible place to look. Coming?" she asked as she strode towards the mouth of the barrow, the musty smell of decay and stale air wafting out into the night. She paused and ran back to the nearest burning building, grabbing a flaming brand to light the way within the tomb. She heard Sigmund shuffle in behind her, and the soft rustle as the multitudes of cobwebs caught fire, the spiders within popping audibly as the flames reached them.

The dark passageway stretched before them, propped up by rough-hewn stone columns, the stench of must hanging heavy in the air, while their shoes crunched over the hard packed earth. It opened out into a small cavern, barely big enough for the two of them to stand upright around the raised stone platform atop which rested an armoured skeleton. "Well, go on then." Skjarla said impatiently, waiting for Sigmund to grab the armour, but he just shuffled his feet uncomfortably. "Look Sigmund, this ancestor is long dead, he has no need of this stuff but you do. If he is your ancestor then he will understand and there will be no shame in taking it."

Sigmund reluctantly began to gather up the scale gambeson and the embossed greaves, but Skjarla's eye was caught by two things, firstly that there was only a single, plain sword, but two scabbards, one of which was far more

28

ornate that the other. The second and more curious thing was the helmet, which seemed to have a step in it, the whole way around its circumference, coupled with archaic etchings. Skjarla knew what this meant, but said nothing to Sigmund. Perhaps there may come a time later when she would be forced to explain, but there was nothing to be gained from it at this time, if indeed this was any relation of his at all. She helped him to pull the armour on over his own clothes, and became irritated when he insisted on replacing the bones neatly on their plinth. She tried to explain that the corpse wouldn't care, but Sigmund was adamant about respecting his ancestor.

They emerged back out under the night sky, the stars clear overhead, save for those obscured by the grimy smudges of smoke from the burning houses, and the moon shining down brightly on them. They trooped back to the inn, Sigmund struggling slightly under the weight of his new armour, which attracted several strange looks from every person they passed. Skjarla passed dozens of piles of belongings where people were waiting to gather up their burdens for the march south. It was a journey of over four hundred miles, which would take even an army twenty days at best, for this rabble of refugees it would be more like forty. Skjarla knew that the chances of every member of the column making Celeste were almost zero.

She silently pushed through the nervous throng assembling outside the inn, fighting her way through to the door and pushing her way inside. The gilded man was in there, eating a bowl of stew while the innkeeper bustled around, directing the serving girls to load things onto one of the many recently repurposed wood carts. She gathered up her cloak, and reached inside to withdraw a deflated skin, she poured the last few drops of water out onto the stained wooden floorboards before making her way purposefully to the bar along one side of the room. She reached behind the bar, searching for one of the many bottles she had heard clinking there earlier. They were filled with a dark spirit, distilled from some of the grain that came north from the Haemocracy, and flavoured with herbs from the forest. She pressed the mouth of the bottle to the neck of the skin and poured the strong alcohol inside, it never hurt to have something to keep you warm for the cold nights in the forest.

"I'll keep in mind that you've got that," said the gilded man, "I might come calling if the nights in the forest get as miserable as this one, and with winter coming, I can only imagine it is going to get worse. I am Accipiteri, might I have the pleasure of knowing your name?"

"Skjarla, a Reaver as you have seen from my markings. You, however, where do you come from, your ears mark you down as having Alfar blood, but your skin is not black enough for Dokkalfar, and I know that there is not a single Ljosalfar left. So what are you?" Her thin brows knotted together as she waited for his answer, wandering over to where she had left her meal earlier, the stew was now cold and the ale warm, neither of which improved the taste, but she was hungry so she sat down to finish the meal anyway.

"You're right, I am neither Dokkalfar nor Ljosalfar. I am one of the Loptalfar, the air elves." He said proudly.

Skjarla didn't even look up, "Horse Shit. I have been to the Windswept Isle and visited the cities of Sky Haven, and I know that you're no Loptalfar. Firstly, they almost never leave their island, although I have met a few on the road over the course of my travels. More importantly though, the Loptalfar have wings, and you do not, so I ask you again, what are you." Her voice was even, no trace of anger in her tone, just the icy impatience of a winter gale.

If she had been looking she would have seen Accipiteri's face fall, but he recovered himself with a grimace and came closer to where she sat. "Well, if we're going to be spending the month together you might as well know. I am Loptalfar, but as you say, I have no wings. It has only happened five times since the cataclysm, but occasionally children are born without wings. These children are deemed to have been chosen by the Goddess for some special task, and as such are given the finest training and armour until their fortieth year, at which point they set sail for the mainland to find their destiny. Two did return, with wings not of feathers and flesh, but of light and fire. The one who is still alive is ..."

"Hjeris. Very well, you are Loptalfar, but that doesn't explain what you were doing here in the arse end of beyond." She said with a nod of her head, still chewing chunks of cool meat.

"I was looking for my calling, and seeing that one of the Fangs was here, and there were innocent people in need of protecting I can be sure that the Goddess sent me here. I have been wandering for years now, and I felt the winds blowing me northwards, the Goddess guiding me." He said this with utter conviction, truly believing in what he was saying.

"Very well, I guess it will help to have one more person along who knows which end of a blade to stick in people. Come, we need to get this ridiculous procession underway." She got to her feet, wrapping her cloak around her shoulders, her helmet hanging from the baldric and the hood pushed back, revealing her head to the air. She carried Dreyrispa and, flanked by Accipiteri and Sigmund she made her way to the doorway. She was struck by the number of people waiting outside for her, the crowd stretch off in every direction, dotted with horse drawn carts and hand sleds piled high with belongings. She held up a hand, and was almost surprised when silence fell across the crowd, she guessed that the people who had been at the mill had passed on the message that she was responsible for their salvation. Bastards, she thought.

"People of Lonely Barrow, we have to leave now, more of the Children of the Dragon will be coming to take this town. I will lead you to the port city of Celeste, but while we march I am in command, and Accipiteri," she indicated the hulking warrior standing at her shoulder with a nod of her head, "will be my second." She walked down to the road, where the track disappeared into the ominous darkness of the forest, the crowd parting silently around the three armoured figures. "Right, let's go." She waved her arm and the people of Lonely Barrow began to follow her down the worn dirt track, the trees casting menacing shadows amidst the moonlight. In miserable silence the townsfolk abandoned their homes and all they had known to some alien invader and marched into the unknown behind just two guardians.

Chapter 3

They had been marching through the interminable forest for four days, eating, sleeping and marching beneath the boughs of the forest, pines giving way to oak and ash as they followed the road south. On the second evening she had called Sigmund over to her, she knew why she wanted to teach him what he needed to learn, but she couldn't give him the real reason. So instead she had said to him that if he refused to give up the Fang then he had to be able to guard the thing properly and began to teach him to fight. Sigmund had been hefting sacks of flour at the mill for years, so he had good strong muscles, but he seemed to be made from wood rather than flesh, he had no flexibility whatsoever. She had held off from using Dreyrispa and instead had used two thick lengths of wood to represent swords. On the first evening, without even trying to she had beaten him black and blue, even when she slowed her speed down markedly. Accipiteri had come over and taken her place, fighting alongside Sigmund and demonstrating with Skjarla how to move with the sword. He was still clumsy, but his technique seemed to improve more for this more gentle approach to teaching.

They camped by the side of the road each night, trying to find a clearing where they could, but often they were simply strung out over a mile along the banks which flanked the road. The fog was always thickest with the dawn, but usually burnt off by midmorning. Skjarla found it tedious, spending days and nights beneath the half light of the forest floor. She had worried about feeding the column, but it turned out that most of the men were handy with their short bows and kept a good stream of fresh meat coming in which was duly roasted over open fires. Skjarla's main concern was that the pace was too slow, she had no idea how far behind the band of Children chasing them were, but they would definitely be closing in. In truth she had already come to admire the people of Lonely Barrow, they bore their forced march away from home with stoic calm, getting on with what needed to be done. Strangely, she found that the nervous innkeeper, Bjarn, was a good leader, organising wood for the people and ensuring that what little food there was was shared around so that no one went hungry.

The march was tedious up until early morning on the fifth day. The fog still sat heavy in the woods, obscuring the path, which was only visibly thanks to the alley carved through the trees. There was an oddly subdued air to the forest that day, with the sounds of birds and animals, the rustling of the forest floor strangely absent. Skjarla marched at the front of the column with Accipiteri and Sigmund, the white tendrils of the mists licking around their legs, the clash of metal from their armour seemed deafening amidst the silence. Skjarla held up a hand, her fist clenched and the column behind her gradually ground to a halt.

"What is it, why have we stopped?" asked Sigmund nervously

"Shhh!" Skjarla glared at him, before pointing out into the path, where the sound of jangling metal and the tramping of heavy steps could be heard. A horse neighed loudly, the sound shrill with terror, out in front of them, still hidden by the shroud of fog. All Skjarla could do was hold the column steady and wait to see what emerged from the mists. She waited for half a dozen heartbeats for another distant sound, but everything was muffled by the mist. The column was strung out behind her over a mile, with most of the strongest men at the rear, always looking over their shoulders for any sign of their pursuers.

She turned to Sigmund, "Wait here," was the only curt instruction that he received.

"But shouldn't I ..." whatever he was about to say was cut off as she backhanded him across the face, nearly sending him sprawling to the ground. He glared back at her, but even though he had nearly half as much bulk as her again he was under no illusion that she could skewer him as easily as a hunk of meat.

"Stay here," The command was repeated in an icy voice, she held his gaze for a few moments until his vision flickered away and he nodded his head in defeat. She stalked quietly down the path, biting back her frustration as she felt Accipiteri fall in beside her, she wouldn't be able to send him back to the column with his tail between his legs. She held a steel clad finger to her lips, the black metal contrasting violently with the flush of her lips and the pallor of her skin, silently urging her companion to keep quiet.

She couldn't quite believe her eyes, the distinctive oblong shields and the crested metal helmets marked the forty men who emerged from the fog, surrounding a single mangled carriage, out as Romans. 'What in the name of Valhalla were Romans doing here?' Skjarla asked herself, the voice within her head both incredulous and intrigued. The new Roman Empire had risen just after Ragnarok, when a legion, calling themselves the Ninth Hispania had appeared from a bank of fog within the lowlands of far off Albion and begun to subjugate the locals. They had assiduously built themselves a large empire, gradually swallowing smaller towns and cities before them. New Rome was an amazing city, Skjarla had been there a few times in her years of wandering, but, as the Sea of Souls was all but impossible to navigate, New Rome was on the far side of the world from here.

She could see two crudely trimmed tree trunks lying near the Romans, one of which had destroyed both wheels on one side of the simple carriage they were clustered around. The terrified horses were still in the traces, straining to pull away from the stricken carriage in their terror as arrows from the trees flickered about them. The Romans themselves seemed far less interested in the horses or their wounded, four of whom lay bleeding on the road, pinned there by crude arrows, than in holding their sheildwall strong, protecting whoever or whatever lay at the centre of that armoured shell.

Those who assailed the Romans from the trees were as much a threat to the column, if not more so given the almost complete lack of armour amongst the men and women of Lonely Barrow. "I'll take those on the left, think you can deal with whoever is on the right?" She muttered to Accipiteri. Fortunately the brigands had not noticed the two of them, so intent were they on the static prize in front of them.

"I'd have thought so," he said with a cold smile, he held a special contempt for those who preyed on travellers. He pulled his sword from its sheath, the broad blade gleaming even in the half light beneath the trees, "Ready when you are."

She nodded to Accipiteri and sprinted off into the trees, screeching a war cry as she sought the bowmen who shot at the Romans. They were simple brigands, armed with crude weapons and clad in stinking furs and leathers. She struck down two of the dozen archers on her side of the woodland before they had even tried to draw their blades. Of more concern than the wild-eyed, underfed brigands were the pair of Abhorrens who seemed to be leading the group. They were both wearing chainmail, bearing the insignia of the Haemocracy, suggesting that they were auxiliaries who had decided that there was more profit in brigandage. Both towered over Skjarla and writhed with muscles. One of the pair had an extra set of arms, and each of his ham-sized fists clutched a weapon of some form.

Skjarla grinned happily to herself beneath her helmet, bearing her teeth in a lupine smile, finally a decent challenge. She had had some spectacular fights over the years, but nothing of any challenge over the past six months. She moved for the two armed one, aiming to keep him between her and the other Abhorrens, dropping to one knee briefly as she noticed an archer loose an arrow out of the corner of her eye. She sprang back to her feet, redirecting the hulking Abhorrens's clumsy lunge, his huge cleaver stabbing into the soft earth of the forest floor. Her momentum kept her going, using the second blade of Dreyrispa to cut overhead down into the corded muscle where the neck and shoulder joined together. She smelt the stinking breath even as the giant collapsed to his knees, huge, dirty, stubby fingers clutching at the wound, blood leaking from between them. The four-armed monster gave a yell of anger and leapt over his fallen friend, jabbing at Skjarla with his two spears, waiting for an opening to use his axes. Skjarla fended off the dancing spear heads, surprised by the speed and dexterity of the raging hulk of muscle facing her.

She smiled, even as she felt beads of sweat trace their way across her skin, soaking the clothing beneath her armour, making it feel clammy against her skin. She was enjoying this, backing away from the Abhorrens, turning briefly to strike down one of the gawping bandits before her attention returned to the flashing points of steel. The monstrous wall of muscle was good, his constant flurry of attacks making it difficult for her to get an opening for an attack. Instead she leapt back from the man as far as she could, landing and going down on one knee, her left hand scrabbling for purchase on the ground, the wet earth bursting from between her slender fingers. She transferred Dreyrispa to an overhand grip, and exploded forward, throwing it like a javelin. Skjarla didn't even look to see if it landed, drawing her blades to finish the monster off.

She was correct in guessing the Abhorrens would have dodged the blow, but it had still carved a crimson furrow across its top left arm. The creature had staggered slightly, giving Skjarla the opening she needed, closing until she was almost chest to chest with the Abhorrens, punching both of her blades through the chainmail over the man's guts and up into the chest cavity. The Abhorrens collapsed in a heap; its lungs and heart eviscerated by the razor sharp Asgardian steel, and the remaining bandits broke and ran at the sight of their captain dead. Skjarla thought about chasing after them, but she felt it would be a letdown after the challenge of that last fight. She knelt next to the fallen giant and wiped the mud from her hand off on his tunic.

Humming cheerfully to herself she emerged from the forest, using a rag she had cut from one of the bandits to wipe the quickly congealing blood from her amour. She held Dreyrispa once again, taking comfort from the worn wood of its haft, she had already cleaned her swords and they had been returned to the sheathes over her shoulders. Accipiteri was already there waving cheerfully as she emerged from the foliage onto the track, while the Romans were nervously emerging from behind their wooden wall of shields. Their commander beckoned her over, and she jogged gently in their direction, the plates and chain mail of her armour jangling as she moved. Behind the officer, Skjarla could see Romans attending to their comrades, washing their wounds and already starting to sow them up with thick, gut thread. Another pair of legionaries were reverently helping a purple-cloaked individual from the ground, gently brushing the dirt from him, which struck

Skjarla as an odd way to treat a man, even if he was soft enough to ride within a carriage.

As one of the Romans disentangled himself from the group she muttered to Accipiteri, "I don't know what's going on here; I don't think they'll attack us though. Go back and fetch the column, but make sure that those at the front have their weapons to hand." A momentary raised eyebrow, invisible beneath the gilded helmet, followed by a barely perceptible nod of the head and Accipiteri strode back down the track, swallowed by the mists.

The Roman officer snapped off a salute, crashing his clenched fist into his breastplate, different to the banded loricas of the other men. "Thank you for the assistance. How far is it to the nearest town down this way?" Even as he spoke she could see the Romans behind him shuffling into a line, glancing nervously to each other, but preparing their steel for an assault.

Skjarla began with an exasperated sigh. "There is nothing left of it, what was the town of Lonely Barrow is now packed into carts behind me," She waved her arm, indicating the column hidden in the mists behind her. "Now what is a group of Romans doing in the outer reaches of the Hierocracy?" She asked, looking pointedly at the officer, who seemed to squirm slightly under her gaze.

The man opened his mouth to answer when a clear, regal voice erupted from the cloak, "Thank you Centurion, I will handle this." The man turned around, clearly having an animated conversation with the cloaked figure, who seemed implacable, she could not tell what was said, but caught snatches of the heated debate. She had her eyes on the Romans and saw a nervous shudder ripple through the tightly packed tines, she guessed the mists behind her must have disgorged the head of the column, The Romans held their ground though as they heard Accipiteri give the order for the strange column to halt, his voice carrying deep into the mists.

The Roman who had spoken to her gave up clearly exasperated, his armed falling to his sides as he glared furiously at the back of his master, whom he followed like a hound on the leash. The pair advanced on Skjarla, standing as a lone island between the two disparate groups, coming to a standstill just out of arm's reach. Skjarla was surprised to see that, as the hood of the cloak was pulled back, a mass of chestnut hair spilled out, framing a very pretty face, dominated by a thin, aquiline nose and two wide green eyes. The woman met Skjarla's eyes, clearly expecting her to bow as all of the Romans did, but Skjarla just stood there, slowly taking in the details of the woman. She began formally, her voice smooth with no trace of an accent, "My thanks for your aid. Now might I suggest that we all continue south together, there is some safety in numbers, and I will explain what we are doing here as we walk?" Behind her were the sounds of grunting and groaning as the Romans manhandled the broken carriage to the side of the road, when they left it piled ignominiously against the bank? There was also the soft thunder as the giant logs were rolled to clear the path for their journey back the way they had come.

Skjarla smiled somewhat maliciously, "Well, for the smaller group there is certainly some truth in there being safety in numbers," she softened her expression slightly, "though seeing as there is only one track I can't see why you shouldn't travel with us." She turned around and waved to the column, "Let's get moving again." She was satisfied to hear the slow rumble as the people of Lonely Barrow got underway once again.

She fell into step with the Roman lady while her men formed a square around them, the centurion lurking close to his mistress like a protective hound. Skjarla couldn't help but notice that despite his leathery skin and badly broken nose he had very kind eyes, a deep blue, like a high lake in summer. He shot a sharp glance at his mistress as she began, "You ask why we're here, and the only answer to that lies in who I am." She took a deep breath, giving herself a moment's pause before beginning, "Well, I am Domitia Aquilia, only daughter of a prominent Roman household." Her eyes seemed to shift slightly at that, suggesting she might be skirting the truth slightly, but Skjarla decided to say nothing, yet. "I am the only legitimate child of my father, but my bastard brother Tarpeus seeks to claim ..." she caught herself before continuing, "... my inheritance. He has sent assassins after me, I left New Rome with close to two hundred men from my personal guard, and as you can see, Centurion Quintus Metellus and his men are all that is left."

"I see," said Skjarla, not entirely convinced that Domitia had told her the whole truth. "Well, I am under contract to escort the people to the port of Celeste, if your men are prepared to help defend the column and not just you, then you may travel with us." Skjarla sounded emotionless as she said it, mainly because she was, what was the difference in having an extra thirty people to look after, and at least these extra bodies would be able to defend themselves. The Romans marched in a square around the Lady Domitia, who was clearly struggling with walking after an hour or so. It was Accipiteri who took pity on her, quietly suggesting that she may be more comfortable riding atop one of the carts. She shot him a grateful smile, and graciously accepted his hand as he helped her up on to the seat beside the driver.

As they continued down the worn forest track Accipiteri asked Skjarla quietly when Sigmund had dropped back for some food, "I've never seen those creatures in the village before. Where did they come from?"

Skjarla looked around, making sure that they were not overheard; she didn't want the people to know what was really after them. When she was certain that there was no one within earshot, "These creatures, the Children of the Dragon, they are not some new evil, they caused havoc with Fafnir in the time of Sigurd. Sigurd's armies drove the beasts back to the northern mountains, but he only crossed the passes with a few of his men. When the Dragon fell the power released was enough to shake the world, all of the passes through the northern mountains were completely ruined. Maybe one or two people could have got through but not an army."

She paused, checking round again and in that silence Accipiteri asked, "But how did they come to be on this side of the mountains then, and why now?"

Skjarla glared at him, "I was coming to that. My guess is that they have been rebuilding their strength over the past centuries, I have no idea how long these things take to breed so I've got no idea how many of them there are. I think they will also have been forced to tunnel through the shattered mountains several times over. They will not have just one way into the Haemocracy but several."

"You make a good point but what I still don't understand is ..." He stopped abruptly as Sigmund rejoined them, passing him a skin of cool water and tearing a hunk from a heel of stale bread.

"What were you two talking about?" asked Sigmund innocently.

Accipiteri opened his mouth but it was Skjarla who answered, "The speed of the march. We're not moving fast enough to keep ahead of those Wyrmlings," she said icily and quickened her pace.

***

They all made camp together at night, and it amused Skjarla to see the small crowd of young men who gathered every night to watch the Roman Legionaries as they trained. Centurion Metellus was a hard task master, but he had invited some of the larger youths from the town to join the training, they had kept the armour from their dead comrades, and he saw no harm in offering that as a carrot to try to recruit some extra guards for his mistress. At one stage Metellus had challenged Skjarla, and she had accepted, using the heavy wooden blades the Romans trained with. He had been well trained, and had a good, quick arm, but she was still able to beat him quickly, if only thanks to the benefit of hundreds of lifetimes of experience. The thing that surprised her the most was how open Domitia was for a powerful aristocrat, she would happily talk to anyone who came to her, although she was still flanked everywhere by at least three burly legionaries who kept their hands on their blades.

One evening it was Sigmund who approached her, nerves burning in his breast as he worried about seeming clumsy or slow in front of such a powerful woman. She just seemed so exotic to him, with her lightly bronzed skin and strange mannerisms. "My Lady," he began nervously with what he thought was a formal bow. It was lucky for him that he had his eyes on the floor or he would have seen the Legionaries all roll theirs.

She giggled charmingly, "There is no need for that here, and we are all members of the same column. What did you want from me?" Her perfect, pearly teeth peaked from between her rosy lips.

He stammered nervously, feeling his cheeks grow warm as he did so, but he pressed on. "I have lived my whole life in Lonely Barrow, and Rome to me is as far off as the moon. So I was wondering if you could tell me about it." He unconsciously clenched his fists to stop his hands from shaking, and then let out a heavy sigh of relief as she smiled and beckoned for him to take a seat beside her, next to the fire where a brace of rabbits hung limply on a spit. He heard the fire crackle as gobs of fat dripped into it, and saw the outsides of the carcass beginning to blacken and burn. One of the legionaries turned the spit slowly.

She waved her expressive hands gently as she began to build the scene within his mind. "Our ancestors emerged from the mists over four hundred years ago, on the day the world was remade. They were lost, but their leader, Lucius Aemilius Carus, was a man of vision, and he began the rebuilding of our people. At first they began to build a city, led by a council of the senior men of his legion, the Ninth Hispania, but then someone pointed out the greatest flaw in the rebuilding Rome. The legion was exclusively male, so Carus was forced to lead his men against the neighbouring tribes to capture their women. It was not an honourable thing to do, but it was important for building the city of Rome."

Sigmund, who was completely captivated by this history of a foreign land, interrupted cautiously, "But what is it like now."

Domitia smiled fondly, "It is a wonder of civilization and learning. People of all races are welcome there; Human, Dwarf and Dark Elf all living together as equals." Skjarla had moved closer and heard this part, and knew how economical with the truth Domitia was being. While it was technically true that Dwarves and Dark Elves, the Dokkalfar, held more rights there than the Haemocracy where they were distinctly second class citizens, they were still far from equal. Domitia had also failed to mention the huge army of slaves who served the citizens of New Rome. She kept silent as Domitia continued, "There are wide stone roads, lined with stalls selling goods from every corner of the empire, fountains and sewers keep the city clean. It is truly a beacon of civilization." Skjarla disagreed, but she could see the Sigmund looked positively awestruck by the images and ideals she had put in his head.

"Then I have one more question my lady. If Rome is such a wondrous city then why are you taking the road through the forest, why not head to the heart of the Haemocracy where you would surely be received as someone of noble blood would expect?"

Domitia gave a sad sigh, "It's not that easy. The threat of assassins is everywhere, and we thought that heading for the east side of the Haemocracy by the northern tracks was safer, even if it did mean spending months in the forest."

Sigmund looked like he was about to ask another question when Centurion Metellus came over and saluted his mistress, "Domina, a word if I may?"

"Very well Centurion. You must excuse me," she said to Sigmund with a radiant smile. She stood elegantly, the cloak parting slightly, revealing the pale, almost shear material of her stola beneath, and Sigmund had to tear his eyes away from the outline of the legs beneath. She withdrew from the fire, her sandaled feet cracking the small twigs which littered the space between the trees they had found. She spoke as gracefully as she could, but she was tired of putting on a show for these country folk, in truth she missed the sophistication of the cities. "Well Metellus, what is the problem now?"

The Centurion looked stern, he may be young, only twenty eight years of age, but he was a fine soldier. "Domina, why do you take such risks, allowing these people so close to you? Any one of them could bring an assassins blade."

She looked at him pityingly, "Metellus, you are a good soldier, but these people have almost never heard of the Roman Empire, there is no chance of one of them being in my brother's employ. I know you seek to protect me, but surely you can see that the benefit in binding these people to me is more than worth the effort." She looked at him pleadingly, in Rome she could have ordered him to do anything she wanted, but here it was more his element than hers.

Metellus looked at her and sighed heavily. He found it hard to deny his beautiful mistress anything; he had fallen helplessly in love with her during the course of their journey together as they fled across the breadth of the world. "Very well Domina, but at least make sure that my men stay near you at all times."

She held up a hand to forestall him, her skin appearing pale in the moonlight as it emerged from beneath her cloak. "No, some things are best done alone. I need to try to gain the support of those two warriors from the column, they may prove useful to my cause." She looked thoughtful then, her face creased by a frown of concentration.

Metellus shook his head slowly, "The man you may have luck with. From what my men have heard he has sworn to protect the boy you were just talking to, appeal to him with the bleak nature of your plight and you may bring him to your service. I get the feeling he is one of those who thrives on being the saviour."

Domitia looked at him pointedly, "I sense a 'but' coming here, Centurion."

"Yes, I do not think it wise to bring the woman to your service, she is one of the Reavers, the worst kind of mercenary. The way that one walks and stares, the dead look in her eye, it's not natural for one so young. It may be that it's just the worrying of a superstitious soldier, but if you knew some of the tales about the Reavers." He let the unspoken warning hang in the air between them. Metellus knew she hated it when he did that but it didn't stop him. Then he noted the disapproving look from his mistress and sighed, reading her response in her face. "If you are truly set on using her, I have heard that this particular Reaver has some interest in the one you were talking to as well. If you really want my advice then I would recommend that you bring the boy to follow you, then the other two will follow him."

She smiled winningly, and Metellus felt his heart melt as she rested her hand on his shoulder, "My faithful Metellus, what would I do without your council." She wandered off into the patchwork of flames formed by the camp fires all around them. Metellus looked at the heavens and sighed to himself, 'Venus's tits,' he thought to himself, 'All that woman has to do is flash me a smile and I would offer her the world.' He shook his head as he walked off to his bed roll, frustrated by how deeply his mistress had got her hooks into him.

Domitia, instead of going to sleep, was already searching for Accipiteri, wandering through the campfires, smiling and nodding graciously to everyone she passed. She found it grating, to have to be so polite and gracious to everyone she met, but the reality of her situation meant that she needed the support of these people, if only to hide herself within the crowd. She found the golden armoured warrior resting against the wheel of a cart, his back propped against the muddy wooden spokes. She couldn't help but feel a certain stirring as she looked at his fine features, the high cheekbones, the curious ear tips just poking out from the curtain of blond hair. As she sat down next to him his eyes snapped open, his hand instantly snapping out like a snake to grasp the hilt of his sword. Then his eyes settled on her and the tension flowed out of his muscles, "Can I help you, my Lady?" he said sleepily.

She looked at him levelly, knotting her fingers together as if nervous and biting her lip slightly, she knew she needed to make this performance convincing. "Well, your name would be a good start." She smiled at him as he chuckled embarrassedly.

"Accipiteri, Domina," he bowed his head gracefully.

She smiled with surprise, "How is it that you know the correct term of address for one such as myself, I didn't think that people from here would have had any knowledge of the Roman Empire?"

"You're right" he said with slight shrug of his shoulders, the armour clanking as the plates slid across one another. "I am Loptalfar, so have had some cause to meet your people. But that doesn't answer my question Domina, why are you here?" He looked innocent enough asking the question, but Domitia could see the keen light of intelligence burning in his eyes.

"As I told your friend, the Reaver, I have been driven here by assassins, sent by my bastard brother to remove all obstacles between himself and my father's property. The centurion and his men are loyal and brave soldiers, but they are not enough to deal with some of the assassins my father's get upon that witch Lucia Petrovia has sent against me. I want you to join my personal guard, I would feel so much safer if you did." She made her lip tremble slightly and moisture seemed to well up in her eyes. Although part of her hated using herself this way, she had to admit that she had a gift for this kind of manipulation, using her youthful countenance to twist people to her will.

Accipiteri sat in silence, his head bowed forward in deep thought, before he replied in measured tones, his voice soft as he spoke to her. "Domina, I have sworn to protect the people of Lonely Barrow, so until they reach safety then their path is mine. However, if you were to travel with them, then there is no reason that I cannot protect you as well, although you may find that which hunts the people of this town is far worse than any assassin. After we reach Celeste then I cannot say what will happen, Skjarla seems to think that there is something here that needs hiding and protecting, and she may need my aid, but I cannot say yet. As such, all I can promise you is that I will protect you while you travel with us." He took her hand and gave it a reassuring squeeze.

Domitia nodded her thanks and then withdrew, leaving Accipiteri to his thoughts, although he was not left alone for long, Skjarla came and joined him, sighing heavily as she warmed her feet by the fire nearby. "What do you make of her Loptalfar? I can't help but think that she isn't telling everything."

Accipiteri nodded gently, "Aye. She may be being economical with the truth, but she is genuinely afraid, I think she is in danger." He gave Skjarla a slightly disapproving glance, before saying coldly, "Besides, if she is a rich man's daughter I would have thought that she would be worth protecting, you could get a goodly amount of gold for it."

Skjarla scowled, which didn't do too much to diminish the cold beauty of her features, "Bollocks to that. I couldn't care less about gold at the moment, you should know the legends of the Fangs as well as I do. We have to get it away from the north, if the Children get a hold of any of the Fangs then it will herald the start of an age of strife."

Accipiteri blew out an exasperated breath, "True, but if they find any of the Fangs then a Hunter will spring up. Do you know where the rest of the Fangs are hidden?"

"No, but if the Children gather all of the Fangs and the Horn then you know as well as I do that Fafnir will rise again and war will be delivered upon all of the realms of Midgard." She paused, weighing up her thoughts before continuing in a whisper. "The other thing I should tell you, although this is not to go beyond us, concerns the boy, Sigmund."

"What about him?" Accipiteri's brow creased with concern.

"His armour was recovered from the barrow in town, his ancestor's apparently. Have you seen the helm, it looks like there should be a crown around it. I think ..."

"You don't think he is the heir to the Iron crown?" Accipiteri interrupted, his voice loud and incredulous, gaining him looks from the surround people who were trying to sleep.

Skjarla glared at him viciously, "Keep your voice down. Anyway, as I hear it it's the rusted crown these days, on account of how no one has worn the damn thing since the days of Sigurd. But yes, I think the Sigmund is Sigurd's heir, the last of his line, if the Dragon does come back then it may be that only he can slay the beast. I'm not sure how much stock I put in the tales of Sigurd's blood being Fafnir's bane though"

Accipiteri shook his head slowly, "That may be the case, but that is so much hot air unless we can get the townsfolk to Celeste, then if needs be we can take ship with Sigmund to the south of the continent and defend him there."

"Agreed. I will leave you to your rest for now, tomorrow we'll rouse the column early, we are moving too slowly and if we don't hurry then we will be caught on the open ground beyond the forest by the Children." With that she got back to her feet, stalking off into the night, leaving an ominous silence in her wake.

***

The column of refugees continued south, leaving the forest on the tenth day of the march, although Skjarla set a punishing pace as they trekked. It was not long before carts began to creak under the strain and the eldest and youngest began to fall behind. Bjarn had led a deputation from the townsfolk to her, begging her to slacken off the pace, but she would not relent. They pressed on even as the autumn rains came again, the chill in the air heralding the winter to come, turning the road to thick, cloying mud which clung to ankles and wheels with a vice like grip. The only comfort that Skjarla could draw from the circumstances, as icy dribbles of water crept down her back, and a howling gale plucked at her cloak, was that the Children would be slowed even more than them by this, the road behind them would be even more churned up by their passing, making for ever slower going. In her heart though, she knew that this was of no real comfort, as their pursuers did not have to deal with carts or elderly people who could barely march a full day.

Accipiteri was far better suited to driving the column on than she was, he seemed to be everywhere, offering encouragement, carrying small children upon his shoulders, lifting spirits everywhere he went. She, by comparison, was being viewed as the grim task mistress, but she had never been in this for their adulation, she knew that her responsibility lay in preventing the Fang from falling into the Children's hands. On several occasions since the rains had come she had considered just taking the Fang and leaving, but her word still remained strong, and her honour held her from that course, for the moment.

It rained almost solidly for ten days, the ditches on either side of the road becoming rivers, every inch of ground was drenched, and all the wood to be found was too soaked to light. The people of the column sat in cold, miserable, shivering huddles, desperately trying to save some of the warmth their bodies generated. Three days after leaving the forest, the first of the villagers died, an old lady. The townsfolk had wanted to bury her, but Skjarla had insisted that there was no time, so she was left where she lay, a gently stiffening corpse, gradually turning blue with the cold.

The number of dead grew steadily over the following days, as they moved away from the river and up into the hills that surrounded the approach to Celeste. Of the three thousand who had left Lonely Barrow, close to one hundred lay silent in the mud of the road, waiting to be picked at by dogs and crows as the spring thaw came around. Skjarla drew comfort from one thing, although the Children of the Dragon would be able to move far faster than the slow moving train of refugees, she doubted that they would actually be able to keep pace. They were on unfamiliar ground, and from what she had seen of their equipment she couldn't believe that they would thrive in the cold. If they could hack the cold then they would have been on us long ago Skjarla though to herself bitterly.

There was a shout from the front of the column, and Skjarla ran to investigate, she had been down at the rear of the column, helping Accipiteri to push the stragglers along. It was a strange feeling, looking out for other people again after so long, in truth she was coming to respect the hardy townsfolk, who silently trudged on, never giving up. The Romans, for their part, had been exemplary, helping to move and wagons which became bogged down in the sucking mud, although Skjarla guessed this was more due to Domitia still being on a charm offensive than any natural instinct to help. She jogged up to the front of the column, icy brown water splashing freezing daggers against her legs. She and the rest of the people were now clad in brown, as the all-pervading mud seeped into every item of clothing. The only one who had so far managed to keep clean was Domitia, although she sat shivering miserably in her thinner clothing. She arrived at the head of the column, pleasantly warmed against the chill wind which blew in from the Empty Sea by her exertions, to see why the people were cheering.

Stretching below them were the walls of Celeste, a pale cream-coloured stone edifice which stretched around the harbour like a giant horse shoe. Thin ribbons of grey smoke crept into the sky from the hundreds of houses enclosed behind the stone gatehouse, and beyond them the tiny twigs of ship masts stabbed into the grey sky. Just beyond the town, which was positioned on the river, a few miles back from the coast, they could just make out the white smear of waves crashing into the shore. Skjarla laughed quietly to herself, as she saw the people of Lonely Barrow hugging one another at the thought of their ordeal being over. There was a gentle hubbub of conversation as the townsfolk chattered excitedly, their carts trundling down the final approach to Celeste.

Chapter 4

The ragged convoy approached the firmly shut gates of Celeste, at this time of year they were not expecting any trade to come in by road from the north, the east gate was open however, connecting the capital to the port city. The refugees began to bunch up around the gate, shouting up to the few bored sentries who lazily patrolled the stretch of wall during that bleak winter's day. Skjarla hammered on the studded wooden gateway as loudly as she could, until finally, the small door set into the gates was opened, and before anyone could push inside the town an overweight official with a thin beard stepped outside.

The man cleared his voice, drawing himself up to his full height. It was still not an imposing sight, with his watery eyes and puffy jowls which spoke of an easy life. Even his thick read coat was lined with expensive furs as oppose to the more common wool. "Who are you and by what authority do you hammer on the gates of Celeste?" he asked pompously, puffed up with his own self importance.

Skjarla's eyes briefly shot heavenward, petty provincial officials were the same everywhere. "These are the citizens of Lonely Barrow, driven from their homes by an invasion from the north. They have come here seeking safety and shelter." Skjarla looked the man in the eyes, fixing as much fire as she could into her gaze, forcing him to look away.

"Well there is no room in the town," the functionary blustered, "You'll have to continue on to the next town to see if they can help you." With that he turned to leave, taking half a step towards the safety of the gatehouse before Skjarla's hand grabbed him by the shoulder, leaving a muddy print on the rich red velvet.

"You're going nowhere, not until these people have food and shelter, if that is not within your remit then you will take me to your superior." Skjarla's tone brooked no argument and the man squirmed under the crushing vice of her grip on his shoulder. His eyes widened as he caught a glance of the shining steel blade the Skjarla half drew from its sheath, a calm fury burning from her eyes.

The look of fear in the man's eyes increased as Accipiteri and the Roman Legionaries pushed their way to the front of the crowd, the blades sheathed for the moment, though hands rested ominously on the hilts. The fat functionary seemed to deflate before their eyes, "Very well, I will take a small party of you into the town, but the rest must wait out here until the city council has come to a decision."

Skjarla nodded severely, "That is acceptable, however you will have bundles of dry wood sent outside; these people have not had a fire in four hands of days." Her tone allowed for no compromise and the red cloaked official could only nod defeatedly as he led Skjarla, Accipiteri and Metellus into Celeste. As she was about to step through the small gate she barked an order, "Bjarn, have a dozen of the sharpest-eyed archers sent back down the track a ways. If they see anything coming down the track then they are to run back and give warning. The only way the Children will come is in our footsteps." She didn't wait to see if he carried out the order, she knew he was as afraid as the rest of them and would do as he was bid. In truth she wasn't worried about a full assault yet, if they had the numbers for that then it would have come already, she guessed that they

55

were waiting for reinforcements for that. The more immediate threat was of a small band sneaking into the camp to steal the Fang, she made a mental note to make sure that there were guards and that her tent was pitched next to Sigmund's.

They stepped through the narrow wooden door, which was slammed shut behind them, separating them from the rest of the townsfolk. The fat official, who had still not deigned to give his name, seemed to recover some of his earlier bluster when the guards clustered around them to escort them to the city hall. The streets were broad and clear of filth for the main part, although there were sewers covered by grates down each side of the road. Metellus whistled softly as he saw the ingenuity, "That is the river water being redirected through the town to wash the filth away; such construction would not be out of place in Rome herself." The roofs of the houses were simple wooden beams, angled so as to deflect any rain away into the gutters, and all of the walls were pleasantly whitewashed. 'This is not a place that knows war or hardship' thought Skjarla to herself, almost envious of their tranquillity for a moment, and concerned about the war she may be bringing to their doorsteps.

There were good reasons why the city of Celeste was used to peace, the Empty Sea well deserved its name, and there was nothing there, no pirates or warships, just thousands of miles of open water. Stories told of giant monsters which lived there, but Skjarla paid little heed to such talk, hunting sea monsters was never something she wanted to try. She knew that in the warmer waters to the south the Sea-Drakes and the Krakenkin were a threat to shipping, and she had no idea what made its home in the cold, black waters of the Empty Sea. The reason that trade flourished was thanks to the merchants of Leopolis and Taureum, who made sure that they were the only avenue of trade between east and west by judicious use of privateers.

These pirates were given the protection of the Isles so long as they only attacked vessels from outside the Trade Guilds, granting the Guildsmen a monopoly. So long as everyone kept to the system they all profited, except for the customers.

The sound of the hobnailed boots clattering against the stone paving slabs echoed from the buildings, the streets were quiet as most of the people had decided that today it was far nicer indoors than in the teeth of a building winter storm. The few people they could see were a fair bit shorter than the people of Lonely Barrow, with black hair far more common and slimmer features; it made Skjarla wonder how much heritage these people shared with the men and women of Lonely Barrow.

The guards drew up outside the imposing, grey edifice that was the city hall, a huge stone facade dominated by the seal of the Haemocracy, a set of scales weighted down on one side by a drop of blood. Accipiteri leant close and whispered to her, "Dwarven work if I am not mistaken, certainly makes a statement if you ask me." Skjarla could only agree, the sharp angles of the ornate work, coupled with the menacing carvings of winged gryphons added a feeling of ominous power to the centre of the Haemocracy in Celeste.

They walked up the dozen steps which led to the arched facade of the building before being escorted through an oak door bound with leaf shaped iron studs. Inside they were led to a small chamber off the main audience chamber, barely having time to take in the blood red decor which dominated the hall, all the way up to the dais which sat below a huge golden copy of the Haemocracy seal. The back wall of the audience chamber, behind the dais so that all who entered could gaze upon it, was a map of the lands controlled by the Haemocracy. This was a ploy to intimidate and overawe all who were called to stand before the council of Celeste and Skjarla could not doubt its effectiveness.

The three of them were hustled through a small doorway into a warm office where a small fire burned cheerfully in the grate; a large desk piled high with papers dominated the room. Someone had already taken the initiative of setting three chairs before the desk, in front of each sat a gently steaming silver goblet, which from the smell contained some form of spiced wine. The wall to the left of the doorway was a large window which led out onto a small garden, which during summer would have been immaculately manicured but was now little more than the skeletons of various plants and shrubs. The other two walls were both dominated by large murals of fantastic men struggling against Abhorrens. A reedy voice from behind the piled papers broke the silence, "Marvellous aren't they, a symbol of our struggle against all that is imperfect in this age of rust and decay."

Skjarla turned around to look at the thin-faced man who sat behind the desk, goose feather quill gripped tightly in his right hand and he continued to sign documents and scan the pile of papers which formed a small wall around him. She frowned at him, "I thought the Haemocracy now had regiments of Abhorrens as auxiliaries for their armies?"

The thin-faced man looked at her with hard, brown eyes, she could see the slight stubble clinging to his narrow jaw. "They may be now, now that we have tamed them and bred out some of their baser instincts." It was no secret that the Haemocracy had, for centuries, been selectively breeding the Abhorrens to ensure that they served their purpose, as slaves to the High Council's will. "Anyway, I have no time to discuss such trivialities," he continued sharply, "Is there a particular reason you have brought several thousand people to my doorstep?"

Skjarla glanced around and looked at Accipiteri who nodded slightly to her before he took up the tale, briefly telling of how the town had been attacked and they had been on hand to help the townsfolk flee. He studiously neglected to make any mention of the Fang in their possession. Skjarla mentally removed herself from the conversation, staring at the fantastically crude piece of art behind the councillor. The portrayal of the dozens of Abhorrens who were fighting against the single pale-skinned, black-haired demigod who represented the Haemocracy was inaccurate to say the least. All of them seemed to be more animal than human; admittedly there were people such as that abroad in Midgard, but not in such numbers as the Abhorrens.

She quietly rejoined the conversation as she heard Accipiteri explaining what the refugees needed. "The people are freezing, their clothes are rags and they have not eaten a good meal since we left the forest, they have been surviving on quarter rations at best. They need to be brought inside the walls and settled somewhere, not least thanks to the possible danger posed by our pursuers." Accipiteri sighed heavily and looked at the inscrutable councillor's face.

The man pursed his lips and made a faint clicking sound with his tongue, "It is a shame to lose the town of Lonely Barrow, and their lumber was put to good use in the shipyards." Skjarla's mouth almost dropped at this crass comment, but she kept her silence even as she felt her temper beginning to bubble to the surface. The councillor continued, taking a sip of his spiced wine and smacking his lips appreciatively, "They cannot come into Celeste. There is, as my junior Breslan told you at the gates, no room to accommodate close to three thousand men, women and children within the walls during the night. However, he may have been over zealous in turning you away. I will send to the high council in Fylkirsblod for further instructions. Until I receive a reply, your people will be given tents for shelter, wood for fire and food that we can spare, so long as they live outside the walls. If they wish to come inside the walls during the day then they must return outside before dark. Of course, certain privileges can be permitted to people of rank. Who else speaks for the people of Lonely Barrow?" The man seemed genuinely helpful, and he smiled weakly at them.

Skjarla rubbed her forehead, she was tired of this, with the people still outside the walls they were still at risk of attack, which more than anything kept her bound to her word and guarding them. At least the people outside would be fed, and she knew just the man to organise it, "He used to be the innkeeper, so he knows everyone, his name is Bjarn and he will be here tomorrow to arrange for food to be distributed to the people." It suited her to send Bjarn, a petty piece of revenge for him landing her with protecting the townsfolk in the first place. She continued, "The tents are the priority, the people haven't been dry in days, so we would hope to receive them today."

The councillor waved his hand impatiently, wanting the interview to be over, "Very well, very well. I will endeavour to get those to you today, but I will not promise you anything. Now, if you have no other demands to make of me, I have other things to attend to. Goodbye." Without even waiting for them to rise from their seats he had returned to his paperwork, and their ears were filled with the harsh scratching as the nib of his quill danced across the paper. The three of them looked at one another and shrugged, filing out through the doorway without another word.

The three of them emerged from the Council Hall to the first flurries of snow, the earlier freezing rain and sleet having now frozen completely. The white flakes settled in Skjarla's black hair like the beginnings of a veil, and Metellus stamped his feet as the freezing flakes found the gaps between the straps of his sandals. Accipiteri was the first to break the silence, his breath leaving steaming clouds hanging in the air, "I think we need to go and make sure that Breslan has not been tight-fisted with the wood for the people." He grinned at Skjarla, "I seem to remember that he had a peculiar desire to stay on your good side in particular." The three of them laughed at Accipiteri's easy wink and walked back towards the gateway, this time ignored by the guards of Celeste, who felt it was far better to huddle around their braziers.

***

It had snowed steadily for three days, earlier snows than usual but not unheard of, a thick white blanket forming atop the sturdy felt hides which had been sent to form tents for the people. Several more of the Celeste militia had stood at the gateway, keeping watch over the rabble who now camped outside. Breslan had been every day, followed by carts of food and firewood which were distributed to the people, but the moment he caught sight of Skjarla in the distance he tried to make himself as scarce as possible. For her part, Skjarla had little interest in the supplying of the refugees; instead she trained with the legionaries, and the growing number of young men and women who insisted on learning the basics of fighting. This profoundly shocked the Romans, who knew of the occasional female warrior, but never in numbers on this scale. To them women belonged as far from the battlefield as possible. The training had to be moved regularly, as the stamping of feet as they fought compacted the snow into a lethal layer of ice. She made sure to rotate those left out in the cold, eyes trained on the road stretching off to the northeast, waiting for any sign of the Children.

Skjarla found herself strangely enjoying the experience; it had been decades since she had last taken any form of pupil, and in truth, it relaxed her. She loved the energy and enthusiasm the people of Lonely Barrow threw into their training, their passion fed by a desire never to be as helpless as they had been again. They only had wooden weapons and the woodsmen's axes with which they had been wrought, but the people revered them as if they were the blades of the gods themselves. Accipiteri was the most popular of the trained soldiers, especially with the two dozen women who had wanted to learn the skills required to handle a blade. Skjarla grinned every time she saw a gaggle of them clustered around where he sat, ostensibly to ask about techniques, but most of them merely sat there gazing at him. Some of the braver souls tried to challenge her, but she was never much of a teacher, often sending them away with fresh bruises and battered pride. Still, several of them kept coming back, earning her grudging respect, but not special treatment. The only person that she and Accipiteri insisted trained every day was Sigmund, they said that if he wished to carry the Fang then he had to be able to protect it.

Gradually people started to slip into the town during the day, rather than spend it huddled around the fires they built between the tents. Two weeks after they had arrived at Celeste, and three days before the winter's Eve celebrations Skjarla found herself inside the Captain's Rest, one of the many inns on the waterfront. She was on her own, drinking flagon after flagon of rich, dark ale. The tavern was a dark place, lit almost entirely by the roaring fire in the hearth next to the wooden bar which ran the length of the room. The grimy windows kept the cold out, but they also kept most of the light out as well. A fug of smoke hung in the room as the fire failed to draw properly; the innkeeper needed to sweep his bloody chimney, Skjarla thought irritably. At least the ale was good, and the mood was raucous without being deafening, the kind of place that Skjarla liked as she could join in the contests or stay out as the mood took her.

She had come here to get away from the stifling nature of the camp, people asking her to settle disputes, to help them with some manner of fighting. Skjarla couldn't understand why the people wanted her help, she was no leader like Accipiteri, even Metellus, with his stolid and staid manner was more use than she was. She had enjoyed the afternoon, so far five flagons had disappeared down her throat, and she had won a small handful of gold in a knife throwing contest. She made sure to keep her cloak wrapped around her; the sight of her armour might alarm the people even more than the appearance of Dreyrispa had.

Unfortunately, as she got to her feet to relieve herself, her thick cloak caught on a nail sticking out of the table and was pulled to the side, revealing her armour, and the horn tied to her hip. Every head in the tavern looked round as she cursed, most of the heads barely spared her a second glance before turning back to their dice and their ale. Skjarla noticed two of the cloaked figures who were tucked deep into the shadows keep their gaze on her for a little longer before pressing their heads together to whisper conspiratorially. Skjarla hastily pulled the cloak back around her, before stalking over to the back door which opened out to the stone seats above the running water which served to clear away the waste. She sat down and shivered as her skin came into contact with the freezing stone slabs. She reflected that the crude trenches beneath a wooden frame found in camp were not as uncomfortable as this.

She was still shivering as she got back inside the Captain's Rest, heading back to her mug of ale only to find that her table had been occupied. She stood, menacingly glaring down at the two people who had taken her table, waiting for them to move. Instead, the short, sturdy one of these two new irritants said, without looking up, "Won't you join us?"

"That is my ale on the table next to you, and I want you two to go and find somewhere else to sit." She tried to keep irritation out of her voice, but alcohol always got her blood up, so her voice had the soft rasp of steel being drawn over stone.

Again, it was the shorter of the two who spoke, "No lass, I think you, my friend and I need to have a little talk. I think we have a lot to discuss." He lifted Dreyrispa off the bench from next to him, his sleeve falling down to reveal heavily armoured forearms and thick, stubby hands which could only belong to a Dwarf.

Skjarla sat down slowly, unsure as to what a Dwarf was doing this far north. Dwarves and Dokkalfar were not made welcome in the Haemocracy, and those who did live there were very much third class citizens, only Abhorrens were below them. Skjarla had long since forgiven them, but the Dwarves and the Dokkalfar had long been shunned as cowards and traitors thanks to their failure to defend Valhalla. As such, in the Haemocracy they had very few rights, but in the west they were far more accepted, especially in New Rome. There were still several great holds in the south, mighty underground fortress cities where Dwarves and their dark elf cousins lived under their own rule, though these were isolated communities.

As she sat down the Dwarf looked at her and said, "My friend and I saw when your cloak was so unfortunately pulled open, and came to ask about that horn which hangs at your side. And I'm afraid our curiosity only grew when we saw this weapon." He gently stroked down the length of Dreyrispa's worn wooden haft. "So we want to know how someone comes into possession of both an Aesir blade and the Gjallarhorn."

Skjarla forced herself to be calm, very few knew who she was in the northern reaches of the Haemocracy, and she wanted to keep it that way. Not because she disliked her past, but if people here knew she had lived with the Gods and was immortal then things would become harder. She was less worried about the Old races knowing about her, they knew she lived and most of them had lived long enough to hear tales of her anyway, but for humans, Abhorrens and other short-lived peoples it was complicated. The Jarls of the south new her tale, if only because they still clung to the old ways, even with their Gods long since departed. She looked into both of the hoods before saying anything, her voice level, "Remove your hoods first; I won't say a word until I know who I am talking to."

The Dwarf reached up first, his thick, sausage-like fingers gripping the worn, dark blue material of his cloak and sliding it back from his head to reveal a broad, round skull, dominated by heavy brows and a thick jaw bone. His green eyes were tired, and his thick red beard was flecked with grey. His most striking feature though, was the thick, angular and vicious tattoos which covered every inch of his face, giving him a fiercely intimidating appearance. The Dwarf held out his arm, which Skjarla gripped in the usual greeting, feeling the forearms, wrapped in metal and hidden beneath the folds of his cloak. The Dwarf's voice was heavy and yet strangely lyrical, "I am Braugr Axehand, and son of Grundin Axehand, my companion will give her own introduction."

The second figure reached up with delicate hands, clad in black leather gloves with studded knuckles, to pull back a jet black hood. "I am Helania," the figure said simply, the voice soft and silky, yet with a line of hidden steel nestled within it. The woman was Dokkalfar, a narrow face stretching from waves of white hair down to a sharply pointed chin. The thin eyebrows were white, contrasting sharply with the ebony coloured skin. Red veins were clearly visible, shot through the inky black skin, which was stretched over proud cheekbones and delicate features. Her eyes were wildly beautiful, a swirl of white and sliver which gave the appearance of winter storm taking place within her irises.

Skjarla looked at them both, taking them in, she couldn't fathom what the two of them were doing together up here, the nearest subterranean kingdom that she could think of was close to two months' hard trek away. She began to speak cautiously, "My name is Skjarla." She took a sip of her ale, looking to see if there was any reaction from her new companions. Neither gave anything away, but she was sure that she could see a flicker of recognition in Braugr's eyes. "As far as you need to know, as far as anyone in here needs to know, I am a Reaver." She said loudly before dropping her voice, "If you truly recognize my things then you will know to stay away from me." Skjarla stood up, grabbed Dreyrispa in one hand and tossed the flagon of ale down her throat before striding to the door and out into the cold.

She heard the door bang shut behind her, then a few seconds later she heard it go again. She shook her head irritably, black strands of hair whipping back and forth with the motion, as she strode powerfully towards the gate. The alcohol gave her a pleasant feeling of warmth, and a soft fuzz to the edge of her thoughts. She nodded to the two gate guards, who stood before the stone edifice, shivering gently as they stood next to a brazier in their crimson uniform, the colours of all who served the Haemocracy. She ducked under the wooden frame of the small doorway carved into the gates and glanced back down the road to see what could only be Braugr and Helania following her. She sighed as she stepped back into the sprawl of the campsite, thinking to herself, before deciding, against her better judgement, to wait for them and then speak to them in her tent. At least that way she would have a little privacy in dealing with them.

The two of them emerged from the wooden gate, Helania stepping gracefully through with feline elegance, while Braugr shifted his heavy frame sideways through the narrow doorway. Skjarla glared at them both, clearly unimpressed by their following her, but simply said, "Follow me." As she turned away she could see Helania grin excitedly and nudge her companion who merely pursed his lips. She picked her way through the tents, never once bothering to look behind her to check on their progress. She entered the small tent she had to herself, bent double and stooped beneath the wooden pole which formed the spine of the felt structure. She picked her helmet off the simple pile of furs and spare cloth which formed her bedding, and perched on the single stool in her tent. She waited until the two of them entered the tent. She gestured to the furs for them to sit upon while she sat with Dreyrispa balanced across her legs and her helmet perched on her knee.

Braugr was the first to break the silence, after he had removed his cloak, revealing more ornate, angular plates of metal woven around his breast. "We want an answer to our earlier question, who are you? I think I know, but I want to hear it from your lips."

Skjarla sighed, her shoulders slumping slightly, "Why, why do you want to know?" Her voice was quiet now, softer than usual.

Braugr looked up at her, "Because Helania and I both seek something, something that we think we may have found with you."

Skjarla's face was blank. She didn't know what to say to this. Her confusion was written plain across her face, so Helania explained, "Purpose. Both of us seek a purpose with our lives, or rather a means to fulfil that purpose. Neither of us are welcome at home, and we have spent several seasons with one of the mercenary companies from Leopolis. That was not what we were looking for, so we caught a ship back to Celeste, where we saw you."

Skjarla looked at the Dokkalfar irritably, "Yes, but you haven't told me what it is that you actually want from me." Her voice had recovered some of its edge. "And what were you doing in Celeste, I can't believe that you were looking for me in particular?"

Braugr took over here, "It was the cheapest route to the Haemocracy. We had planned to wait out the winter here and then travel south to the lands beyond the Black mountains. It seems that we have one thing in common with these people around us, the need for a new home."

Then she paused, as she noticed something for the first time. "Braugr, how is it that you come to have both the arms of the Hearth Guard and the tattoos of the Shattered?" The Hearth Guard were the elite Dwarven units who were charged with defending the Dwarven kings and were usually the crack units of any Hold's army. The Shattered, though, were Dwarves who had been disgraced for some great failing of their honour. These Dwarves were shunned by the rest of Dwarven society and often chose to leave their Holds.

Braugr looked at her sadly, she thought she could see tears welling up in the corners of his eyes, before he responded heavily, his shoulders slumped at some internal defeat. "My daughter, I lost my daughter through my own stupidity. Please, do not ask me to say more, I know we are asking you to trust us, but the memory is still raw even now."

Skjarla thought the Dwarf seemed honest, and it heartened her to see Helania give her travelling companion's shoulder a reassuring squeeze. She made a decision and spoke, "I am, or rather was, a Valkyrie. But what would you want from a sell-sword who once lived and fought alongside the Gods?"

Helania was the first to reply, her voice overflowing with excitement, "Ha, ha," she whooped, slapping Braugr on the back. "If you were just a simple sell-sword we doubt that you would still be protecting these people, so therefore there must be something keeping you here. What we want is to help you achieve whatever it is you're doing."

Skjarla's eyebrows knitted together and she stared incredulously at the dark elf, "What? You don't even know what I am doing, you have never met me before, and why would you want to join me?"

Helania's eyes lit up as she spoke, hurriedly and excitedly with great passion in her voice. "You must be doing something great, and I want to follow you because it will help my people to regain their honour, no one can question that the Dokkalfar are courageous if one of their number completes some great quest."

Skjarla ignored Helania's patently bizarre argument, whatever her true reasons she was clearly hiding them, she stared at Braugr who nodded as if to verify what Helania had said. Skjarla spoke softly, "And you, what do you want out of helping me?"

"Honour," the one word was spoken with heavy emphasis.

Skjarla got the feeling that both of them were stretching the truth as to why they wanted to help her in whatever she was doing, but she was tired of this foolishness. She needed every trained arm she could get, and even if she couldn't trust them completely she decided to let them stay, for the moment. "You said you had both fought for one of the Leopolitian companies, which one?"

Braugr answered her, reaching into his cloak to withdraw a medallion which he handed to Skjarla. "We both served for six years with the Highland Irregulars, the medal bears their seal. Helania may be young but you should see her shoot, and her swordplay does not lack for much either, you have my word that she will not be a burden."

Skjarla nodded quickly, "Very well. You can help with the refugees for the moment; I will not know what the plans are for the people until the courier returns from Fylkirsblod. I do not know where our journey will take us, but I can promise you that we won't be going back north, so it should at least be in the direction you need. Until we are forced to move on you are welcome to come to the camp when you wish to, we train with weapons every day, so you will be welcome to join in with that. Now, unless there is anything else ..." her voice tailed off as she let the hint that they should leave hang heavy in the air. They both got the message, rising to their feet they bowed to her and left the close confines of the tent, pressing out into the cold winds which whipped through the camp. If they had checked about them in the gathering gloom, they would have seen one of the Roman legionaries who had stepped closer to Skjarla's tent from his position guarding Sigmund's tent for the evening. Silently the man went back to his position, finishing his shift before casually walking away from the tent to report the conversation to his mistress.

***

There was peace in the camp for the next three days as people prepared for the winter's Eve feast; Breslan had been to pass on the message that the townsfolk would be welcome in Celeste for the whole day and night, to enjoy the celebrations. Skjarla was beginning to appreciate that even though he was bound by bureaucracy Garret, the high councillor of Celeste, was at heart a good man who was genuinely willing to help.

Winter's Eve was a day and night of drinking, feasting and celebrating the end of winter, going from the shortest day of the year. From what she had heard down in the many taverns it appeared that some fishermen had braved the crashing waves and taken their boats out. They had been rewarded for their courage by landing some of the biggest tuna that Celeste had ever seen, one of them measuring over eight feet long. There had also been cattle and pigs slaughtered to feed the people of Celeste.

The people of Lonely Barrow had been cobbling together gaudy clothes to wear, sharing scraps of colourful clothing between themselves. Skjarla was growing to admire their sense of community and their drive to help each other during this difficult time. Skjarla, for her part had managed to buy a crimson cloak in Celeste. She knew well that the black armour was not the right colour for Winter's Eve, but given that there was no safe place to leave it she wore it anyway.

The day of the feast came, and so far there had been no sign of the Children of the Dragon, Skjarla was beginning to hope that the cold weather had driven them back under the mountains or at least confined them to Lonely Barrow. The townsfolk and their few guardians were welcomed into Celeste, Breslan opening the north gate to them. There was a festive mood in town, and although there were large flakes of snow falling it was a relatively still day, so the white flakes added to the holiday mood rather than ruin it. Skjarla glared around as a snowball whipped out of nowhere to strike her behind the ear. Everyone around was studiously avoiding her terrifying gaze, but she could not see who had thrown the offending ball of ice. She continued on her way, the fresh snow crunching beneath the heavy metal of her boots and a red hot glare carved into her features.

***

If she had been able to pick out the figure in the crowd, she would have seen Sigmund hurriedly wiping his snowy hands on his cloak while Accipiteri chuckled next to him. Sigmund had come to like the giant warrior's company, the Loptalfar was only matched in his weapon craft by Skjarla, but his manner was far nicer than hers. For all his travelling in the fifteen years since he had left the Windswept Isles he had not encountered a winter's Eve fair in the Haemocracy before, so Sigmund felt that it was his duty to show his friend its delights. Large banners of coloured cloth hung across the streets, slung between the houses. The streets themselves were a riot of colour and revelry. Even though it was barely two hours past sun up, many of Celeste's more committed citizens were already rosy-cheeked from alcohol.

As one of the many young women holding trays of steaming drinks, the speciality being a clear alcohol mixed with honey and herbs to make Joldrykkr, winter's Drink. He took three and handed one to Accipiteri and another to Metellus who had joined them, though he was still keeping a watchful eye on his mistress. The girl smiled at him as he handed her a small handful of battered Orichs.

Sigmund took a small sip of the scalding liquid, then spluttered a laugh as Accipiteri clutched at his throat, he had tried to swallow a large mouthful and had nearly burnt it. Metellus, having seen Accipiteri's discomfort was more careful drinking his Joldrykkr. He sniffed at it suspiciously, before taking a small sip, his face split by a large smile, "Not bad, Bacchus's Balls that's a good drink for a cold day."

"So long as it doesn't burn your throat out," Accipiteri muttered ruefully.

Sigmund slapped his friend on the back, "Come on, we'll get you something to soothe the burn." He led his two companions through the throng, gently but firmly pushing their way through the crowd, heading for the main square by the Council chambers. Outside the building, on the broad, cobbled square, were dozens of stalls selling steaming slabs of meat and bowls of rich fish stew. There was a sudden shift in the crowd's mood, and Metellus instantly reached for his sword, alert to any danger.

Sigmund's hand gripped his arm and gestured simply to the steps, where two men were about to entertain the crowd by breathing streams of fire above their heads. The three of them stood there watching with open mouths, enjoying the spectacle until one of Domitia's legionaries grabbed Metellus's arm, explaining that their Roman mistress wanted him for something. Metellus smiled to Sigmund and Accipiteri, shrugging his shoulders by way of apology for leaving them.

"Ah well, what else is there to do on this festival?" Accipiteri asked as he saw Metellus disappearing into the crowd.

Sigmund stroked his chin thoughtfully. "There will be more of this sort of thing, jugglers and the like. Other than that most of the inns will be open, people will be dicing and throwing knives, arm wrestling and things like that. Any of those interest you?" Sigmund looked up at Accipiteri, who was a few fingers taller than he was.

Accipiteri smiled to himself, "I am not usually one for gambling, I would prefer to wander around and take in the atmosphere of this feast day, but if you want to go to the inns I am more than capable of surviving on my own. Oh, and I forgot to congratulate you earlier, that was a fine throw with that snowball." He grinned broadly, but Sigmund suddenly looked pale as he smiled thinly.

"Thanks, just never tell Skjarla that it was me, she'd beat me black and blue, wait for the bruises to go down and then beat me again."

"That she would, but don't worry, your secret is safe with me, provided you find me another of those Joldrykkr." He said with a wink.

Sigmund had no strong desire to go to any of the inns, partly because he thought it was more interesting out on the streets, partly because he wanted to avoid Skjarla. She hadn't been keen to let him into the town, she warned him about the Fang being stolen. For the life of him, he couldn't understand why she put such store in an old tooth. He didn't believe for one minute that it was the fang of some ancient dragon who would rise from the dead if it was returned to him. He was confident that it was from some forest beast, and no more than a simple family heirloom. Still, he knew it was more than his life was worth to Skjarla if he lost the tooth, so he kept it close to his chest and found himself constantly closing his fist around it.

He and Accipiteri enjoyed the day, wandering around and sampling as many of the stalls as they could, spending a good few Sanguines in the process, the Loptalfar was generous with his coin. The sun was low in the horizon by the time that most of the people of Lonely Barrow were slinking back to their tent city, many propping each other up. They arrived to find Helania, who had quickly become a favourite of the younger people who had survived the trek south thanks to her bubbly manner and otherworldly appearance, and a mob of children. They had set up walls of snow, and as the adults emerged from the gateway they were pelted by a hail of snow, which exploded in brilliant puffs of white as it came into contact with them.

The battle by the gateway raged for nearly an hour, until the sunlight became too poor to see by. The adults picked up all the snow they could find and assaulted the defences with shrieks of laughter and flung armfuls of snow at the children and youths. Sigmund was especially surprised to see Skjarla emerge from the gate, smile and plunge into the fray, lobbing snowballs left and right. 'So, there is a heart in there after all,' he thought to himself. His moment of reflection, standing still in the middle of the melee earned him a snowball straight in the face. He heard Skjarla's voice from through the crowd, "Haven't I told you enough not to stand still in the middle of a fight?" There was laughter in the voice, but also the hint of reproach. Sigmund couldn't help but wonder if she knew that it was him who threw the snowball at her in the morning.

The snowball fight broke up gradually, with people slinking back to their tents and excited shouts from the children as they told their parents about their part in the fray. Helania was touched when Bjarn came over to thank her for making the day so special for the children. She had known that after the hardships of the march and the shock of being in a strange place they would need some fun and a break from their grim situation. There was a satisfied calm which hung over the tent city, and although everyone else was fast asleep and there was a peaceful silence, Skjarla couldn't help but feel nervous. So much so that she got to her feet, and as silently as she could, stalked through the tents. She sat in the snow, watching the road which disappeared into the night as it wound its way north. She couldn't help but feel that today's peaceful revels had been but a brief interlude in the struggles of the people of Lonely Barrow.

Chapter 5

Skjarla's grim predictions were proved right nine days after the winter's Eve feast. The day after the feast had been met by near silence as the peoples of Celeste and Lonely Barrow slept off the effects of the previous day. It had then been back to business as usual for the people, surviving on the charity of Celeste as they waited for their fate to be decided in Fylkirsblod. Skjarla, Accipiteri and Bjarn were summoned to the Council halls by Breslan, telling them that Garret, the high councillor who had authorized the gifts of food and shelter, had news for them. The three of them trooped through the city, which was still festooned with decorations of winter's Eve, looking decidedly more ragged for ten days hanging in the snow and wind. There was a feeling of nervous apprehension among the group, but for very different reasons. Bjarn was hoping that the people would be allowed to stay, letting them move into the city and become part of the community. Skjarla worried that the situation would not be resolved as all she wanted to do was to get Sigmund away and to protect the Fang from the Children of the Dragon. Accipiteri was worried that the first chance he had found to truly serve the Goddess might be taken away from him, his chance to earn his wings.

They were escorted through the audience chamber, back to Garret's study, which did not seem to have changed at all since Skjarla had last seen it. There were still the same stacks of paper, piled high around the man, still a roaring fire in the grate, and still the same tasteless murals on the wall. Garret gestured for the three of them to sit down, and Skjarla took it as an ominous sign that there were no cups of spiced wine before them, only one in front of Garret.

Garret cleared his throat and began severely, "I have had word from Fylkirsblod. It arrived by courier yesterday." He looked at the three of them grimly. "The High Council of the Haemocracy have decided that there is no evidence of any assault over the mountains by anything at all, all of the other forest towns are still in one piece. They have therefore decided that the people of Lonely Barrow should not have left, and must be returned to the town to continue their logging work. I am ordered to cease all aid to the people of the town, and to close the city to you. You are either to return to the town or starve." Garret's face looked as if he was chewing something unpleasant, he clearly did not like the orders he had been given, but who was he to question the orders of the High Council?

Skjarla was the first to recover herself, "What? That is outrageous." She thought to herself, 'They've responded to Garret too quickly to have even bothered to check. They have just assumed that because the whole of the north is not in flames then there can't be a problem.'

Accipiteri, however was more studied in his response, "What if we chose to do neither of those?" everyone in the room looked at him. "Well, what if we go beyond the lands of the Haemocracy, then they cannot order us to do anything." Bjarn looked uncomfortable at this, but he knew in his heart that he would rather go anywhere than back to the ruins of Lonely Barrow.

Garret pursed his lips slightly, "I would offer you the opportunity to take ship from here, but I am under orders to close the city to you, and I cannot go against the will of the

77

High Council on that. However, there is nothing I can do to stop you if you were to take your case to Fylkirsblod and petition the High Council directly." There was a grim smile which accompanied that last statement. "However, by my orders, your people must quit the city by the end of the day. I recommend that you go and prepare your people to march, wherever that may be."

Accipiteri and Bjarn led the way out of the room, but Skjarla lingered for a moment. "Thank you for this. But I warn you, for all the blindness of the High Council, the creatures who drove them out of Lonely Barrow will come here. I would look to your supplies, and keep a strong vigil on the northern wall. At least you will have the ships to flee in if it comes to that." Garret looked at her, thinking of batting the comment away, but then he saw the heavy look in her eye, and merely nodded his agreement.

With that she turned from the room and headed back to the campsite, seeing Accipiteri and Bjarn in conversation as they walked a hundred yards in front of her. She jogged down the street, her metal studded boots clanging against the stone paving slabs, and she could feel the Gjallarhorn bouncing against her leg as she ran. She caught up with them just in time to hear Bjarn say, "We hadn't expected our supply to get cut off quite like that, we have enough food for maybe three days if we stretch it, after that we are going to start losing people." He noticed Skjarla and looked at her, his lips drawn together in a thin line, "What about you? Are you staying with us? I do not feel I can hold you to our bargain any longer. You've done right by us, though I won't deny you'd be useful on the trek."

"Where are you going?"

Bjarn raised his hands skywards and shrugged his shoulders fatalistically, "Well, we can't bloody go back up to Lonely Barrow, those rich bastards on the High Council may not believe us, but we know damn well what attacked us. We'll follow Accipiteri's advice and head for

Fylkirsblod, we'll take the coast road to the port of Bloodwater, then head east to the capital."

Skjarla thought carefully, trying to ignore the pointed glance being shot at her from behind Bjarn by Accipiteri. She wanted nothing more than to grab the Fang and get away from there, but she also felt a strange sense of duty to these people, a desire to protect them. Her voice was hard as she replied, "I will accompany you as far as Fylkirsblod, then we shall see. I shall return to camp in an hour or so, but our supply problem will be solved when I return."

"Do you need my help?" Accipiteri asked, taking a step towards her. She shook her head as she turned on her heel and headed back into town. She had seen the seal of the Haemocratic Bank inside the Council Hall, and she had decided to make a withdrawal. It had been one of the advantages of her long years of fighting monsters with such a mercenary attitude, she had amassed a considerable fortune, most of which she had no need of and sat with various banks. Some of those funds had been on account for centuries, she only used what she needed and that was less than half of what she earned. She pounded up the steps into the building, turning right at the audience chamber rather than left. She burst into the quiet room; the only sound was the gentle sigh of breathing paired with the insistent scratching of quills.

She headed to the desk at the head of the room, where the bespectacled clerk peered at her, "Can I help you?" he asked with a sniff, certain that this woman, wearing armour was unlikely to be someone with any money whatsoever.

"Yes, as a matter of fact you can, I wish to withdraw five thousand Sanguines from this account." She leant forward and snatched the quill from his hand, before scratching out the name she had used to create the account, and the associated account number. She enjoyed the feeling as the clerk's eyes widened as she wrote out the details, then the look of absolute shock as he saw how much remained in the account even after the withdrawal. She didn't bother to thank the man as she gathered up the heavy purse of gold and hurried off to the warehouses and granaries. Once there she arranged the purchases of breads, grains, dried meats and cheeses, things which would not spoil on the month long journey to the town of Bloodwater where they could resupply. The real problem would come when they hit the Skien, the middle river by which the Scath opened out onto the Empty Sea. There was no bridge there, only a simple rope ferry. Since most of the traffic between the two went by sea, as far as the councillors of the two ports were concerned there was no need for an expensive bridge.

Once she had seen all of the supplies loaded onto carts and led by draught animals out to the campsite she checked her purse. It was still heavy and jangling when she hefted it, and she guessed that there was still close to one thousand Sanguines left in there, all in fifty Sanguine coins. She chewed her lip, an idea growing in the back of her mind, but she would have to go and see if it was possible. A part of her raged at wasting all this money on these people, but a different part of her knew that the money would never be spent otherwise. She wandered over to where there were lines of smoke climbing into the sky, the sound of hammers coming from the four forges which supplied the people of Celeste with metalwork. Given that they also supplied the ships which came into port, Skjarla thought that there was a good chance that there would be a collection of blades and weapons she could get her hands on for the people.

Her eyes lit up as she walked past the first of the forges, a line of plain blades, spears and axes were up against the wall, waiting for some ship's captain to decide that he needed a bit of extra insurance against pirates. She strolled into the forge, feeling the blast of hot air as the glow of the furnace hit her. Eagerly she reached for one of the swords and gave it an experimental swing, she wasn't expecting much compared to her usual blades, but she could tell that these were very poorly made. There was a worrying degree of flex in the blade, telling her the steel hadn't been quenched properly, and the balance was all wrong, slightly off to one side which meant the blade wasn't even. With a snort of disgust she replaced the blade and tried her luck in the next forge, where a burly man was hammering out a ploughshare against his anvil. This man didn't have as many blades as his neighbour, but the ones that were there were of good quality.

She walked over to him, but he took no notice, continuing to beat out a rhythm on the red hot metal blade in front of him. The ringing of metal on metal began to grate on her nerves, and she cleared her throat, only to be ignored. Skjarla growled and went to lean against the door frame, her arms folded and a face like thunder as her eyes bored into the back of the blacksmith's head. She was sorely tempted to leave, but it felt to her like a test of wills – who would crack first. She waited, steadily growing more and more irate until the blacksmith finally drove the glowing sheet of metal into the bucket of water next to him, from which erupted great gouts of steam. She lost sight of the blacksmith through the cloud of steam which filled the forge, the heat sending drips of sweat pouring down her back.

"What do you want?" The smith asked grumpily, which momentarily put Skjarla on the back foot.

Then she recovered herself, "Trying to buy some of your bloody weapons, but if you're going to be so fucking difficult then I will take my business elsewhere." Indeed, the only thing that kept her there was the knowledge that this man's blades were superior to those of his neighbour's.

She turned to walk out the door, but was stopped by the smith's hand grabbing her arm. His voice was no less surly, though, it contained a degree of smug self-satisfaction. "You could, but Norris can't forge to save his life, Bergen is a drunk and Harald is a pirate. You want good blades, you pay my price." The smith shrugged and pursed his lips, inviting Skjarla to walk away.

Despite herself, Skjarla found herself warming slightly to this prickly individual, he looked to have seen more than fifty winters, his grey hair and beard shining orange from the glow of the coals. His hands were covered in calluses and were similar to his craggy face, both worn and weathered by years of tending the forge. Skjarla looked the smith in the eye, "I need every blade, spear and axe you have. How many of each do you have, and what is your price?"

The smith made sure to keep the gleam of pleasure out of his eye, already mentally counting the coins he was going to earn from this. "Sixteen blades, three dozen spears and eleven axes. The blades will cost you seven hundred Sanguines, four hundred each for the spears and axes. Fifteen hundred Sanguines all together."

Skjarla scoffed, "I know the price of steel, and that lot is barely worth five hundred Sanguines."

"True, but I won't get any more steel until the first shipments come in from the smelters at Tormelist, so you're paying for my loss of business until the new season. But maybe I could give you a small discount, fourteen hundred," The smith said with a cold, serpentine smile.

"Six."

"Twelve."

"Eight"

"One thousand, I will go no lower." The smith finished, turning away from Skjarla, as if to go back to work.

"Nine hundred Sanguines, or I walk away."

The old smith made a show of chewing the inside of his lip, wringing his hands as if struggling to come to terms with the price, but they both knew that he was getting more than fair price for these weapons. Ordinarily Skjarla would have stormed out after the smith had named such an exorbitant price, but part of her respected the smith's attitude, she saw a shadow of a true Norseman in this man. She was gratified when she saw the smith nod his head, "I will be back within the hour to collect them, I want you to check the edges before I return."

The smith waved his hand, acting incensed at the suggestion that his blades would not be in good condition; the dance between every shopkeeper and customer the breadth of Midgard complete. Skjarla paid the man, then left the shop, jogging back to the warehouses to redirect one of the wagons via the forge. She arrived to see a hive of activity around the wagons as stout men heaved sacks of grain and joints of smoked meat onto the wooden wagon, the shaggy draught horse which was attached between the traces stamping its feet impatiently. She crossed over to the foreman and gave him instructions for the wagon, then waited until it began to trundle through the streets of Celeste toward the forges. Once there, Skjarla and the wagon driver spent ten minutes driving off the cold by carrying armfuls of heavy weapons and heaving them into the back of the wagon. Skjarla could tell that the smith was pleased by the deal, given how warmly he greeted her when she returned to forge.

Once the blades were loaded onto the cart they headed for the north gate, Skjarla enjoying taking a last look at Celeste for the time being. She had been here before, nearly three centuries before and it amazed her how much the city had grown in the years between her visits, she wondered what the place would look like next time she passed by this way. The solid northern gates protested as they opened, squealing on their hinges as the heavy wooden doors swept across the snow, piling it up against the sides of the arches. The dozen carts she had bought to carry the supplies creaked as they started to move forwards, inching out onto the path between the tents where the north road lay.

Accipiteri came bounding up to her, exploding out of the crowd. Before she could stop him he lifted her bodily off the ground in a huge bear hug. He could hear her grinding her teeth in his ear, but he didn't let her down, instead explaining, "By the Goddess, what is this? I thought that Reavers were meant to be the most selfish people on the face of the earth, but that can't be true after this. You have saved these people; I only wish I had been able to do it, that surely would have brought me favour with the Goddess. You truly are a wonder Skjarla." He put her down, but before she could give him a savage tongue lashing she was swallowed up by a tide of people slapping her on the back and cheering her name. She had no desire to be the heroine, she knew that, 'but, then,' she asked herself, 'why did I bother to buy them all of these things if I didn't want to be their heroine?'

After a few minutes the crowd broke up and the people began to break up their camp, dismantling the tents and loading them onto the carts they had brought south with them. She saw a hive of activity around Domitia's tent and went to investigate. Metellus was directing a hive of activity as his disciplined legionaries expertly dismantled their camp and loaded it all onto carts. She called out, careful to keep her question casual, "So, you're coming with us?"

Metellus shrugged, "It's the only way we can go. I daren't stay in the ports any longer in case a ship lands bearing agents from Rome on the lookout for my mistress. As far as I can gather the only route open to us is into the centre of the lands, towards the capital of the Haemocracy."

It made sense to Skjarla but she couldn't help but wonder, "Understandable, but what do you hope to achieve in Fylkirsblod?"

Metellus's tone became more guarded, "As I said, it will be harder for agents from Rome to move against my mistress. She has her own reasons for wishing to travel that way, but it is not for me to speak for her." That seemed to bring their brief conversation to an end, leaving Skjarla more than a little frustrated by the constant evasiveness of the Roman when it came to his mistress. She had too much to worry about to dwell overlong on Metellus, and at least having the Romans along would mean they had a few more well trained swordsmen.

While the rest of the people were dealing with the camp, Skjarla held a council of war. She and Accipiteri led the conversation, with Metellus, Sigmund and Bjarn weighing in, along with Braugr and Helania. Skjarla was issuing orders and listening to advice, trying to organise the march. "Bjarn, I want you in charge of the food distribution, it will take at least a month to march to Bloodwater, so make sure that the supplies can stretch to six weeks. We have to be wary, as the thaw sets in, it is possible that the Children will pick up our trail. We have the sea to guard our right flank, so Metellus, I want your men at our rear. Sigmund and Accipiteri, you and the rest of us will march down the left flank of the column with the recently armed townsfolk. The main thing is to reach the Skien ferry as fast as possible; if we can cross there then we force the Children to go over three days' march upstream to the nearest ford. Any questions?"

Metellus was the first to speak, "I am happy to keep most of my men at the rear, but I want at least four of them in the centre of the column with my mistress."

"Agreed, anything else?"

Accipiteri this time, "What hours are we going to march? I would say that we should be underway as soon as the sun comes up, then halt for the night as it goes down. That way we'll have light to make camp by, and light to continue training the townsfolk." There was a general murmur of agreement.

Then it was Helania who spoke up, "How many archers do you have? If they need any pointers I have retrieved my bow from the Captain's Rest."

Bjarn answered this question, "We've got close to two hundred men who can shoot a bow. Mainly hunting deer and the like, but they know how to shoot."

Skjarla interrupted the conversation, "They need to stay in the middle of the column, we'll use them if we have to, but there will be time to gather them if we get warning of an attack, and if we get ambushed then they'd just get in the way of our few trained fighters. Bjarn, can you let the people know that Helania will happily help people with their archery if they so wish. Now, if there is nothing else, we must get the column moving. We need to be away from here by nightfall." Everyone got to their feet and filed off to their positions within the column, except for Metellus, who stood, waiting for her to be alone.

She sighed, tired of dealing with other people's problems, "What is it Metellus?"

The centurion looked around apprehensively before he spoke, "I am nervous about going through Bloodwater, I spoke to some captains down at the harbour, and apparently a ship carrying Romans arrived in the port just before the winter storms sealed them in. The likelihood is that they will still be there, and that they are Roman agents sent after Domitia. She is going to need close protection, and she asks that you and your friends provide it."

Skjarla was tired but she sensed an opportunity, this was a chance to find out a little more about why Domitia was being hunted. "Very well, but if I am going to protect your mistress I need to know more about her. What is it that she is meant to be inheriting which is so valuable that her illegitimate brother is sending assassins the breadth of the world to kill her?"

Metellus looked like he was about to say something, but then thought better of it. Skjarla could see him struggling with something, it clearly sat badly with him, not telling Skjarla why his mistress was putting the column in danger. She thought she might have cracked him, but he recovered himself, his Roman discipline overriding his natural honesty and conscience. He looked shamefaced as he said, "I am sorry my friend, that after all you've done for us I still cannot tell you, but it is my mistresses tale to tell. I will pass on your request to her, but do not hold out much hope." He turned and headed back to where the rest of the legionaries were helping to clear the last remnants of the campsite. Skjarla gently stroked her chin, standing in deep thought. Metellus's refusal to reveal all had been an admission of sorts. It told Skjarla that her suspicions had been correct, Domitia was not simply the daughter of some rich family, there was more to her than she let on.

Chapter 6

The column marched slowly east, Bjarn carefully rationing the supplies and Accipiteri running the training with Metellus. Skjarla tried to help, but in truth, she had spent too long fighting alone to be comfortable with fighting in any formation. She still worked with Sigmund regularly and she had to admit that the boy was improving, both in technique and stamina. He had had big shoulders and strong arms from years of hefting sacks of flour, but the work with the sword was adding fresh layers of corded muscles and strengthening him enormously. It was strange, in this young man, she could see an echo of all those brave Einherjar who had stood with her at Ragnarok, and he had the same stubbornness if nothing else. He was becoming capable with the sword and the spear, though the axe was proving beyond him.

They marched along the coast road for several days, the mood in the column becoming steadily more depressed. There was enough food to go around, but the weather was still cold, and the memory of the flight from Lonely Barrow weighed down upon them. The Romans, who were normally jocular and good company were also twitchy, given the fact that they knew that they were marching into danger at Bloodwater. There was a cold wind blowing salty air in from the sea, whipping Skjarla's hair about, her black locks clashing against the pure white of Helania's as they walked together. Simply to make conversation Skjarla broke the silence as she leant into the wind, "Where did you get that bow? Few enough people have ever even seen a Whorl Root bow, let alone drawn one."

Whorl Root was a very rare plant which grew underground, surviving from the heat emitted by underground rocks. It was brilliant white, thanks to the complete lack of sunlight, but it was very strong and pliable. Helania smiled softly, her hand stroking the smooth limbs of the Whorl Root, "My father's," she said proudly. "It is the last thing I have left of him, apparently he died during one of the Blood riots a few decades back, I was barely an infant at the time." The Blood riots were when the High Council of the Haemocracy had blamed the food shortage on the Dwarves and the Dokkalfar. They who were considered sub human by the council, and therefore a convenient target for the people's rage. Thousands had been killed in the riots; the High Council had waited for the crowds to sate their bloodlust before halting the massacres.

"Where did you learn to shoot it?" Skjarla wasn't really interested, but she was bored of walking in silence.

"I did a little back at home, but really I got most of it when Braugr and I were with the Highlanders."

This did actually interest Skjarla a bit, she knew the Highlanders by reputation. They were a tough mercenary corps and they would almost never take on people with no experience of soldiering or life in the field. "What made them take you? Braugr I can understand, but I can't imagine you would have had much to set you apart from everyone else."

Helania smiled slightly and looked a little shy, "Braugr got me in, once they found out he had been in the Hearth Guard, they were keen to have him."

"I can imagine." Skjarla interrupted with a knowing look. All of the nine famous and reputable mercenary companies had approached her on several occasions. She had even spent a few seasons with some of them and kept contact with some the captains even now. The companies were always a good source of news and gossip from around Midgard. They would all be after a member of the Hearth Guard, Dwarven royal guards did not appear for hire often, and they were very handy in a fight.

"He made a condition of his joining them that I join as well. They weren't overly happy, but once he pledged us both for four seasons they relented." Helania seemed cheerful, chattering away in her musical voice.

"Did he say why he was so insistent on helping you?" Skjarla couldn't help but wonder what would compel someone to do so much for a stranger, even if they were a fellow exile.

"We had travelled together for a while, I like to think he was inspired by my dream of changing my people's standing that I wanted to make people see us as we are, not just as cowards." Her voice was full of idealism, but Skjarla couldn't help but think it sounded a bit hollow, she refused to believe that anyone was truly that idealistic. She also suspected that the real reason Braugr had been so keen to help Helania was that her naivety probably reminded him of his lost daughter.

The conversation lapsed back into silence, and they plodded onwards, marching through the wind as winter turned to spring. The column broke up for the evening and everyone sat, eager to get the weight of their feet, and preparing for the next day's march. The only thing that the townsfolk found good about getting through their supplies was that as the march wore on, more and more space opened up on the wagons so they could rest and take turns riding in the carts for a while.

The following day, twelve days out from Celeste, they crested the final hill, and before them, stretching across the frost stained earth was the ribbon of the Skein. Skjarla could just pick out the brown blob of the ferry, resting on the near side of the river. Then she heard a scramble and one of Metellus's legionaries appeared next to her, panting heavily.

"Domina, the Centurion wants me to report that there is a dust cloud behind us. Maxentius has seen the flashes of steel beneath it. The Centurion is sure that those things that are chasing these people have caught up with us, they'll be on us before nightfall." Skjarla's mind whirred, it had been years since she had had to command a battle, she could feel a degree of panic rising up her gorge, but she choked it down.

She began to issue commands, "Legionary, tell Metellus that we'll have a fight on our hands soon. He'll get his orders shortly but for now he is just to keep moving towards the ferry." The legionary snapped a salute, but she had already turned away, bellowing loudly. "Accipiteri, I need you here. Bjarn, get these wagons moving faster, they need to be crossing the river now. Braugr, get down to the front of the column, persuade the ferryman to work fast, we'll join you down there and set a defensive line around the ferry and hold it until everyone's across the Skien." She saw the Dwarf break into a lumbering run as he hurried down to the ferryman's hut, just then, she heard Accipiteri come up beside her.

He was panting heavily, having sprinted through the new shoots of spring grass which were starting to emerge through the thawing ground. "I gather we have company on the way," he said calmly.

"That we do, now, I want your advice. How would you position our men to defend the ferry?"

Accipiteri rubbed the back of his head nervously, "I have a few ideas, but if I am honest, I have never actually commanded a battle before. I mean, I had the theory drummed into me for years, but that is not the real thing. Surely you know how to deal with this?"

Skjarla glared at him, "The last battle I fought in was an unmitigated disaster where everything I knew and loved was destroyed, not much of a recommendation for me to command here." She saw the light in his eyes shine with curiosity. He had no idea what this great battle was; he couldn't think of anywhere that had been wiped out in the last five years, if Skjarla had fought in it, it had to be recent. Accipiteri made a mental note to ask her about it later, 'if they survived', he thought with a grimace. "There's no time for dealing with the past," she continued, "what ideas do you have?"

Accipiteri stood in silence, his eyes sweeping the area as he tried to get an idea of the terrain, trying to imagine where he would station their meagre forces. "We need to get down there, then we can get a better idea of the lay of the ground, although it looks very flat from up here." The two of them ran down the hill at breakneck speed, pounding past the horses and oxen who were straining against their harnesses. Bjarn was already yelling at people to get their wagons moving faster and Helania was running down behind them, looking for something to help with.

Just as Skjarla and Accipiteri came to a halt Helania caught up with them, "What can I do?" she said breathlessly, her chest heaving as she fought for air.

Accipiteri's face hardened as he formulated a battle plan, "Gather all of the archers and put half of them on either side of the road. Tell them to hold fire until I give the order, and then to fire as fast as they can. Go now." Helania turned and ran back up the column, pulling men and women with bows out from between the wagons and sending them down to the riverbank in a steady stream. By now the first two wagons were being loaded onto the flat topped pontoon and the ferryman and his sons heaved on the thick cord of rope which was slung between the banks. The ferry worked its way out into the strong current, a wave building up around the upstream edge of the pontoon as the water pushed against it.

Skjarla looked at Accipiteri, "I take it you have a plan." She smiled thinly with slightly raised eyebrows, her hands on her hips as she waited for him to elaborate.

"I have the beginnings of a plan, but in truth, given what we have to work with, all we can do is try to hold the line until we can get everyone across the Skein. The Romans will have to take the last trip, simply because they have our only shields. If those bastards out there have bows or more of those blowpipes then anyone else would be defenceless. We just hold the line and try and drive them back, buy time for the wagons to cross the river."

Skjarla nodded, pulling off her cloak in one fluid, swirling motion and tossing it onto a passing cart. "Sounds like a good plan, but Sigmund goes across as soon as possible, if the Fang falls into the Children's hands then all is lost. Braugr," her eyes flickered to the Dwarf before returning to Accipiteri, "You and I will be in the centre of the line. We'll break their charge around us." Accipiteri nodded grimly, slightly alarmed to see the look of bloodlust which crept over her face at the thought of being in the front of the battle. He copied Skjarla and tossed his cloak into a passing cart, pleased to see that the first wagons were already being unloaded on the far side.

One of the Roman legionaries came jogging down the path, saluting Skjarla and Accipiteri, "Domina, Dominus, the Centurion sent me to say that the pursuers will be on use soon, they are about two miles away."

Skjarla looked at Accipiteri with a worried expression, "We aren't going to get these carts across in time, and we need to slow them down." She turned behind her and cupped her hands around her mouth as she bellowed, "Helania, get your archers up to the ridge." She turned back to Accipiteri, "Keep the wagons moving, I'll keep an eye on things up there. Get the rest of the fighters ready for battle, we'll need to hold the beachhead for a good twenty minutes." She turned and ran back up to the top of the hill, pursued by the archers and Helania.

They got to the crest of the small ridge, turning back to see the ferry working its way back across the Skein, having just unloaded another pair of wagons. Below them, back on the river banks, Braugr was yelling at the ferryman to load more of the carts on each run, and the response that anymore weight would sink the rickety old ferry. Skjarla stepped out in front of the two hundred archers, each had about twelve roughly cut arrows, but they would do the job of slowing down the Children. She spoke, projecting her voice to the edges of the line of bowmen, "Hold fire until my order, we need to stop their charge, so fire one volley, then fall back to my position. We will then fire by halves, everyone on my left fires a volley while those on my right retreat, and vice versa." She dropped her voice a little. "Helania, I want them to form on the flanks when we get down to Accipiteri and the Romans."

Helania looked a little nervous, but then she seemed to steel herself before the coming combat. She was realizing that fighting with untrained villagers was very different to having a trained mercenary corps at your back. She nervously shuffled closer to Skjarla, "Aren't you going to give them an inspiring speech, fire them up before the fight?"

Skjarla looked at her, "Speeches are not my strong point, plus, these people are fighting to defend their friends and families, if that is not an inspiration to fight hard then nothing is."

Helania looked put out, but she said nothing, taking her place next to Skjarla as she waited for the Children of the Dragon to close with them. As they drew near, Skjarla could pick out some of the characteristics she had missed fighting against them in the dark. Their head crests were a riot of colours, with the larger beasts having larger, horned crests. Their armour was as cobbled together as she remembered; a mismatched collection of leathers and iron work. In the light of day she could see that more of the Children were heavily muscled, and more heavily armoured than she remembered. She could still see many of the scrawny ones, but she guessed that these were the scouts, and the proper warriors were the bigger, more heavily built individuals.

The swarm of creatures were at the bottom of the ridge, Skjarla and the archers staring down at them. The largest of the Children stepped out from the ranks, clad in heavy iron plates with viciously curved talons shining dully in the morning light. Skjarla turned to Helania, "Does your bow have the range to hit that beast?"

"Just, but it will be a difficult shot. " Helania said quietly, already looking through her arrows to select the straightest of them.

The monstrous Wyrmling shouted to the lines on the hill, its crude words carrying with hissing menace through the cool air. "Give us ... Fang. And you may ... Live." This was greeted with looks of confusion amongst the people of Lonely Barrow, none of them knew anything about the Fang. Skjarla cursed herself for not telling Helania to take the shot earlier, but she did so now. Skjarla heard the soft groan from the limbs of the Whorl Root as the tension of the draw pulled against them. She heard Helania take a long, steadying breath before she loosed the arrow, which went streaking away into the sky, tracing a high trajectory as it arched down towards its target. The large Wyrmling noticed the arrow at the last moment, twisting its body to the side with inhuman speed. Even so the arrow still struck deeply into its shoulder.

Every man and woman on the ridge heard the roar as the Children of the Dragon surged up the slope, screaming for blood. Skjarla took two paces forward, swinging Dreyrispa menacingly, then raised her left arm overhead, shouting at the top of her lungs, "Hold." The Children were two hundred yards away. "Hold," one hundred now. At what she judged to be fifty yards, "Fire." The arrows whipped forward with a soft hiss, and the front rank of the foe stopped as if they had run up against a stone wall. Before they had even checked to see if their arrow had hit, the archers had already turned and were haring back down the slope, Skjarla drew half of them to a halt after fifty yards. A ragged volley slowed the pursuit and gave the archers time to turn and flee again, covered by their companions further down the slope.

Barely half of the arrows caused casualties, the hunting bows didn't have the power to punch through the iron plates, and the simple iron arrow heads bent against the metal. Some shots found gaps though, and the bodies of the dead and wounded fouled the charge of their comrades. The archers split in front of the warriors, going to the sides and, as Helania had taught them, drove their remaining arrows head first into the hard earth. It was a trick she had learnt with the Highlanders, it made knocking the next arrow much faster. A quick glance told Skjarla that the last of the wagons was just being unloaded onto the other side of the Skein. They had to wait for the ferry to come back, load up most of the archers and then take them across the river before coming back for the rest of them. Her eyes told her that they were up against nearly two thousand of the Children, far too many for them to win.

The legionaries in the centre were clustered around the great white crest of Metellus's helmet, standing in a thin line, ready to gut all of the Children who reached them. Braugr was on the right, with a collection of the armed townsfolk, while Accipiteri was with the rest on the left. Skjarla pulled her helmet from where it hung on her belt and slid the cold metal down onto her head, her world becoming muffled and her vision dimmed slightly. She stepped out in front of the ranks of defenders. She had meant what she had said to Helania, speeches were not her forte, all she could do was raise Dreyrispa and let out the most blood curdling roar she could. The cry was taken up by all of the men and women standing with her, the sound of their roar engulfed by the crashing impact as the Children hit their ranks.

Skjarla was three paces in front of the Roman lines, splitting the charge as she swung Dreyrispa in vicious, scything arcs, the Children falling around her like heads of wheat. The Romans were doing well, their short, sharp gladii punching into the guts of the Children, cutting through viscera and arteries alike, building a growing wall of corpses in front of them. Skjarla felt sorry for the people of Lonely Barrow. Although they had heart and a burning desire to fight, they lacked any form of armour, and so she knew that casualties would be highest with them. They were only saved by the fact that the Children were so desperate to cross the river that they were throwing all their weight against the centre of the thin line.

She heard Helania's shout, and as she spun in an arc of death saw men of the archers sprinting to the ferry, packing onto the wooden platform and lending their weight to the braided cable as they hauled the ferry across the Skein. The remaining defenders clustered closer to the landing, the Romans in front, and the growing number of wounded huddled behind the shrinking shield wall. Still Skjarla stood alone, breaking the impetus of the charge, and indeed, a space was opening up around her as the Children feared to press too close to the wickedly spinning blade. Accipiteri was using his broadsword to good effect too, although the shield he had slung from his shoulders was battered and splintered from the rain of blows. Braugr was wreaking havoc, his axe shattering legs and bringing screaming Wyrmlings to the ground, where they lay with dark blood pumping from between their clawed fingers.

There was a shout from the ferry, which was coming back for them. It momentarily broke Skjarla's focus, and she took a heavy blow from the rough iron club wielded by one of the larger Children. Its claws scored a blow against the side of her armour, the plates of Aesir steel screeching in protest and the talons ground against it. Skjarla threw a wild punch, swearing as she hit bone. It felt like she had broken a knuckle or two, but she dug her thumb into the small, beady eye, causing the muscled creature to shriek in agony and back away from her. The press of bodies was pushing her up against the Roman shield wall, which duly parted, letting her slip through before closing up again. She could see that about a half of the townsfolk were still fighting, and of the rest, less than half of those were still alive, binding one another's wounds behind the ever shrinking line.

The whole group heard the loud thud as the ferry bumped against the landing, "Everyone aboard," yelled the ferryman, clearly terrified by the fighting going on in front of him,

"Flanks give way, Roman's to give ground steadily." Accipiteri bellowed, and already the wounded and the men defending the banks of the river started to edge back towards the ferry.

"You heard him, you dogs. By Mars if any of you breaks ranks I will cut your balls off myself. Show these blond bastards how real Romans fight." Metellus roared to his men, his shoulder set to his shield, pushing against the crush. Skjarla could see the sinews straining in the man's calves, even as he jabbed his blade between the gaps in the shield wall, plunging the cold steel into any exposed flesh. He was red up to the elbows, as was every Roman; it looked like they had been working in a slaughterhouse. There was a steady flow of men and women pressing onto the ferry, and the crowd defending the bridgehead gradually shrunk until the last people left were the trained fighters. As one, on a roared command from Metellus, the Roman legionaries swept their shields before them, giving them a split second to turn and sprint for the ferry.

As they leapt aboard, every person standing next to the braided horsehair rope heaved against it with all of their might, pulling the ferry away from the bank of the Skein. The Romans stood at the edge of the pontoon, their shields built into a wall of wood and iron. The sound of improvised missiles clattering against the shields was audible to all on the ferry, each of whom stood there nervously, waiting for a lucky shot to claim their lives. Suddenly, all those, including Skjarla and Braugr, who were heaving the ferry along its tether felt a tremor through the cable. Braugr's voice bellowed from the stern, "They're cutting the cable, hold her hard." Skjarla understood what he was trying to do, the ferry was nearing the centre of the Skein, if they held tight to the rope, and the current should swing them against the bank.

With an ear shattering crack the braided horse hair of the cable gave way, and the ferry was quickly swept downstream. The people holding the cable felt the skin on their hands and fingers giving way and tearing as it protested against the strain of holding the ferry against the current. However, slowly but surely the ferry pivoted around its tether on the far bank, picking up speed until it slammed into the bank, sending people flying to the floor. Already there was a cheering crowd of townsfolk running down the bank to help. They were cheering the fact that the Children had been stranded on the opposite side of the bank. They arrived to help pull people from the warped and now blood stained boards of the ferry. The wounded were quickly loaded onto carts. Those who were badly wounded hadn't managed to make it off the other bank, so there were only walking wounded with the column now. The Romans proved amazingly adept at field medicine, sewing up wounds and applying poultices to the ragged gashes of the wounded.

Bjarn came over to find out what the body count was. Three Romans were dead on the other side and two dozen archers had been hit by darts, all poisoned and all dead. Of the sixty three townsfolk who had fought face to face with the enemy, only forty four had made it across the river, twenty of them with deep wounds. Skjarla was more irritated by the fact that their weapons were still sitting on the far side of the Skein, now useless in the defence of the column. Their casualties had been kept down by the small frontage they had fought over, and the delaying work of the archers. The people of Lonely Barrow did not waste time, quickly putting things together and getting moving again as soon as they could, eager to put as much distance between themselves and the Children of the Dragon as possible.

To complete the mood which hung over the column, the heavens opened and a thick curtain of heavy rain fell upon them, drenching them all and adding to the grim sense of isolation. The grasses around the road glistened as the water droplets formed on them. Sigmund had been roaming up and down the column, but he finally found Skjarla, and he was so bitter and distraught that he did not fear her wrath. "Why? Why would you humiliate me by letting everyone else fight and sending me across the Skien on the first ferry?" His eyes glittered with angry emotion and the veins in his heavily muscled neck bulged beneath his trembling jaw. Skjarla could see his fingers clenched in rage, but she frankly didn't care, too many good and irreplaceable people had died for her to feel the need to soothe one person's troubled ego.

"Those people we left on the other side, they died for you!" she spat at him. "Do you realise the consequences if that Fang falls into their hands? Do you? Well I'll tell you, they will take the Fang back to the bones of Fafnir and plant it in the earth there. From the earth one of the

Veidrmadr, the Huntsmen, will rise. He will be drawn to the other Fangs, and will bring them to the Dragon, along with its horn. Once the pieces of the Dragon are assembled Fafnir will be reborn, and he and the Children of the Dragon will begin their quest for what Fafnir desires most. There will be a generation of fire and blood and death. The Dragon will seek everything of value and try to take it from others without care for them," She paused, looking him in the eye while her voice became soft and deadly serious. "That is why I sent you across first, because I know that the end of the world is not a place that you want to be."

Skjarla emerged from her rant and cursed to herself over and over again, the townsfolk around her were standing still in open-mouthed silence, the raindrops cascading across their worn faces and running off the waxed surfaces of their cloaks. She realised that she had let slip the real reason that she was with the column, giving the people a reason to be even more frightened than they were and worst of all had given them the idea that she may not just be a simple Reaver.

She was so furious that as Sigmund started to argue, he got out the words, "You've taught me to fight," before she knocked him to the ground with a single punch. Leaving him sitting in the mud with a badly broken nose, blood flowing down over his chin and swiftly adding a red tint to his brown shirt, she stepped over his body and stalked off down the column. Those who saw her go could see people further on making way for her, knowing well enough not to tangle with the Reaver in this mood.

Later, once night had fallen and the tents had been pitched, Skjarla got a visit from Accipiteri. They sat together in the small tent, the rain pattering against the leather as Accipiteri sat there smiling openly at her. She couldn't help but find his calm smile irritating, he clearly wanted to say something, but he was waiting for her to break the silence. She wasn't going to give him the satisfaction, she was still livid at her earlier slip, and was dwelling on the moment, chasing it round and round within her mind. There was silence outside, as the other families and groups packed into their tents and huddled in depressed silence, out of the rain which had followed them since the battle at the ferry. The mood in camp was subdued to say the least, news of Skjarla's rant had gone around the column like lightning, and although some had gossiped about who Skjarla really was, most were in silence as they digested her revelations.

Accipiteri finally broke the silence, an exasperated sigh cracking through his veneer of calmness, "You're going to have to talk about it sooner or later. Look, it doesn't matter to me, but I think you should at least apologise to Sigmund. It wasn't just his nose that you broke; you also bruised his pride quite badly." His head was tilted to the side, a twinkle of laughter in the corner of his eyes.

Skjarla scowled at him, Accipiteri couldn't understand how someone with such a pretty face, such young, expressive eyes, could have such an old soul. "Maybe I should apologise to him, but if the idiot doesn't want to get hit then he shouldn't pick a fight."

Accipiteri clapped his hands on his knees, and then reached behind him to the small sack he had brought with him. Skjarla had erected her tent and then retreated inside it to avoid the questioning glances from the people around her. He knew she hadn't eaten, so he had brought a small wedge of cheese and a slab of cured beef which he passed across to her. Skjarla nodded her thanks, and then began to break off small hunks of the cheese which she gracefully popped into her mouth. Once she was eating he started talking, his voice soft and conspiratorial. "The people are worried, not only have you scared the life out of them with your revelation about the Fang, they are not sure if they can trust you."

"What? After I used my own money to buy those supplies and weapons, they doubt that I want to protect them?" She exploded into life, her voice raised and Accipiteri had to raise a placating hand, trying not to draw more attention to their conversation than was necessary.

"Look, I know that you have done more than you are obliged to to help the people of Lonely Barrow, but scared people have short memories. They are shaken by the deaths today, once we reach Bloodwater then they will be fine, and the shock will have worn off by the morning. Anyway, that is not what I came here to talk about." He sat back and leant against the leather wall of the tent, the material creaking ominously.

"Well, spit it out, I need to get outside before the rain finishes. And if you go through the wall of the tent then Sigmund won't be the only one with a broken nose." Accipiteri looked quizzically at her. She rolled her eyes and explained, "A lot of blood got through my armour and soaked me to the skin, I need to wash it off, and seeing as there is no water nearby I have to make do with the rain." Accipiteri was still young enough to blush at that comment. He may be sixty years old, but that was young for his people, a few of whom had been alive since the changing of the world four hundred years ago.

Accipiteri recovered himself and began. "I have been speaking to Helania and Braugr, trying to find out how they knew you and what they knew about you. They were evasive to say the least, which was an answer of sorts. I want to know who you really are, I mean, you barely look twenty five and yet you have experiences that date back centuries. I know about the Fangs, those stories reached us in the Windswept Isles, but I don't know about you."

Skjarla looked irritated, and tried to brush him off with a wave of her hand, "Why do you want to know so much? What possible reason do you have for wanting to know my secrets?" In truth, if any of the group had to know about who she was, she would prefer that it was him, of all of them he could understand how she felt. He was not allowed to go home until the Lady gifted him with wings, if he ever did.

"Skjarla, I can't imagine what secrets you have buried in your past, but if you are running from something, I pledge myself to protect you from whatever it is you are hiding from." He looked so genuine, so fervent in his desire to protect her that she had to throw her head back and laugh. He looked affronted by her laugh, "My Lady, do you not think that I am capable of helping you? Am I that laughable?"

His voice had such a hurt tone to it that she gave another chuckle before holding up her hands. "Accipiteri, there is no one, living or dead, who can save me from my past. Memories and guilt are something you carry with you forever; this is something you'll learn eventually. You really want to know who I am. I am someone like you, someone who can never go home, although you at least have hope to cling to, I don't even have that luxury."

Accipiteri was getting impatient, "Yes, fine, whatever you say. You still haven't answered my question though. Who are you?"

She looked at him, their eyes locking, and the highly trained Loptalfar saw something in her eyes which frightened even him. Echoes of war, death and chaos burning like the smouldering embers of a dying fire, lay in there, full of menace. "You really are set upon this path. Very well, I am Skjarla, last of the Valkyries, I have watched everything I know burn as the fires raged over Valhalla. The only thing I had left to me was my gift, war, and as such I became the killer I am, the first Reaver. You ask why I still look so young, it is my curse. I am cursed with immortality. Do you have any idea what that feels like? To watch everyone you know and befriend grow old and die in an endless cycle, when all that you pray for is to trade places with any one of them." She fell silent, and Accipiteri sat stunned, the passion and emotion laced into her voice had shocked him. In truth, he couldn't understand it, living forever when all you wanted was to die. He was amazed by her strength, to keep going under such a dragging strain.

"Skjarla, I can't imagine what it must feel like, and can offer only one piece of advice. Try to find something, anything that makes your immortality more bearable. If there is anything I can do then just let me know."

She replied, more softly than he expected her to, "Thank you, but in four hundred years there has been nothing permanent to ease the passing of time. I have long since given up any hope of there being something. I have accepted my new life; please do me the favour of doing the same." She looked down at her feet, and he could swear that he saw the sparkling drops of tears splatter against the trampled grass floor, but he knew better than to say anything. In silence he headed out into the night, but not to his own tent; he wanted to talk to Braugr and Helania. If anyone would know about Valkyries they would be from the elder races. The Loptalfar may be of similar stock to the Dokkalfar but they had been created in the cataclysm unlike their black skinned cousins who had survived it.

He heard the tent flap slap behind him once again, as Skjarla stalked off into the rain. He knew that she was going to wash herself clean in the rain, but it would be a brave man who decided to try and catch a glimpse. He walked through the crowded walkways of the subdued camp, stepping over the tangle of guy ropes and stacked belongings. Normally there would be the gentle murmur of conversation coming from within the tents, but tonight there was nothing being said, just occasional sob of grief coming from those who had lost loved ones at the Skein ferry. Through the dark he picked his way to Braugr's tent, which he shared with Helania. The two of them had spent so many years sharing a tent on campaign with the Highlanders and just kept the same habit now. He felt the rain pitter-pattering off his armour, washing away any of the grime which still clung to it; they would still be a sorry sight by the time they reached Bloodwater.

He emerged into the bright interior of the tent, squinting as his eyes adjusted to the sudden change. He looked down to see that the two of them were sitting beneath the tent pole, Braugr twirling his finger in his beard irritably as he considered his next move. The two of them were playing Jarls, the board game based on a twenty by twenty grid, with the objective of capturing the opponents Jarl. The game was made more difficult by the fact that neither player could see which of the other's pieces were facing them. Only you knew the disposition of your pieces. Accipiteri was surprised; Braugr had tried a skirmish advance, a row of cheap pieces in front of a knot of his best troops. It was a good tactic, difficult to counter unless you could bluff well and play quickly. Unfortunately it turned out that Helania was good at both of these, and had ambushed Braugr's pieces, leaving her in an almost unassailable position. He watched as Helania's counters pushed Braugr all the way back and finally captured his Jarl.

Braugr didn't look up as he said irritably, "That's the third time this evening she's had the better of me."

"Maybe you should play a different game then?" he said, giving Helania a sly wink, he knew that the Dwarf was prickly at the best of times, no more so than when he had just lost a game. Accipiteri liked both of them, they were a strange pair certainly, but they were good company. Helania was always cheerful but she could be very innocent at times. However, she had picked up too many soldiers habits from her time with the Highlanders for Accipiteri to believe that some of it wasn't put on. Braugr was another mystery. He was good company, but always politely declined to join anyone for drinks, and a Dwarf who would not touch ale was about as common as snow in the desert.

"Piss off you long eared prick." Braugr thundered at him. Accipiteri knew this wasn't helping him in the eyes of the Goddess, but it was entertaining nonetheless. The Dwarf took a deep breath to calm himself, "What do you want? I presume you didn't come just to poke fun at me?" He sounded calm, but there was still a dangerous hardness to his voice, and he cracked his knuckles ominously for emphasis.

"I wanted to ask you about the Valkyrie. Your people are among the old races, surely you must know more about them." He looked carefully at each one of them, looking for any hint of dishonesty. His eyes lingered on Helania, sweeping over her fine features, she was very beautiful, and the curious lustre from her black, marbled skin gave her a particular allure.

Helania looked at him, her face cool, not displaying any emotion, "She told you then. To think of it, one of the Aesir still walks the face of Midgard, it's incredible."

Braugr was more direct in addressing the question, "We can tell you about the Valkyries themselves, lad, but as to this particular one, she is as much a mystery to us as she is to you. The Valkyries were the warrior maidens, daughters of Odin All-Father and gatherers of the dead. They would bring the souls of slain heroes to Valhalla, where there would be drinking, feasting and merriment until the Ragnarok came, the end of the world. It was said that all were fated to die on that fell day, but our peoples did not take part in the battle, to our lasting shame. We had heard that all had perished, but our kind still recognize the weapons forged in the fires of Asgard, and that was how we recognized Skjarla. How she came to survive the battle is her tale to tell, and I suspect she will take it to her grave." The tent was eerily silent after that gloomy pronouncement, but Accipiteri couldn't help agreeing with

Braugr. He wouldn't want to be forced to relive the events which had destroyed his homeland, so he couldn't imagine Skjarla would want to either.

Helania piped up, as she suddenly remembered something, "There is one interesting thing though. She has an artefact which should have been destroyed, but she managed to save it." Accipiteri looked at her quizzically, his brow furrowed with confusion as she continued, "The Gjallarhorn. The horn that summoned all of Asgard to battle, blown by Heimdall when he caught sight of the fearful throng of Loki's minions. What power the horn still holds, if any, I do not know, but there must be a reason she carries it around with her." There was nothing to be said to that. All that Accipiteri could do was mull over what the two of them had said, and compare it with the things he had found out about Skjarla from their earlier conversation.

It annoyed Helania greatly that even though Accipiteri was clearly miles away, lost in thought he still beat her twice at Jarls without even really trying. Braugr tried to give the Loptalfar a game, but was soundly thrashed and gave up, muttering darkly about Elven games.

The next morning the march continued, but the people were still giving Skjarla dark and mistrustful glances, afraid of her intentions for them. They had also ostracised Sigmund to some extent, blaming him for their misfortune. A small minority were for driving them both away and returning to Lonely Barrow, but most of the townsfolk were against this. Accipiteri was pleased to hear Bjarn, stood atop a wagon and addressing a crowd who were walking behind it. He was explaining that the Children thought that they had the Fang, and even without Sigmund, they would still hunt the townsfolk. They were committed to this course now, they were bound for Fylkirsblod, but first they must make for the safety of the walls of Bloodwater.

Accipiteri had been right about one thing, by the time the walls of Bloodwater hove into view, nine days after the battle on the Skein, the people had forgotten all about driving Skjarla away. He was glad of that, for all her prickly nature she was the one he'd want with him in a tight spot. Bloodwater was a far grimmer city than Celeste, its walls carved from a curious local stone, the colour of clotted blood, which gave the place its name. When they arrived, the streets were quiet and subdued beneath the dark walled buildings. There were stories of how in years past, when the slave trade in Abhorrens was rife, the stones had been coloured by the blood of murdered slaves. Once again the majority of the people had been left outside while they built their tent city. Skjarla and a few others, including Accipiteri had been allowed to enter the city to trade for supplies. The city of Bloodwater came to life near the docks, where the shouted commands of foremen loading and unloading ships were only matched by the cries of the many whores who worked the waterfront.

Metellus had insisted on coming into the city, leaving his men to protect Domitia, but he was twitchier than they had ever seen him, and given the nature of most of the people in the city that was not a good thing. Everyone in the town of Bloodwater was armed, owing to the large number of mercenaries travelling through the port. Most were either heading back to Leopolis and Taureum or looking for employment in the Haemocracy. People were casting lingering glances at the stocky centurion, whose thumb was nervously caressing the pommel of his gladius. They split off in various directions once they reached the wharf. Metellus took Accipiteri with him and headed off for one of the many taverns, trying to find information about the Romans who had arrived in Bloodwater. Skjarla shook her head disapprovingly; she knew those two would stick out in any of the dives along the waterfront. She sent Braugr after them, at least he would know how to fit in in a place like that. Helania stuck with Skjarla as the two of them headed to the nearest bank, once again needing to draw on her own funds to feed the long column of refugees. It had irked her, their ingratitude and hostility after the battle at the Skein, but she still felt she had a duty to them, and it made it much easier to keep an eye on Sigmund.

In truth, she was beginning to worry that she would not be rid of the people of Lonely Barrow for some time yet, but the seeds of an idea were starting to sprout within her mind. She had realised that short of taking the Fang herself and wearing it, she had no way of protecting it for years. What she needed was to find a city or citadel where the Fang would be safe, and people who would be willing to protect the bearer of the Fang. She thought that the people of Lonely Barrow would be a good start, but they would take some convincing, and she had no idea where she could lead them. She hoped that they would be able to be left behind the supposedly impregnable walls of Fylkirsblod, but if they couldn't for some reason, then she'd just have to think of something. Helania got the impression that her companion was deep in thought and had the sense to remain silent. She focused on the buildings around her, which were more haphazard in construction and organisation than the neat, ordered streets of Celeste. Here as well, the noisome fug of pollution hung over the streets, where the open air sewers lacked running water to wash away the filth. Even to Helania, who had grown up underground, the way that the deep red of the stone seemed to drink in the light and shine as if a crimson liquid were running down its surface made her spine shiver.

She watched in awe as Skjarla withdrew another small fortune and instantly spent the lot on supplies for the column and more weapons. There was a far greater supply here in Bloodwater with dozens of smiths supplying all of the military ships lying at anchor within the great stone breakwater. There were a mix of wide bellied trading ships, a single mast and a dozen or so oars one either side, or several sleek warships. The warships were thinner, with banks of oars and two solid masts, and the shining metal of their rams just poking above the water. There were even some Triremes from the trading isles, bigger than any other ship in the harbour, with great towers fore and aft. The Triremes were the secret of Leopolis and Taureum's power, with their fleets they were able to completely control trade while defending themselves from any threats. And that was only their legitimate fleets, both cities had hundreds of privateers they could call upon to protect their interests if they so chose.

With the supplies ordered and instructions issued to send those to the refugees outside the walls Skjarla took Helania to one of the inns along the waterfront. "If you ever need information then the Weeping Maiden is the place to go. Information is as good as currency in there, plus you can find all manner of useful characters." Helania took in the seedy front of the inn, the badly chipped and faded paint of the sign, and suppressed an urge to scoff. If Skjarla said this place was useful then who was she to argue? Aside from her years with the Highlanders she had spent barely a year above ground.

They walked through the worn door and onto the sawdust strewn warped planks of the floor. The entire place reeked of stale ale and there was a hush on the room as the two of them walked in. In an instant tables were pulled back from the centre of the room and the crowd of drunks and gamblers formed a hollow circle. Skjarla cursed. Her badge had been recognized and there must be another Reaver in the room. She started to stretch as the crowd cheered, she could hear the excited chatter as wagers were placed and money changed hands. She handed her cloak to Helania, along with the Gjallarhorn, they were accompanied with a stern look, that told Helania the cloak and the horn were more valuable than her life. The other

Reaver stepped out of the crowd, and the reaction was not what Helania expected. She expected Skjarla to frown as she took in the lithe man before her. The man's head was still hidden beneath the hood attached to his soft leather armour, a distinctive giant shoulder guard on his left side. Instead, Skjarla's face was split with a wide grin, but she did not say anything, dropping into a low stance, knees bent and balanced on the balls of her heels.

The two of them charged into one another, the blades flickering around in wide arcs, the stranger's broadsword flying in a whirl of steel as he fended off Skjarla's vicious twin-headed spear. The light from the fire and the torches cast strange patterns on the crowd as it was reflected by the shimmering steel. The two of them dance around each other, their movements becoming more and more frenetic as they sought advantage. Skjarla finally got the better of her opponent, deflecting his thrust off to the side and stepping in to slam her elbow into the side of the hood. The crowd went silent; they were eagerly anticipating the death blow.

There was a sigh of disappointment as Skjarla offered her hand, "How many times do you have to be told Iskander, the weapon is not the only thing you can strike with."

"Always once more." He took her hand, grunting as he got to his feet. "Drinks are on me Skjarla. Again," he sighed melodramatically. The tall Reaver led her over to his table, set in a small alcove in the wall, and beckoned to one of the worn, buxom serving girls who worked the floor. Skjarla waved Helania over, taking the cloak from her and replacing the Gjallarhorn on her hip. "Who is this? It is rare that someone can match your beauty my lady."

"Iskander, this is one of my travelling companions, Helania." As she continued Iskander took Helania's hand and planted a small kiss upon it. Skjarla rolled her eyes with a smile. "Helania, this is Iskander, a Reaver from

Taureum and the most incorrigible rogue that I have ever had the fortune of meeting."

"I must say Skjarla, the waterfront is abuzz with news of your latest travelling companions, all three thousand of them." He became serious, "Skjarla, what have you gotten yourself into, I've known you to work with other Reavers on occasion. Damn it, you've even worked with me once. I know some of our kind do protection work, but not the good ones. How did you end up protecting a column of refugees?"

Skjarla sighed and rubbed at her eyes tiredly, she took a mouthful of the lukewarm ale which was plonked down in front of them. She saw Iskander slide a few worn Orichs across the table, which swiftly disappeared into the meaty fist of the serving woman, one Sanguine being worth ten Orichs. "It's a long story Iskander, and not one that can be told in a place like this. All I can say is that I have very good reasons to be with these refugees, the townsfolk are decent people who need protecting." She could see that he was not convinced by this explanation, but he accepted that the Weeping Maiden was not the place to reveal secrets, not if you wanted them kept at any rate.

"Well what did you come in here for?"

Helania was amazed by the conversation, the now quick and businesslike exchange clashed with what had almost sounded like familial concern a moment before. To her the Reavers were most definitely an odd bunch. Skjarla carried on talking, leaving Helania out of the conversation, "We have friends making inquiries about a ship load of Romans who arrived a few weeks before the winter's Eve feast. Also, I have had no news from the west for some time, what is the latest story?"

Iskander leant back against the wall and grinned softly at Skjarla, "That'll cost you. Looks like you'll be buying my beer for the rest of the day if you want all of that."

Skjarla laughed, "Iskander, you may be a rogue, but at least you're a cheap drunk." Iskander feigned looking wounded, all the while keeping his gaze on Helania, a suggestive glimmer veiled behind the dark eyes.

"Well, my Ladies, the west is much the same as it has been for the last twenty years. The followers of the Red Father and the New Roman Empire still wage war. The Isle of Ryhm remains a bloody stalemate where the two pour men and money in and get corpses back. Both sides continue to court the mercenary companies, but aside from Lachlan's Blackhearts going over to the Red Father there is still little change and likely to be little. So long as the trade cities remain impartial, which is where their profit lies, the war will not progress at any great rate." He paused and took a long, deep swallow of his ale, smacking his lips happily as he placed the battered metal tankard down upon the weathered table. "As far as your other enquiry goes, there are close to three dozen Romans in Bloodwater who all arrived on a Leopolitian ship around the time you mentioned. They've kept to themselves for the most part, making discrete enquiries about a woman and her Roman guards. Why, are you mixed up in that too?" he looked excited now, Helania was unsure as to whether that was at the prospect of having some good gossip or something else.

"She is under my protection." Skjarla intoned ominously, emphasising every word, "What do you know about these Romans here?"

"They have no legion insignias, which tells me something. That lot are usually big on which legion they're from, so I would guess either an elite unit or specialist assassins, maybe hired in. They go armed everywhere, and they look handy with it. Why, do you need help?"

Skjarla sat in silence for a moment, her eyes gently shut, as if sleeping, but if you looked closely you could see the slight twitches of the muscles beneath as her eyes moved with her thoughts. Finally, she opened her eyes, a light shining within them, "Yes, but not with this. Iskander, you aren't under any contract at the moment are you?"

"No, just finished dealing with a band of Raptores," The black winged birdmen who were more crow than man, "So I am a free man. Why? What do you need me for?"

Skjarla's gaze flickered across to Helania. She grabbed her ale and tossed it down her throat in one go, she smiled, burped loudly and handed the empty flagon to her Dokkalfar companion. "Helania, I seem to need a refill, you wouldn't do the honours would you? You understand, Reaver business." Helania couldn't keep the disappointment from her face, but she got reluctantly to her feet.

She was about to move towards the bar when Iskander caught her arm with a grin. He too tossed back his ale like it was water, "While you're up, love?" She found herself disarmed by his charming smile, any temptation to refuse dying on her lips. She took up his flagon and made her way through the crush to the bar.

She still had half of her ale at the table, so when she finally caught the eye of the harassed looking man behind the bar she simply said, "Two ales, inn keep." The man nodded and went to refill the two flagons. As she waited at the bar she noticed something wrong, an added pressure next to her.

She turned to see what was causing it and was irritated to find that it was a man, probably a sailor with long greasy hair who reeked of stale beer. "How much for a quick tumble?" he asked with a drunken leer as his stinking breath rolled over her. Helania stood there speechless, shocked out of her momentary lapse as she felt him clumsily squeeze her behind. Without a second thought she smacked her forehead forward into his nose, feeling a satisfying crunch of bone and then getting a welter of blood in her face and down her front for her troubles.

The sailor staggered back into his friends who laid hands on their knives, ready to draw blood in defence of their shipmate. These two companions though, were not so far gone as their friend, so they recognized the deadly intent in Helania's eyes, and the half-drawn rapier at her hip told them that this was not a fight they would win easily. They gathered up their bleeding comrade and beat a retreat while Helania coolly turned back to the bar, wiping the blood from her face, slid four Orichs across the stained and ale soaked wood, before going back to their table. She set the brimming flagons down, irritated to see that whatever conversation the other two had been having was drawing to a conclusion.

Iskander nodded slowly, "Very well, I'll do it." There was a slight pause while he grinned mischievously, "For a kiss from you, beautiful lady." Skjarla rolled her eyes, but she smiled at him as she leant across the table to give the dark haired man a peck on the cheek. Iskander pretended to be affronted, "You call that a kiss? I should know better than to trust your value of a kiss, my Lady." He got to his feet, drained his ale and wandered out of the Weeping Maiden.

"Is that normal?" asked Helania, a mystified expression etched onto her features.

"Iskander is like that, very dramatic, but an honest man. You'll find no man better than him among the Reavers."

"Why does he do it, I mean, he seems so charming, so soft, I would have thought he'd be a poet in some noble's house somewhere, seducing noble ladies and the like."

Skjarla laughed at her companion's earnest expression, then tilted her head to the side thoughtfully, "Yes, I have thought the same of him on occasions. I think he loves the adventure, I think he would view being a poet as some form of gilded cage, something which would ultimately destroy him. One of his favourite sayings is, 'We are most alive when we are closest to death.' Personally, I don't agree, but it is the sentiment of a lot of Reavers. That was well done at the bar by the way, I would have helped but you seemed able to handle it yourself."

Helania couldn't help but smile at that, but when it came to the Reavers Helania wasn't sure what she thought. All she had ever heard of the Reavers was that they were mercenaries of the worst sort, and honourless thugs to boot, but that was not what she was seeing. To her, the Reavers seemed to be a close-knit family, a brotherhood which it was exceptionally hard to get into, but if you were good enough then there was a great degree of respect among members. "Should we tell Metellus about what we found out?" she asked, simply to fill the silence.

"No need for the moment, I suspect the assassins will come to us before too long. The workers who deliver our supplies will take the news of a group of Romans travelling with the refugees back into the town. I suspect tonight will not be a quiet one. I am looking forward to it."

Helania's mouth dropped open, how could this woman seem so eager for bloodshed? Even after her time with the mercenaries her guts tied themselves into hundreds of knots before a battle. "Why?" she breathed softly.

Skjarla continued, "I am looking forward to the chaos, and the fury, the rush of battle. Most of all though, I am looking forward to catching one of those assassins and finding out what secret our little Roman damsel has been hiding. There has to be some special reason why forty Romans have crossed the world to kill her." With that she got to her feet and swept out of the dingy inn, trailed by Helania.

The two of them made their way back through the city, heading back for the north gate. The road ran alongside the town, not actually going into the narrow streets of the port city. They wandered through the throng, people wandering back to their homes for the evening meal before spending their day's pay in one of the many drinking establishments.

The two of them passed through the Blood gate, the only break in the continuous walls which enveloped the city. The people outside in the tent city cheered as they saw the pair, the wagons of supplies having been welcomed with open arms. Skjarla shook her head at how fickle the hearts of a crowd can be, one moment you are their worst enemy, next you are the darling of the mob.

She did not see Accipiteri among the townsfolk, but that was no surprise. He was not going to be as overjoyed about the supplies for a second time. Plus, he had other things on his mind, what with the need to protect Domitia weighing heavily upon him. Skjarla decided to go to the Roman heiress and speak to her. She knew that at the moment they were in the middle of the camp, but if they stayed there then the assassins may well kill townsfolk as they tried to get to Domitia. 'Also', thought Skjarla, 'it would be much easier to deal with these other Romans out in front of the camp, where we can trap them against the wall'.

Domitia was sitting in her tent, the largest of all the tents in the small enclosure. The two legionaries standing out on guard snapping a salute, the ringing clang as their clenched fists thudded into their armoured chests echoing out through the air. Skjarla ducked through the low door flap, emerging into the warm space where a fire burned in the centre of the tent. Domitia sat upon her travelling chest, her rich clothes looking worn and threadbare after so long on the road. Skjarla knew that she had asked to go into the city to buy new clothes but Metellus had forbidden it. "Domitia"

Domitia looked at her disapprovingly, "Skjarla, when will you learn that the correct form of address for a Roman Lady is Domina. What can I do for you?" She had been sitting brushing her hair with an ivory comb, and went back to it while she was waiting for Skjarla's answer.

"Domitia," Skjarla put emphasis on the name, and was rewarded with an exasperated sigh from the other woman in the tent. "I want you and your Romans to move your tents to the edge of camp nearest the city wall. From my contacts in the city, there are Roman assassins in the city, and I don't want to risk one of them slipping through our guard and hiding amongst the tents. This way I can be sure that we get them all in one fell swoop." She had no intention of giving the real reason and therefore giving Domitia an opportunity to say no.

Domitia hesitated for a moment before taking a deep breath. "Very well, Skjarla, but I assume that you and the rest of the armed people of the town will be on guard, I would hate to think that I am being put at risk for no reason." Domitia licked her lips nervously and Skjarla realised that she was genuinely frightened, that the mask of calmness was beginning to crack as the assassins drew nearer.

She suddenly felt sorry for the calculating Roman. She was young and just doing what she felt she had to to survive. "Don't worry Domina, I will be outside on guard this evening." With that she got up and left Domitia's tent. If she had looked behind her she would have seen a small smile creep across Domitia's face. 'I have done it', thought Domitia, 'I have bound her to me, she and those other warriors who follow in her shadow will protect me, and maybe one day, help me reclaim what is rightfully mine.'

The people of Lonely Barrow watched in silent confusion as the Roman legionaries disassembled their camp, only to put it back up again barely one hundred yards away. They saw that Skjarla and all of the other experienced fighters were patrolling the area close to the Roman tents, and decided to move away from there. They could smell bloodshed on the wind and did not want to get caught up in any more violence than they had to. The Roman legionaries were on edge that evening, most sitting in grim silence, the only sound being the gentle rasp of their whetstones as they honed their blades. They sat and diced in subdued silence, waiting until night fell. Everyone was agreed that the assassins would most likely be coming tonight. Metellus and Accipiteri had come back to report that there were indeed a crowd of Romans in Bloodwater, Metellus had recognized them as being members of the Praetorian Guard, the Emperor's own bodyguards. They were sure the attack would come tonight, the Praetorians were not known for their subtlety and they wouldn't want to give her an opportunity to escape.

Torches were lit and legionaries began to patrol around the edge of the Roman enclave, their heavy shields clanking noisily as the metal rims banged against their greaves. There was suddenly a strangled cry, not from one of the torch bearers, but from up on the walls. A sentry must have discovered the Praetorians coming down over the wall and been silenced. Two of the Roman legionaries lobbed their torches in the direction of the shout. They arced through the air leaving trails of sparks like shooting stars, when they crashed to ground they illuminated the scene of the final few Praetorians climbing down ropes. The Roman assassins were lit up by the eerie orange glow, and before they could react there was a guttural roar from Domitia's men as they surged forward. Skjarla joined them in their charge. They must have looked like daemons, their eyes shining in the fiery glow, their armour flickering as it reflected the dancing flames of the two torches.

The Praetorians recovered themselves quickly, forming a line as they drew their blades. These men were supposedly the elite of the Roman army, but without their shields they were at a serious disadvantage against the line of Domitia's legionaries. Most of the Praetorians threw themselves against the line of wood and steel, but ten of them slipped around the flanks, sprinting for the one large tent they could see. Skjarla yelled to Metellus, "Your men hold them here, we'll get the rest." And she charged off, without waiting to see if any of the others had followed her.

She chased after the Praetorians, hamstringing the first one she chased down, sprinting across the flattened grass between the walls and the tents. She saw the four legionaries who had been defending the tent mouth standing in a wall, sheltering behind their shields as blows rained down upon them, seeking out any flesh they could. Skjarla fell upon the rear of them, seeing an axe appear next to her and Braugr charged out of the darkness. She felt Helania appear as well, her rapier flickering about like a snake's tongue as it danced in the darkness. Skjarla admired the Roman skill, but the much greater reach of her weapon meant that they couldn't get close enough to score the killing blow. Between them they cut down the Praetorians, leaving bloody, purple clothed mounds of flesh lying in a gradually spreading pool of blood before Domitia's tent.

While they were moving the corpses away from the tent flap Skjarla stalked back into the darkness, heading for the prone shape of the Praetorian she had hamstrung. The man was groaning softly, his knuckles white as his hands gripped the wound, trying to staunch the steady flow of blood weeping from his thigh. "Come to finish it then?" said the Praetorian gruffly, baring his throat as he did so. Skjarla was impressed by the man's courage.

"That depends, you tell me what I want to know, and you will be allowed to live." She spoke in a soft, friendly manner, but as she spoke she wiped the blood off Dreyrispa with the man's own cloak, leaving him in no doubt as to her seriousness.

"Very well, ask your questions." The man's face was tight and the words were forced between clenched teeth.

"First of all, who sent you?"

"Servius Tarpeus Aquilius."

"And who are you hunting, or rather, why are you hunting her?" She looked at him severely.

The Roman laughed, then winced at the pain, "You don't know?" he asked incredulously. "Only the bloody daughter of the emperor, half sister of my master and first in line to the Imperial throne."

Skjarla's eyes bulged briefly, but then things started to click; Domitia's evasiveness, Metellus's refusal to divulge why she was here. It explained a lot, but as to what she would want from the people of Lonely Barrow, who she was increasingly trying to bind to her, Skjarla could only guess. She could hardly use them to take on an empire on the other side of Midgard. If it weren't for the permanent bad weather which gave the Sea of Storms its name then travel between the Haemocracy and Rome might be manageable. Those storms meant that all trade, news and travel was forced to go via the trade cities, which in turn made any invasion of Roman lands impossible without their permission. She would have to see what happened over the next few weeks, but as it was they were all going to be marching for two months towards Fylkirsblod. She snapped from her reverie as she heard Metellus come over.

"I thought I heard voices," he said simply, as he knelt down next to the Praetorian lying prone on the ground. Before Skjarla could do anything, Metellus had drawn his small dagger and cut the other man's throat. As the body spasmed and red arterial blood spurted over the pair of them Skjarla leapt across the corpse. She pinned Metellus to the ground, her left arm grinding the bones in his wrist until he released the dagger, while her right hand held her own dagger to his throat.

Metellus had never seen her as angry as she roared in his face, "I gave him my word. Who do you think you are to break my vow?" Her voice dropped to an icy whisper, as sharp as her blade as the words rasped out from between her teeth, "Give me one reason why I don't recover my honour in your blood."

Metellus tried to look as unconcerned as he could; keeping his eyes on Skjarla's so as to stop himself from looking down at the eight inches of razor sharp steel which rested gently against his rhythmically pumping carotid. "He had to die, he would have followed us, or simply taken a ship back tell his master where Domitia is going."

Skjarla looked at him steadily, "Metellus, you know that is absolute crap. It would take him almost four months to go back to the nearest Roman city, then another four months to get to Rome itself. In sixteen months we could be anywhere on the face of Midgard. So why did you kill him."

"He would have followed us," he said simply, "And I will not allow any threat to my mistress. If that is wrong, then cut my throat, and let that be the end of it. Otherwise let me up and remember that I will not allow any threat to Domitia to continue a minute longer than it has to." He lay there, calmly looking her in the eye as he waited for her to make up her mind. Eventually she glared at him and hissed loudly before sheathing her knife, leaving Metellus on the ground as she got back to her feet and stalked off into the night, the shadows swallowing her up. Metellus let out a huge sigh of relief. He had looked into Skjarla's eyes and had seen death in there. His heart was hammering, but to him that was a good sign, it meant he was still alive, which he was still struggling to believe. He took a few deep, calming breaths before heading back towards the rest of the Romans.

Chapter 7

The butcher's bill for the battle outside Bloodwater had been seven dead Romans, bringing the number of Legionaries down to just nineteen. Metellus had stripped the armour from the bodies and taken some of the best fighters from the townsfolk and started to train them as legionaries. Skjarla hadn't told anyone what she had found out about Domitia, saving her knowledge until she needed it, instead using it to put Domitia's actions into perspective. The column had been advancing along the paved road which ran east, straight towards Fylkirsblod and the river Ranr. It would be a minimum of two months travelling, and for the first three weeks they made good progress, chased by the occasional late spring shower. The grasses and crops in the fields around the road steadily turned greener and grew taller, until they were up to the knees of the few people who chose to walk alongside the road instead of on the stone slabs.

Metellus had regarded Skjarla with suspicion for a few days, but after she had kept her silence his attitude to her had thawed once more. Ten days out of Bloodwater they had encountered some of the Raptores that Iskander had mentioned, the black feathery winged people, covered in dirt and grime which lent their thin faces and beak like noses a hellish appearance. Over fifty of them had dived out of the clouds which had dominated the skies that day.

Once that would have been a problem, however, since they had been able to stock up with weapons in Bloodwater there were enough people with spears and bows to drive the Raptores away with very few losses. The only injuries had come when the few surviving Raptores had pulled back into the sky and begun to rain arrows from their crude short bows down upon the column. However, once the creatures had realised that there was little of value to be taken and that the price in lives would be too high they gave up, cawing noisily as they disappeared into the clouds.

Since then it had been relatively peaceful on the march. There had been some grumbling about the monotony of the rations, but none of it serious. Accipiteri had continued to train Sigmund and the rest of the townsfolk who were willing to learn. More and more people had been taking up some form of weaponry, mainly out of boredom, but they were definitely getting better with their weapons. Skjarla continued to pace up and down the column like a caged lioness, worrying about what would be waiting for them when they reached Fylkirsblod. She also made sure that they kept moving as fast as possible, fearful that the Children of the Dragon would close up behind them. They had lost two days going around Bloodwater, but at least the Children would have to give the city a wide birth as well.

They had passed through three farming towns so far, and in all of them Accipiteri had taken it upon himself to warn anyone who would listen about the threat the chasing Children posed. Most had laughed at him, but when they came to leave there were always a few extra wagons on the end of the column. She wondered what had happened to the towns since they had passed through. Part of her, the idealistic part, hoped that the Children would have hurried past the towns, but the realistic part of her knew that the likelihood was that they were burned to the ground by now, their people nothing but ashes and bones. She was worried about this stretch of the journey, over the endless plains, fields and gently rolling hills which dotted the countryside between Bloodwater and Fylkirsblod. Every time that she went to the top of one of those small mounds of earth she was terrified that she would see the telltale dust cloud on the horizon which meant that the Children of the Dragon had caught up with them.

She voiced her worries to Accipiteri, "We need to move faster, no matter how fast we get these carts moving the Children are always going to be moving faster than us."

Accipiteri smacked his hands on his legs in exasperation, "How many times are we going to have this conversation Skjarla? You know that we can't get the column moving any faster without starting to lose people, and the longer the column gets the slower it moves, we take longer to break and set camp every time we pass through a town. If you have any new ideas then that is great, but if you have nothing new to say on the matter I have got the rest of it memorized." Every night for the last five days they had had this conversation, and Accipiteri was fed up with the discussing it by now.

"I know I know, but we have to do something. One idea I did have today was that we should look at putting higher sides on the carts, at least that way we could use them as a defensive wall if we are attacked. You know that if they catch us it is all over for the column." She said fatalistically, her voice low so as not to worry the townsfolk around them.

"That's not a bad idea Skjarla. I disagree about it being all over for the column though, the men and women have put in some good training and we still have twenty odd legionaries."

Skjarla shot him a filthy look, "That is wishful thinking my friend, you know that there were at least two thousand of them still standing after the battle at the Skein, even if the men and women we had here had half a dozen campaigns under their belts it would still be a difficult fight. Yes, they may be learning which end of a blade you point at the enemy, but neither of us have any idea how the new ones are going to respond in combat. At least the ones who fought with us at the ferry will have bit more steel in them, but we are up against animalistic killers, no pity, no mercy, just the urge to hunt."

Accipiteri glared at her, "I know that, Skjarla, of course I bloody do, but I have to believe that stuff, if I have no hope, then what chance do I have of giving the people any. I have to keep the faith, because if mine fails then I worry that the faith of all those who follow us will also fail."

Skjarla's shoulders slumped as she spoke sadly, "Accipiteri, I accept that, I really do. You are still young, but seem to have read every military manual ever written, I mean who was that one with the strange name you were spouting the other day?"

"Sun Tzu?"

"Yes, him. He would see that this is not a pitched battle we can win; we need to do this on our own terms. I fear that may well mean leaving with Sigmund, or if he won't leave then we need to take the Fang. I want to save as many of these people as possible, but when you have been around as long as I have you learn that sometimes all you can do is pick the lesser of two evils."

It was a heartfelt speech, full of emotion, but Accipiteri's only response was, "Bollocks." He got up quickly, but as he strode into the night, his cloak swooping around him like the set of wings he so desperately craved he turned back to her. "You don't always have to take the choice you're offered, you can make your own choices." He was then swallowed up by the shadows, leaving Skjarla alone as she stared into the dying embers of the fire.

***

They reached the midway point of the march to Fylkirsblod when the hills of Njorden rose into view. Here the climate was quite dry, far from either of the two great rivers in the north of the Haemocracy, the Skein and the Ranr, and the land was given over to orchards instead of crops. On the south facing slopes of the hills she could see the endless tracts of neatly organised vines. From a distance they gave the hillside the appearance of having been ploughed by a giant, the shadows of earth between the vines looking like huge furrows. The rest of the hillsides were covered with trees, olives and other twisted, gnarled varieties which could survive with less water. The summer sun was high in the sky by the time that they reached the orchards, and against Skjarla's advice, the column was called to a halt. The people gratefully spread out among the narrow trunks of the grove, seeking respite from the baking sun beneath the leaves. Skjarla knew that around here somewhere would be the local Haemocrat's estate, complete with its horde of low paid Dokkalfar and Dwarven workers.

She leant against the trunk of an olive tree, nestled between two roots which disappeared into the earth, thinking about the Haemocracy as the leaves rustled over head. To her it was one of the most bizarre systems of allocating power ever devised, when the true power lay not in the hands of great warriors or men, or even in the hands of the High Council themselves. In truth, the power of the Haemocracy was held by the Keepers of the Blood, a group of scribes and bureaucrats who kept the ledgers and histories of every marriage and child between the families of the Haemocracy. In order to keep their standing, people had to marry others whose blood was deemed to be at least as pure as theirs. It was a strange world, where the merest hint of illegitimacy, an unknown father, could completely destroy a family for generations. The system was used in part to ensure that the Dokkalfar and Dwarves who lived above ground were kept at the bottom of the social hierarchy. Those who knew the system knew that the real powers behind the Haemocracy were the Keepers. If a member of the High Council was too outspoken, then the purity of his breeding was called into question.

Skjarla was unsure as to how such a system had ever come into being, even with the proliferation of Abhorrens after Ragnarok, how the quill had become mightier than the blade in this Empire of Blood. Such a thing would never have happened in the old days, and at least in the Roman Empire people still knew how to lead. She was amazed that there weren't more insurrections against the High Council, but then she remembered the brutal way in which the early rebellions had been put down. Battles were won by the brutish Abhorrens auxiliaries who were then given freedom to obey their basest animal instincts on the survivors. Tales of people eaten alive, burned to cinders while their tortures laughed at their screams, of women raped to death, were more than enough to quell the most rebellious of hearts. Those of the old races who hated their existence above ground would flee to the great underground holds, but the lack of any wealth and the innate suspicion of outsiders in the holds meant they were merely trading one poverty of another.

Her musings were interrupted by the loud clang as Sigmund sat down next to her. "I hear from Accipiteri that you are worried about the column. Look, I know that this isn't what you're used to, and that you are really only here to protect this thing hanging around my neck, but thank you nonetheless. I don't think that we'd have even made it to Celeste without your help." His voice was soft, it sounded as if a heavy weight was pressing down upon him.

Skjarla was feeling unusually sympathetic, perhaps because what he had said had seemed so genuine, but she asked him, as kindly as she could, "Is something bothering you?"

Sigmund chewed the inside of his lip nervously and fiddled with the straps on his armour before replying, "Skjarla, am I to blame for all of the deaths on this column? I just feel that if I wasn't with them, then the people would be safe, and the Fang would be safer too."

Awkwardly she rested a hand on his shoulder, she wished that it were Accipiteri dealing with this, he would know exactly what to say. "Look, don't blame yourself, even if you left now the Children of the Dragon would still hunt down the townsfolk to try to find out where you had gone. Until they find one of the Fangs and raise one of the Hunters they cannot truly sense the Fang unless they are very close by. As to those who have already fallen, there is nothing you can do to change the past, so there is no point in dwelling on it, you just have to make do with what you have now." She tailed off, unsure what else to say.

She was extremely surprised when he turned to her and said with a watery smile, "Thank you Skjarla, I'll try to remember that." He got to his feet and slunk off, alone with his thoughts as he passed through the crowd of people grabbing food from one of the wagons for the midday meal.

Skjarla was trying to return to her thoughts when she heard Accipiteri's voice as he stepped out from behind the tree. "That was good of you, to try to reassure the boy, but it would be better of you took the advice yourself." He left her no room to reply as he turned and headed into the crowd as well.

Further along the road, where the Romans had stopped their march, Metellus and Domitia were in deep conversation. "Domina, is everything all right? You seem very preoccupied today." Metellus's voice was full of concern, which Domitia put down to his protective nature, rather than his feelings for her.

She smiled thinly, "Yes Metellus, everything is fine thank you. It is just that seeing these trees and vineyards reminds me so much of the lands of my father, the imperial estate outside Avenicum. We have mountains covered with olive trees, and row upon row of vineyards, it is truly a great place." Metellus held his tongue, choking back a comment about the reason it was so immaculate and neat was the thousand slaves who were used to keep it that way. "I guess that I just miss my home, that is all," she continued, "What about you Metellus, do you ever miss Rome?"

"Domina, I do miss Rome herself, but there is nothing there waiting for me, I have always been a soldier, and will always be a soldier of Rome. So long as I have my duty to do and you to protect then I am content with my life." This was an outright lie. Since he had first begun to serve the heir to the Imperial throne he had been unsatisfied with his life. He remembered that first time that he saw her. As a reward to his century for rescuing Domitia from a group of the Red Father's men they had been made her guardians. It was thought that the plan had been to kidnap her and use her as leverage to extract concessions from the Romans. Her carriage had been chased by horsemen, her guards all slain, and his men had been lucky enough to be coming the other way down the road. The men of his century and another, travelling to rejoin their legion after a two day patrol, had parted to allow the carriage through before reforming the line and driving her pursuers off. He, as the commanding officer had had the honour of checking who was in the carriage. When he had pulled back the heavy velvet curtains he had seen her in there, sitting silently. She had been clothed in the dignity of a Roman heiress, her face calm and not the slightest trace of fear in her eyes. He had been struck dumb by her beauty and her courage and had loved her from a distance ever since.

They had served faithfully for three years, but once her illegitimate brother Tarpeus had started to build his power base for an assault on the Imperial throne they had become even closer, with the young Roman relying on him more and more. It had come to a head during one of the food shortages which had plagued Rome over the last few years. A mob had descended on the residence where Domitia was staying that night, baying for her blood. Metellus had no doubt that they had been sent to drive her from the city and they had succeeded in that. His men had had to form a thick square to cut their way through the mob. He had been amazed by the courage she had shown as he had ordered her to gather those few things most precious to her and flee the city. Once they were outside the city they had been chased by assassins, driven from Rome, fleeing the concealed blades of her brother.

Over the months of their flight he had become closer to her, as she started to rely on him more and more for advice as they were hounded away from Rome, steadily losing men during the nights. Soldiers would disappear, their bodies found the following day further down the roads, the corpses showing the signs of hideous torture, a warning to the fleeing heiress as to what she should expect. His affections had betrayed him on the night before they had taken ship to Taureum from the port of Salvitium. They had been in a grim inn, Domitia taking over the top room of the inn, the only one which was even close to worthy of the daughter of the Emperor. Most of the survivors of the guard were already waiting on the ship, but as the ship was not to sail until the next morning Metellus had decided to hide Domitia in the town. He and the four best swordsmen in the remaining half century had been in the room next door, all of them on edge as they waited to hear any sound of a disturbance. Metellus had been standing outside the door on watch when he had heard a loud crash, the sound of the window shutters exploding against the walls.

He had roared his loudest, and he remembered with painful clarity the scene which had greeted him as he burst through the door. The worn green shutters lay on the floor, splintered and broken by the three assassins who had forced their way in. Domitia was standing at the foot of the bed, her worn, pale stola wrapped around her to keep the chill off, as she wildly swung the sword he had left with her, trying to keep her assailants at bay. Metellus remembered how they had looked as he had charged at them, the thick black clothing, covering every inch of skin beneath their soot smeared loricas. They were clearly Romans, given the confidence with which they held their short, heavy gladii, the menace with which they stalked towards their prey spoke of cold killers. He could remember the hard thuds as the nails in his sandals bored into the floorboards as he propelled himself across the room, the smell of damp that came from the worn fabrics in the bare room. He could remember the jolt of pain in his shoulder as it had crashed into one of the assassins, the jarring sensation in his wrist as his blade punched through one of the assassin's armour. It had been over in seconds, his rage had dredged up previously unknown reserves of strength as he cut down those threatening his mistress in a welter of blood and hewn limbs.

The other legionaries had only just burst into the room when he was wiping his blade on the dark tunic of the final assassin. He was still consumed by the red mist of battle, his blood thundering in his ears and his vision reduced to two narrow pin points, when Domitia had dismissed the other legionaries. He had been about to follow them when she had bade him stay, and gently washed the blood from his crimson stained hands. His heart had been hammering against his ribs at the unexpected intimacy, even more so when she wrapped her arms around him and sobbed softly into his armoured chest. She had wanted comfort, closeness, and they had lain together that night. He may not have intended it, but his heart was hers now, totally and utterly, until the last breath left his body.

However, since that one night in Salvitium they had not lain together, and it was becoming close to a physical pain for him. His love for her burnt all the stronger for the distance between them, and he felt the need to prove himself worthy of her in everything he did. In his deepest heart he knew that it would never be, she was the heir to the Purple, he was merely a centurion from the II Legio Mithyria, but he still clung to a fool's hope.

"Metellus?" Domitia brought him back from his reverie, his head shaking violently as he snapped back to the present.

"Sorry Domina, I was miles away, thinking about life back in the Empire." He said quickly, hoping that she wouldn't pry too deeply into his thoughts. "I had meant to ask, how is your plan going? Are you any closer to binding these people to you?"

She smiled at him, her front teeth just peeking between her perfectly formed lips, he fought not to stare. "Well, given that they came to my aid in Bloodwater, I would have said that the important members of this rabble will follow me, and if they will come, then all the rest will follow them. However, we still need a place to build a position of strength from which I can begin the quest to regain that which is rightfully mine." Her eyes shone with light as she held the image of sitting upon the imperial throne in her mind.

"Domina, if I may, why not merely pay Skjarla to assassinate Tarpeus, I would have thought she'd have the skills for it, and the inclination too." He paused for a heartbeat, "A word of caution though Domina, I fear that you must prepare for a long wait," he kept talking as she started to object angrily. "I only say that so that you do not die of disappointment if it takes more than a year. I have sworn to you that I would die to see you back upon the Imperial throne, and I stand by that."

She seemed to deflate slightly, "Thank you Metellus, I am glad to hear that I have one as loyal as you with me. Rest assured though, I do not intend to be away from civilization long."

Metellus smiled at her as she turned to go, walking off between the olive trees and staring wistfully out over the gently shifting vineyards as they blew in the breeze. In truth, although he wanted nothing more than to make his mistress happy, he didn't want to go back to Rome any sooner than he had to. He knew that once they were there, any chance of his love for her ever bearing fruit would die, but on the road like this there was always hope. He stood there, staring into the distance as he struggled to bully his emotions back into line, masking it behind his stiff veneer of military hierarchy. He found himself glad to see that some of the new legionaries, townsfolk he had stuffed into the armour of the legions, were struggling to place their packs correctly on their shoulders, with gear falling to the ground in a cacophony of sound. He roared at them, the pain in his heart morphing into roars of anger as he bellowed at the hapless recruits. The Romans were already preparing to march, and it was not long before the shouts were passed down the column, calling for people to start moving forwards.

***

They had only been marching for three hours when Skjarla was called up to the front of the column. She had been walking at the back, her eyes constantly scanning the horizon as she waited for signs that the Children had caught up with them. By this time the sun had sunk low against the western horizon, forcing her to raise her gauntlet to shield her eyes from the glare. She puffed out her cheeks and jogged up to the front of the column. Taking her helmet off she strapped the heavy steel to her baldric, next to the

Gjallarhorn, where it clanged noisily against her hip. She had dispensed with her cloak, it was getting too hot for that and she was grateful for the cool wind that washed the sweat from her brow and rustled softly through her hair. As she ran past the townsfolk, she felt people falling in behind her, Accipiteri and Helania, who had taken to walking together most of the time, stepped into her shadow. Braugr and Sigmund also joined the small group as it passed them. At the head of the now halted column she found a small band of horsemen, led by a figure clad in the finest crimson robes she had ever seen, sat atop a perfectly white mount.

They studied the figure as the two parties stared at one another between the endless groves of trees. Their cause wasn't helped by the fact that people behind were taking advantage of the halt to strip fruit from the trees, in this case a strange orange coloured fruit with a waxy skin. The skin itself was as unpleasant as the flesh within was sweet and juicy. She and the others had given up on trying to get the people not to strip the trees of fruit completely. Although this was one of the main roads within the Haemocracy there were almost never large groups like this making their way along it, so the fruit trees were safe even though they were planted right up to the stone surface. Her eyes scanned across the party behind the rich lord, they were all sheathed in gleaming golden steel, the metal seeming to flow like water across their skin as was the fashion at the moment. There were over two dozen of them and they looked like they knew their trade. She knew that the guards of some of the great Blood Houses were second only to the Lupine Guard, the cream of the Haemocracy's armies.

Before her mind could wander any further one of the soldiers kicked his horse forwards, until he was halfway between his lord and master and the people of Lonely Barrow. "By what right do you travel this road?" His voice boomed out across the short distance, his large, bucket-like helm giving his voice a metallic rasp.

Accipiteri was the first to answer, "This is a council road, and by that right anyone can use it," his voice already angry thanks to the tone of the mounted man. Skjarla shook her head slightly, aristocrats everywhere were a prickly bunch but those of the Haemocracy were particularly full of themselves and their god given right to rule.

The mounted warrior responded haughtily, "These may be the highways of the Council, but the right to travel on them is still held by the local Haemocrat. My master has been told of damage to his crop of olives, and of a sudden reduction in the number of apples and oranges along the roadside. He is curious as to what caused these shortages. Perhaps you'd be able to tell him?" There was no hint of the expression beneath that blank metal faceplate, but the voice held the smug edge of someone who took a vicious pleasure from their discomfort. Skjarla was already measuring distances within her mind, she imagined covering the five paces which separated the two of them and getting her shoulder underneath the mounted man's foot. She would then cut the girth on the rich leather of his saddle and flip him off the horse's back. She half smiled at the image of the man wrapped in gilded steel falling to the ground with a deafening clang, his limbs knotted within the red and gold material of his clothing.

The silence stretched onwards until Sigmund took a pace forward. Skjarla reached out to haul him back but he had begun speaking before she could. "We are travelling to an audience with the High Council; surely your master would not want to stand in the way of such business?" The helmeted head jerked backwards as the man processed this new information, the horseman turned back to his master, looking for instruction.

The two of them conversed softly for a few heartbeats before the supercilious voice returned, washing over them like a wave of oil. "My Lord says that you are free to continue along his section of the road." There was a pregnant pause. They could all sense that he was waiting to finish his statement. "However, My Lord wishes for you to put right the damage you have done already. He will accept a fee of fifty thousand Sanguines to replace the stolen fruit and treat the damage to the trees."

Sigmund surprised them all and did a very brave thing, he laughed, long and loudly in the face of the warrior. They couldn't see what was going on beneath the steel helmet of the nearest man, but the face of the local lord was swiftly turning as crimson as the material of his cloak. Hands went to swords among his body guard and Skjarla began to scan the orchards on either flank, in case there were more of the lord's soldiers hidden there. When Sigmund had recovered himself he spoke again, his voice cracking slightly as he kept the laughter from his voice, "Sir, all we have you see behind you, and if all of the contents of the carts behind me are worth more than ten thousand Sanguines then I will eat my own shoes." That elicited a nervous chuckle from the crowd forming behind them.

The warrior on horseback did not seem particularly amused, though, and squeezed his sword hilt as a way of showing his fury at this mockery of his master. "In that case, my master will need people to work on the orchards, to pay off the damage done by you thieves," the man was spitting mad now, every word ejected with violent force. "As such, unless you pay, or give him two hundred souls, all younger than thirty summers, to work the fields until they die; you shall not pass any further along this road."

The man sat back smugly, his posture relaxed as he saw the look of shock pass over the faces of the people before him. Skjarla knew that this was clearly a cruel lord. Benevolent rulers will not keep cruel men in their pay, but cruel rulers attract vicious men the way corpses attract flies. She sensed a shifting behind her, but resisted the urge to turn around, instead gently checking the balance of Dreyrispa in her hands, she prepared for combat. It would make them hunted outlaws if they cut their way through this obstacle, but then, they were already hunted so what was the difference there. Out of the corner of her eye she could see Helania slide her rapier an inch or so out of its narrow, plain leather scabbard. She was sure that Braugr and Accipiteri would be doing the same thing. They all wished that the Romans would come up to the front, their numbers would help to put the haughty Haemocrat on the back foot, but no one had thought to summon them.

Sigmund's mind was whirring, he could feel the blood pulsing through his hands as adrenaline surged around his system. He could see his companions preparing for combat and had no desire for that, Accipiteri had told him how precarious the column's situation was, and they did not need the blood of a lord on their hands as well. Before Skjarla could slip her leash of civility and leap into combat he roared to the guard, a good deal more confidently than he felt. "I offer a challenge, if one of us can defeat your master's champion then you let us pass unmolested."

He waited as the silence stretched out, seconds dragging on as the river of time slowed to a dull trickle. Then the Haemocrat himself rode forwards, the powerful muscles of his brilliant white horse clearly visible as they bunched and surged beneath the gleaming coat. Up close Sigmund could see the lines on the thin face, made more angular by the thin, pointed beard which was apparently all the fashion among the nobles of the Haemocracy. The man's robes were a rich crimson, the material shimmering as it moved with him as he rode the horse. His eyes were a vibrant blue, but there was no warmth in there. His voice was serpentine and full of rage a he hissed sibilantly, "Well boy, you shall have your wish, but it will be you to face my champion, and when you fail I will take the entire column into slavery. You have damned every man, woman and child here, I want you to know that before you die."

Sigmund looked the man calmly in the eye, straining everything to make sure he didn't flinch as he said nonchalantly, "Name your champion."

"Dane, come and teach the whelp to die. Slowly." He waved his right hand, the heavy rings on his fingers glinting on his fingers as they caught the light. Sigmund felt his guts clench with the horrid convulsions of fear, as one of the bodyguard spurred his mount forward. Skjarla and Accipiteri shared a worried glance with Braugr as they saw the champion approach, he was a nondescript individual in scarred armour, which told them this was a cold, experienced killer. Some champions were all bluster and tales, others were screaming psychopaths but the most deadly were the quiet ones, who methodically got on with the business of killing.

Accipiteri jogged to Sigmund's side and said quickly, "Remember what Skjarla and the others have taught you, he's probably quick so make sure you make use of all that extra reach you have."

Sigmund snapped at him unkindly, regretting his challenge, "Can't you offer something more practical than that?" he ignored Accipiteri as he started to draw his weapon, trying to remember all of the things that Skjarla had pummelled into him over the last four months. The champion bowed slightly to him and Sigmund felt he should return the favour. He found his eyes tracing the scars in the plain steel armour which encased every inch of his opponent. He saw the smooth sinewy motions of the man's flesh and realised he may have made a catastrophic mistake. They faced each other across the space, the hard paving slabs of the road providing a firm footing for their duel, the trees on the roadside rustling gently, the calmness jarring with the coming brutality.

There was no sign, no sound, but Sigmund found himself presented with a whirling stabbing wall of steel as his opponent's broadsword sought out the gaps in his defence. Sigmund found himself wishing that he had a shield, even though he had cursed the weight every time he had trained with the damned thing. He tried to follow the training he had had, sweeping the blade to the side, but desperately trying to keep the razor sharp edge away from his flesh. He was grateful to his ancestor for the armour, the ancient steel taking many blows but the shining scales turned aside the champion's blade. He felt his eyes drawn to a flicker of movement and nearly got impaled for his lapse in concentration. He had noticed Skjarla frantically miming as she grabbed her elbows and tapped her knees. The lesson that she had tried to drill into him from day one, 'Your sword is not your only weapon.'

With that in mind he started trying to get inside his opponent's reach so he could use his superior bulk and power to end the contest. He stepped in close and felt his ears ring as a crashing blow from his opponent's fist rattled his helmet. He staggered back, ears ringing and vision swimming as he tried to groggily fend off the storm of steel which raged about him. His armour finally gave against the blows, the scales over his right shoulder parting as the champion's blade bit deeply into the flesh of his shoulder, coming to rest in his collarbone. He screamed as the fiery pain consumed his body, followed by a second wave as his opponent tried to pull the blade free from his flesh. However, as much as the man tugged, the sword was stuck fast, and all Sigmund could do was roar with rage, the moment of bloodstained fury fuelling the strength in his arm. He lunged forward with his left arm, feeling his collarbone snap as his body twisted, a fresh stab of pain engulfing him. He felt the tremor run up his left arm as he punched his blade through the steel, heard the wet, visceral sucking sound as flesh parted around the steel, saw the gout of red which spilled over his arm. He remained standing just long enough to feel the champion go limp, the weight of his body dragging his sword out of Sigmund's hand.

There was a stunned silence as the two fighters crashed to ground, one after the other. Then the people of Lonely Barrow rushed forwards to aid Sigmund whose blood was pouring from his wounded shoulder. The Haemocrat looked stunned, the blood draining from his face as he watched his Champion's lifeblood start to seep through the cracks in the paving and running down to stain the earth red. One of the villagers was sent running for the Romans at the back of the column, they were the best healers they had, at least when it came to battlefield wounds. Skjarla had surprised the others when she had torn off a length of clean material from the tunic she wore under her armour and used it to staunch the bleeding. She hadn't had the gentlest of touches, and Sigmund had screamed as if his bones were on fire as she clamped the cloth to his wound, applying as much pressure as she could.

One of the Roman legionaries, Appius, arrived followed closely by Metellus and Domitia. Metellus and the legionary instantly started to scrutinise the wound, while Domitia tried to get a handle as to what had gone on. Skjarla tore her eyes away from Sigmund's snow-white face to watch as the Haemocrat's men silently gathered up the remains of their fallen champion and silently rode off into the trees. She heard Metellus's voice ring out in his trademark parade ground roar, "Get a fire going, we need to cauterize the wound and set the bone before we can stitch him up." Ironically the first place that people went for wood was the surrounding trees, hacking branches off to build a small fire. She watched as they worked, the torn cloths steadily turning a rusty red as the blood soaked through them.

Within minutes there was a small, crackling fire alight on the stones, the soot staining the stone paving slabs as the fire burnt fast and hot. She saw Appius draw his pugio, the small dagger all legionaries carried with them, and push it into the heart of the fire, where the embers pulsed with a fiery glow. The group waited in a stagnant silence as the metal began to gleam, before glowing a dull red, then brilliant orange before it was withdrawn from the heat. "Hold him down," Appius said grimly, "He's going to fight against this." Skjarla and Metellus pinned his limbs to the road's surface, with Braugr lying across his legs.

Appius took a deep breath and pressed his hand close to the deepest wound, the one in Sigmund's shoulder. Without warning he pressed the still glowing blade into the cavity of the wound and Sigmund screamed, his body arching as every muscle clenched in a rictus of agony. Metellus was nearly thrown clear and clung on for dear life, pressing his bulk towards the road, trying to hold Sigmund down as the smell of burning flesh pervaded the air. As Appius withdrew the blade Sigmund's body relaxed, but only until Appius pushed the still steaming blade into the other wounds still weeping blood. He finally withdrew the now cold metal from Sigmund's body, the blade covered with crusted blood and his hands stained with gore. Sigmund had passed out, and now lay unconscious on the stones, his chest rising slowly with each shallow breath. His clothes were shredded and stained with blood, his armour laying scattered about him like an abandoned shell.

Domitia surprised the crowd by helping to lift Sigmund's body and carry it to one of the empty carts, ones that had once been full of provisions which had long since been eaten. She sat in the cart beside him and gently stroked the young man's hair, using some of the column's water to wash the swiftly clotting blood from his flesh. Skjarla wandered down to the cart and peered in, someone had thought to erect a leather cover from one of the tents, to keep the worst of the sun off Sigmund and whoever was watching him. She was annoyed at herself, she should have stepped in quicker to fight the duel, and Sigmund had no right to fight when she was far better at it that he was. She also couldn't help but wonder why the heir to the imperial throne was caring for Sigmund, what she hoped to gain from it. Over the course of the afternoon Appius returned several times to see the state of his patient and was looking increasingly worried as Sigmund began to sweat, his skin becoming hot to touch as he writhed in his fevered sleep.

The mood was subdued as they halted for the evening, the tale of the duel and the reasons for it had spread up and down the column like wildfire and while everyone was grateful for Sigmund's service they were worried about him. Skjarla found herself sitting in silence by a small fire with Accipiteri, the two of them united by their concern for Sigmund and the worries over the consequences had he failed. They had discussed the fight briefly and spoken of ways to improve Sigmund's technique. It was clear that they could not shelter him from violence, and he must be able to protect the Fang should it come to that. They had sat in silence for some time before Skjarla spat angrily, "I should have been quicker and issued the challenge before he could." She shook her head slowly.

All Accipiteri could do was smile thinly, "He has a good mind, to see a route out of that confrontation, and you have to admit he did well in the fight."

Skjarla laughed hollowly, "He will carry the scars he gained today for the rest of his life, and as far as fighting well, he nearly died. He only won thanks to the luck of the blade becoming wedged in his shoulder." She stared into the fire, waiting for the feeling of hopeless irritation to end.

The silence dragged on for a while before Accipiteri asked softly, "This seems so new to you, have you not had to do something like this in all the years since the cataclysm?"

Ordinarily she would have silenced such a question with a scornful glance or a sneer, but on this night she answered. Maybe it was due to the sense of community and purpose she had found in the column or maybe it was that she felt a certain degree of kinship with Accipiteri. "No, I have found that the life of solitude is far preferable to the alternative. Think about it, I become great friends with you all, and what do I have to look forward to? Watching you grow old and die while I remain young forever." She waved her arms expressively, even as she felt the salty sting of tears well up in her eyes. "Immortality is my curse. No matter how hard I tried, I could not die. When Hel cursed me as Ygdrassil burned, the power scarring my armour and my body, you know my hair was not always black, it used to be as golden as ripe wheat, but now ..." Her voice tailed off and she looked down, not wanting to meet Accipiteri's eye.

Accipiteri looked around the grove in which they sat, taking in the small trees which encircled them, the silhouettes of the rest of the column moving about as they spoke and ate together. The smell of the orange trees hung heavy in the air and the light of the fires could be seen glinting off their waxy skins. In the dim light he noticed something, and looked more closely. He spoke slowly to Skjarla, as if carefully considering each word as it escaped his lips. "Skjarla, I will not deny that what you suffer is torment beyond description, but do you not think that there may be some way of breaking your curse?"

"In truth I have always had this immortality, as you well know, but that which I once considered a blessing is now a curse. All Hel did was to force me to survive Ragnarok and stop me from killing myself, as I so wanted to do."

Accipiteri tried to sound cheerful as he squeezed her shoulder reassuringly, "Then surely the only thing you can do is to try to make your immortality more bearable. It will not end your life as you so wish, but it may at least break the curse."

Skjarla laughed hollowly, he could feel the muscles moving as her shoulders heaved with the movement, "Accipiteri, if you can reason out a way of doing that then you are far wiser than I."

She rose to her feet to go but Accipiteri snatched at her gauntleted hand, before saying softly, "I think you already have," holding gently onto her left index finger. "Look," he said, somewhat breathlessly. Skjarla held the finger up to the light and felt her heart race as her eyes took in what lay before them. White veins shot through the armour over her finger, looking like spears of lightning against the night sky, cracks in the soot black exterior that Ragnarok had burnt onto the once flawless metal. She couldn't say a word, just stood there, staring in wonder and amazement at the sight. Accipiteri left in silence. Glancing over his shoulder he could see that she was still standing there, turning the gauntlet around in the firelight, studying the splinters of light.

Chapter 8

The summer sun beat down upon the column, the earth around the road becoming increasingly dusty. Away from the hills between the rivers there was less rain, not enough to support the verdant orchards which had carpeted the landscape there. Instead the land was one endless, arid plain, where beasts grazed during the winter before they were moved to the summer pastures along the river Ranr. The column was silent, save for the soft slap of shoes against the stone road and the gentle squeaking of poorly greased cart wheels, turning lazily about their axles. Sigmund was still in the back of a cart, his mind returned, but his body still weak. It had been nearly a week before he had recovered from the vicious fever that had claimed his strength. Ten days since he had returned to himself and he was still too weak to stand, but Appius pronounced that the wounds were healing cleanly now, and that the collarbone was knitting well.

From what Skjarla knew of the Haemocracy, they were still about fifteen days march from Fylkirsblod and the only thing that worried she was the lack of water. They still had several dozen leather skins filled with fresh drinking water, but the last well had been poisonous, a dead bird had been floating on surface, and they all knew that drinking that water was the quickest way to enjoy a very painful death. No one knew how far it was to the next well and so they were strictly rationing the supplies they had. Since they had left the orchards they had not seen another living soul, but this was not surprising, given the time of year. Most of the caravans tended to set off at the end of the autumn, travelling during the cooler months to ensure that their goods were in the market for the following spring.

She smiled as she thought of what had gone on in the last two weeks, how regularly she had seen Accipiteri and Helania in deep conversation, laughing together and seemingly growing closer to one another. Braugr was always there, at a discrete distance, not interfering but clearly protective of Helania. It made Skjarla chuckle at how unnecessary it was. Yes, most men would be trying to toss Helania on her back at the first opportunity, but Accipiteri was not most men. Skjarla had known him long enough to know that his undeniably good heart was backed up by his religious adherence to honour, and as such Helania was safe. Skjarla remembered Helania asking about Accipiteri, after all, Skjarla had known him for longer than the Dokkalfar had. It had been an odd conversation, for all that Helania seemed to be interested in Accipiteri, and she seemed reluctant to admit any feelings to him, as if she was afraid of being defined by such a decision. It was all part of the mystery which surrounded her real reason for being at war, and she was still none the wiser as to why Braugr was selling himself as a mercenary.

Domitia had continued to tend to Sigmund, much as that seemed to annoy Metellus. Skjarla was increasingly beginning to dislike the Roman aristocrat, who seemed to be out for every advantage she could get, and seemed to attempt to achieve them by wrapping any man who would follow her around her finger. So far as Skjarla knew, she had not yet used her sex yet, but seemed to trade on the unspoken promise of future trysts. She felt particularly sorry for Metellus, who followed his mistress around like a love struck puppy, with his hopelessness plain to all except him.

Braugr and Accipiteri were frequently to be found in animated conversation. Mainly discussing not only how to improve the training and equipment of the Lonely Company, as the armed townsmen had taken to calling themselves, but also how to quickly return Sigmund to full health. They all knew well that it was a delicate balance, the longer that he lay there the more muscle that he lost, but to stress him too soon would be to set back his recovery. He should be pressed, but not too hard, so they had quietly asked that Skjarla not take part in his training until he was fully fit again. In truth she hadn't been worried about that, preoccupied as she was trying to plan the dealings in Fylkirsblod. She still felt a desire to do right by these people, odd as it still seemed to her, but she knew that she had to keep Sigmund with her, and how to do that was causing her problems.

She hoped that the task to which she had detailed Iskander would be successful. If it all went badly then they would have need of his help. The other thing which still caused her wonder was the lightning strike upon her hand, which now crept up to her knuckles from every finger on her left hand. Other people were beginning to notice and remark upon the strange appearance of her gauntlet. There was much that needed to be prepared. She was anxious as it was almost certain that the angry and humiliated Haemocrat whose estate they had pillaged would have sent a man to the council demanding vengeance. If the two and a half thousand people remaining in the column reached the walls of Fylkirsblod to find their passage barred by a large army then they were doomed.

She heard the heavy crunch of hobnailed sandals, one of the Romans, almost certainly Metellus as he was the only one who regularly came to talk to her. She didn't look around, only asked, "Everything alright, Metellus?"

Metellus kept his peace for a moment, as if plucking up the courage to ask something. He took a deep breath, and then began, his footsteps falling into step with hers as he spoke. "Skjarla, before I say any more, I ask that this conversation go no further than the two of us." He looked around, seeking people who might be listening, but there were none; they were a good twenty paces in front of the first cart in the line.

Skjarla tried to suppress her interest, hoping she sounded nonchalant when she said, "Of course Metellus, I would have hoped by now you knew me well enough to know I guard my honour jealously."

The Centurion seemed relieved by this, but then he seemed to tense up again, bracing himself for the consequences of what could happen. "Skjarla, I wanted to apologize for something I have had on my chest for too long. One of our legionaries overheard you in conversation and told Domitia and I about where you're from." This wasn't strictly true, the Legionary had been listening out for her, trying to ferret out secrets which would aid Domitia.

"Go on." Skjarla's voice was razor sharp and Metellus glanced at her nervously, acutely aware that he was close to triggering Skjarla's legendary temper.

"As I said, I apologize for that, but what I wanted to ask you is this. Since I found out that you were a goddess it has made me wonder, are the gods of my forefathers real, or were yours the true gods?"

Skjarla wanted to be angry, she wanted to yell at him and send him away, but, for all the faults of his mistress, Metellus was a good and honourable man. She shook her head, partly in answer to the question, partly at her own weakness in not sending Metellus packing with her boot print on his arse. "Metellus, look at Accipiteri. He believes in his Goddess of Light and Sky, she did not exist before the cataclysm, but in the ancients of his people there are manifestations of her power. I was not a goddess, but I know that the Aesir were not the only Gods there were. I don't really know, but I think that if enough people believe in the gods then they become real and gain their power through the worship of their followers. Think of the Red Father, the God he claims to speak for is also a being of the new world. No one had heard of the Wounded God before Ragnarok. So in answer to your question, I think that your Gods are still watching over you."

Metellus was silent while he digested all that she had said. In truth, Skjarla wasn't sure what she had said was true, but it seemed to soothe Metellus. It was her best guess, but no one in Valhalla had given much thought as to why the Aesir were there, enjoying their immortal existence and preparing for Ragnarok. Still, at least it seemed to have sufficed for Metellus. She suddenly wondered if Metellus was trying to work out if she knew about Domitia's real situation. Maybe he was using this honesty to try to elicit some frankness from her. She kept her peace, not wanting to lose the advantage she had, letting Domitia continue to act as if her secret was safe.

The two of them walked in silence for a while, the awkwardness becoming more and more evident. In the end Metellus was the first one to break the oppressive silence. "Do you think that we've lost those creatures that were chasing you?"

"Not while we have the Fang." She stopped, swearing silently in her head, a tirade of invective ringing between her ears. Skjarla was furious with herself for that lapse in concentration.

Metellus looked at her carefully, "What is the Fang?"

"Nothing important," she said lamely, hoping in vain to pass it off as a slip.

"Really, if those creatures chased you all the way to Celeste and beyond then I suspect that what they want is a good deal more important than what you say. Look, I couldn't really care if you were carrying the key to Venus's bed chamber, but if it is something which puts my mistress in danger then I want to know what it is."

"It is nothing, save to say that if it falls into the hands of those chasing us then a tide of blood and death will be unleashed upon the world. Enough blood to make your wars against the Red Father on the Isle of Ryhm look like a bloodless skirmish. If you feel that you are not so safe with us, then by all means leave. On this road though, you are stuck with us, the only water is further down the trail."

Metellus's eyes glittered slightly as he said softly, "You know my men could take the water carts if they chose, and then where would you be?"

Equally softly, but even more dangerously she replied, "We would be cleaning your blood off those same carts, I would kill every last Roman without a second thought." As Metellus met her chilling gaze he was in no doubt as to the truth behind her threat.

Further down the column Helania and Accipiteri were chatting happily with Sigmund who, unknown to Skjarla, was walking alongside the cart which he had rode in. He was resting his damaged arm on the wooden side of the cart, trying to take as much weight as possible from his shoulder. They were talking light heartedly, although Sigmund couldn't help but feel slightly superfluous given how close Helania and Accipiteri seemed. He felt the first stabs of jealousy as he saw the way which she clung onto his arm, staring up at the tall, imposing figure with starry-eyed happiness. He doubted that anyone would look at him like that, at least not someone as beautiful as Helania. It gave him some comfort as he reached up and squeezed his fist around the Fang, still hanging from a leather thong beneath his tunic. If there was one blessing to be had from carrying such a dangerous artefact, it was that it meant that he would never just be a face in the crowd, for good or ill, he would be someone.

"It's good to see you back on your feet," Helania smiled at him cheerfully.

"Well, it would be better if my legs didn't feel like sacks of month old flour," he said with a frustrated raise of his eyebrows. The other laughed gently. They were happy to see him back on his feet.

Helania continued, "I would stay away from Skjarla for a bit though, she's still pretty furious with you for fighting like that. Although we can't tell if she's more irritated by the fact that you fought instead of her or that you got so badly torn up. I mean, Braugr and I were talking about it, and we only saw a handful of people lose as much blood as you and live in all our time with the Highlanders."

Accipiteri was grateful for the chatter next to him, it gave him time to think. He could still feel Braugr lurking nearby. He wasn't sure why the dwarf was so protective towards Helania. He didn't begrudge it, but it was strange. His mind wandered onto Helania, she was extremely attractive, and he would not deny it. Accipiteri got the feeling that she was of a similar mind to him though. They enjoyed each other's company, and were probably more than just friends, but there was nothing physical between them. An unbidden 'Yet' sprung into his thoughts but he closed his mind to it. He wasn't sure what held her back, but he knew that his doubts came from his service to the Goddess, his desire to be true to his quest, to earn his wings. He then shifted onto Skjarla, again, undeniably beautiful, but beautiful in the way of the Gryphons which inhabited the high eyries of his home, dangerous for all their majesty.

"What do you think Accipiteri?" Helania's voice broke his contemplation.

He shook his head as if he had been drenched with cold water, "Mmm?"

"You weren't listening," Helania said with exasperation. "Sigmund wanted to know if you would be willing to tell us about your homeland."

"Why?" He asked, confused by the request, which seemed a little odd to him.

It was Sigmund who answered, "It's my fault Accipiteri. I, and the rest of the people, are further from home than we have ever been; this new landscape is so inhospitable to us. We have lived in the shadow of the mountains, beneath the endless boughs of the forest. From the little you have said about your Isle it sounds like a great place, and I wanted to hear more, if only to see in my mind's eye something more than this endless plain of brown grass and browner dust."

Accipiteri walked in silence for a while, Sigmund opened his mouth to speak but Helania laid her hand upon his arm and forced his silence with a sweet smile and a soft shake of the head. Finally, Accipiteri began, his voice rich and full of emotion as he spoke of his far off home, "The Windswept Isle. It is quite something. The Isle has a spine of high mountains, the peaks of which are almost always obscured by cloud. Our cities are carved into those peaks, and on days when the clouds dip below them, then you stand atop a small island, looking out over an ocean of white. Other times the storms will come, the skies will turn the colour of lead, and the forests which ring the mountain holds will shift and roil like a living beast. The rains are cold, and there is often snow in our harsh land. Harsh, but beautiful can barely begin to describe it." He smiled warmly at them both, "Maybe one day you both will see the eyries for yourself." Then his smile faded and his face became pale as he said softly, "If I ever see them again."

They walked on in silence, Helania occasionally opening her mouth to say something, but thinking better of it and swallowing the words back down as she waited for Accipiteri to cheer up again. Sigmund managed to walk alongside them for another half an hour before his wounds and the loss of strength the fever had taken from him forced him back into the cart, sweating profusely. All that Helania and Accipiteri could do was fall into step at the rear of the cart, trying to keep Sigmund's spirits up by talking about all manner of things.

Chapter 9

They held council that night, on the hills which flanked the large plain dominated both by the Ranr and Fylkirsblod. The lights in the towering city in the distance seemed like a beacon of fire, with the great man made mountain of stone twinkling in the distance, the light dancing back from the Ranr even at this distance. Sigmund found it strange, that for the first time in his life he could not see any of the stars. Accipiteri thought that it was because the city was too bright, but this was clearly nonsense, how could one light snuff out another. At least the moon was still there, though, that was some small comfort of normality.

The nights were still warm, even though the summer solstice was well behind them and the nights were beginning to eat into the days. The eight of them sat out on the grass, looking over the final few miles of road which stretched out before them. Bjarn was talking nervously, "What happens if they do close the gates of the city to us? There's no way we have enough supplies to get to somewhere we can buy enough to feed everyone if we cannot get them here."

Bjarn was a good man, but his worrying was beginning to get on everyone's nerves, especially as he had been doing it for the past three days. Domitia said as amicably as she could manage, "Bjarn, that is a bridge we'll cross if and when we come to it. Worrying about what might be when you cannot change it is as pointless as hoping to change the weather by shouting at the sky." They sat in silence then, the only light coming from the moon and the far off city. The meat was cold, as was the stale bread and hard cheese; it had been since they left the orchards. The land had been plains of grassland and wheat fields, not a tree to be seen in any direction. They chewed in silence, the cold meal sitting heavily in their stomachs. At least they had plenty of water, Metellus thought to himself, they had been able to fill up everything which could hold water at the first well they had come to. Where there supplies would come from now was a problem, but at least they could get water from the river. They would have to be careful though, Skjarla had been to Fylkirsblod before and had explained how the sewers ran straight into the river, so they must gather water from upstream of the tide of human filth.

There was a long, low howl from the night, and the sound of something large moving across the undulating sea of grass below them was unmistakable. Everyone was on their feet in an instant, hands going to blades and Helania notching an arrow to her Whorl Root bow, its white limbs glowing softly in the moonlight. They were all braced for an attack, when they noticed the glimmer of a torch against the road, about a quarter of a mile towards the city. They waited in silence, hands clenched over weapons while they prepared their bodies for a fight, if that was what came their way. Those who had armour were wearing it, although Sigmund's still bore the marks of the Haemocrat's champion. All except Skjarla recoiled in terror as they were able to pick out the details of the figure riding towards them.

Out of the night air, beneath the flickering glow of a burning torch was a knight, one of the famous Lupine Guard. His armour, which covered every inch of his body, was covered in wolf designs, the helmet studded with fangs and the heraldry bearing a snarling wolf's head against the blood red colours of the Haemocracy. The most startling thing though, was the beast between his legs, a giant wolf, taller than any horse and snarling like a wild beast. These giant wolves, Fenrisians, were one of many products of the Cataclysm, but they were almost always wild beasts, the top predators in the lands of the Haemocracy. She had heard that to train the beasts, the prospective member of the guard got the Fenrisian as a pup, and raised it for five years before the two of them were allowed to join the guard. The men who rode the wolves were fiercely protective of their mounts, not only because they were almost like family, but because if your mount was killed then you were out of the Lupine Guard.

"Who is the leader of this column," the voice emerged from beneath the visor with disdainful arrogance, sounding more than anything irritated at having to ride out of the city during the night.

The group all looked at each other, and Accipiteri found himself the centre of everyone's gaze. Irritably, he sucked a breath in through his teeth, standing with his hands on his hips, grateful that he was still in his armour, which glinted magnificently in the orange glow of the torch. "I am. I presume you come bearing a message. If you will dismount then we will happily hear it."

The rider sat like stone; then his voice boomed out, the metallic echo from the helmet was eerie, as was the total, perfect stillness of the rider. "The city of Fylkirsblod is closed to these people. Two of the Haemocrats have made complaint to the High Council. A small group, five strong, no more, no less, may enter the city to answer these charges. If you fail to enter the city then the High Council will interpret this as an admission of guilt, and as such the guard from Fylkirsblod will be sent after the column, and all will be put to death." The rider simply tugged at the reins and turned the grey Fenrisian as he rode back towards the city, leaving a stunned silence behind him.

"Fuck," was all that Skjarla said.

Nervously, Sigmund asked, "What is so bad, surely we just go and defend ourselves."

His eyes widened with fear as Skjarla rounded on him, grabbing his arm, her fingers painfully digging into the still soft muscle of his bicep. "Firstly, you are not going anywhere near that city, if they find out that you have a Fang it will be the chop for you, and the Fang will go into the vaults of the Haemocracy. Secondly, why do you think they invited five of us in?" She paused while he shuffled sheepishly, before resuming her tirade. "They want the ringleaders to appear in the city, present themselves to be executed as a warning to the rest of the people."

Metellus shook his head, "That is probably true, but if we can't go in there and get our hands on supplies then we will have condemned the people of the column to death as surely as if we flee from here this night."

"Aye," Braugr joined the conversation, "It is a pretty bind we find ourselves in. Is there anyone who disagrees that five of us must present ourselves tomorrow?" There was stony silence, all knew that he was right, but none wanted to think about the likely consequences of venturing beyond the walls of Fylkirsblod.

Bjarn looked at them nervously, he knew that he wouldn't be one of those going into the city, but he needed to make a point here, "We need to get inside, get some more supplies."

"I know," Skjarla said fiercely, her temper rising, straining against the shackles of her will. "I think we all agree that we have to go into the city, but we need to work to how to get supplies out. Those of us who go in will probably be watched, so I won't be able to slip away and get at my funds, which are a lot lighter now," she muttered pointedly. "If we're lucky then Iskander may be able to help, but I doubt it."

Braugr shook his head, rubbing his forehead wrinkled forehead. "So we're all agreed that we need to go in. The only thing left to decide is who, and how we're going to get out of this in one piece."

Accipiteri stepped into the centre of the loose circle, "I'm going, and Skjarla, I'm guessing that you're going in as well."

There was a shocked silence as Domitia raised her hand, stepping forward, "I'm going, I may be able to help in this circumstance." Everyone apart from Skjarla, who looked very suspicious, stared at her incredulously.

"What can you do?" Braugr asked finally, once everyone had recovered from their surprise.

"I have my ways, and I think that I'm better suited to this than you, master Dwarf."

As Braugr bristled Metellus interrupted to prevent any slur against his mistress, "If you're going Domina then so am I."

"Who's the fifth then?" Asked Accipiteri, looking around the remainder of the group, "We know it's not you Sigmund, so Braugr, you or Helania?"

Braugr was once again talked over as Helania burst in with, "I'll do it," a small smile flashed at Accipiteri.

Braugr grabbed her arm, "Girl, you don't have to do this, the likelihood of seeing anyone who walks in there again is practically nil." He thought he was being quiet, but their conversation was clearly audible not only to the group at the head but most of the rest of the column as well.

Helania looked at him angrily, her teeth bared slightly as she glared down at him, "Braugr, I can do this." Her voice softened slightly, "Look, you've seen what I can do, and if Skjarla and Accipiteri aren't able to look after me no one can. I'll be fine." That last part was almost pleading with the Dwarf who stared at her sternly.

Finally he shook his head and looked darkly at the other four going into Fylkirsblod, "She'd better come back in one piece, or I swear, by Stone and Dark that my shade will chase yours through all eternity." With that the Dwarf stalked off down the column, clearly angry at how things had gone. Skjarla was interested to know what drove the Dwarf to be so protective of his Dokkalfar companion, but that was a question for when they returned from the city. If they returned from the city.

Accipiteri looked around his small group of nervous men and women, puffed out his cheeks with a noisy breath and ran his fingers through his yellow white hair as he had a habit of doing when he was nervous. "I think we should get some sleep, I intend to be at the gates at dawn."

There was a low mutter of agreement, and the group broke up, each of them heading off to their own tents, which they had pitched on the firm ground around the road earlier that evening. Accipiteri was nervous as he returned to his tent, not only about the possible danger of the next day. He was very fond of Helania, he cared for her deeply but he worried about this evening. With death such an ominous shadow, a real and almost certain eventuality for the next day, he worried that Helania would try to act on her feelings for him, if they existed as he thought they did. It was not that he didn't desire her just that he worried that his Goddess would not approve of his laying with a Dokkalfar. His only comfort was the fact that Braugr, who was so protective of her, still shared a tent with her, and he doubted that he would let her out during the middle of the night. Braugr was strange, Accipiteri could not work out why he was so protective towards Helania, seemingly for no reason whatsoever. These thoughts still worried at the edge of his consciousness even as he fell into a restless and fitful slumber.

They rose before dawn the next day, meeting at the edge of the camp and began to stride along the road towards Fylkirsblod. There were the sounds of cattle off to the north, where one of the herds was being driven to the river to drink their fill, perhaps before some of them were taken for slaughter to feed the hordes of people who lived within the walls of Fylkirsblod. The sky was just beginning to lighten, with the inky blue black of night giving way to the pale reds of the dawn sun creeping over the horizon. The city clearly slept, the touring inferno of torches and fires had burnt low, and the last of the night stars were visible once more against the sky. There was a slight pall of smoke hanging over the place, as the last of the fires died their slow deaths before they were stoked once more for the following day's activities.

The city was a great artificial mound, the people had built the false hill atop which the high halls of the High Council sat. It was resplendent with their decorations of gold and rubies, which seemed to catch fire as the morning sun caught them. The other building in that small, exclusive enclosure was the House of Blood, where the keepers of the Blood kept their records, and wielded the power behind the thrones of the High Haemocrats. That hillock though was not just a statement of power, it served as the largest barrow in the kingdom. For beneath the Halls of the Council lay the resting places of all of those deemed pure born by the Haemocracy.

The rest of the city was hidden from their view by the mighty walls which ringed the place, the pale yellow stone of the wall topped with the dark pinpricks of soldiers keeping watch, shuffling from position to position as they endlessly marched the length of the walls. The walls were broken up by towers at regular intervals, squat, square, brooding structures which loomed over all who would come before the walls of Fylkirsblod. The gates themselves were just as ominous, but more ostentatious, designed to subdue all who passed through them with a sense of wonder, the gold and rubies again showing the power of the Haemocracy. Looking up they could see the thin lead tubes emerging from the stonework, pipes which would unleash a torrent of boiling oil down onto any who thought to breach the gates.

Skjarla knew from previous visits that this was the more attractive side of the city. Beyond the walls on the far side of the city were the slums of the Old Races, where they lived and died in poverty, while their neighbours enjoyed their wealth and comfort. The Elder Races were not deemed to be pure bred by the Haemocracy, and as such were banned from entering Fylkirsblod except by special invitation from the council. The people in those slums were completely trapped, as unpleasant as their lives were on the surface; they were deemed to have abandoned the old ways. As such they were not really welcome in the Holds either, so they were trapped in their status of second class citizen on the surface of Midgard.

Accipiteri saw that the gates were open, and a small squadron of footmen emerged, all wearing shining scales of steel and with heavy pikes gripped tightly in their right hands as they waited for the small group to reach them. Not a word was spoken as they formed a small, hollow square around them. Accipiteri set the example and they walked with such pride and dignity that it looked more like they had been given a guard of honour rather than marching as prisoners. Helania's face wore a look of wondrous amazement, stunned by the opulence of the place. The others found the city just as stunning but were better at keeping their expressions passive.

They were being escorted down a wide thoroughfare, the street paved with perfectly flat stones, the cracks filled with small pieces of lead, forcing the rains to run off into the drains on either side of the road. The crowd of people was almost like a tide sweeping those unlucky enough to be caught in the centre along no matter where they wanted to go. There was a gentle hubbub of conversation, but as the regular soldiers of the city watch passed there noise subsided slightly. The majority of the army which was stationed near Fylkirsblod was kept in a barracks outside the city. Those soldiers were the Abhorrens auxiliaries, bred through generations for strength and obedience, it sickened Skjarla. There were other Abhorrens inside the city, led by their masters, carrying heavy loads like dumb beast of burden. She had heard the saying that every stone in Fylkirsblod is locked into place with the blood of an Abhorrens, and didn't think it was too far from the truth.

She remembered the subjugation of the Abhorrens, selectively breeding them like cattle or dogs, choosing the ones that exhibited the traits they most wanted in a race of slaves. There had been uprisings, but the brutal way in which the hulking and slow Abhorrens were punished for the slightest hint of rebellion helped to pour cold water on any smouldering fires of freedom. They had built this city on slave labour. The most important buildings and the walls designed by the most skilled Dwarven engineers and masons, but the actual work of carrying the heavy stones to their proper place was done by those Abhorrens. Behind the facade of normality, of a peaceful city, prosperous and happy with merchants selling their wars from all across the vast lands of the Haemocracy there were slaves doing every menial task that there was.

They couldn't deny that the city was beautiful, with trees on every corner, running water through the drains to flush away all the effluence, keeping the air smelling sweet. They marched in towards the High Council at the centre of the perfectly circular city. The Dwarves had designed the city like that, as a wheel with spokes reaching out in perfectly straight lines from the High Council atop their hill, as if you were being drawn towards the seat of the Haemocracy's power. The road began to climb, and the houses became mansions as they entered the areas where the truly wealthy citizens of the Haemocracy lived.

Amongst this warren of mansions the vicious struggle for power and status within the Haemocracy was an everyday game. Youngest sons and daughters were despatched to become scribes and clerics of the Blood, working carefully to protect their own houses as they kept their records of the people's bloodlines. Older children would be pushed to excel, either directly in politics or bought commissions in the army. The quest for glory was one of the reasons that the Haemocracy had been so brutally energetic in its quest for new lands, until it had run up against the deserts of Vfar and the conquests had ground to a halt. The commanders were constantly trying to show off, to impress their superiors and the people of Fylkirsblod. They were reckless, especially when they had command of a regiment of Auxiliaries, they simply didn't care about the lives of the Abhorrens under them.

There was no time for reflection as they reached the central circle of the city, the one which ran around only two buildings, the Halls of Blood and the High Council itself. Both of them stretched up into the sky, a looming statement of the power of the Haemocracy. The buildings had the same angular designs as the Council Hall in Celeste had done, but everything was grander and much more ornate, almost vulgarly so. The facade of the Council Halls was a riot of colour as precious gems vied for attention with the gold leaf and marble stonework. Members of the Lupine Guard stood watch at the doorway, their armour polished so that it shone and gleamed even in the shadow cast by the building. One of the guards collected their horde of weapons, Skjarla found it particularly hard being without Dreyrispa, which she barely ever let out of her sight.

Inside, before they were taken through to the Council itself they stood in the reception chamber, a vast cathedral of a room, stretching on for over a hundred paces. Indeed, it did remind Skjarla of the Cathedrals of the Red Father, far away to the west. Banners hung from the pale stone of the walls, to which were fixed all the trophies taken from other fledgling kingdoms before the Haemocracy had gained supremacy. The floor was polished marble, alternating hexagons of white and crimson, which bounced the sounds of their footsteps up into the high, vaulted roof as they marched towards the High Council at the far end of the chamber.

The door to the council was an unsurprisingly ostentatious portal, seemingly cast from a single slab of gold, and adorned with rubies the size of Helania's thumb. They were led through the doorway by one of the soldiers, Accipiteri first, followed by Domitia and Metellus with Skjarla and Helania bringing up the rear, followed in by another of the soldiers. There were four other members of the Lupine guard stationed within the room, standing still as statues, but their eyes could be seen roving over the room's new occupants from within their helmets. The room looked out over the city, through giant glass filled windows, the view sweeping across the buildings, down to the walls and beyond, over to the river Ranr and the plain filled with grazing beasts. The small room was dominated by a single, ornately carved wooden table, the details in the carving picked out in gold paint and other vibrant colours. The high backed chairs beyond the table were padded with crimson cushions, and atop the high backs they held the heraldry of their occupants, plain for all to see. There were the seven men of the High Council, enthroned atop the polished stone floor looked across the table at the five standing before them, and received equally careful, appraising glances themselves. All bar two of them were older men, with hair already having changed from grey to white, but in most of their eyes there was still the light of fire and ambition.

The one in the centre shuffled his notes and twitched his nose at them as if they brought some odious stench into the room. His hands were craggy and seemed to struggle gripping the paper properly, shaking softly as he did so. He squinted as he read the notes before beginning in a voice surprisingly full of power, strength and authority for someone in his state of physical decay. "Lord Boros of Celeste and Lord Corval of the High Marches have both issued complaints against the people formerly of Lonely Barrow." That didn't sound good, as if they had been pronounced exiles already. The Councillor continued slowly, "Firstly you have been charged with abandoning the lands of your village in the North Forest, thereby depriving your rightful master of the revenue from the wood processed there. You are charged with fleeing his lands without paying taxes and dues owed to your lord. The second charge is one of theft and assault. You are charged with stealing produce and causing damage to the orchards in Corval's land, and then with assaulting and killing one of his personal guard."

He paused and sized them up, looking each one in the eye. "If you plead guilty now, then the people outside will be spared punishment, merely returned to Lonely Barrow to continue their work, providing lumber for their lord. If you refuse to admit your crimes then you will be put to death, and so will every man capable of bearing arms out beyond the wall. The women and children will be sold into slavery."

The heavy silence hung in the air and the only voice heard was Domitia, smiling sweetly, but with steel in her voice. "I am the daughter of the Roman Emperor, heir to the throne of the Imperium, and as such I ask that you show mercy to these people who I had paid to protect me. If you will look at this," she withdrew a small onyx seal bearing the Roman eagle, "The Imperial seal should be enough to prove my identity."

There was an excited shuffling amongst the council, and the men leant together, examining the small seal and whispering furiously. One of the younger members of the High Council got to his feet and spoke quickly, "High Lord Skjeddr, I move that there is a stay of execution for that one. Kill the other four to appease the other lords, and let me bind her to me in marriage. That way the Haemocracy will be able to make claim to the throne of the Roman Empire," He finished triumphantly. None of them noticed Domitia smile slightly, to her it was not such a bad end to things, she was sure she would be able to manipulate any husband who thought to ascend to the Purple through her.

The five of them tensed at that one as another leapt to his feet, "No, It should be me who marries her, my family is truer than yours, so will give the Haemocracy greater strength when we claim the Roman Empire."

Another one chimed in, "Ha, My son is a better man than either of you."

Skjarla had had enough of this. Regardless of what they decided she and the others were dead. She nodded to Accipiteri, hoping that he guessed what she was about to do. She lunged at the nearest guard, wrestling for his blade. She butted her head against him, it hurt like mad but she felt the satisfying crunch as his nose gave way beneath the blow. As his hands instinctively reached up for his broken nose, already gushing blood, she wrenched the short sword from his hand, launching back to her feet to be confronted by nothing. Instead the Lupine guard quickly hustled the Council out of the room, ignoring the small band threatening their masters.

"Run," Skjarla roared at her companions. "Head for the main door and get our weapons back, and then we run for the gate, and pray that they haven't got a runner there fast enough to close the gate." She set off at a dead sprint, pounding across the silent marble reception chamber and heading for the main doorway, not bothering to check if the others were following her. She heard a shouted order and saw the two guards standing next to their pile of weaponry turn around quizzically. She was on them in an instant, the tip of her stolen sword opening the throat of the one on the left, turning quickly to smash down the guard of his companion. Her third blow hammered into his skull, releasing an explosion of gore which spattered over her, dripping to the floor even as she and the others, who had caught up, grabbed for their weapons.

They ran through the great doors, still trying to get a proper grip on their weapons even as they continued their headlong flight out of the city. They came to a halt, noticing the sound of soldiers running towards them from round the circle, boots pounding on the stones. Quickly they were surrounded by over a score of grim-faced men, their weapon's pointing unwaveringly at the fugitive's hearts. The circle began to close in about them, as the small band prepared to sell their lives as dearly as they could. Skjarla couldn't help but laugh, even as their doom closed about them, it was to be a second Ragnarok then, fighting against hopeless odds for a glorious death. It was too bad that her plan had failed to come to fruition.

Without warning the soldiers crumpled to the ground, revealing black cloaked figures who had appeared, as if from thin air, behind them. The newcomers' strange assortment of weapons each dripping crimson trails onto the stones beneath their feet as they now moved to surround the nervous looking group. One of them drew back their hood, and Iskander's face emerged, split with a cheerful grin. "Skjarla, you don't do things by half do you?" Relief flooded through her and Helania, but the other's still looked worried, they had never met Iskander or heard of his and Skjarla's plan. She had told him to be in place with as many Reavers as he could gather, insurance in case their meeting with the High Lords of the Haemocracy had gone badly.

"Leave it, Iskander, we don't have time. We've got to get to the gate as fast as possible before the soldiers catch up with us." She pushed past him, running down the main road, trying to shove her way through the thick crowd of shoppers who clogged the city's arteries. "Move," she bellowed, shouldering her way through the crowd, sending unsuspecting people flying to the ground with her headlong charge. Panic seemed to flitter through the packed masses, and they started to stampede away from the running, blood stained fighters.

There were screams as people were pressed against the market stalls, the rending snaps as the pressure of the human tide splintered the wood of the stands, sending trinkets and produce flying onto the floor. They could feel the pressure in front of them slackening, as people charged down the side roads and alley ways, their screams still audible to the sprinting group.

All that Domitia could hear though was her burning breath, and the thundering of blood in her ears as she pounded along the paved streets. She could feel herself slowing, as her body naturally refused to go any faster, her hands rising to hold her chest, trying to hold in the lungs which were trying to burst out from her ribs. She was flagging and she knew it, but she had not the breath to ask for help. She could barely managed a shocked gasp of surprise, shock and fear as strong arms swept her off her feet, lifting her and throwing her over a muscular shoulder. Plates of metal dug uncomfortably into her midriff, but looking down over the armour covering the back of her rescuer she could see carefully tied sandals. Metellus was carrying her to safety. She could hear his increasingly ragged breath, but she did not have the wind yet to order him to put her down, let alone to continue their flight to safety.

"Hold on Domina, I can see the gate," Metellus panted, each word carried out on a ragged gasp of burning air. If she had been able to look around, she would have seen Accipiteri, Skjarla and Iskander put on a last burst of speed and strike down the few guards who were struggling to quickly close the giant gateway, pulling at the great winch concealed within the masonry. She heard the crash as their limp forms collapsed to the ground, the armour ringing out against the stone, and saw the ground beneath them darkening as they passed into the shadow of the gate. She lifted her head and saw behind them, sprinting down towards them, a tide of crimson and steel clad warriors, all baying for the blood of the small group who ran before them.

'Horses, where are horses when you bloody need them?' Skjarla thought to herself, even as she jumped in alarm at the sound of metal pinging off stone. The archers patrolling the walls high above them had started to fire down at them, the arrows, long as her arm, were worryingly close to hitting them. One of the people who had joined with Iskander yelped in shock and pain, pulling up with an arrow transfixing their calf. The Reaver instantly spun on the spot, drawing their blade and placing all of their weight on the uninjured leg, fully intent on buying time for the others. Skjarla was all for leaving them, acknowledging the man's sacrifice but leaving them to die. Accipiteri had other ideas, she heard him swear in frustration and anger as he turned and ran back, throwing the wounded man over his shoulder, staggering under the weight but gradually building up speed as he chased after the group.

Skjarla had no time for Accipiteri's naive stupidity, she was more concerned by the fact that the column of people from Lonely Barrow seemed to be closing with them much faster than it should be. A quick glance over her shoulder told her that the pursuit had stopped, if only to give themselves five minutes in which to organise a proper hunt. She ran up to the column to see a truly agitated Braugr, who only seemed to relax a little when he saw that Helania was still in one piece.

While Accipiteri loaded the wounded Reaver into one of the carts Braugr spoke breathlessly to Skjarla and the others. "Bloody Hellfire, you really kicked a hornet's nest this time didn't you? That's not the only problem, there's a huge dust cloud coming in from the Northwest."

"Fuck. Fuck it all," was all Skjarla could manage for a moment. "Right, get the column off the road and moving south as fast as we can, if we're lucky we can run long enough that both sets of our pursuers run into each other, that should give us time to choose our next move."

There was no time for discussion, all Braugr did was turn back and bellow at the top of his lungs, his deep voice carrying through the air like the beating of the drums. "Turn south, get off the road, we're running for the south." There was a brief hubbub, but the news of the dust cloud to the north, now barely two miles away meant that everyone was ready to move already, and the convoy started to move south as fast as they could. The oxen and the draught horses could put on a burst of speed, but could not maintain anything faster than a walk for more than an hour. Men and women who could jogged beside the carts over the uneven ground in an effort to save the beasts for as long as possible.

Glancing back to the shrinking form of Fylkirsblod, Skjarla could see a stain spreading across the land as the pursuit burst forth from the gates of the city like a river unleashed from a dam. She ran next to Braugr, looking at the ground ahead of her as she loped along next to the Dwarf, hearing his shorter legs pounding along in a jangle of armour as he tried to keep up. "We need to get these people to safety, if we're still on the run tomorrow evening then we've had it. I wouldn't ask you this lightly, but I need to know where the nearest Hold is."

There was a heavy silence, Braugr's panted breaths giving him an excuse not to answer as he chewed over her request. His voice was weak as he finally responded to her, "Please, don't ask me to do that," he begged, glad that he did not have to meet her eye.

She kept her voice soft, difficult enough as she ran in her armour, "Braugr, I don't know why you chose to leave the Holds, but surely it must be something that we can help with. Have you not got the finest companions in all of Midgard?" She knew in her heart that she would not be so gentle were it not for the fact that she respected Dwarven honour so deeply. "Braugr, I will not force you, and these people will run until we are forced to turn and fight like a hunted stag, but the Holds are our only hope of safety."

Braugr mumbled, the legendary strength of the Hearth Guard almost completely absent from his voice, "Very well. Follow me, although Helania may find this even more odious than I do." He looked up at the sky, and at the surrounding hills, trying to get his bearings. "This way." He led Skjarla to the front of the column, and angled the march off to the west, into the land of the setting sun. Skjarla frowned to herself, even as the sun crawled up to its zenith, the change of direction likely meant that their pursuers would be far enough apart that they would not get in each other's way, more was the pity.

The column ran on, the two clouds of their pursuers separated by a low ridgeline, keeping them separate as they hounded the people of Lonely Barrow. Skjarla had had the time to run alongside Iskander and the seven Reavers he had brought with him. It had been what she had sent him on ahead to Fylkirsblod to do, to gather some of the Reavers as a small insurance policy, in case things went against them in the capital. Four of them she knew, all of them from the lands of the Haemocracy. Like almost all of the Reavers, they were wedded to a life of travelling, with no real sense of loyalty to their homeland. She didn't know how their loyalties would hold, there had never, to her knowledge, been such a large group of Reavers together at once, but they would be useful in any fight, and might just give them an edge. Surprisingly they seemed happy enough with the arrangement, it seemed that they actually enjoyed the company of some of the few individuals they considered their equals.

The word had quietly gone around the column that they were heading for one of the Holds. This news had produced an excited chatter, mainly from the young and the old, who, seated atop the carts, still had breath to talk. They had heard tales of these underground cities, stretching many miles beneath the surface of Midgard, the home of the Dwarves and the Dokkalfar. The huge tunnels lit by Whorl Root and stone mined from deep within the flesh of Midgard which glowed with a bright, yet cold, blue light, as if they held the essence of the sky itself.

The people of Lonely Barrow ran on, chased by the ever growing columns of dust, at the base of which were the flickering flashes of shining steel the weapons and armour of those who would do them harm. Even Skjarla, bred for war with a body honed to muscular perfection by centuries of combat was panting now. They had been running since the morning and already the shadows were lengthening to signal the advent of dusk. The beasts pulling the carts were lathered in white foam as they sweated at the traces. There was little speech, even those riding in the carts were forced to silence by the pressure of the situation.

"Down there," Braugr said, pointing down the ridge to what looked like a small cave, a rocky mouth in the side of a small hillock to the east of the ridgeline. There was a symbol, angular and shaped like an hourglass, carved into the stone at the very peak of the arch.

Skjarla turned to Helania, who had been running alongside them for some time now, a nervous look on her face which Skjarla put down to fatigue and the events of that morning. "Helania, I want you to take your bow and go on ahead. I think that Caerleon and Brynja, two of the Reavers that came in with Iskander have their bows with them, I will send them down to join you. As the column hits the cave it will slow down, and we'll need cover in case the enemy catches up with us before we're on the way to the Hold."

"Very well." Helania panted noisily, dropping back down the column to grab her bow from one of the carts, then lengthening her stride to run past the tired people and beasts. Skjarla was not so worried about the Lupine Guard catching them. Yes they were faster, but if they had been committed to the hunt then they would have been on them by now. No, she was more worried about the Abhorrens Auxiliaries, fit, fast and relentless; they would single-mindedly pursue the column until they were brought to a standstill by cold steel. She knew there would be a fight, but at least in the narrow confines of the cavern the odds would be fairer to them than out here on the field.

The heavy carts picked up speed as they rumbled down the side of the ridge, the overworked axels squealing in protest as they turned faster and faster. The oxen and draught horses bellowed in fear as the carts began to push them down the slope, forcing them to move tired legs into a gallop even as the terrified animals sought to arrest the descent. The grass out here was brown at the end of the summer, waiting for the autumn rains, and the ground released small puffs of dust as they thundered over the ground.

Sigmund hobbled out of the column to speak to her, "Where is my armour? You'll need every man and woman you can get for this."

Skjarla was tempted to agree with him, but she could see from the way he walked that he wouldn't be anything other than a liability in the shield wall. She clapped him on the shoulder, seeing his wince she knew she made the correct decision, "Don't confuse bravery with stupidity, fighting when you aren't able is the latter rather than the former." All that he could do was nod his head and head back to his place in the column. In his heart of hearts he was relieved, he knew that he was in no fit state to fight properly, but at the same time he still craved Skjarla's praise desperately.

Accipiteri gathered all of the fighters they had at the rear of the column as the carts began to slow on the valley floor, trundling into the darkness of the cave. Braugr had explained that it was at least the same distance as they had already come again beneath the earth so there would be no support for them at the mouth of the cave, but at least in the narrower confines they could try to make their opponents think twice about chasing them. The fighters all stood, chests heaving as they sought to catch their breaths. At the mouth of the cave, just off to one side and standing atop some boulders were Helania, Caerleon and Brynja, ready with their bows to cover the retreat into the cave.

The Romans were clustered around Metellus, hefting their shields and swinging their swords in small circles, loosening up tight and stiff muscles as they prepared for combat. The people of Lonely Barrow who had been training with blades and spears for the past few months stood in small groups. They had been blooded but were still nervous of the coming fight, perhaps more so for it being the second battle. They lacked the enthusiasm of people who have not been exposed to the hell of combat, they had seen friends killed in battle, and knew what their chances were.

They gradually stepped towards the mouth of the cave, the dark maw into the underworld, keeping with the final cart as it slowly inched forwards. The Abhorrens who had been set loose to chase them down had closed the gap and were jogging determinedly down the valley, the almost perfectly uniformity of their steps making the earth tremble beneath them. The only positive was that they could see the dust cloud behind the Abhorrens on the far side of the low ridge, which meant that if they could hold for a little while, hopefully the crazed Children would fall into the combat. Unless, that is, they were smart enough to let the other two forces batter each other to a standstill. In which case, it would be a bloody and painful end for the people of Lonely Barrow, far from their home in the northern forests.

They were about one hundred paces from the entrance to the cave when the Abhorrens lengthened their stride to build up for the final charge, the earth shuddering under the weight of their hideously over muscled skeletons. The Roman line in the centre braced itself behind a shield wall, while those on the wings readied their spears to try to take away the impetus of the charge. Arrows streaked overhead as Helania and her companions found their range. It was these more than anything which saved the defenders, as such was the size and speed of their pursuers that when one fell it fouled the charge of not only those behind but those to the side as well. Those Abhorrens which were not slowed by the hail of arrows hit the lines like an avalanche, their arms raining down blows with their heavy blades as they knocked the defenders flying. The line wavered under that charge, people looking over their shoulders, searching for a way out. But the roars of the leaders kept them there, and they swiftly learnt that, as strong as the Abhorrens were, and as quick, they could not think fast enough.

Skjarla felt the familiar rush as the blood flowed and let slip the leash on her anger, moving forward, flowing under the swinging swords as she wrought crimson carnage with Dreyrispa. The Abhorrens were drawn to the combat like bees to honey, and she was the eye of the cyclone to which they gravitated. Every one which threw itself at her pulled them away from the frontline, already twenty paces behind her. Skjarla didn't care, she howled for the joy of it, the release and the freedom of battle, continuing to sow death and carnage as she moved like smoke through the combat.

"Skjarla, the last cart's safe, come back." She wasn't sure who the voice belonged to, and it was barely more than a breath stroking the edge of her consciousness, combat was all she knew at that moment of time. She ignored the sounds and lived in the moment, unaware of the heated conversation going on behind her.

Accipiteri was straining to go forward, "We have to save her. Without her this whole column will fall apart."

Metellus was shouting back, even as he sheltered behind his shield, splinters of wood flying past his helmet. "We can't waste men rescuing someone who doesn't want to be saved. You want to save her, you do it." He turned his head back to the front, "Come on, you sons of Mars, fight as if he were watching you," he roared to his men.

Accipiteri took a pace forward, driving from his legs as he shoved against his shield, his broadsword held in one hand as it sliced off fingers which grabbed at the rim. He felt the heavy steel blades hammering against his armour, piercing it in several places on his back, the hot blood flowing down between his shoulder blades, unpleasantly sticking his leather gambeson to his skin. All the while he was yelling, "Skjarla," at the top of his lungs. The press got denser and his advance slowed as the Abhorrens swarmed around him from all sides. He found himself lost in the storm of combat, the swords and spears around him flickering like tongues of lightning.

He felt the press weakening to his left, and heard Skjarla's voice, "What are you doing here Loptalfar?" She asked with a smile, "Come to join the fun?" Her appearance was truly startling, caked from head to toe in gore, the black metal beneath giving the blood an even more sinister appearance, but strangest of all was her smile. Plastered across her face was a huge grin, her mouth split in a laugh as she continued to fend off their opponents, laughing slightly maniacally all the while.

"The carts are safe Skjarla, we can go back." He said through gritted teeth, even as he opened the guts of another of the Abhorrens, punching his sword through the chainmail hauberk.

Skjarla shook her head, "Not yet," she ducked beneath a wildly swung blade and drove Dreyrispa into her attacker's armpit. "The Children of the Dragon have not joined the battle yet, if we can't distract the Abhorrens then they'll chase us into the cavern."

Accipiteri was amazed, and almost dropped his guard for a moment. How could she do it, seem so lost in the bloody slaughter yet still be so calculating? There was nothing more to say, so he merely returned his focus to the battle, swinging against the swirling blades, his shield becoming little more than a chipped and cracked plank of wood. Finally he heard a whisper from Skjarla, "Time to go." They tried to cut their way back as fast as possible, but they had no way of knowing how much of the force of Abhorrens had got past them. They were retreating because the last of the Children had finally dropped below their line of sight on the Ridgway and had joined the battle.

They could feel the tide of Abhorrens flowing around them as they rushed to meet the new threat. Skjarla and Accipiteri cut down the final few Abhorrens in their way, small precise movements, almost mechanical in their efficiency, built their passage to freedom. The two of them slipped into the darkness of the cave, stepping over the bodies of Abhorrens and the defenders who had given their lives in that determined effort to protect the rest of the column. They both took a last glance over their shoulders, looking at the swirling melee they had left behind them, Accipiteri's expression was one of relief, while Skjarla's was worryingly close to lust.

As they jogged down the tunnel, nearly tripping over the corpses hidden by the darkness, Accipiteri had nagging concerns about Skjarla. As skilled as she was, he couldn't help but worry at the possible consequences of her perpetual flirtation with death, although, the stories of the Gods of Asgard he had heard as a boy were equally bloodthirsty, full of gore and violence and sex. Maybe she was just holding true to the legends. He allowed himself a small half smile; he had forgotten that not everyone was as devoted to the Goddess as he was.

Chapter 10

There had been silence in the column as they walked onwards, everyone clinging onto the carts which had been tied together with whatever could be found. The only source of light they had was Helania's Whorl Root bow, which glowed softly in the darkness, allowing her to lead the column through the endless passages. The stones here were rough and looked natural, although the floor of the cavern was well packed with earth, and while not completely flat it was far smoother than was natural. The unwavering light of the bow, held high above Helania's head cast ominous shadows across the rocks. Everyone who had light to see at the front of the column was looking around in fear, especially suspicious of the stone roof above their heads. It was worse at the tail of the column, where there was no light at all, and people just stumbled on, trying not to fall over any of the rocks peeking from beneath the packed earth.

Skjarla and all the others who had fought were particularly uncomfortable. The blood of those who had fallen in battle was splattered all across them, drying in sticky clumps which painfully adhered clothing and armour to their skin and hair. There were mutters and people emptied their canteens in a vain hope to scrub the stench of carnage from their skin, but it would need a lot more water than they had for that. At least there had been no more combat, the battle may still be raging outside the entrance to the cave, and there had been no sound of a pursuit. Maybe they had been lucky and both groups of their attackers had fought one another to a standstill.

She saw some of the refugees upending their skins of water over their heads, trying to wash off the gore, "Stop now! We don't have the water to waste on washing." She roared at the small group, her voice drawing the attention of those nearby who might have thought to do the same.

"You expect us to march, eat and sleep caked in gore? You should wash, too, that blood will start to smell soon."

Skjarla looked at the man coldly, raising her voice so that everyone in the cavern could hear, "What would you rather, a little smell or dying of thirst in the dark, when we have come so far already?" There was a soft grumbling of assent, people returning the water skins in their hands to the carts with heavy shoulders. They all knew the truth in Skjarla's words, but that didn't mean they were happy about it.

Skjarla made her way up to the front of the column, struggling against the sense of foreboding the dark engendered in her. She had been to the Holds before, but she much preferred to be on the surface of Midgard, where she could see the sky far above her. They called a halt for the night, the food supplies were reduced more than usual that night, people exploiting the dark to come back and get extra helpings. The warriors were the most uncomfortable, the clotted blood was beginning to itch their skin, and most of them rubbed their bodies against the rocks in a vain attempt to get to the places their hands couldn't reach. Hair was matted in uncomfortable clumps which prevented any of them sleeping peacefully that night. Most of them gave up after who knows how long tossing on the ground, and talked in low, soft voices so as not to disturb those around them.

It was impossible to know how long they rested for without the sun or moon to mark the passage of time. After some time Helania passed up and down the column, using her bow to light the way, shaking people awake and preparing for the final push of the march onto the Dwarven Hold before them. Thinking about it, Skjarla didn't even know which of the Holds they were heading to. As far as she knew there were at least eleven Holds, hidden beneath the earth, but there could be many more. They pressed on in silence through the darkness, only the occasional curse heard as someone stubbed a toe against the rocks.

The tunnel began to grow gradually brighter, light spilling down it, gently at first, but as they rounded a corner it became such that people were force to shield their eyes from the sudden glare. There were some shrieks of pain, followed by the soft sighs of relief. Light meant civilization, which meant that they had arrived at one of the Holds of the Dwarves. The carts pushed on through the tunnels, with the lights becoming brighter and brighter as they advanced, the squeak of wheels and axles echoing down the passageway. The stone became more managed, the packed earth of the surface replaced with flat stones, the walls carved into square pillars, each one bearing the mark of the Dwarf who carved it. From the vaulted ceiling hung iron chandeliers, which on closer inspection turned out to be giant baskets filled with the glowing stones which bathed the passage in their eerie light.

They walked on in wonder, the sound of their approach echoing along the walls, meaning that there would most certainly be an armed welcome turned out for them. She looked at her friends at the front of the column, noticing the soft sheen of sweat on Helania's brow and the agitated flickering of Braugr's eyes, like a beast seeking to flee. She thought to ask something, but then they were presented with the gateway to the Hold.

It was a magnificent thing, built into a domed chamber, almost perfectly circular and carved into patterns and pillars around the walls. Hanging directly from the centre of the room was a giant chandelier. Against the glare you could just pick out the chain running down behind the wall, so that it could be lowered and refilled. The ceiling was far higher than that of the passageway down which they had just come. It showed just how far beneath the surface of Midgard they were, that the ceiling could stretch over a hundred paces above their heads and still not reach the air far above them.

The walls which stretched across the ground were equally menacing, curved so that every archer who stood atop those crenulated stones could focus their arrows onto the tunnel exit. The walls themselves seemed to be made from a single block of stone, so flawless was the construction, the work of more than a generation of Dwarven masons and architects. The gate at the centre of the wall was a plain affair; the only ornamentation being the carvings upon the gates, none of the jewels or ostentatious gold leaf that had been seen on the gateway to Fylkirsblod. There was a soft groaning as the heavy wooden planks of the doorway slid across the stones, the thump of the locking bars dropped into the floor still echoing around the chamber. Figures could be seen atop the wall, tall lithe shapes which marked them out as Dokkalfar, their bows pointed unwaveringly at the people of Lonely Barrow.

A delegation of Dwarves came marching out, having seen that there was no attack coming from the people who were still flooding into that cavernous space. There were over forty of them, their stout frames hidden behind angular plates of steel, perfectly overlapping to prevent a single gap from occurring in their armour, no matter how they moved. Axes of various sizes, along with swords and hammers sat easily in the Dwarves' hands as they advanced. Not one of them wore a helmet. Their magnificent beards, most replete with gold and silver rings, marked them out as veterans of the Blood Eye. This was the arena where champions of the Holds competed to prove themselves and for the honour of their clans.

One at the head of the group raised his gauntleted hand, the echo of the metal fingertips clacking against the palm of his gauntlet reverberated around the chamber. There was a crash like thunder as the Dwarves came to a stop in a single pace. "Who are you, and why do you come before the gates of Sundark Hold?" the imperious voice rang out across the space.

"We seek refuge here—" Skjarla was cut off as one of the Dwarves recognized Braugr.

"Braugr, what are you doing here?" he asked accusatorially, glaring at him.

"Enough." The lead dwarf glared at the one who had spoken out of place. "My lady, you, Braugr and the Dokkalfar with you will enter the city to provide reasons for your arrival to king Jori. The rest of your group will wait outside." He waited for the three of them to walk across the space between the two groups. They may have wanted to run, to bring others with them, but they had no choice.

Skjarla got strange looks when they saw the state of her armour, "Do you always travel caked in gore? Do you care so little for your steel?" one of the Dwarves asked in disgust.

Skjarla decided that the best response possible was merely to stare down her nose at the Dwarf, ignoring his comment and striding on into the Hold. They all looked round as they heard the grating sound of the gates closing behind them, the image of their companions being slowly swallowed up by the gates as the gap between them shrunk. They finally came together with a loud clunking sound, and they were sealed inside the Hold. As they were marched through the streets, Skjarla had little time to admire the architecture, she was distracted by the glares and angry glances that were directed at Braugr and Helania.

They were led to a high building, almost shaped like a half pyramid, with steps carved into the front of it. Those stairs led up into the palace which was carved into the very walls of the cavern which held the city. Skjarla was sure that the view from there would be truly amazing, but she did not have time to think about that as they were led into the audience chamber. The walls were entwined with lengths of Whorl Root, which made it seem as if the palace had been made in the roots of a giant tree. There were rich rugs upon the floor, blue and gold, at Skjarla's best guess the colours of Sundark Hold. The king was seated atop his throne, which in turn sat atop a dais at the far end of the room. His beard was brown, with only small flecks of grey, he was young for a king. His twin-headed axe rested head down against the stone arm of the throne, his fingers twiddling the haft idly, making the light dance as it bounce off the gold rings which covered his hands. His robes were blue and gold, voluminous and edged with black fur, giving him a brooding appearance. His eyes were bright, and they dominated a kindly, but lined face, aged prematurely by the responsibilities of leadership.

"Braugr, you stand before us once more?" the king asked once the three of them had bowed alongside their Dwarven escort. He turned to Skjarla, "Tell me, woman, do you know why the two people were travelling the surface?"

Skjarla stood in silence, not sure whether or not she should say anything. In the end she decided that the best choice was to say, "When I met them they had just completed a term with the Highland Irregulars. They offered their services in protecting the column and have proved honourable and capable travelling companions. We were under attack, and the only place we could find safety was here, so they kindly led us to the Hold of Sundark."

King Jori looked at her closely and scowled. "Do not try to dodge the question. Braugr was a member of my personal guard, the Hearth Guard, my champion in fact, but he chose banishment as he could not live with his shame." He took in Skjarla's blank expression. "You did not know why he took the mark of the Shattered? He drank often here, as many do, but he had a particular fondness for ale. That coupled with a love of gambling led to trouble. The fool wagered his daughter against one of my nobles and lost. That is why he walked the surface and that is why he is not welcome here. She," he pointed an accusatory finger at Helania, "Is wanted across all of the Holds, for breaking the terms of a contract."

He waited, again gauging Skjarla's impression before continuing, "Nothing again? She was bought by one of the madam's of the Nightfast Hold's companion houses, for delivery upon her fortieth birthday to begin no less than fifty years of servitude. These were the terms by which her mother bought their safety from the strife of the surface. Instead she fled the Hold and is to be returned." His guards moved closer to Helania, not close enough to grab her, nor to trigger Skjarla's temper, but enough to put them on edge. "And who are you that brings these two to my halls, followed by a tide of surfacers who have nothing to offer save empty bellies?"

Skjarla looked the King in the eye and said slightly mischievously, hoping that she hadn't misjudged the man. "I am known to your people, and I think that you'd be able to recognize me if I was able to make use of the famed Dwarven Bathhouses."

The king looked at her for a second, then threw his head back and laughed, long and loud. "Lady, you may not know how to address a king but at least you have spirit." He turned to the guards next to him and whispered some instructions. The guard bowed to the king and scuttled out of the audience chamber. The king smiled warmly at her,

"One of my guards has gone to prepare my own baths for you and your friends, and I owe Braugr the courtesy of one night's hospitality for all the honour he won for my family in the Blood Eye. However," his voice became stern once more, "You will tell me your name."

She simply said, "Skjarla."

The King's eyes widened with surprise at the name. He turned and whispered to his guard, who began to walk towards her. "You will hand Dombrek your weapon." His tone brooked no argument.

Skjarla silently handed Dreyrispa to the Dwarf who reverentially carried the twin headed spear up towards the dais. The King's eyes gleamed softly as he took the weapon in his hands, raising it to his eye level and turning it slowly in the light, seeking to admire it from every possible angle. His voice was hard as stone when he asked, "Where did you get this from?"

Her voice was equally steely as she replied, "It is mine, and always will be." Their eyes remained locked, Dreyrispa held between them like the prize for a duel. Skjarla knew that Jori coveted the weapon, one of the last remnants of his people's heritage, from a time before Ragnarok. But she also knew that he had guessed who she was, her existence was far less of a secret among the Elder Races, and as such he feared and revered her in equal measure.

He blinked his eyes slightly and ran his hand lovingly over the blade one last time before saying sadly, "Dombrek, return the weapon to the Valkyrie, she is our honoured guest." The Dwarf's face was struck by wonder as he approached the living embodiment of a time when the Dwarves were respected on the surface of Midgard. Skjarla relaxed visibly when her fingers closed around the haft of her spear, looking the king in the eye.

"What of the people outside your gate? What is your plan for them?" she was well aware that either the Abhorrens Auxiliaries or the Children could well be coming down the tunnels even as they spoke. It was a difficult situation, she knew that the king would be anxious to frame some deal in such a way as to gain Dreyrispa. Such an object would elevate him above all of the other Dwarven lords, he may even be able to proclaim himself High King of the Dwarves. At the same time she couldn't afford to leave the people of Lonely Barrow out there too long, not with their water supplies running dangerously low.

Jori looked at her darkly, he was a king who did not like to be questioned, "I have been generous enough already, not seizing the Dokkalfar girl you brought before me. Personally I have no feeling one way or the other as far as she's concerned, but I have treaties which I should respect. Do not test me."

Skjarla thought carefully, her mind whirring as she tried to find a solution that might be acceptable to the curmudgeonly king of Sundark Hold. "At least let them travel through the city and stay in the Hidden Ways," the passageways which connected the Holds beneath the surface of Midgard.

The king tilted his head to the left, looking through her as he asked, "Why? Why are you so desperate to move them away from the outer wall of Sundark?" he reached across with his left hand and twiddled one of the rings on his fingers, spinning it around the digit as he seemed to wrestle with something. "Your people may cross the city, but there will be a cost, added to the reckoning when you and I meet tomorrow. I do not do this from the goodness of my heart, but there are stories in my family about you, I believe you killed a Hyrrstein in the Ways for my great grandfather, so I will grant your request. However, you and the other two will remain in the city tonight, and tomorrow we will discuss the price for that and whatever else you have come here for."

Skjarla knew she should hold her tongue but she couldn't help the snide remark, "Are we staying as your guests or your hostages?"

The King leapt to his feet, his fingers clasped tightly around the arms of his throne, the knuckles white as fingers gripped the stonework as if he was trying to choke the life out of it. He took a deep breath before responding, "You, my dear Valkyrie, are to be my guest, but if you say one more word then exile and the whore will be spending the night in the cells where they belong. Now, I suggest you follow Dombrek before you earn your companions a most unpleasant night." Skjarla wisely beat a retreat, followed by a pale looking Braugr and Helania.

They were not led out of the palace, instead they were taken deeper into the warren of tunnels and passageways, and all lit by the harsh white-blue light of the glow stones the Dwarves mined. The carefully carved and tailored stone passageways led out into a small hallway where a slim Dokkalfar servant instructed them to disrobe, explaining that their clothing would be washed and returned to their rooms. For all that this was just a kingdom of the Elder races, with no humans to sneer down at them, there was still a clear hierarchy between the castes. Braugr went an embarrassed pink as the three of them pulled off their clothes, his and Skjarla's having to be uncomfortably pulled away from the skin where dried blood had adhered it to them. The plates of armour clanged to the floor next to a pile of soiled clothing which the bath house attendant stared at with distaste. He wrinkled his nose at the thought of having to carry the mountain of stinking cloth through the palace. Helania guiltily thought about the fact that none of them had had the water to wash their clothes in well over two months, not since they had gathered some rainwater two days after the orchards had been put behind them.

The attendant gathered up the piled clothes, armour and weapons, earning himself an angry scowl from Skjarla as he dropped Dreyrispa onto the floor. The three of them grabbed soft lengths of cloth which they would use to dry themselves. Braugr was grateful that the two women allowed him to walk in front of them; the height difference was particularly awkward for him, as he was at eye level with their breasts. They were a pretty liberal people when it came to nudity, but there were some like Braugr who were less comfortable with it, especially when they were both good friends and not fellow Dwarves. They went through to the first room, a steam bath, which almost instantly had them bathed in sweat as the clouds of steam billowed up from beneath grates in the floor, heated in the rocks deep beneath the Hold. The steam baths and the hot water for the rest of the bath houses were piped up from deep beneath the Hold, where the water seemed to boil out of the rocks themselves.

Helania enjoyed the feeling and gloried in the opulence of their surroundings. The walls were covered with smooth carvings which seemed alive as the steam condensed on them and rivulets of water ran down them, making it look like it was raining. She compared that to the few times that she had been in the baths back home in Nightfast Hold; the faded, peeling paint, the leaden tang to the steam and the general feeling of neglect in the poorer areas of the Hold. She was surprised by how unabashed she was, given how quickly she had had to change her approach to nudity on the surface, where people were much more sensitive to that sort of thing. At least it hadn't been too bad with the irregulars, since everyone was living in the field so there wasn't so much room for niceties like separate jacks for men and women. She couldn't help but glance across at Skjarla' marvellously smooth skin, her legion of scars becoming even more pronounced as her skin flushed red with blood, the white slashes standing out vividly.

The three of them sat in silence in the steam, with both Helania and Braugr silently worrying about what Skjarla would say as to the reasons for their being on the surface. Helania was particularly down; she had worked so hard to build up herself as a warrior, a fighter, a strong person. Yet still she found herself being dragged down by her past, by being sold as a whore by her own mother. Braugr had been the only one who knew her secret, he had forced it out of her when they had met on the surface, in Leopolis. He had wanted to know how someone with a Whorl Root bow, who had clearly been raised beneath the earth, had ended up on the islands.

It had been strange at the time, she had expected his scorn and revulsion, but instead he had taken her under his wing. He had never told her why he was on the surface, and to begin with she had been worried that he would try to take payment for his care with her flesh, but he had never come near her. Now she understood his treatment of her, he had viewed her as a surrogate for the daughter he had lost. Most strangely to her was the fact that she did not hate him now that she knew about his daughter, instead she respected him all the more. She knew now why he did not drink, why he did not dice with the others, and all that she wished was that there was something she could do to help him find his daughter.

Braugr was equally downcast, worrying that he had lost the respect of two of his friends, and that he would lose a lot more once the news of his shame fired its way around the camp. He waited in silence for one of the other two to say something, anything, but they just sat in the steam, the grime forced out of their skin by their sweat. Eventually Skjarla got to her feet, her black hair plastered to her neck by the sweat, and stalked out through the steam filled archway into the next room, one which was entirely filed with water, there was no way through without getting into the water. Although given that the water was heated from far beneath the Hold you wouldn't want to just rush through it, it was too luxuriously warm, and there were stone benches carved beneath the electric blue water. People would sit and discuss business, matters of state or just life in general as they let the warmth relax their tired muscles.

Skjarla sighed contentedly as she relaxed back against the stone bench, her eyes closing gently and a soft smile playing across her face. Helania and Braugr followed suit, sitting gently on the stone benches, the water rippling across the surface as they lowered themselves into the warmth. Eventually they could take it no more and Helania burst out, "Will you say something, anything, about what the king said?"

Skjarla lazily opened one eye and peered at them both from beneath her fine eyelashes. With a grunt she pressed herself into a more upright position as the water comfortably moulded around and she looked intently at each of them. "What do you want me to say? Do you want tirades of anger at what you've done? Sympathy?"

Helania looked defeated and lowered her head, "Anything, but the silence is just torment."

Skjarla sounded scornful as she replied, "I am not here to make either of you feel better, although you, Helania, I can't see why you're so ashamed." Helania's face sagged with relief as she continued, "I see no shame in trying to improve yourself, and taking your destiny in your own hands and turning your back on a life on your … you know what I mean."

Skjarla choked as a wave of water rushed into her mouth, caused by Helania throwing herself across the width of the room to give Skjarla a hug for her kind words. After a few seconds she released the fuming Valkyrie who then turned her attention on Braugr. "Braugr, I cannot respect or condone what you did," she paused for a moment before continuing in a more gentle tone, "But I am grateful to you for leading us here, even though you knew the shame that awaited you."

Braugr stirred and said softly, "Thank you for saying that, Skjarla, it's been hard being back here." He hoped that that would be the end of the matter, but Skjarla continued to ask questions.

"What was her name? And have you tried to get her back?"

He shot her a quick glare which quickly subsided back beneath his bushy eyebrows. "Aetria. Her name was Aetria, and of course I bloody tried to get her back. Brodri Iron-Tongue was never a friend of my family though. I was drunk and he challenged me at dice, I had been lucky all night, and suddenly my luck deserted me. I wagered more and more and more, trying to win it all back every time." Now that he had started the tale was pouring out of him involuntarily, like a river in full flow once the dam has been breached. "Eventually I had nothing more, so he challenged me to wager that which I held dearest, to which I laughed and said that I wagered my honour. He won, when it should not have been possible for him to do so. I was drunk and asked him how he intended to take my honour, and he responded by claiming my daughter as his property."

Helania burst out with, "But didn't you try to stop him?" All it earned her was an angry glare.

"Course I bloody did," he roared before recomposing himself. "When I had recovered the next morning I went to his home and begged him on bended knee not to take my daughter from me, but it seemed to give him a perverse pleasure to inflict such suffering upon me."

Skjarla's question was a more reasonable one, "What did her mother think to this?"

"Aetria, the girl I loved since the day we first met, died giving birth to our daughter, so the only thing I could do to keep her name alive was to give it to my daughter. I want to find that girl more than anything, but the Iron-Tongue has spirited her away from me, and there is no trace of where she has gone. I have tried everything but there is no way to melt the ice that has replaced his heart."

Skjarla looked at him, impressed that his gaze was unwaveringly focused on her eyes, steadfast determination writ large across his face, and said seriously. "If there is anything I can do, my friend, then just tell me."

"Thanks," he said softly, barely even a whisper. The uncomfortable silence returned as they sat there, no one else knowing what to say to try to lift the mood. They sat in the water, the skin on their fingers gradually wrinkling up, growing ridges and valleys as the water soaked in.

***

Outside the luxurious confines of the palace there was a heated discussion going on at the column of refugees. They had been escorted through the hold by a cordon of Dwarves, all of them covered in menacing armour, no inch of their skin visible beneath the dark metal. They had been unceremoniously bundled out of the gate and left on the road beyond the walls of the Hold. At least, they thought, there was a city full of Dwarves and Dokkalfar between them and anything chasing them. There were increasing grumbles from the people of the column as they tried to work out which army, if any, might be coming after them. They had been running for nearly a year, and they were beginning to wonder when, and where it would all end. Many of them had taken their concerns to Bjarn, who seemed to be the only one willing to act as go-between with the warriors who were leading the column. He had heard tales of several loud disagreements, mainly between those who had fought and those who were either too old or too weak to fight.

Overhead the light was dimming, telling the people that on the surface it was getting towards dusk. One of the Dokkalfar had come up with an ingenious mechanism of doing this, the giant Sun Stone globes which were suspended from the roof of the Hold were encased in gradually rotating globes. These globes were made from two hemispheres of glass, one clear, the other a dark, smoky colour which dimmed the light source dramatically. As the sun dropped below the horizon the darker hemisphere would block the light, and as dawn broke on the surface the clear glass would replace it. There were numerous examples of the engineering brilliance of these people who dwelt beneath the earth. Even down to the small pipes which brought fresh air down into the caverns, on some days even creating the faintest of breezes which stirred the fabrics hanging across windows.

Near the gateway there was an animated conversation going on under the watchful eyes of the Dokkalfar sentries on the wall. Voices were lowered but still the odd murmur burbled up to reach their ears. "Great, we're trapped here now, thanks to that stupid bitch." Domitia said, her customary veneer of calm cracking. She recomposed herself and lied glibly, "Apologies, I have never been good with being underground." In truth it had never bothered her, but she needed to keep Sigmund and Accipiteri on side, she never knew when she might come to need their support.

Sigmund glanced at the Roman noble, amazed by how graceful and commanding she could look, even with her clothes torn, stained with mud and dust, her hair wild and unkempt. "Domitia, I am sure that they will come to us with a plan, they have to." In truth he was not sure if that would happen, and he had no idea what the plan would be if there ever was one, but he felt a strong desire to be seen to be in control by Domitia.

"Well, all that I know is that we're running low on water. Unless we go to half rations of water then the urns will be dry by the morning. We got through the water faster than we thought with everyone having to run here and through the tunnels." Metellus said glumly, "If we don't get access to some supplies soon then it doesn't matter where we go, we'll all be dead within three days."

Accipiteri looked at them all wearily, "Look, I don't like it any more than the rest of you, but without either Braugr or Helania to guide us through the tunnels we're doomed. So as far as I can see the only thing we can do is wait for the three of them to return to us and see what happens then."

Domitia looked around angrily, quietly annoyed by the lack of spine she felt her companions were showing. "We should have tried to cut our way to some supplies when they were taking us through the city."

Sigmund scoffed, "We'd have been dead in minutes. I may not know much of war, but even I know that two hundred tired and worn out people who are barely warriors cannot take on a city. We'd have been dead before we got off the road."

"I have to agree with the boy," Accipiteri added. "Look, at least we're safe from attack here tonight, so why doesn't everyone just try and get some rest alright?" He wandered off, knowing that he was too tired to do anything about arguments even if the other three wanted to have one.

Domitia looked sideways at Metellus, "Centurion, would you give us a minute." Metellus looked absolutely furious but he was too well trained as a legionary of Rome not to obey his mistress's command. He stalked off, sending a rock flying down the tunnel with a stab of his sandal, a curse echoing as he caught his toe on the stone.

Sigmund looked nervous, his entire body tense as Domitia stalked closer to him, like a wolf closing in for the final kill. "Sigmund, I am going to need your help with something one day, so I would like to offer you my support now."

As he gazed down at her lovely face, drawn into her eyes and the gentle swell of her lips he found himself lost, all he could mumble was, "I don't understand."

She smiled softly at him, her hand coming up to caress his cheek as she looked into his eyes. "Sigmund, I don't think that the others bothered to tell you who I really am, did they?" His blank expression told her that they hadn't and she sensed the tiniest gap in which to sow the seeds of discord. Domitia had realised that some of the group would never follow her in her quest to regain her throne, so it was important to separate them from those, such as Sigmund, who could be useful to her. "I can tell you that I am the heir to a great kingdom to the west, but what I want to know is what makes you so important to Skjarla." She was tempted to try to use her beauty to get the answer out of him, but at the last moment decided that it would be better to save that for the moment. 'After all,' she thought to herself, 'Once he has had me then I will have lost the leverage of the first time, better to save it for something truly useful, if it comes to that.' "Is it that the two of you are lovers?" she asked lasciviously.

Sigmund laughed awkwardly. In truth he had thought of Skjarla in that way, but at the same time he couldn't believe that any other man had failed to admire the sensual curves of her body. "No, no it's nothing like that. I just have something that she thinks she needs to look after."

Domitia carefully filed that information before continuing, "I can't believe that she's not just trying to keep an eye on you, I've seen the way she looks at you." Skjarla clearly had no interest in him, but Sigmund didn't know that. Now Domitia decided to go for the throat, casually tossing in the line, "I can understand why she's interested in you, if you weren't spoken for I know I would be." She went up on her tip toes, her breasts just brushing lightly against his chest as she gave him the softest of kisses on the cheek, yet one full of unspoken promise and desire.

Sigmund watched her disappear back down the tunnel towards the Roman encampment where they had already set up a tent for her. His head was spinning slightly and he couldn't help but wonder what in the God's name had just happened to him. If he read it correctly he had just had the heir to the Roman Empire making advances on him, something that would have been laughable this time last year, if he had even heard of the Roman Empire back then.

Chapter 11

Back inside the Hold, Skjarla had requested an audience with King Jori, who forced her to wait for the best part of an hour until he concluded a meeting about improvements to the sewage system in the Hold. She had waited in silence, sitting motionless as a statue, not wanting to give the difficult king the satisfaction of seeing her frustration. He was difficult to read, this king. He seemed so honourable, keen to respect someone who had served his family and upheld the honour of his people as Braugr had, yet at the same time greedy and petty. Maybe it was a function of growing up in a situation where your word was law, but she still felt that the young king's parents could have done a better job. She thought about the system employed in the old kingdom of Leske when she had visited there, before it had been swallowed up by the Red Father. The children of royalty and nobles had been sent anonymously to neighbouring lands to teach them the value of their own labours, rather than trading off the name of their parents.

Jori emerged and took up his throne, shooting her a dirty look as she only gave the most perfunctory of bows. "What do you want now?" he asked tetchily.

"King, I wish to leave the city for an hour or so, to visit the refugees."

He leant forward and looked at her intently, his fingers fiddling with his beard as he spoke, "Why? Why do you need to visit them now, rather than after we speak of your plans tomorrow morning?"

She sighed and ran her fingers through her hair, brushing a few stray strands away from her face. "I know what my plans are, but I cannot speak for the rest of the refugees, which is why I want to go and get their permission to speak on their behalf."

"Very well, but again, when the reckoning comes I will remember my generosity. Dombrek, go and fetch one of the Way Watchers to take her out to the people and bring her back. The Valkyrie is to be watched at all times." He turned back to Skjarla, "Braugr and the girl will remain here until you return, just in case you had ideas of slipping your leash."

Skjarla bowed before following the Dwarven bodyguard out of the palace, down the steep stairs into the Hold. She could see the three chambers leading off from the main room, one leading the way they had come, up to the surface, another down into the Ways and a third off to the Under-Hold. The Under-Hold was where the engineers dug down for new veins of the light-giving Sun Stones and maintained the water pipes. Off in the centre of the hold she could see the squat, imposing shape of the Blood Eye, the great arena in which the house champions battled for honour and bragging rights.

Dug into the far wall, and looking slightly neglected was a single, lonely temple, a small flame burning outside. That was the Beacon, the flame to guide the old Gods of Asgard back to their temple. It was a nice belief, thought Skjarla, but it had been so long now that everyone knew that none of them were coming back. To look upon it sent waves of crushing sadness over Skjarla, reminding her of just how alone she was. If she had glanced down she would have seen the brilliant lights snaking up her arm dim noticeably, not gone but definitely duller.

The young Dokkalfar escorting her did his best to be chatty, giving his name as Fjoraen, clearly awestruck at meeting the only surviving link to the Old Religion. She was not in the mood for conversation, and after a while of getting nothing but stony silence from her he shut up as well, walking her to the inner gate. On the way through the Hold he led her past the various stone benches which were placed on the sides of the road, holding various wares as the Dwarves and Dokkalfar behind them called for business. There seemed to be quite a rush of business going on, with furious yet good natured haggling going on almost everywhere she looked. The houses were a mix of low, square designs and taller, more ornate buildings, which seemed to flow together. They may live side by side but the Dokkalfar and the Dwarves clearly had very different places they liked to live.

They emerged behind the wall at the side of the Hold leading into the Ways, not as tall as the one defending the Hold from the surface but still a substantial obstacle to any who hoped to take Sundark Hold. "Open the gate," Fjoraen said grumpily, "The King orders that she should be allowed out for an hour, I'll shout when we need to come back in."

One of the other men on guard scoffed a laugh, "Off to go and slum it with the peasant surfacers out there Fjoraen? Be careful you don't come back smelling as bad as they do, some of them were still caked in blood, the savages." The guard's gaze was brought smartly round as Skjarla cleared her throat noisily. The Dokkalfar guard did not recognize her completely, but knew she was one of those who had come in from the surface. He glared at her for interrupting and Skjarla felt a strong desire to rearrange his features for him, but Fjoraen quickly moved between them.

"Drava, the gate?" he said, gesturing to the giant slab of metal-clad wood which separated the Hold from the Ways.

Muttering darkly to himself Drava beckoned one of the other guards to him and the two of them worked the winch mechanism which withdrew the three giant locking bars. She watched them throwing their weight against the windlass which gradually, with much screeching of hinges, moved outwards, throwing up clouds of dust as it scraped across the floor. Skjarla and her guard stepped out into the darkness, not hearing anything behind them. Clearly the guards were so unconcerned about the safety of the Hold that they didn't even bother to shut the gateway.

Fjoraen whispered to her, "I'll wait here, you go on ahead. I have no desire to wander amongst your people."

"As you will," she replied tartly before striding off down the passageway. It was wide and well carved, with a high, vaulted ceiling, the walls set with chunks of the glowing Sun Stones, their harsh light illuminating the surroundings. It made a pleasant change from the inky blackness of the tunnels down from the surface. She knew that if she carried on down the tunnel away she would find one of the many Way Houses, small inns run by one or two families for a few years, catering to those who travelled the Ways. This was not always the safest business, with monsters of all descriptions occasionally emerging from the stone, from the small and stunted Smaparmar to the fearsome Hyrrstein.

This close to the Hold there would be little danger though, and she hoped that their luck would hold for once. There was little warmth to greet her arrival, people came to look at her but would not stand too close, their expressions blank with fear. Skjarla shook her head softly as she walked closer, heading for the nearest of the carts. As she approached it she called out, "Gather everyone around here. I need to address the whole column." There was a degree of trepidation in their reaction, but word was passed around and from her new vantage point atop the cart she could see a steady trickle of people joining the gradually swelling crowd.

She scanned the crowd, her eyes finally alighting on the person she was looking for. "Sigmund, come here," she called, and the young man started to nervously edge his way through the crowd. She began what was the most difficult thing for her that she had tried in the last four hundred years. "People of Lonely Barrow, many of you are wondering why we are here, far beneath the surface of Midgard."

"Too bloody right," a voice called out of the crowd.

"From here, we can use the Ways of the Dokkalfar and the Dwarves to go beyond the reaches of the Haemocracy if we chose to. Some routes will lead us back into their lands, and I do not think that is something which can be done safely. Therefore I believe that there is only one option open to us, one thing that it is our duty to do. However, if any of you feel that the plan I offer you is not right then speak up. I will not guarantee the safety of those who intend to stay here or in the Haemocracy, but nor will I try to stop you from leaving."

She paused for breath as Sigmund arrived at the back of the cart, reaching down to offer her hand and pulling him aboard the wooden deck where all of the assembled crowd could see him. "All of you know this man. He is one of you, but he is more than that. It is my belief that he is the Heir of Sigurd, the armour found in his ancestor's tomb says as much."

A different voice bellowed out of the crowd, from behind her, causing her to whip around, "Half the town claims descent from the nameless warrior, what makes him anymore a king than me."

Skjarla didn't like this, she knew that to convince any of them to follow Sigmund then she was going to have to put all of the cards on the table, and she didn't like the thought of this new information going into Domitia's plots and plans. "Because he holds one of the Fangs of Fafnir," that prompted a mutter of worried chatter, "It is why we have been hunted by the Children of the Dragon all this way, they seek it, as a drowning man seeks air."

"So if we killed him and left his body with the Fang then they would stop chasing us? Who's with me?" There was a murmur of agreement around the speaker, but more faces looked at Skjarla with fear writ plain across them, waiting for her reaction.

"You do that over my dead body, and trust me, I will take many of you with me if you try." She paused, gauging the feeling of the crowd. They were subdued, well believing the violence behind her threat. "I propose that we head south, beyond the lands of the Haemocracy, beyond the deserts of Vfar to the Black Mountains where the Blackstone Castle still sits on the pass of Shrieking Winds. From there we will be safe."

"That place is a ruin, if there's anything there at all." Scoffed a voice, "What waits for us there except a freezing death, after crossing the burning heat of the desert."

Skjarla's temper finally snapped, "Well if you have a better idea then you are welcome to come up here. The journey will be as safe as possible. We will travel beneath the land, along the Ways, it will be as safe as I can make it. I don't ask you to decide this moment, but I must return to the city within the hour. Think, discuss it with those dearest to you, and then make your decision. As I said, I will not hold it against any who wish to remain here, or try for passage to somewhere within the Haemocracy, but we are better off if we stick together."

She sat down heavily in the cart, engulfed by a wave of noise as over two thousand people began talking at once. She tried to ignore it as the group broke up, but she was snapped from her reverie as a throat was cleared. The young men and women who had fought with her and the others were already clustered around the cart and one of them seemed to lead this group. She fumbled for his name, Striggr, Striggr Wotadsson was his name. The young man with his fierce expression clashed his fist against his chest, snarling to accompany the hollow thump. "Mistress, whatever these others decide, we are with you to the end. To visit Sigurd's keep would be something worth seeing, and protecting a Fang of Fafnir is something worth dying for."

She smiled at him warmly, more so than she had in a long time, "Thank you Striggr, it's good to hear that there will be more than just a few of us making the journey south." She was happy. These people, these ones standing before her seemed to have something which she had thought lost, the Viking wanderer spirit, the lust for adventure which seemed to have been replaced by a lust for gold across much of Midgard. None of them noticed, but the pale cracks in her armour flared brighter, and the shards of lightning snaked further up her arms, now half way up the forearm on the left and up to the wrist on the right.

The Romans followed suit, or more precisely Domitia decreed that they would also be supporting Skjarla and coming south with the refugees. Skjarla had no doubt that the woman saw an opportunity of some form there, a chance to set in motion a plan to regain her throne, but the girl was not always bad news, just determined to regain her throne at any cost. Also, the few remaining Roman soldiers would be useful if they found Blackstone Castle already occupied.

She heard Iskander and the other Reavers shout their support from across the crowd of soldiers, which she felt incredibly grateful for. They all knew the legends of Fafnir and his Fangs, and if there was a Fang to protect then they viewed it as their duty to help the Ancient Reaver. So far Skjarla had been surprised by how well the Reavers had been doing with the people of the column. They were all used to a life on the road, alone with their thoughts. They were by nature a combustible bunch but they had yet to start a fight with each other or the refugees, although they had all made point of challenging the Romans, wanting to see how these warriors from the west fought.

Gradually, in dribs and drabs the people of Lonely Barrow made their way back to her podium, waiting quietly for her to speak again. Once again she got to her feet, looking out over the expanse of heads; she rubbed wearily at her forehead, waiting for final silence. "Raise your hands if you wish to accompany me and the others to the south." There was a soft finality about her voice, a sense that she was not worried how many came with them, so long as the decision was finally made.

A few hands went up at the front of the crowd after a few seconds of pregnant pause, and others followed suit, a ripple spreading through a sea of rising hands. Unconsciously she sagged with relief, which shocked her more than anything, to realise that she actually cared about what would happen to these people. "Very well, I must head back to the city tonight, but I will try to have supplies sent out to you tomorrow."

She hopped down from the cart, grateful that for once she was not clad in heavy plates of metal as she landed on the ground, and stalked off towards the gates of Sundark hold. There was no cheering from the crowd, no slapping her on the back, just a quiet acceptance that their ordeal was far from over, and a grim determination to meet that challenge. She emerged from the throng, which was already starting to break up as people headed back to whichever spare piece of ground that they had found to sleep on, to find Fjoraen still waiting for her.

He looked at her with quiet intensity as he asked, "Are you ready to return to the Hold my Lady?"

"Yes Fjoraen, thanks for waiting." She replied, even as she fell into step with him as they walked back towards the still open gate. They passed through the narrow opening and left the two sweating and swearing Dokkalfar behind them to reseal the gate for the rest of the evening. The Gates to the Hold tended to be kept sealed, as most travellers planned their visits months in advance, usually leaving notice of when they would return on the previous visit. Otherwise they would just open the gate when someone turned up, but the traffic between the Holds was minimal at best.

She was led back through the streets of the hold, Fjoraen maintaining a respectful silence. The roads were noticeably darker, as the darker hemisphere inched across the globes, dimming the light on the streets. Shop keepers were busily packing away their goods for the night and urchins, children of the poorer members of society, were busy fighting over the food which had been discarded at the end of the day. She felt an unmistakeable weariness in her thighs as she hauled herself up the gargantuan flight of stairs which led to the palace. And was grateful to be handed over to one of the palace servants who led her through the labyrinthine maze or corridors to where Braugr and Helania. The two were sat around a small stone plinth, atop which sat platters of partially eaten food.

The two of them were sat on plump cushions, and Braugr gestured to an empty one while saying, apologetically, "Sorry we started already, but we weren't sure how long you were going to take."

Skjarla waved his apology away even as she reached for a chicken thigh, covered with aromatic spices. "I would have started too, don't worry." She took a mouthful and spoke happily, trying not to shower her companions with chunks of meat. "Ah, finally something other than dried meat and cheese." There was a hearty laugh from the other two, then Helania, whose black marble cheeks seemed to have an odd sheen and be flushed with blood, held up a gilded flagon.

"And they have given us wine!" she exclaimed happily, clearly having gotten stuck into that as well. "You know that Braugr doesn't touch the stuff anymore, so there's plenty here for the two of us." She giggled slightly as she handed the heavy flagon to Skjarla, who quietly wondered how much of the flagon Helania had drunk already.

Braugr was still his usual dour self and refused to touch any of the wine, unsurprisingly, but his mood did seem to be lifted by Helania's levity. For her part Skjarla was also grateful for the Dokkalfar's high spirits, helping to distract her from the earlier struggle of trying to convince the people to follow her. She had never liked doing that even in Valhalla, preferring just to get on with the business of fighting, something she knew and was good at.

The evening wore on and the now empty platter of food was silently cleared away by the palace servants, who also continued to top up the flagon of wine. Some time later, Helania had fallen into a deep sleep, and Braugr's head was beginning to nod as well. "The young can't handle their drink these day s can they?" he said with a sad smile and a shake of the head.

Skjarla stifled a yawn as she nodded her head, her hands coming up to sleepily knuckle her leaden eyelids. She swore softly to herself as she got to her feet, wobbling slightly as she did so, before heaving Helania over her shoulder. One of the servants silently led them to the guest wing of the Palace, directing them into three rooms. Skjarla laid Helania down upon her bed, a stone plinth topped with furs and a straw packed mattress to make it more comfortable, before heading back to her own chamber. She was delighted to see her armour hung spotlessly upon a frame, with her clothes neatly folded next to it. Dreyrispa was resting on a rack at the foot of the armour stand, along with the two swords she carried with her. She couldn't resist walking over to caress the worn, smooth wood of the haft before collapsing on the soft furs of the bed. She felt the long strands of the fur tickling against her skin, and was annoyed by the amount of dust which seemed to be trapped in there, puffing up in a small cloud every time she moved. It irritated her throat, making her cough noisily, and the last thought she had before drifting off was that she envied Accipiteri outside in the relatively fresh air of the tunnels, away from the politics which would greet her tomorrow.

**

The false dawn of Sundark Hold brought an uncomfortable pounding headache to the fore of Skjarla's consciousness. If she was feeling this bad then she didn't want to imagine how Helania was coping with the abuses of the previous night. Fighting the urge to vomit she reached down to collect her under clothes, pulling them on and taking a deep breath, bracing herself as she reached for her armoured boots. The room swam slightly as she righted herself and began strapping the remnants of her armour onto her body. There was a very specific order to put the steel plates on, as often one would cover the seams and gaps left by the one beneath.

When she was eventually back in her armour she wandered outside, to be met by a cheerful looking Braugr and a very pale looking Helania, who was almost clinging onto the wall for dear life. The three of them made their way into the palace in search of a servant to lead them to the throne room. By chance they found themselves there without having seen anyone at all, although the room was empty. Skjarla cursed herself for not thinking that the palace might not rise as early as they did. The column had been in the habit of starting with the dawn and not coming to a halt before the sun dropped below the horizon. In the summer that would be far earlier than the palace's day.

All they could do was resign themselves to waiting, so they positioned themselves against one of the walls, sliding down so that they were all seated, legs out in front of them, backs propped up by the cold masonry. Helania closed her eyes and went to sleep, her breathing heavy and reeking of alcohol fumes. Skjarla and Braugr were both practised enough soldiers to take sleep where it was offered, and both quickly drifted off into very light sleep.

They were awoken by one of the guards shaking them awake, looking sternly while the king chortled from up on his throne, "I don't normally allow beggars to sleep in my throne room." He became serious as he sat down, resting his shining axe across his knees as he began, and "So, I will hear what you have to ask from me before I give you my terms."

Skjarla chewed her lip and glanced to the side, grateful for a small nod of the head from Braugr. At least there was some support there. She cleared her throat and then began. Standing in front of the throne, everything seemed sharper to her as the adrenaline flowed, the lines of the stonework seeming crisper to her. "King Jori, the people of Lonely Barrow beg your aid, they wish to travel to the south through the Ways, to emerge in the Black Mountains, or as close to there as possible. To do this we will also need supplies and a guide. I have money on the surface, but none with the Dwarven banks with which to pay for the goods we need."

King Jori shook his head, "Money is not something I need. What I need is something easily given by you. It is fortunate for you that the eldest son of King Turil Hammerhand is coming of age in the next month." He took in her blank look, and knew he had to keep talking given the sudden worried expression on Braugr's face. "He is holding a contest in the Blood Eye of his Hold, Moonshadow. I had planned on entering Dombrek or one of the other members of the guard, especially since my finest champion now walks the surface," he shot a pointed look at Braugr. "Therefore, especially given that the

Moonshadow hold is beneath the borders of the Vfar desert and so on your way south, I will give you what you wish if you agree to represent my Hold in the contest."

Skjarla chewed at the inside of her cheek, Braugr opened his mouth to say something but was silenced by a gesture from the king. Finally she spoke, "Very well, I have one further condition though."

"Name it," the king said in a bored and irritated tone.

"Pardon, or if that is not possible your protection while we travel south, for Helania."

"I cannot pardon her, but you have my word that she will not be harassed in any way while she travels to the south. If that is acceptable to you," he said sarcastically, "then leave a list of what you need by way of supplies with one of my guards. We will not be leaving for the south for about ten days. Now if there is nothing else, this audience is over." He got back to his feet and walked out of the chamber looking thoroughly pleased with himself.

Before he could open his mouth Skjarla turned to Braugr to ask, "It has to be at least a two month journey to the edge of the Vfar desert, how does he expect to do it in less than two weeks?"

"Not entirely sure, my guess may be that he is planning on going ahead with some people and will wait for the rest of the column to catch up. After all, they are not needed to take part in the rest of the festivities which will be going on down in Moonshadow Hold." His face darkened as he continued, his arms flailing slightly as he angrily yelled at her, "Couldn't you see I was trying to stop you from doing this? If this is a coming of age contest then it will be more than just a straight duel to first blood, these contests always are. Furthermore they will view you as king Jori's champion, his pet, and as such some of the Holds will try to sabotage you. A few broken ribs before a fight may be just enough to tip it against you."

She smiled back at him, which only served to further enrage his temper. "Well, at least I shall have a glorious death in that case, something I have been searching for for many lifetimes. Plus, was there honestly any other way to get the supplies we needed and secure passage through the Ways?"

Braugr sullenly replied, "No, I suppose not." The three of them headed out of the chamber to find one of the servants. The Dwarf led them to the palace steward, the Dokkalfar whose duty was to control the supplies and finances of the court. The man was surprisingly friendly and clearly in awe of Skjarla, although a good deal cooler towards Braugr, whose shame was well known around the Hold. She explained what they needed, and he promised to provide the provisions required for the long journey to the south.

They were leaving the palace together when the sight of the long drop stretching before them finally got the best of Helania, who peeled off to the side of the path and vomited noisily. She returned to the others looking wobbly and thoroughly wretched.

***

The ten day period before they left passed relatively without incident. Skjarla was often required at the palace as they insisted on making up a whole series of garments for her, including a surcoat for her armour, all bearing a golden orb on the blue field of Sundark Hold. The refugees were generally welcomed, allowed into the town during the day, and many took advantage of the Dwarven baths dotted around the place. They were not exactly warmly greeted by the locals, but there was none of the animosity or tension which existed between the races on the surface. The only real problem for the people had been that there was no sewage facility outside the walls, so they could only use the jacks when they were allowed into the city, during the day. It was not the greatest hardship, but any ill will was assuaged by the regular arrivals of food and water, provided from the central stores of the Hold.

Sundark, like all of the Holds grew everything beneath the land and even raised some small herds. The animals had learned to graze on a fast growing yet lush lichen which sprouted like a weed everywhere underground. They had also used the same infrastructure that they did before the cataclysm, with the Sun Stones being used to grow huge expanses of green produce, with vegetables and grains grown in abundance. It was a marvellous system, supplemented by the lands of the surface, often grown in secluded valleys where there was little chance of discovery, or through trading with the Haemocracy.

Accipiteri made sure to keep the soldiers of the column, the Lonely Company as they liked to refer to themselves, in training. His hope was to stop them from putting on any weight and losing any condition as they camped outside the Hold. They were running drills for the most part of the day, Accipiteri and the Romans trying to introduce the idea of formation fighting, much to the amusement of the guards patrolling the wall, lazily keeping an eye on the people before the wall. The only bonus from the long months of marching was that it had hardened the soldiers, giving them wind beyond anything they had known before, and steel-like cords of muscle in their legs.

The day of departure grew nearer, and the people of Lonely Barrow started to pile supplies onto the carts. Bjarn went everywhere with a nervous expression on his face; he had been entrusted with the various chits which would give the column the right to draw stores and water along the Ways. Such items were immeasurably valuable, and Bjarn kept patting the side of his trousers where his purse was, trying to feel if they were still there.

The thing which amazed them all the more was how well most of the people were taking to being below the surface. Braugr had seen merchants who came down from the surface on occasions constantly glancing up at the ceiling, desperate for the open skies again. By contrast the refugees had taken to it rather well, but then, Braugr supposed, that was a consequence of not having any other option in the matter.

Fjoraen appeared at the edge of their camp on the day before they left for Moonshadow Hold. He sent someone into the camp to search for Skjarla. It was strange, the man was a well trained warrior and had been protecting the hold for over fifty years, but seemed very nervous and unsure about entering the camp full of surfacers. He seemed to relax more when she arrived, telling her that the king wanted to see her one last time before they set off.

As they walked together, for once she spoke to him, mainly out of curiosity rather than a desire for idle chatter. "Fjoraen, how does the king intend on travelling to Moonshadow Hold so quickly? I've heard that on foot it would take several months, but we need to be there in less than two weeks."

Fjoraen looked at her strangely, then smiled knowingly and nodded his head. "Ah, you haven't been told then. I guess Braugr must have left just before we started building the thing. One of our engineers came up with what is basically a powered cart. There is a large boiler which drives the wheels, I'm afraid I don't know more than that."

Skjarla looked at him sceptically, trying to work out if the Dokkalfar was having a joke with her. "A mechanized cart?"

"No word of a lie mistress. I have never had the privilege of riding the thing. None but the King and his favourites have as the stones which heat the water for the steam are incredibly expensive. Believe me, it is a rare honour to ride in such a vehicle. They say that it can travel across the smooth ground of the Ways as fast as a horse can gallop. It helps that the Ways are dead straight, for the most part, it means that the thing can just pick up speed and go." He finished off with breathless excitement, a light buzzing in his eyes as the Dokkalfar thought of the adventure of such a trip.

"Why haven't we seen it then? Surely if it is so valuable then it would be kept within the walls?"

"Well, it would be, but the King doesn't want anyone going near it if they don't know what they're doing. It is supposedly incredibly noisy, so can't come too near the Hold without deafening everyone. At least that's what we're told," He finished with a shrug.

She spent the rest of the journey to the palace trying to work out how such a contraption would work. Surely the people of Sundark hold had not managed to come up with something as farfetched as all that. She was once again escorted into the throne room, the king pacing before the throne as he waited for her impatiently. "Ah, my champion has arrived," he said with a smile.

Skjarla bowed gently before asking, "You summoned me King Jori?"

"Yes, I wanted to tell you that there will be room on the Balfara for you and three of your companions. Any others you may wish to bring will have to travel with the refugees and catch up when they can. You have told me that some of them can defend themselves, therefore I will only be sending a few of my people to act as guides for the journey to Moonshadow Hold."

Skjarla's mind was miles away as she tried to decide who to take with her and who should be left to lead the column. Her voice was remote as she asked, "Is there anything else?"

"My Lord. Is there anything else, My Lord?" he corrected her sternly.

Internally she sighed but said wearily, "Is there anything else My Lord?" More and more she was regretting this deal with the king, but if she still wanted to protect the refugees, which she was beginning to doubt was worth it, she had to keep up the charade.

"No, though you will have to start wearing the colours of my house before we arrive in Moonshadow. You may go." He waved his hand, dismissing her. Skjarla knew that there was no need for her to be summoned here to receive that message, the King just liked having a Valkyrie at his beck and call. Strangely, she wasn't furious, just weary of all this politicking. It had been years since she had spent this long in the company of others, and she missed the solitude and peace of the road. She felt like she had no time to think, no time to breathe, but that second one may just have been the slightly stale tang to the air in the Hold.

Fjoraen interrupted her thoughts, "My lady, are you alright? You seem distracted."

She shook her head softly, she could not voice her concerns to one of the Hold's warriors, so instead she simply said, and "I was just worrying about the supplies for the column. It's nothing too serious though."

He smiled at her warmly, his brown eyes seeming so soft, even in the harsh glare of the light stones. "Your compassion is not something I ever thought to see in one of the Maidens of Death come from legend."

Now she laughed long and hard, with a trace of regret, "I haven't been one of those for an age, but you're right, I would never have done something like this in the old days."

Fjoraen knew that the Valkyrie was leaving tomorrow, and the chances of his being chosen as one of the Royal guard were zero. In Holds like Starfall and Whiteshadow where the rulers were Dokkalfar the Royal guard tended to be Alfar rather than the Dwarven Hearth Guard. It was a shame he thought, the chances of him going on an adventure such as these people were on was almost nil. He knew that at dawn the next day the two parties would start their respective journeys to Moonshadow Hold, so he took the chance at the gate to say a final farewell to Skjarla.

"My Lady, I wish you luck in your trials ahead. It has been an honour to meet you in person."

She smiled at him genuinely, "Thank you Fjoraen, I wish you all the best for all your coming challenges," and then seeming to read his mind she added, "Don't worry, adventure will come to you one day."

The Dokkalfar thinned his lips in a sad grimace, his thumb nursing the pommel of his sword as he replied, "Kind of you to say so, but I really don't think it will. Not in a place like this." He glanced sadly around his small world, the high ceiling suddenly seeming more like a prison than anything else.

They parted company at the gateway, Fjoraen waiting in the small gap while Skjarla passed out between them, heading back towards the small encampment without a second glance. Once she had crossed the short distance, rolling her stiff shoulders and giving her neck a satisfying crack, she called the others to her. They sat upon the dusty flagstones a distance away from the camp, hoping not to be overheard by everyone else. Skjarla explained what the king had said to her and then looked around the group. She knew she had no power to make a decision, but if she phrased it right she could probably get her way.

Accipiteri was a strong fighter and a loyal man, a fine leader. If he came then it would be one less person for her to keep an eye on, but at the same time he was the one she most trusted to lead the column. Domitia wouldn't be particularly useful in a fight but at least she knew politics and Skjarla would frankly rather have the Roman spider where she could keep an eye on her. Braugr couldn't come, the king had made it clear that he would not arrive with one of the Shattered in his party. Metellus would have to come if Domitia did, but he was too honest to be much of a threat. The real conundrum was concerning Sigmund. She didn't want the Fang in the middle of a place like that in case anyone tried to steal the thing, but at the same time she didn't want to let it out of her sight.

She addressed the group of her closest companions, "As I say, I can only bring three of you with me, I would like Accipiteri to stay here and lead the column, is that acceptable to everyone?" There was a general murmur of agreement before Domitia piped up.

"I would like to visit the Hold and see what the state is in the Dwarven Kingdoms, I can act on behalf of my father, so hopefully gain some influence in the court."

Metellus joined in with a stony voice, "If my mistress is going then so am I."

Domitia continued, "I would have thought that a Valkyrie will be welcomed in the court in Moonshadow Hold, so on the trip I could maybe help you to appear a bit more lady-like."

Skjarla snarled angrily at the suggestion as the rest of the group fell over laughing at the thought of the proud warrior trying to be lady-like. Braugr choked on the words as he tried to say, "Domitia, you've got more chance of getting water to run uphill than getting Skjarla in a gown of any form."

"Yes, yes, it's hysterical," Skjarla drawled angrily once they had finally quieted down enough to hear her, "Back to the matter at hand. So far I've got Domitia and Metellus coming with me. Iskander, how do you feel about it?"

Iskander stroked his sharp chin, humming thoughtfully to himself before replying, "As much as I want to come and spend the next six weeks in your company as the guest of the king..." his voice tailed off as he raised a suggestive eyebrow. "I think that I had best stay here, the others seem to be more comfortable with me around, and we can't have them getting the impression that I'm your favourite now can we." Skjarla laughed lightly, she had missed Iskander's irreverence and wry sense of humour for the last few months.

"Very well. Sigmund," the young man perked up at the thought of travelling on ahead with her, "You and Helania work it out between yourselves as to who comes with me." He sagged slightly, then turned to Helania.

"Do you want to go with Skjarla?"

"Yes and no, it will be an incredible experience but I worry about causing problems, especially with the people from Nightfast Hold." She finished sadly

"But they won't recognize you, surely?"

"No, perhaps not, but I can't be sure, and what if one of the king's guards let slip who I am?" she paused for a moment, "But perhaps you shouldn't go. I mean, do you think it is really sensible to take the Fang into such a place. The Lords of the eleven Holds are always competing for power and status and getting their hands on such an artefact... Well, it would give whoever gets their hands on it a huge boost against the others."

"I suppose you're right, much as I hate to admit it, and I feel I should hang onto the Fang for some reason, otherwise I'd just get someone else to carry it and travel ahead with Skjarla. You should go." His face was low as he replied, trying to hide the disappointment in his eyes. If he had looked up he would have seen the quiet nod of approval shared by Accipiteri, Braugr and Skjarla, impressed by the young man's maturity in such a situation.

Skjarla glanced at Helania, "Alright, you and the two Romans are coming with us in the morning. Be ready to leave camp as soon as the orb starts to change from dim to light. As I said earlier, I want Accipiteri in charge of the column until we are back together in Moonshadow Hold." She realised as she said this that she had inadvertently become the leader of their sorry band. It was not something she had wanted or sought, but increasingly the people were looking to them, and her in particular for answers to all their problems, simply because she had provided them in the past.

As their little meeting broke up she collared Accipiteri, "I need a word." They waited patiently for the rest of the group to shuffle off, back towards the refugee camp before continuing. "I am sure I don't need to tell you, keep an eye on Sigmund; he's carrying the most important thing in this group. Watch out for whoever they send as your guide, it's quite possible that they'll try to steal the Fang to curry favour with the king. They may not know about it now but they're bound to find out about the Fang over the course of your journey. Other than that, protect the people and we'll meet in the Hold to the south."

"You know I will keep an eye on things Skjarla, and you look after yourself. If what I've read about Dwarven politics is right you'll be stepping into a true nest of vipers, almost worse than the squabbling of the Haemocrats."

"Thanks for the warning, I'll keep an eye on it, but I've never met anything that Dreyrispa couldn't cut me out of." She finished with a cold, dangerous smile as she left, heading back to the camp site.

Skjarla spent the evening alone, and Metellus and Helania were doing much the same thing as her, polishing their armour and preparing their gear for the next day's travelling. The cold rasp of their whetstones stropping against the edges of chill steel resounded from the walls, putting the whole camp on edge. Eventually silence reigned on the camp, now bare of almost everything as supplies and comforts had been packed onto the carts, leaving only the sleeping blankets still on the ground. There was no need for the waxed leather tents beneath the earth.

They were woken the next morning by the loud squeal of the gate being pushed wider, to make room for the Royal party to pass through in comfort and style. Glancing through the gate they could already see a crowd of people lining both sides of the road. Sigmund leant close to Helania and whispered, "Do you reckon that they are coming out to see their king, or looking forward to seeing the back of him for a time." Helania stifled a giggle, then stepped forward to join Skjarla and the two Romans. All of them had their arms buffed to a high shine, they had even found some wax to apply to the leather straps of their harnesses.

"All ready to go I see," the King said cheerfully as he approached them. He was understandably upbeat; he believed he was going to claim all of the honour for his Hold by winning this coming of age tournament with an unbeatable champion. "Fjirsk and his men here," he gestured to a group of three Dokkalfar, "Will lead the refugees to Moonshadow Hold, where you will continue south with them, once you have won the tournament for me."

He breezed past them carelessly, "Bring your friends to the Balfara, we have a long journey ahead of us."

Skjarla shrugged to the other three and fell into step with the rest of the Hearth Guard, towering over the heavily armed Dwarves who travelled with their king. Beyond the guards she could see a dejected looking Fjoraen, standing with his fellows at the gate, waiting to close it behind the heavy wagons of supplies following the king. As they disappeared down the tunnel, leaving the people of Lonely Barrow and Sundark Hold behind them, Skjarla heard the screeching of tortured metal as the heavy gates were winched back into position. She felt a weight ease from her mind as she left the burden of the Lonely Company behind. Although she still felt the Fang as a nagging presence at the back of her mind.

The group headed down the paved road of the Ways for the best part of an hour until an object appeared down the tunnel. As they marched they were bathed in a harsh light, the mechanisms for periodically dimming the lights in the cities were too cumbersome and complicated to be fitted the length and breadth of the Ways. There was a thin mist as condensation dripped from the ceiling, they must be near the steam engine. Skjarla fought against the unconscious quickening of her pace, she would not break step with the guards and give the king the satisfaction of seeing her curiosity. She noticed that the Dwarves and the Dokkalfar were chattering in quiet excitement, clearly they were as amazed by the construct as she was.

It looked like a giant sled fitted with wheels. It was nearly fifty paces long, each side set with five giant iron wheels, the front two of which were fitted with an alarmingly complex array of pistons. The steam gathering against the ceiling of the Ways was being pumped out of a gigantic boiler mounted at the front of the sled, while the back end was covered with a heavy felt tent. The tent was covered in silver and gold thread, while the interior was filled with soft cushions and silk hangings, one of the most opulent places that Skjarla had ever seen.

Skjarla noticed one flaw with the smoking monstrosity, it was facing towards them. However, the remedy became readily apparent. While the king climbed aboard Skjarla and the others were set to work with the entourage throwing their weight against the wheels to push it around. It was back-breaking work and Skjarla felt sweat dripping from the tip of her nose and down her spine as she set her weight against the screeching metal of the wheels. Inch by inch they shoved the steam cart around until it was facing the other way.

Skjarla asked one of the other travellers as they were climbing aboard the iron and wood contraption, "What happens if we're not perfectly straight going down this passage?"

The Dwarf responded without looking, concentrating on the wooden ladder fixed to the side of the cart. "They can turn very slightly from upfront, something to do with braking on one side or the other, but I don't know the details." It was a gruff response, but it satisfied Skjarla that they weren't going to die on this trip.

As they started to move Skjarla was disabused of this notion. The noise sounded like the birth of the world, while the rattling and shaking was truly horrific; she felt as if her eyes were about to be shaken from their sockets. At first she was afraid she was going to die, after ten minutes of the punishing ride and the hammering sound of the pistons she was afraid she wasn't going to. The only vague relief came when the king ordered the heavy felt curtains of the tent flap drawn closed, which helped to muffle some of the noise, but did nothing for the shaking, as every imperfection in the stone surface of the Ways seemed to be magnified a hundred fold.

She would have liked to talk to someone to help pass the day, but she could see that the Dwarves and everyone else inside had their hands firmly clamped to their ears, trying to shut out the racket. They passed the day in noisy silence as the heavy steam cart thundered towards Moonshadow Hold, leaving the column of refugees far behind them.

Even the evening halt offered little respite, as the noise left a ringing in everyone's ears. The Dwarves explained that it was the only reason that they stopped, because no one could physically sleep on such a contraption. They had come to a halt outside one of the many Way Houses which were dotted along the Ways. It was carved into the wall of the road; the door and a few windows the only suggestion that there was anything here apart from the stones of the road. Inside it was much like any inn that Skjarla had visited on the surface, there was a large courtyard behind the inn, apparently accessed from just beyond the inn to either side. The Balfara was simply too big and too unwieldy to fit into the courtyard so it was left out in front, clogging most of the Way. 'There are some perks to being royal,' Skjarla thought wryly.

The interior of the building was comfortably furnished with solid wooden chairs, tables and benches set around a room, one wall of which was dominated by a long bar. Behind the bar a burly Dwarf was busily wiping the pewter tankards with a dirty rag. His face had lit up at the sight of the Royal train and the thought of the coin it would bring in. Skjarla missed the roaring fire which would have been the centrepiece of any inn on the surface, but with nowhere for the smoke to go that simply wasn't possible underground. The walls were the same plain, pale stone as the walls of the road outside, and the hissing boiler of the Balfara could be heard within the common room

They were packed into the rooms; Skjarla ended up sharing hers with Helania, the Romans and a surly Dokkalfar, clearly aggrieved at being forced to share with the surfacers. A meal of rich meat pie had been prepared by the royal kitchens and merely been heated up by the staff at this Way House. The usual fare here being much more like what Skjarla was used to, dried meats, cheeses and other long-lived foods. Apparently there were sometimes fresh provisions, but usually only just after one of the supply convoys had passed through.

The Way Houses were interesting, paid for by the sales of food and board, the families that ran the place then had to buy their supplies from the crown and pay rent to their local lord as well. It was a hard life, requiring no small degree of bravery, given that bar the occasional patrol there was little in the way of protection from anything dangerous which chose to emerge from the rocks and tunnels. Sleep for the travellers that night was nearly impossible though, loudly as all of their ears were ringing, the clanging and hissing of the boiler seeming to be right there with them.

The cycle of rising early, spending a torturous day being shaken to pieces on the back of the Balfara then trying to drown out the misery with strong Dwarven ale before passing out was dull and repetitive. Skjarla and the others had swiftly followed the example of the Dwarves after the first night; alcohol did indeed help you sleep. Domitia though was not as used to strong drink as the rest of them, and found that the journey the next day was even more intolerable thanks to the pounding in her head.

On the fourth evening of their travels, as Skjarla and Metellus sat together downstairs, tucked into a corner of the common room, both nursing large flagons of ale, a thought occurred to her. She glanced around the crowded room, they had met a trade convoy going the other way, back towards Sundark Hold which had meant the Way House was packed. Domitia was upstairs, already trying to get some sleep before Metellus came in and started snoring like a rutting boar.

"Metellus."

"Mmm?" was the only response she got.

"I was wondering, how many legionaries do you have left?"

"What do you mean," he asked with a shake of the head, "Men in the uniform, or men from Rome?"

"Well, both I suppose," came the weak response, slightly apprehensive as to the reply.

"I have just twenty three men in legion kit. Of those only eight are from Rome herself, the rest are village lads who we've squeezed into the armour."

Skjarla let out a low whistling breath, earning her a scowl from Metellus. "Is Appius still with you, the one who treated Sigmund after his duel with the Haemocrat champion?"

Metellus shook his head before taking a long swallow of ale. "He died in that fight outside the caves, I saw him take a spear to the gut as we retreated; nothing we could do. He bled to death beneath our feet."

"Shit. I'm sorry to hear that. He was a good soldier." She finished lamely.

"That he was." Metellus raised his tankard and Skjarla followed suit, "To Appius, and all the other Romans who went before him, May we meet again beyond the Styx." He drained his ale and Skjarla followed him in his grim toast. Metellus seemed to consider her for a moment before, as drunk people often do, saying something incredibly true without realising it. "I feel sorry for you, girl. We Romans cling to our Gods, and our belief in the old ways. We believe that when we die there will be something waiting for us on the other side, that our souls will go somewhere, will still be. You, you know what comes at the end. I've heard what happened to your kind Valkyrie, how can you fight so much, knowing there is nothing after it all?"

She smiled a grim, dangerous smile, the embers of a cold sadness glimmering in her eyes. "You ask how I can be a Reaver knowing that my death is the end? The true question is how I cannot be a Reaver. When all you know is dust, all you seek is an end to it all. You ask if I am afraid of the nothingness, in truth I welcome it. I shall greet my end as an old comrade, one whom has walked beside me for many years."

Metellus couldn't think of anything to say to such a grim, final statement. Sheepishly, timidly he made his way upstairs, leaving the Valkyrie in silence to contemplate what they had just said. He glanced back down at her once, from the top of the stairs. He couldn't help but wonder at her beauty, but found himself terrified by the cold veneer which lay atop it, like a sheen of ice atop a lake.

***

Nearly a week's march back down the stone passage stretching the length of the route between the Holds Accipiteri was facing very different problems. He had been forced to put the people onto low rations, which led to a general feeling of discontent. He had no other choice, the supplies they had been given were insufficient for the whole journey, and there was not enough in the various Way Houses to supplement the diet of the whole column. The landlords did their best, but were not likely to be especially generous to surfacers. After the first one had turned him away he had resorted to sending Braugr to claim the food and supplies, but with the brand of the Shattered on his face he had little more success.

The guides, a trio of Dokkalfar who shared their races graceful forms were an isolated bunch. There were two men, Fjirsk and Torae, and a woman called Tomani. They all seemed to know the Ways like the back of their hands, but were resentful of the thought of having to escort the lumbering column all the way to Moonshadow Hold.

On just the second day Torae had pulled him to one side and quietly asked, "How many soldiers do you have with the column?"

Accipiteri remembered being confused by the question, but he had told the Dokkalfar, "Nearly half of them know what they're doing with a weapon, but that is only because we rotate training. The real problem is that we only have arms for around two hundred and fifty of them."

Torae had nodded severely before saying darkly, "Make sure they keep their weapons to hand, the smell of the waste from all of these people and animals will draw beasts to us like moths to a flame. If we're lucky then it will just be the odd pack of Smaparmar, if we're not then it might rouse a Hyrrstein against us."

He had left it at that, even though Accipiteri had no idea what those things where or how they got into the Ways. He had asked Braugr about it later on, and the Dwarf had explained that the Ways were not always the neatly carved tunnels that everyone thought they were, other, natural caves branched off from the Dwarven Ways.

Regular patrols helped to keep them relatively clear, but monsters such as the small, grey-skinned Smaparmar or the fiery Hyrrstein often broke into the tunnels, occasionally causing havoc against the convoys which frequented the Ways. It was the main reason that each of the Holds had to be self sufficient, they could not rely on trade and goods from any of the other Holds. Iskander had been a little comfort, saying that the Reavers knew enough of these beasts to be able to drive them off, although he admitted that none of them had personally done so before.

He had not slept soundly after that, worrying as to what could happen during the night, worrying that the guards would fall asleep. Not that there was much darkness to fall asleep in, the lights along the walls burned constantly, their unwavering glow covering the Ways, whose smooth walls offered no shelter. It was quite sickening, even after just four days. If it really had been four days, with no sun to mark the passing of time it could have been two days or two weeks. All he knew was that the column had to keep pressing forwards, heading towards Moonshadow Hold and trying to catch up with Skjarla.

Chapter 12

Skjarla gratefully dismounted from the infernal Balfara which had been driven right up to the gates of Moonshadow Hold. If king Jori was trying to make an impression then he failed, every other ruler had had the same idea, each arriving in their ostentatiously decorated Balfara, their guards turned out for parade. Skjarla had felt particularly resentful towards the Dwarf Dombrek, who had made a point of telling her and the others to ensure they dressed smartly for the occasion. Domitia had been happy as she had been given a new dress to wear while in the Hold, but the others had just glared at the black-eyed Dwarf.

Two nights ago Dombrek had tried to have his way with Helania, saying that she was a whore and therefore should spread her legs for his coin. He had been quite insistent and had only backed down when Helania gave him a black eye. He had been about to jump on her when Metellus had come across the scene, forcing the Dwarf to back down. Helania had been an odd mix of grateful for his support and irritated by it, affronted by the inference that she couldn't look after herself. The centurion had shaken his head as she stormed off, knowing that the greatest mystery in the world remained the same, and women.

The walls of Moonshadow hold were different to the creamy stones of Sundark. Here they were orange in hue and very grainy, like sand. Skjarla realised that they must be beneath the desert of Vfar, they had already come a long way south. Skjarla was grateful that they had several hundred paces of rock between them and the baking sun which cooked anything which tried to cross the deserts. There were only a few scattered tribes of nomads who scratched a living from the shifting sands of Vfar, chasing the small oases of water and defending those they owned with an intense fervour.

They were led through the city, Skjarla feeling more like a hostage or a sacrificial lamb than an honoured guest, even with the screaming crowds and the coloured lengths of cloth stretched above their heads. The people were cheering, but she still managed to hear Metellus whisper to Domitia behind her back, "Now I know how the gladiators feel in Rome." Unlike Sundark Hold this one was based in a bowl shaped cavern, with all the buildings able to see the giant, ziggurat shaped palace which squatted menacingly at the centre of the city. The entire city was built out of the red sandstone of the walls, and given the dark hemisphere was already moving across the sun globes affixed to the roof, the stones on the far side of the city seemed to have taken on the ominous hue of blood.

They followed the road down towards the palace of Moonshadow Hold, tall Dokkalfar standing guard at the base of the stairs leading up into the palace. They stood up perfectly erect and stationary, still as the stone which they guarded, except for their eyes, which relentlessly swept the crowd, searching for any threat. The crowd had grown thicker around them, the news of surfacers travelling with him had created the stir that King Jori had hoped for. There was cheering and roaring from the crowd, but also a number of suspicious glances. Given the treatment of their folk on the surface, it was not surprising that most of the folk who dwelt in the Holds viewed outsiders with grave suspicion.

They marched up to the top of the stairs, the majority of Jori's guards peeling away to their chambers, led by one of the Moonshadow Hearth Guard. There were ten of them, the four from the surface, Jori and his five finest guards, who were allowed into the throne room. They could see the throne at the far end of the room, carved from black marble and chased with gold filigree. The normally empty expanse of the throne room was filled with benches and tables on this occasion, already groaning under the weight of food and strong ale. There was a passage between the tables, leading up to the high table where the King and his eldest son sat, greeting all of those who came to partake in the tournament. Turil was a strong man, a face like it was hammered from iron, and his immense black beard glimmered with the light of over a dozen rings, honour won both in battle and in the tourneys. His son was an equally sturdy Dwarf, although his beard lacked the ornamentation of his father. Both had weapons close at hand, the hafts just peeking above the table. A whole roast pig stood in front of them, one of the creatures which flourished underground, feeding on the fungi which grew there.

"Ah, Jori," King Turil bellowed, getting slowly to his feet, "Here at last." He paused and looked quizzically at the king, "Why do you bring surfacers into our midst? They have no place at Tyril's coming of age." He roared across the room, his head turning red as his legendary temper came to a boil.

"Peace, Turil, peace." Said Jori calmly, raising a hand to forestall any rage on the part of his fellow monarch, "May I present to you my champion; Skjarla, the last Valkyrie." Jori's face was frozen in ice as he fought to keep the smug grin of satisfaction from his face, pleased by the stir his announcement had caused. Indeed, there was a moment of stunned silence at this pronouncement, followed by a rippling wave of excited whispering.

"Who are the other two? I have never seen their like in my dealings with either the Haemocracy or the Nomad tribes." The king responded, still tetchy, glowering at his rival who had sought to steal his thunder.

Domitia interrupted, "I am Domitia, and the heir to the Roman Empire, with me is my guardian, Centurion Metellus." King Jori shot her an angry glare for her interruption, but Turil seemed satisfied by this response.

He turned his attention back to Jori and Skjarla, "You claim that this woman is the last Valkyrie, the Ancient of War, what proof do you offer?" His voice held a trace of scorn, clearly unconvinced that this woman could be of Asgard.

Jori simply nodded to Skjarla, they had agreed about this beforehand. All she did was to raise Dreyrispa high above her head, the light catching the twin heads of the spear. There was a rush of air through the chamber as all of its occupants gasped as one. The other kings, including Turil looked darkly at Jori, envious of his champion.

Turil did his best to swallow his pride, and said as graciously as he could, "I congratulate you on finding such a champion, clearly it will make Tyril's coming of age an event to live long in the memory of all who gather here."

Jori nodded to the king, and was led to his seat by one of the stewards, gratified to hear that the topic of every conversation which drifted to his ear was Skjarla, the Valkyrie. He leant across to Dombrek, "Ask around, I could only see seven of the Kings here, find out what has happened to the others." The surly Dwarf nodded to his master before getting to his feet and making his way through the crowd of Dwarves, off in search of one of the servants who may actually know something. Jori turned happily to Skjarla, "Ah, you will win me much glory in the coming weeks. I don't know what the format will be, but I am sure that you'll be up to the challenge." He laughed and slapped her heartily on the back.

Skjarla was not that worried by the prospect of fighting in the Blood Eye, she had done prize fighting of this sort before, as distasteful as it was to admit it. She looked around the room, noting how the other champions were now obviously noticeable, carefully studying her, or anxiously talking to their masters. She knew that it would be an interesting contest, and as to the format of the thing, Turil had been playing his cards very close to his chest. The strangest feeling was that, with the room so dominated by Dwarves, she towered above the crowd, save for the lone islands of graceful Dokkalfar. After years on the surface it was a peculiar sensation.

Dombrek returned, "I've just spoken to the Steward, the people from Hiddenwave Hold have refused to come, and no one has heard from Sky's End in a generation, so they are unlikely to be here either. Nightfast Hold is expected tomorrow." He grinned nastily as Helania who he saw flinch at the news, worried that someone would recognize her.

Jori nodded, "Well, that is of no real bearing on the contest, Hiddenwave have never been fighters and frankly the absence of the smell of fish is a blessing rather than anything else. Sky's End is different, but they were always a solitary bunch anyway, who knows what's going on up there. You've served me well Dombrek, grab some ale and meat. We'll discuss the other champions later; there can't be any who can hope to take on a Valkyrie." Skjarla found that she did not share the Dwarf King's high spirits; she suspected that with her such an obvious threat, the other Kings and their champions would try to find a way to level the field.

She turned to Helania, "What do you know of the two Holds who have not come, I cannot remember ever visiting those cities."

Helania seemed grateful for the opportunity to take her mind off the impending arrival of the representatives of

Nightfast Hold. "Hiddenwave is on the coast to the east and far to the south, just north of the Black Mountains and at the end of Darkwater Bay. It is said to have an internal lake in its cavern, where the sea comes into the cave itself. It is meant to be quite spectacular there. Sky's End lies in the other direction, on the north eastern edge of the Haemocracy, beneath the mountains there. They are a grim people, constantly believing that they're under threat, always preparing for what they call the second Ragnarok. Most of the other Dwarves think they're crazy."

Skjarla interrupted quietly, "Given the rise of the Children I think they may have a point."

"True, but they are mainly worried about the Haemocracy seeking to expand into their territory. While the main bit of the Hold is below ground, they have a lot more people on the surface than most of the other Holds."

Skjarla worried that the reason that no one had heard from Sky's End in a generation was because no one was left, and if that was the case then it was possible the whoever had destroyed the Hold would have access to the Ways. That was a terrifying thought. The Haemocracy with the ability to go beyond the deserts of Vfar, or the Children of the Dragon able to pop up anywhere on the Continent that they so chose.

The festivities continued into the night, emptied platters of food instantly replenished by the well trained staff, and regular toasts to the coming of age of the young Dwarf Prince. There was little to do that evening besides drinking, until the festivities came to a close when Turil got unsteadily to his feet and proclaimed in a loud voice. "Friends, the evening is drawing to a close, Go to your chambers and rest in all of the comfort and splendour that Moonshadow Hold can offer. Tomorrow, at midday, we will hold the presentation of the Champions to the people of the Hold, down in the sand of the Blood Eye. Kings and Queens of the Dwarves and the Dokkalfar, this will be a tourney to remember, this I promise you." Jori was taking that to mean that the presence of a Valkyrie would make it special, but Skjarla read some darker threat into those words. She knew that Dwarven honour was all that kept open fighting from breaking out between the Holds in a place like this, but at one fell swoop a man could eliminate half of his rivals, if he so chose.

The rooms they were allocated were indeed well appointed, Skjarla had again found herself sharing with Helania, which was no problem to her. The pair of them had had to wait until they closed the door once they found out that poor Metellus was to share a room with only his mistress before bursting into a fit of giggles. They knew how shy Metellus was where his mistress was concerned, and they both had a good idea as to his true feelings for her. That coupled with the Roman aristocrat's desire for properness and her love of privacy meant that this could be an awkward couple of weeks. At least there were separate beds in the room, which was a small blessing.

Helania ran her hand against the red sandstone walls of the room, enjoying the feeling of the rough stone against her skin, a few grains tumbling onto the floor. It still amazed her that she, a woman who had grown up in such poverty that her mother had been forced to sell her services, was now sleeping in a palace and had visited far of cities like Leopolis and Taureum. She sometimes wondered if she would go back and try to find her mother, but she doubted it. She meant little to her, ever since she had revealed that they had sold her body to the highest bidder. She felt little but contempt for her, but while she did understand that their circumstances had forced them to such a situation, she couldn't forgive her mother the decision though.

The beds they had been provided here were again little more than stone plinths, covered with a straw filled mattress and topped with rough cloth. Not the luxury that one might have expected in a Dwarven Palace, but at the same time, they both knew that the very best furnishings would have been reserved for the visiting Kings and Queens. The two of them were merely grateful for the fact that they were not choked by dust that evening. Instead, they were able to sleep through until the clarion call of a horn sounded across the city. They were being summoned to the morning meal, and then Skjarla would be presented to the crowds in the Blood Eye.

As they were led through the corridors of the palace, the red walls glowing with a strange, pinkish-purple hue as the blue light of the glow stones shone upon them, Helania leant close to Skjarla. "I guess you're looking forward to this challenge?"

"Not really," Skjarla whispered back, "I can't really win. If I win then it is expected, and if I lose then the reputation of the Valkyries will be shattered. Plus, everyone will view me as the biggest threat, so by fair means or foul, they will be trying to even things out."

"You don't think they'd do that do you?" Helania asked slightly breathlessly.

Skjarla sighed at the naivety of her companion. "Helania, you of all people should know how protective the Old races are about their honour, and there is much honour at stake here. Can you honestly say that you wouldn't suspect some people of trying to win the contest by any means?"

Helania was about to answer when they came into the main room and caught sight of Domitia and Metellus at the edge of the crowd. Both of them walked over to their companions, forestalling any further conversation. Domitia was looking quite pleased with herself, "I have been speaking to one of the Dokkalfar rulers, and I think her name was Estraela. She knew what was going on in Rome at the moment, apparently their Hold was recently visited by a trader who had been there several months ago. The latest news is that my father still lives, not only that but Tarpeus is apparently in disgrace, barred from the bosom of Rome until it is known for sure whether or not he had some hand in my disappearance." So that was why she was in such a good mood.

Metellus interjected, earning himself a reproachful glance from his mistress, "Yes Domina, but nothing has yet been done about his network of supporters. While they still live you're in danger. Plus that news is several months old, and it will take a few months to get back to Rome, the situation could be completely different by the time you return." He looked at her imploringly, "Domina, we must return from a position of strength, able to dictate terms if the situation demands it, any other way is madness."

Domitia's face fell and she looked as if she had just eaten something sour as she pulled a face. "I suppose you're right Centurion." She looked around the room, her eyes making note of all of the rulers and lords assembled there, "And if I am going to build support for my attempt to reclaim what is rightfully mine, then I can think of few better places to start doing it." She finished with a flourish and headed off into the crowd to mingle with the rulers, Metellus at her heels like the loyal hound he was.

Skjarla couldn't help but be revolted by the naked ambition of the other woman, even though she admitted that this was very much Domitia's element, rather than her own. It must be strange in the upper echelons of Rome, the constant jockeying for position, having to read beyond what was said to you. She had been to that city several times, but almost always just to do a job of some form, never to get embroiled in the murky world of Roman politics.

She was interrupted in her thoughts as Jori came out of the crowd to grab her, saying cheerfully, "Skjarla, I trust you had a pleasant night's sleep." Adding more quietly, "Do you have to spend so long in the company of the whore? People from the Nightfast Hold delegation have recognized her from the description given by her madam and are anxious to get their hands on her." Skjarla started to tense and he laid a calming hand on her, "I have explained that she is under my protection for the time being, but it does not make me look good if my champion is spending all her time with a whore." He glared at her seriously, trying to threaten the Valkyrie who made a point of looking at him as nonchalantly as she could.

"Jori, you asked me to fight for you in the Blood Eye and I agreed, but at no point did you say that I had to abandon my friends." She looked down at the Dwarven King pointedly, feeling a flash of satisfaction as his gaze slipped away from hers.

He had looked like he was about to make an angry retort when king Turil got to his feet, standing in front of his throne. "Friends and Champions, the time has come. We will travel through the city to the Blood Eye, to introduce the champions who will be competing for glory at my son's coming of age. King Jori, your champion will do me the honour of walking with me." A quick glance down showed that Jori was not happy with this arrangement; his champion would be seen walking with Turil rather than him. It didn't matter that she would be presented to the crowds as his champion, their first memory would be of her marching down the main road of the Hold beside their King.

The gathering formed up just inside the palace, at the top of the steps. Tyril in front of his father and Skjarla at the head of the column, Jori just behind with the two Romans, then the other kings and queens. Helania had been banished to the back of the column, but that did not worry her overly much, she was quite happy to be away from the dark looks of the delegation from Nightfast Hold.

At a signal from Tyril horns struck up and the procession lurched into motion, steadily making its way down the palace steps to the road, each side of which was packed with cheering crowds. At the front of the crowds there were small groups of people looking more closely at the champions than anything else; Skjarla guessed that these were the book-keepers. They would be trying to work out what odds to offer on the champions before the contest had even started, trying to work out how best to part people from their money.

As she walked beneath the streaming cloths and between the throngs of cheering Dokkalfar and Dwarves she couldn't help but chuckle at the festive atmosphere, which was to be bought with the blood and sweat of the champions. Turil do not look up, still waving to his people as he asked, "Does something amuse you Valkyrie?" his voice carefully neutral.

"No, but I am confused as to why you are so happy to have me in your son's coming of age tourney."

She glanced across and saw the merest flicker of a smile beneath that thick black beard, "Because it suits me. Jori thinks that all the honour will be his through having you compete in his colours. Why you chose to do so I don't know or much care, I'm sure you have good reason. He doesn't realise that the people are unlikely to remember who the Valkyrie fought for, they will only remember that on the days when my son came of age, a Valkyrie fought before him." She heard the Dwarven King chuckle mirthlessly, "Honestly, the fool Jori has done me a favour, but then he is like his father, only looking for the short gain."

The conversation fell silent as they continued along the main road, people calling out Tyril's name for the most part, but Skjarla was surprised to hear more than a few cheering her as well. The palace servants must have got the word out about her. She had to wonder if the canny Dwarf next to her had ordered that they do so, to create extra anticipation of the coming tourney. It didn't matter, they were approaching the Blood Eye, in this case a worryingly apt name. The champions entered through a round tunnel which, when carved from the dark red sandstone did indeed look like a bloody eye socket. The rest of the crowds were pushing their way into the tiered banks of seats which stretched high above their heads.

Skjarla heard Domitia's voice behind her, "I never thought I'd be entering something so close to the Colosseum from this angle." There was a strange similarity between the Dwarven Blood Eye and the Roman amphitheatre, the steep banks of seats for the public, the enclosed area for the rich and powerful members of the Hold. The subterranean societies were highly stratified, and nowhere was this more apparent than at the Blood Eye, where your seating went hand in hand with your rank. There were small children running the length and breadth of the stands, taking bets and calling out the odds as they went. Elsewhere tradesmen were doing a brisk trade in food and especially ale, the Dwarves especially were fond of strong drink with their contests and bloodshed.

Tyril had broken away from the front of the column, strolling casually out into the red sand of the Moonshadow Blood Eye as he soaked up the applause and cheers of the crowd. As the audience began to quieten down again the announcer started up, his voice booming around the stands, no artifice needed for it to reach every ear. "This Tourney has been provided by the magnanimity of our king Turil Hammerhand in honour of his son Tyril Hammerhand. On this day, to celebrate our own prince becoming a man in the eyes of the people," Skjarla tired of listening to the blathering platitudes of the announcer and allowed her mind to wander.

She came back to the present when Jori jerked her arm, the two of them walking sedately into the sands of the Blood Eye. Skjarla was surprised to see that they were the last in the ring, but this meant she was not surprised to see a red tint to Jori's face, the King was clearly furious at what he deemed as a snub. Skjarla realised that it was more to the benefit of the other Holds that they had been held until last, if she had been the first in she doubted that any of the other champions would have been noticed at all. She heard the announcers voice bellowing as she walked out into the centre of the arena. There was silence as he spoke, the populous shocked at the appearance of someone other than a Dwarf as the champion of a Dwarven king.

"People of Moonshadow Hold last, but most definitely not least, I present to you your final champion. Fighting on behalf of King Jori, lord of Sundark Hold, the Ancient of War, the last Valkyrie, and Skjarla." She could see his mouth still moving but the words he was trying to get out were drowned out by the excited chatter of every single member of the crowd. Some doubted the veracity of his statement, others were talking about how excited they were to have the opportunity to watch what should be a unique event in the history of their people.

She took the opportunity to cast a cursory glance across the champions who occupied the ring with her. Of the eight other champions, five were Dwarves, and the other three were Dokkalfar, two of whom were women. That wasn't the surprise, Dokkalfar girls were often fine fighters, and Helania was proof of that. No, the shock was the champion from Daybreak Hold. A female Dwarf, clearly a solid fighter or she would not have been made champion, the fact that she was made champion at all spoke volumes as to her ability. Some of them wore heavy plate armour, clad from head to toe in shining steel, others looked to be more agile, more leather than metal on them, what skills they had to use the blades which hung by their sides would soon be apparent.

She was surprised as they were ushered out of the arena, their tourney would begin the following day; Turil wanted to give his people more time to slaver over the list of entrants. They marched out of the Blood Eye, chased out by the sounds of the crowds roaring cheers. Skjarla found that she missed the rush and anticipation of real battle, to her this whole thing seemed so artificial. Still if it was the price for the safety of the people then she was happy to pay it. Life in the palace seemed dull though, as she was escorted back to the palace, it was very strange after years of living hard and frugally to be presented with such opulence. She didn't envy the others, back down the Ways, but she knew she would feel more comfortable back there, a more honest life.

***

At that moment Accipiteri and Sigmund were deep in conversation, the column had been pushed hard for the last few days, chased by yipping, hooting calls echoing down the walls of the Ways, seeming to emerge from every crevice and imperfection in the stonework. Their three guides had been nervous, they knew what was going on, and had told the few leaders of the column. Smaparmar were gathering for an attack on the column, and the calls that were making everyone jumpy were them summoning more of their kind to the feast. Torae had explained that it was not the Smaparmar which were the problem, it was if they lured in the bigger beasts, the Hyrrstein or Jormungandrr that was when they'd really have problems. The other major issue facing the people of the column was that the lights in the Ways had no dimming cycle, it was bright as the noonday sun all the time, there was no respite, no relief. It was beginning to wear on some of the people, making most of the normally kind people of Lonely Barrow short of temper and quite aggressive. As Accipiteri rubbed his forehead exhaustedly he couldn't help but think that a fight might be a good way to burn off some of their pent up aggression.

The Way houses were defensible, but there would not be room to squeeze all of the refugees into one of them, and he didn't want to subject some innocent families to danger on their account. The problem with the Ways was that they were dead flat and dead straight, there was nowhere that really qualified as a readily defensible location, and all they could hope to do was to out run their pursuers. It was seventeen days out of Sundark Hold that they lost their first person. With the perpetual shrieking of the Smaparmar as they chased through the rocks and passages alongside the Ways, and the permanent bright lights of the glow stones set into the walls, exhaustion had claimed its first victim. It was one of the eldest members of the column, but to lose their first person to fatigue after having been through so much together was hard on everyone.

The old woman, a grey-haired individual by the name of Helda, had been found dead after the evening rest period, her life having simply expired. She was found upon the ground, her eyes open and staring blankly out into the nothingness of the Ways beyond them, her face relaxed, as if every care had been lifted from her. It made Sigmund look more closely at the people he had known all throughout his life. The changes had been so gradual that he had not noticed what had been happening to them, it was only noticeable when he compared them to what they had been like when they had left their home. The people were thinner, many of those who were as old as his father would have been were going prematurely grey, and everyone's cheeks were hollow, their eyes slightly sunken. It was even more pronounced among the warriors; they ate no more than the rest but burnt extra energy training with their blades. The only difference between them and the others was in their gaze. While the majority of the people's eyes were tired and worn out by their journey, the soldiers had a steely glint to their eye, a hardness that was frightening in its coldness.

The thing that really stuck in the throats of everyone that day was that there was no time to bury Helda, all they could do was move her corpse to the edge of the pathway and continue on their journey. Each person who walked past her took a long look at the body, and the sight of that pathetic mound of flesh stiffened their resolve, gave them the will to survive. The true horror though, pursued them down the stone passage, the sound of breaking bones and the excited shrieks as the Smaparmar found the corpse and began to feast. The people of Lonely Barrow and their guardians quickened their pace, hurrying along the Ways as they tried to out run their pursuers.

Sigmund fell in beside Tomani, trying not to focus on her mesmerizing white eyes, to ask, "What will happen to the Way Houses we leave behind us."

"It will depend on how hungry the beasts are. So long as they seal up the gates then they will be fine, the Smaparmar will not want to let a feast such as this escape them, they will chase hard and are unlikely to stop for long."

"That is good," said Sigmund with heartfelt honesty. When Tomani glanced at him curiously he shrugged somewhat sheepishly for expressing such a sentiment, "Enough people have died to protect us, I would not have more blood on our hands."

"Death is but a fact of life, your people have just not realised that all they are doing is postponing theirs," She said this with no malice, just a bored fatalism that Sigmund found incredibly disconcerting.

"How can you say something like that? How can you believe something like that?" he asked incredulously.

She smiled thinly, her face cool and chill, "I knew my grandfather, and he lived through the Cataclysm. That taught my people that the end is something that comes, but that you can choose the manner of your end. You cannot imagine how it feels for all that was known and comfortable to you to be changed, gone forever in the blink of an eye."

"Neither do you," Sigmund said, somewhat more harshly than he meant to.

She looked at him stonily, "Maybe not personally, but there are still a few Dokkalfar alive who lived through Ragnarok. They tell the stories of the earth shifting on that terrible day, of families buried alive. For you humans it has been over a dozen generations, for you the Ragnarok is just a distant memory, a story to be told on cold winter nights, for us it is our very recent history, it is our everlasting shame." She paused for breath, looking at him levelly, he had to break the eye contact, and he felt so ashamed of his outburst and the reaction that it had provoked. It seemed even worse to him because she didn't seem that angry about it, more worn out now that she had finished her tirade.

He fell back from her, feeling embarrassed and trying to disappear into the crowd of the refugees, but she wouldn't let him, dropping back with him, until they were both standing at the rear of the column. She looked at him, a twinkle of laughter in her eyes, "I shouldn't have snapped like that, now come on, we cannot fall too far behind; I have been told that you are the one we really need to look after in this column."

"I can take care of myself," he said, realising just how childish he must sound saying something like that, his voice must sound so whiny.

"I do not doubt it, but we have heard the whispers of what you carry. It is a precious burden that must not fall from your fingers." She looked very serious as she spoke, the turned and jogged to catch up with the back end of the column, glancing over her shoulder as she said, "If we're lucky we'll run into a patrol before too long, extra swords never hurt anyone."

He shook his head and pumped his legs a little fast to catch up with the rear of the column, offering his encouragement to those who were flagging. He thought that, as bad as it was, it was a good thing that Helda had died, she had spurred the others to fight harder to hang onto every spark of life that they had. There were still over six weeks of travelling ahead of them, and there was almost certainly violence and death waiting for them before they reached Moonshadow Hold.

Chapter 13

Back in Moon shadow Hold Skjarla was preparing for her first appearance in the tournament. All of the Champions would be fighting at once today, against a number of monsters that had been captured and smuggled into the Hold. This was so that the crowds could get an idea of the challenger's abilities. Money would change hands after today, as those who knew when to bet had held their money until they had seen the champions in action for the first time. They well knew that the finest armour could disguise a poor warrior, just as a great warrior could thrive in unadorned steel.

The champions had surprised her quite a lot; they were all out to win the tournament, but at the same time there was no overt malice towards their competitors, they appreciated skill as much as the audience. Indeed, most of them seemed surprisingly thrilled to be competing against a Valkyrie, as the representative from Starfall Hold had said. "You might as well compare yourself to the best, there is no honour in challenging those beneath you, but against a Valkyrie there is honour even in defeat." It was a fair comment but it meant that, as Skjarla had worried, everyone was out to beat her.

She waited for the rest of the champions to make ready for the first challenge, apparently there would be eleven challenges through the weeks of the tournament, one for each of the Holds. Skjarla couldn't help but wonder if any of them would be left by the end of the contest. The wooden doors to the arena opened and all thought ceased, she bared her teeth in a lupine smile, her blood rising as she relished the thought of the coming combat. The small group jogged out into the middle of the ring, most of them saluting the crowd, although Skjarla kept her eyes focused on the other doorways into the arena, the blood red sand soft beneath her feet.

There was no word from the announcer, just a hushed intake of breath from the crowd as the doors swung open, and out of the darkness beneath the spectators burst forth the worst that the lands beneath Midgard had to offer. Three giant Hyrrstein emerged from the darkness, their fiery bodies flaring angrily as they took in the scene, sighting their prey in the arena. Hyrrstein were elemental creatures, beasts of fire and stone, implacable destroyers, made so by the very nature of the elements from which they were crafted. The rough, angular stones of their bodies were just visible beneath the fires which smouldered across their forms, the joins of the stones were the only weakness, and bringing one down was an almost impossible task. Beneath the glowing flames you could make out the vaguely human shape of the stones, but far bigger, standing nearly four paces tall. They held no weapons, but they needed none, a single blow from those crushing fists would certainly be fatal.

Skjarla roared her battle cry and sprang forward, her footsteps kicking up puffs of sand as she drove against the yielding surface. She didn't bother to look around her to see if the others were following her in her mad, headlong dash towards the three Hyrrstein. She threw herself into a headlong slide between the legs of the middle creature, the sand cushioning her landing as she rolled beneath its legs. As she came into a low crouch she swung Dreyrispa in a low arc, scything the blades against the backs of the creature's legs. One of the heads bit deep into the back of the creature's knee and it roared in agony, the sound making the whole of the Blood Eye shake with the pain of it.

A sword of fire flared in the Hyrrstein's hand and slammed into the sand next to her. The creature was limping badly, but the magics in its body stopped it from toppling. She flung herself to the side as the next Hyrrstein converged on her, a flick of her gaze showed her that the rest of the champions were still standing at the far side of the arena. So much for the unity of the champions, she could see that they were studying her moves for a while, working out where her weaknesses lay. She was lucky in that one of the Hyrrstein seemed more interested in the other Champions than her, but she knew that two of them would present more of a challenge than she could meet.

She danced away from the two Hyrrstein as they advanced on her, one charging forward, the other dragging its wounded leg, digging a furrow in the sand as it did so. With one slower than the other they weren't able to pin her against the walls of the arena, but their size meant that she could barely get close enough to strike a blow. She fended off one strike, almost dislocating both her shoulders as the absorbed the impact of the overhead swing, a lesson that deflecting them was far easier than stopping them. She tried to use the same trick that had worked against the Abhorrens back in the woods near Lonely Barrow, using one to block the other, but that merely had a terrifying result.

There was a juddering, screaming sound as stone grated on stone, a whooshing as fire licked across the surface of the stones with renewed vigour. The two Hyrrstein moulded into one, a gigantic mound of stone and fire, whose head was well above the parapet at the top of the arena, level with the first few rows of seating. There were screams of panic from the crowd; no one had ever seen

Hyrrstein do anything like this before. As the rocks and boulders of the giant Hyrrstein settled themselves into position Skjarla beckoned to the other champions, most of whom were fused in place by shock.

They swiftly came back to their senses, three of them keeping the attention of the smaller Hyrrstein while the other five came to join Skjarla for the formidable challenge of the giant pillar of stone and fire. The thing was swinging scything blades of fire, leaving glowing trials in the sand as it tried to strike out at its attackers. Luckily the thing was a clumsy as it was big, its movements were easily read and avoided, but they all knew that if the Hyrrstein got a clean blow on them then they were dead. She flung herself to the left as one of the two flaming blades plunged into the ground next to her, flames licking across the sand, the landing jolting every bone in her body.

She shook her head to clear her vision only to have to throw herself to the left once again, this time to dodge the smoking body of one of the Dwarven champions sent flying through the air where she had just been. The body clanged against the wall of the arena, then fell to the ground with a fleshy thud, to lie smoking and unmoving on the blood red sand. "Go for the knees," She screamed at her companions, "Bring it down." The only way they stood a chance against the hulking behemoth was to strike for the neck, not something they could do while it was ten paces above their heads. The Dwarves set to, one with an axe and another two with their heavy mauls, striking at the joints as they desperately tried to avoid the blows of the blades. Finally one of the hammers shattered the right knee joint, the creature screaming and toppling to the side, an inferno bursting forth from it as it hit the ground.

Skjarla knew she had moments to finish the beast before it recovered itself, even on the ground it would be a truly formidable opponent. She leapt onto its body, trying to ignore the flames licking up her calves, and the horrible burning sensation in her feet as she sprinted across its body. She was so glad that she had dispensed of her cape, as one of the two Dokkalfar women's one caught fire. Her screams were heart wrenching as she tried to tear the burning cloth from her back before it touched the flammable grease which had burnished her leather armour. Skjarla forced herself to put it all out of her mind as she leapt into the air, plunging down, and all her weight behind Dreyrispa's point as she drove the spear into the gap where head met body.

There was a soft rushing noise as the flames atop the rock guttered and died. Skjarla lay where she had fallen, cradled in the neck of the dead Hyrrstein. The only thing in her senses was the constant pain in her legs, the slightest movement of her left sending shockwaves of agony coruscating up her body. She hoped that the other Hyrrstein was not beyond the other champions; she knew that she didn't have the strength to rejoin the fray. There was no noise from the crowd, and Skjarla was barely aware of being lifted from the red sand, carried back to the palace on the shoulders of the other champions. They felt guilty about leaving the Valkyrie to tackle two of the Hyrrstein by herself, and the deaths of three of their number weighed heavily upon them.

Helania pushed her way nearer to Skjarla once they returned to the palace, the Valkyrie was still barely conscious, the pain from her burns blocked all else. Outside the crowds were already laughing happily as they relived the moment of her suicidal bravery. It sickened Helania that they seemed to have no concern for the Valkyrie's health. There were three Dokkalfar healers clustered around the foot of her bed, her armoured boots and greaves lay discarded against the wall. The air was thick with the sound of muttering voices and the pungent smell of their unguents. The one on the far side of the bed held an alabaster jar in his withered right hand, while the left smeared the powerful smelling substance gently across the burns. It tore at Helania's heart to see the Valkyrie, the proudest woman she had ever met, the closest thing she had had to a role model, flinch at the lightest touch.

The doctors finally left the room to treat the other wounds sustained by the champions, although none were as serious as Skjarla's burns, they had either died or come through relatively unscathed. Helania perched on the edge of her bed, peering across the gulf at her companion. The Valkyrie's forehead was beaded with sweat, and every time she tossed in her narcotic induced sleep her face creased with pain. The most nauseating thing on the way back to the palace had been Jori, ecstatic at the fact that Skjarla had killed the giant and anxious to return her to the ring so she could represent him once more.

***

Five days later Skjarla was on the mend, the healers had been to visit on a regular basis but they had declared that although the skin was pink and oozing that the wound was clean and that there was no infection. All that she needed was a few weeks rest and she would be back to normal, they brought a special salve to rub on which would prevent the skin from tightening up too much with scar tissue. Skjarla was getting increasingly irritated, her burnt feet meant that she could not walk to the jacks, and instead had to have one of the servants clear away the night soil pot twice daily. She found it humiliating; Helania could understand but still thought that her friend was being ridiculously proud.

She heard a rap on the wooden door to their shared room and went to answer it. It was king Jori, rubbing his hands anxiously, "So, what did they say? Is she able to fight, the next round of the challenges is next week and she needs to take part."

Helania choke on a scowl before responding sharply, "The healers agreed she needed several weeks of rest, so no. She won't be able to fight."

Jori sucked in an angry breath and then hissed at Helania, "Well you'd better find some way of motivating her, and she needs to be on the sand of the arena in six days time. You can start by telling her that if she isn't there then I'll be handing you over to the Nightfast King, and then we can see how much she really cares for her friends," he added cruelly.

Helania slammed the door in his face, but her time with the irregulars and Skjarla had taught her one thing, panic solves nothing. Her mind spun as fast as it could, chasing thoughts through the maze like passages of her brain as she tried to find a way out of the problem. She had no doubt that Jori was serious in his threat. Suddenly it came to her, how she would get out of this, but she would have to be so very careful so as not to give anything away, what she was planning would certainly result in her death if they found out what she was doing.

On the day of the next challenge Skjarla presented herself at the front of the palace, her helmet already on, a thin piece of cloth woven over her face where the helmet left her mouth exposed. She explained that the dust was irritating her throat and she didn't want any more problems with her body. The other champions laughed uncomfortably, still feeling guilty about their treatment of her. They processed down through the Hold, Skjarla waving to the crowd as they cheered her name, soaking up the adulation, twirling Dreyrispa in front of her, carving swirling patterns of light in the air. The other champions were looking at her suspiciously but she took no notice.

Once they reached the tunnel beneath the Blood Eye, waiting to run out into the blood red sands she kept apart from the others, silent as she prepared for the coming challenge. The horns blared their triumphant call, summoning them out to battle; they all knew that this was going to be hideous, given the need to build the spectacle further from the previous challenge. From the darkness of the far end of the arena there was a low, sibilant hissing sound, and out of the darkness slithered an angry Jormungandrr.

The creature was rare even beneath the Holds, preferring the black subterranean pools and damp, dank, dark pits to make its lairs. This one was a monster, its green scales turning white with age, nearly twenty paces long from snout to tail, and the two arms growing out of its serpentine body tipped with claws which dripped poison. At least it did not have the venomous breath of Jormungand from Ragnarok, one of the small blessings to come out of the cataclysm. The red eyed head, almost one pace long was almost completely jaw, filled with razor sharp fangs; pieces of meat could be seen trapped between them.

The champions fanned out, the Dokkalfar pushing to the sides while the heavily armoured dwarves stood in the centre of the line with Skjarla. She could feel her palms sweating beneath the leather lining of her armoured gloves, her heart racing as she stared at the Jormungandrr. She noticed that as she swung Dreyrispa lightly in her hands the nightmarish creature tracked her movements, swaying from side to side hypnotically.

Suddenly the creature lunged forward, moving incredibly quickly for something that size, the sand making a hissing noise as the Jormungandrr shifted across it. One of the Dwarves shifted to the side, the talons on the left hand gouging three furrows in his shield, the poison smoking slowly as it ate away at the metal. The others instantly converged on its tail, hoping to sever the creature's spine and cripple it. Instead one of the Dokkalfar was sent flying through the air to crash against the wall of the arena by a flick of its giant muscles. The man got unsteadily to his feet, still alive but clutching his side in pain, some ribs must be broken. There was no time to worry about him as the Jormungandrr turned its baleful eye on Skjarla, its thin pink tongue licking its teeth malevolently.

She stood on the balls of her feet, light and ready to spring in any direction, Dreyrispa braced against her forearm, angling up alongside her body. The Jormungandrr snapped forwards, she spun to the left, the spear licking out like a tongue of fire during the pirouette, leaving a smear of inky black blood leaking from the scales in its side. The creature screamed with rage rather than pain and chased after her. She dodged again, Dreyrispa shooting out once more as the Jormungandrr shot past her. Her lungs were burning, the cloth over her mouth meant that she could barely breathe, especially now that it had become soaked in sweat but she couldn't spare a hand to rip it off. Every inch of her consciousness was focused on keeping her away from the razor sharp teeth and talons that were so intent on ending her life. With every pass the creature was working out her strategy, swinging its arms wider and wider in an attempt to knock her to the ground where it could finish her. On the fourth pass Skjarla only dummied her movement this time but it was enough to fool the creature who flung its arms wide. Instead she dropped into a low crouch Dreyrispa pointing unwaveringly at the charging monstrosity.

The Jormungandrr twitched its head to the side, avoiding the point of Dreyrispa and locked its teeth onto her shoulder in a death grip. However, the thing couldn't stop its heavy body from crashing forwards onto the point of Skjarla's spear, the shining Asgardian metal punching through its pale belly to pierce the vital organs. The creature collapsed to the side, pulling her with it, the weight of its head dragging on her shoulder, the teeth scratching the steel. One of the other champions came over and used his hammer to smash the monster's jaw, allowing Skjarla to escape the vicelike grip of the razor sharp teeth.

The crowd were cheering as the champions saluted the crowd and then marched from the red sand of the arena. Skjarla was tired and still barely able to breathe beneath the sweat soaked cloth across her mouth, but frankly she didn't have the energy to pull it away. She walked on with slumped shoulders, tiredly carrying Dreyrispa next to her. It was surprising how tired she felt now that the burst of adrenaline had worn off.

She returned to the palace and made her way back to the room she shared, and pushed open the door. As soon as the door was closed she started to peel off her armour, glancing over at Skjarla lying asleep on the bed. Helania had had to drug her food to make sure the Valkyrie would sleep through the contest. She felt bad about it, but there nothing Skjarla could have done to fight today, and there was no way that she was being handed over to the Nightfast Hold people. The Valkyrie had barely moved, but given the new scars on the pauldron of her armour, she didn't doubt that Skjarla would discover her deception. It had been lucky that she had been able to fit into the Valkyrie's armour; she had had to wear an extra layer of clothes underneath to stop the armour from rattling round. Reverentially she cleaned and replaced the armour on its stand next to Skjarla's bed, gently placing Dreyrispa next to it, caressing the worn wood of the haft one last time.

It had been the proudest moment of her life so far, wearing the hallowed armour, the last link to her people's long dead gods. She knew none of her generation would ever come so close to the divine. The adulation of the crowd had been incredible, but so had the fear; she had never realised how brave the Valkyrie was facing down such things without hesitation. She knew she couldn't have done it for four centuries. She looked down at Skjarla, sleeping peacefully, the narcotic still calming her system, she would have been annoyed if she had burnished the reputation of any other that day. Helania felt that it was her who had been done a service by just once being able to experience what it was to be Aesir. It was a memory she would cherish until the moment she died.

***

They were three weeks out of Moonshadow Hold and they were flagging. The column was now one of the walking dead, hollow cheeks and sunken eyes were evident on everyone's faces. They had lost over seventy people to exhaustion, many of them the oldest members of the column. The more worrying fact was that for the last few days the majority of the Smaparmar calls had been coming from beside the column, and now they were starting to echo down the Ways from in front of them. Torae had grimly explained that this mean that the Smaparmar had gathered in sufficient numbers for the cowardly creatures to consider attacking. They had had now moved in front of the column and were now just waiting for the people of Lonely Barrow to come to ground of their choosing.

Accipiteri had done all that he could, moving the majority of his warriors up to the front of the column, ready to break through any blockade that was thrown up. What worried him more was that the walls here were pitted with fissures and small crevices, the Smaparmar could hit the entire length of the column at once if they so chose. Braugr came to him one evening to give him some advice, "I have ordered the strongest of the draught animals moved up to the front of the column. We might be able to get them to pick up enough speed to break through a barricade; at the very least a stampede would flatten a few of the grey-skinned bastards." He spat noisily on the floor.

Accipiteri wearily raised his head, wrinkling his nose as a blast of air from inside his stinking armour hit his nostrils. "That's not a bad idea," he said exhaustedly, "I think that whatever is going to happen will hit us in the next day or so." He paused and looked around to make sure that there was no one listening too closely but everyone else was busily caught up in a world of their own fatigue. He looked hard at Braugr, "If it all goes to Hel then I want you to make sure Sigmund gets free. As much as I want to save these people nothing matches the importance of the Fang."

"Agreed, though it pains me to say it and I hope to whoever is listening that it will not come to that." Braugr shook his head angrily, his beard twitching as he did so.

The halt that day was called outside a Way House where they could refill their dwindling stocks of food. They had ceased to travel in days and just did it by the Way houses. There was no way of telling time in this infernal place, and when there is no respite from the glaring lights and the shrieking howls those journeys seemed endless. The people had long since given up on laying out their sleeping mats, just collapsing and trying to pass of into the blissful serenity of sleep as fast as they could. Sigmund and Accipiteri had been trying to keep the soldiers more disciplined, but there was only so much that they could do. The only ones who seemed unaffected by the whole thing were Iskander and the other Reavers who seemed relatively cheered by the coming prospect of a fight.

'I should have expected it,' Sigmund sighed to himself, 'Skjarla's great and really good to have around, but she's mad as an enraged bull, just like the rest of them.' He wouldn't have minded having the bloodthirsty Valkyrie here, but she definitely scared him. She was so remorseless and so focused on the Fang to the exclusion of all else. He leant against the wall of the Ways and allowed himself to slide down it, the stone grating against his dust-streaked armour. He was asleep before he hit the floor, and was being shaken awake before he even realised he had been asleep.

People were already getting numbly to their feet while others drifted amongst them handing out dry loaves of unleavened bread. Most of the food was simply taken from the carts and eaten as they walked; there was no time for anything else, not with them trying to escape from the shrieking Smaparmar. Sigmund had a small brainwave and went to find Iskander, who was walking easily and chatting with the other Reavers.

"Iskander, I need your help."

The others looked at him suspiciously but Iskander came to him easily enough, "What's the matter lad?" His head tilted to one side quizzically.

"I want you and your Reavers to go ahead of the column, we need some form of warning when we are going to hit the Smaparmar, give everyone a chance to prepare. Don't get yourselves killed; I only want a warning of what's ahead."

He could see the others nodding grimly behind Iskander, already slinging the less useful of their gear onto the carts. "That's a good idea, we'll go on ahead," Iskander grinned and clapped Sigmund on the shoulder, "Don't you worry, lad, we'll win through this one, should be a bit of a laugh." Sigmund shook his head as they loped easily down the cavern, passing by the front of the column. Reavers were mad to a man he thought.

They were not gone for long. The column was just drawing their day's march to a halt when Iskander and the others ran back to them. "There's a crude barricade set up about an hour's march down the Way. Pretty crude, but from the noise there's a lot of the little bastards down there."

Accipiteri looked to Braugr, "Any suggestions?"

The Dwarf smiled grimly, "Hit them hard, if we can shake them then the cowardly little sods will panic and run for it. But give them a sniff of victory and it's all over for us."

"Agreed," Iskander nodded solemnly.

Accipiteri thought for a moment, feeling the weight of expectation pressing down on him. "Stand everyone down, and give them double rations. There's no point in them dying on an empty stomach. Move the heaviest carts up to the front; we'll use them as a ram to break the barricades. We'll let everyone get a proper rest before we set off, but we can't wait for too long. The longer we wait the more Smaparmar that we'll face."

The others looked at him blankly, he could see how tired they all were, and the trials of the journey had pushed most of them to the limits of their endurance. He knew that, as exhausted as he was, he had to set an example to the others. He wished Skjarla was here, although she was not much of a people person she was a rock, utterly indefatigable and the people would follow her anywhere. He wasn't sure he had that kind of support yet.

The people were grateful for the break, and collapsed to sleep almost instantly. Accipiteri rested with them, but roused himself before the others. He in turn roused some people to break up one of the carts and cook some of the food up for the people; he knew that they would fight better after a warm meal. There were delighted cheers as the smell of food reached famished nostrils and woke the refugees. The people ate in silence, desperate to stuff down as much of the food as they could. Two of the heavy carts were wheeled up to the front of the column, and when everyone had eaten their fill they got underway. The Legionaries, there weren't enough veterans to think of them as Romans, and the Reavers in the front, the razor sharp point of the column, supported by over half of the fighters. The rest of the fighters were spread down the column, ready to deal with anything coming out of the walls, although he hoped it wouldn't come to it.

Accipiteri went to the head of the column, on the left of the two heavy carts with the Reavers, while Sigmund, Braugr and the legionaries were on the right. The carts rumbled slowly forward, the column silent as people prepared for the very imminent possibility of their deaths. It was horrible, waiting for the coming combat, fighting the urge to run in the opposite direction as fast as possible. The shrieking of the Smaparmar was getting louder, they could smell the column coming towards them and their bloodlust could be heard on the air.

When they could see the barricade Accipiteri gave the order to the two legionaries who were driving the carts to whip their beasts into a run. The oxen lowed in pain as the Romans set their whips to their hindquarters, breaking into a run as they tried to escape the stinging strikes. The column broke into a loping jog beside the carts, the legionaries raising their heavy wooden shields as the crude bows of the Smaparmar came into view. The roof of the Ways meant that the bows only had a range of about thirty or forty yards, enough for one volley before the lines crashed together.

Accipiteri hoped that the first charge would be enough to send the Smaparmar fleeing back into the darkness of their caverns, if not then it could be the end of the column. He and Braugr both knew that if nothing else, they needed to make sure they got Sigmund clear, the Fang must not get out of their sight. There was a soft rushing sound the prelude to the coming storm as the Smaparmar arrows whistled through the air, their feathered shafts hissing softly. The Reavers shifted under the shafts, most of them whistling overhead to smack dully into the flesh of the men and women behind them. A chorus of screams burst forth from the people behind. This sound was followed by the dull thud and the terrified bellows of the oxen who had crashed into the flimsy barricade. The wood splintered and the stones they had used to anchor the base shifted and gave, a gap opening up in the wall, into which the legionaries charged.

The Smaparmar were hideous from this close, their mottled grey skin looked like lichen covered stone, while their crude plates of jagged black iron gave them a menacing look. Beneath pointed helms viciously sharp teeth grinned in smiles thick with malice, while red eyes seemed to burn with crimson hatred. The creatures were well known for their cowardice, falling back from the unfamiliar fighting style of the legionaries. While their gangly limbs made them taller than Dwarves they barely came up to the shoulders of the burly legionaries, whose short swords were soon wet with thick green blood.

The fighters cut their way deep into the packed ranks of the Smaparmar, pressed on by the weight of the people behind them, crushing any fallen bodies beneath the stamping of panicked feet. "Spread out," bellowed Braugr, "Open a corridor for the column." The legionaries were quick to take up the call, forming a line while Braugr yelled at the people of Lonely Barrow. They formed an uneven line, holding open a barely passable corridor through which the refugees streamed.

Sigmund looked around him; he could tell that his people, the men and women of Lonely Barrow had barely two dozen shields between nearly one hundred and eighty souls. They didn't have the skill to hold a line with just their ragged assortment of blades and spears. Sigmund's gaze flickered around to Accipiteri, the Loptalfar cleaving heads with each swing of his mighty sword, even as he sheltered behind his polished round shield. His friend had had one made especially in Sundark Hold to replace the one ruined in their flight from the Abhorrens. "We have to push forward," he called desperately. The only response he got was a roar from Accipiteri who began to batter his way deep into the ranks facing him, swinging with wild abandon. A cheer went up from the people who followed his example, starting to cut their way forward, leaving the bodies of the wounded behind them to be loaded onto the passing carts.

Sigmund couldn't help but feel a stab of jealousy, he doubted that people would ever follow him the way they followed the gilded Alfar or the menacing Valkyrie, but he tried to dismiss such thoughts. He heard Braugr's voice above the din of combat, the sound of metal on metal ringing in his ears as people fought for their lives. "Last cart's through lads, fall back. Fall back." The people of Lonely Barrow turned smartly on their heels and pelted back to the column as fast as their feet would carry them. The legionaries were made of sterner stuff and pulled back in a more orderly fashion. They needn't have bothered, the carpet of grey bodies, dotted with the occasional human corpse, gave the Smaparmar pause. The creatures backed off, contenting themselves with hostile shrieking, the piercing noises rising and falling as they echoed the length of the passage.

There was no time to count the butcher's bill as the column swiftly continued down the passage with the warriors at the rear casting nervous glances over their shoulders. They had managed to collect all of the wounded, which was a blessing, but the sound of breaking bones as the Smaparmar descended upon the corpses was still sickening. They left the ravening beasts far behind them as they hurried on their way, the carts bouncing over every imperfection in the surface, eliciting pained groans from the wounded. Sigmund, at the rear of the column, could see the slender trail of blood drips where they had fallen between the floors of the carts, leaving a trail for the Smaparmar to follow if they had the nerve.

Accipiteri called the groaning column to a halt, the people breathing heavily as they pulled to a gradual, relieved halt. He looked around the group, the Reavers had already stopped to bandage and stitch each other's wounds, while the few legionaries were doing the same. The fighters from Lonely Barrow all bore the marks of the short, violent fight. Paying the price for their lack of armour, those who had managed to get their hands on one of the looted sets had fared better. They did their best to treat the wounded before they continued their seemingly endless journey into the infinity of the tunnel.

Chapter 14

Skjarla groaned as stiff muscles protested angrily at her exertions. The skin around her legs was still tender but was getting back to its usual, pliable self; she had been pushing herself in her training ever since she had been able to rise from her bed. She was preparing to fight in the final bout of the tourney. The horrendous attrition rate of Champions meant that the tournament had been cut from the planned eleven rounds to just three. Much as it irked her to be fighting at the beck and call of the stuck-up Dwarven king it at least gave her something to do. They were expecting their fellows from Lonely Barrow any day now, and yet there was no sign of them, not that there would be until they entered the final stretch of the Ways towards Moonshadow Hold.

She had taken to training more and more with Helania, dancing the spears with the young Dokkalfar. She smiled at the memory of her reaction when Helania had explained what she had done while Skjarla had been locked into her drug induced sleep. She had initially been horrified and angered, ordering a cowed Helania from her presence, but once Metellus had given her a full account of what had gone on she had mellowed a little. In truth it was a good idea, one that smacked of Loki cunning. Such things gave her hope that the old ways, of devil and cunning and bravery were not completely dead. The two of them were dressed simply in rough Dokkalfar robes, loose garments which reached down to the calf but left the arms bare, perfect for sparring. They danced around the soft sand of the training arena, simple lengths of wood in their hands knocking together in a deafening staccato rhythm.

As they came to a pause in the dance of spears she saw the ominous sight of King Turil waiting impatiently at the edge of the sandy training arena. Here there were no benches for him to sit upon, just the plain columns which held the high roof of this part of the Royal Palace, clearly something inspired by the Gymnasiums of the Roman Empire. Turil silently beckoned Skjarla over to him, his eyes colder than she had ever seen them before. It was strange, she thought as she brushed some stray black hairs from her sweat drenched brow, the King had always seemed amused by her competition in the Tourney, why the sudden grim look?

Quite roughly he took her by the arm, pulling her after him into one of the dusty corners of the colonnade. "Listen to me, as I am sure you well know the six remaining champions will fight one another, but what no one else knows is that the winner of that bout will face my son, who will win the honour of his own Tourney."

Skjarla looked at him suspiciously, her mind already knowing the answer, but she wanted the king to damn himself in her eyes on his own. "Why tell me this?"

He looked at her as if she were a simpleton, "Because I have no doubt whatsoever in my mind that you will win the bout of six, but you will," and he put deliberate emphasis on the word, "lose to Tyril."

Skjarla glared at the Dwarven King, her eyes boring down at him from over a foot above his bearded head. With an edge of steely menace in her voice she ground out, "And if I decide not to throw the fight?"

A cold, triumphant smile lit up Turil's face ominously; Skjarla felt her insides tighten slightly. Turil spoke calmly, as if discussing the weather. "Then I shall regretfully mistake the crowd of scruffy humans at the gates for an invasion and order my guards to bar the doors before driving the lot of them back into the tunnels with arrow fire." His eyes locked onto hers, before he waved his hand nonchalantly, "Of course, after my son has won I will be able to give proper consideration as to who could be at the gates of Moonshadow Hold, but until that time ..." He tailed off and grinned at her nastily.

Skjarla looked at the King scornfully before an icy stream of words slipped from between her tightly drawn lips. She was quivering with rage as she told Turil, "I swear this, upon everything I have ever held dear. For every one of those people who dies needlessly, I will exact the blood price from your son's flesh. I swear that you will watch him die the slowest, most painful and dishonourable death I can give him if you break your oath."

Turil shrugged, then looked at her coldly, "If by that I am to take it that you agree to our little bargain then you have nothing to worry about." He turned to leave, heading for the exit of the Gymnasium before calling over his shoulder. "Oh, and Valkyrie, make it convincing."

Skjarla returned to the arena, her knuckles white as they were clenched against the wood of her staff. She tilted her head slightly, concern writ large across her brow, "What was that all about?"

Skjarla shook her head angrily and snarled a single word, "Begin."

Some hours later Helania was slumped up against one of the pillars of the gymnasium, every inch of her body aching and some bruises already starting to come through, no doubt more would follow. She had no idea what had set her friend off, but the cold fury of Skjarla's rage had been truly terrifying. Even more annoying to Helania than her injuries was the fact that she had been disabused of the notion that she had been catching up to the Valkyrie.

Clearly she had much more to learn, given the ease with which her friend had disarmed her and floored her again and again. The most irritating part of that was not that Skjarla was better than she was, it was that she had been holding herself back to make the contest more even.

Helania spat out a sticky wad of phlegm, all she wanted was some water, but she was far too tired to move and get some. Metellus came to her with a flask and let himself slide down next to her. The soft expression on the usually stern face of the centurion invited her to vent her frustrations. "What am I supposed to do?" Her voice was heavy with bitterness, "I have studied her, trained with her, and how am I meant to get as good as her."

Her eyes scanned the room in the silence, tracing the carvings on the walls, the puffs of sand being throw into the air by the next group sparring. She felt Metellus give her shoulder an affectionate squeeze, "Helania, I've seen how much you want to be like Skjarla, and I can understand it, but think about it for a moment."

She razed a thin, quizzical eyebrow as she waited in silence for him to continue, determined not to get drawn into this conversation. "She's been around since the world shifted," Metellus continued firmly, "And she was around for ages before that. Now you're what, thirty?"

"Fifty nine," she corrected him with a frown.

Metellus smiled calmly and bowed his head slightly, "Apologies, I still find it difficult to gauge how old you Alfar are. Anyway, as I was saying, you've got barely fifteen years of experience behind you, she has likely got more than fifteen hundred years of experience, probably much more. So don't feel too depressed about your sparring."

Helania took a deep breath, she had to admit the truth behind the words, "I suppose you're right," she hoped to leave it at that, but as she started to pull her legs under her to get back to her feet, Metellus grabbed her arm.

"Wait, just listen for one more moment. I may be younger than you, but I have fought on the Isle of Ryhm, and I've seen people like Skjarla. They may not have the endless experience or the immortality, but they are the same as her, and I don't think you want to be like that."

"Why? Why wouldn't I want to be as good with a blade as she is," She asked indignantly.

Metellus smiled sadly, "For people like Skjarla and those legionaries who I knew that were like her, it is not a question of experience. It was the kind of person they were, a cold detachedness, and a person for whom killing is second nature. I am not even sure if you can train to be a person like that. It is just something which you grow into, and I sincerely hope that you don't." He smiled softly and dropped his gaze away from her eyes as he finished, "You're too good a person to turn into something like that."

Helania's jaw dropped slightly and her eyes widened with shock as she digested the Roman's words, was he displaying some affection for her, or merely trying to protect her. Words tumbled around inside her head, all clamouring to be uttered, but in the end she said nothing, merely got to her feet in silence and stalked out of the gymnasium. If she had glanced over her shoulder she would have seen Metellus's eyes following her, and the sad shake of his head as he worried that his message had failed to get through to her. He knew that she could well turn into another Skjarla, but he doubted she would be able to handle it. Many who carried so much death around with them went insane, either overwhelmed by what they had done or lashing out at anything which came close to them. Few were able to follow Skjarla along the knife edge of sanity and death, the fine line between madness and clarity.

For the next few days Skjarla was like a chained tiger, pacing furiously and burning with barely restrained fury as she trained with Helania and Metellus, often both at the same time. Metellus had been up onto the red stone walls of the Hold and had confirmed that the column was indeed camped up against the foot of the giant stone barrier. They were being fed and watered on pallets lowered over the walls, but the gates of Moonshadow Hold remained stubbornly closed.

A few shouted greetings from the walls told them that Accipiteri had made it safely with the column, as had Sigmund, but that was about all they could manage to shout to each other. The eyes of the people on the wall told them that the column had suffered a hard journey, the numbers had shrunk dramatically, and many of the survivors were still carrying wounds. Metellus had told Skjarla how odd it was that there were so many guards on the wall by the refugees, and she had practically bitten his head off in response. As the final day of this coming of age tourney drew closer people learnt to treat Skjarla as they would a smouldering volcano, approaching only with the greatest care and prepared to flee any moment.

***

Skjarla's eyes roved around the arena, the sands bathed in flickering light from hundreds of sputtering torches. For reasons only known to him, Turil had ordered that the light globe hanging over the city be dimmed and the fight be lit only by the fires of the torches. As unnecessary as it was Skjarla had to admit that it did add something to the atmosphere, the sand seemed to roil like a sea of blood, while the shadows of the champions flooded across the surface. The crowds packed into the stands, more than had been there so far, stood in crushing silence as they waited for the bloodshed to begin. From behind the Royal seats, shrouded in crimson fabrics, a lonely trumpet began its mournful clarion call.

As Turil, his son and all of the visiting dignitaries took their places Skjarla felt herself relax, as if floating several feet above her body. She took in the six remaining champions as she calmly waited for the start of the contest which was at least only to first blood. Two Dokkalfar, one man and one woman were still there. The man seemed calmer, older, but the woman was visibly gripping the hilt of her sword, clearly nervous. Skjarla could admit to herself that she felt less comfortable without Dreyrispa; the champions had been told that they would all have the same weapons, just a simple longsword. The three dwarves, all male were encased within their heavy armour, standing patiently as they waited for the battle with the torchlight flickering off the sharp angles moulded into the steel.

The swords were supposed to make the contest more even, but Skjarla thought she could read in Turil's eyes, even from this distance, the desire to handicap her. She had no doubt that the others would seek to take her out of the fight first before squabbling amongst themselves for the right to fight Tyril. As the sad notes of the trumpet grew to a mournful crescendo she managed to find Helania, Domitia and Metellus. Her Dokkalfar friend looked nervous, as did the Roman centurion, while Domitia's face was a study in icy aloofness.

The music of the trumpet ceased with one last, tumbling note, and all was still. Some of the crowd had no doubt expected the fighters to spring into action, tearing at one another like dogs, but there was not an inch of movement, all waiting for one of the others to break the spell. In Skjarla's head she could hear the relentless, melancholy yet exhilarating pounding of the drums of war. She started to sway slowly from side to side, a snake waiting to strike as it began its beautiful yet deadly dance of death. The others seemed to lower their weapons slightly, hypnotised by the sinuous, almost sensual movements of the Valkyrie's body. If they had been able to see into her helmet they would have seen her wide pupils suddenly contract to the merest pinpricks, black dots nearly indistinguishable against the green irises.

She spun on her left foot, two paces taking her close to the Dwarf to her left. The speed with which she reached him left him dumbfounded, and he crumpled as she hammered her metal boot into his groin, grabbing for his blade at the same time. She felt the bones in her toes give way and grate against one another, the excruciating pain masked by the flood of fire surging through her. The Dwarf collapsed to his knees, both hands cradling his groin. Casually she drew a small line of crimson on the back of his hand, in the gap between gauntlet and bracer before turning back to the rest of the champions. They were still stood stock still, but then they recovered from their shock and exploded into motion.

Skjarla could feel the weight of the two long swords pulling at her wrists, the tremors of each contact reverberating up her arms. They were fine blades, but not even close to the quality of the two she had kept from Valhalla. She was forced to throw herself to the ground as five swinging blades all sought out her flesh, but she kept moving, striking out at any exposed skin she could see. She felt the blows against her armour, but the flowing movement of the body beneath meant that they glanced off the black steel. The two longswords spun in wide circles, seeking out exposed flesh where they could draw the bloody lines that would bring this fight to an end.

Before she had realised it, Skjarla was standing alone in the centre of the arena, surrounded by a deafening silence which hung heavy in the air. The other champions were lying on the ground, all still breathing, but bleeding slowly into the sand of the Blood Eye. Blood dripped from the points of her blade, the sound of it hitting the sand was the only thing she could hear, her breath coming in soft gasps.

The drumming within her head had ceased by the time that Turil got slowly to his feet.

His voice echoed out across the crowd. "People of Moonshadow Hold, I give you the champion of Tyril's coming of age."

Those words broke the spell that was holding the people, and thunderous roars of applause burst out from every side, washing down the tiers of seats and breaking over Skjarla. She did not move a muscle, watching coldly as Turil raised his hands for silence, his gold ornamentation catching in the light of the torches. "I have an announcement to make," His voice roared out once the crowd had quieted. "There will be one further bout. Your champion, my son, will face the Valkyrie for the honour of this proving. The bout will be to first blood in one hour's time." He paused for dramatic effect, seeing the excited look on the faces of his people, "Until then, the ale shall flow freely from the royal cellars, drink your fill until the final contest begins." This last pronouncement was met with thunderous applause and cheers. Skjarla turned on her heel and stalked out of the arena, not bothering to salute the royal seats, glimpsing Helania leaping out of her seat and heading for the exit.

She headed down into the dark areas where combatants would wait before their fights and began to strip off her armour. By the time her three companions had arrived she was just standing there in her sweat-stained clothing, the material which shielded her skin from the abrasive steel.

Domitia looked confused, "What's happening, why have you taken your armour off?" Her expression became even more concerned as Helania began to peel off her own garments while Skjarla began to take off the last few bits of clothing. Metellus went pink and turned around fast, the metal of his Lorica Segmenta and the chainmail he wore jangling loudly.

Skjarla didn't say anything, handing her clothes across to Helania, so Helania spoke up instead, using a flat, monotone voice, clearly displeased with what she had to do. "Turil has threatened to kill the refugees if Skjarla doesn't throw the fight against his son."

She was about to continue before Domitia interrupted, "But that doesn't explain why you're taking her place. Why can't she throw the fight herself?" Sneering contempt was writ large in her voice. Skjarla said nothing but walked silently behind Metellus, whipping his pugio, the short Roman dagger, out of its sheath and offering the hilt to Domitia.

Coldly staring at the heir to the Roman Empire she said calmly, "Try and stab me, I want you to try and kill me." Domitia looked confused and terrified, while Metellus seemed to be fighting the urge to turn round and assist his mistress. "Do it!" Skjarla yelled loudly, and Domitia lunged wildly for her chest. The dagger came up against her chest and came to a dead stop, Domitia's body crumpling as her arm hit what felt like a stone wall. As Domitia looked in awe at the dagger, and the unbroken surface of Skjarla's skin, Skjarla spoke, slowly and pointedly. "I told you, I cannot choose to die or be harmed, so I cannot let that dwarf win. Hence why Helania has kindly agreed to take my place in the fight, for the safety of our friends trapped beyond the walls and for the survival of those of us stood here."

She turned to Helania, who was busily strapping on the greaves and the thick plates covering her thighs. "Thank you for doing this, I can't think of anything worse than throwing a fight. It takes a warrior of rare courage to lose on purpose." After she had pulled on some of the plain, drab clothing that had been brought down for her she wrapped Helania up in a large hug, grateful for the sacrifice her friend was making. As they broke apart she threw a hooded cloak about her shoulders and grabbed the wrapped bundle which held Dreyrispa. She allowed herself a small smile as her hand reached inside the worn cloths to caress the well worn wood. Helania was busy tying a scarf across her mouth to hide the red-veined jet-black skin of her face.

Metellus turned around once he was sure that his friend was decent and gave her the traditional military salute, crashing his fist into the chest plates of his Lorica. Skjarla bowed her head, please to see that the enchantments on the armour were still holding strong, the small nicks becoming less ragged and the dents softening out. Helania nodded to him and the others before she picked up one of the two longswords, now stained with crusting blood, and stalked back out into the arena. Skjarla pulled up the hood of her cloak and followed Domitia and Metellus back out into the stands of the Blood Eye.

By the time they made their way back down to their seats at the very edge of the arena Helania was at the centre of the sandy arena, gently stretching her muscles as if she had already fought once today. Skjarla could see that Helania was working to favour one leg, 'the girl missed her calling on the stage,' she thought with a wry smile from within the dark embrace of her hood. The Dwarf Prince Tyril was swinging his axe in wicked circles, the movement of the air around the blade audible over the crackling of the torches. The gilded armour the dwarf wore seemed to shine like the sun in the warm light of the burning torches, while his opponent's black armour drank in the light. It looked like one of the fabled clashes between champions of good and evil from the old tales.

After about fifteen minutes of this Turil got to his feet, waving the two combatants to their marks, then called out to the crowd. "My people, I present to you the Heir to the Throne of our mighty Hold, now come of age. He will prove this by showing all of you the strength of his arm against this relic of the Old Kingdoms." He paused as the crowd roared their approval of these words, Skjarla's knuckles whitening as her fists clenched, livid at being described as a relic. He raised his arm theatrically into the air, "Begin!"

Tyril waited, taking one step forward, waiting to see what his opponent would do. Skjarla found it strange, watching herself, seeing the palpable aura of fear that that menacing black armour lent to the figure beneath it. Helania felt the sand shift slightly beneath her feet as she sprung forward, her blade seeking out the thick metal of Tyril's pauldron, no danger of cutting him there. She found it strange, but she agreed with something Skjarla had told her when they had first devised this plan, it is far harder to fight trying to lose than trying to win. It was requiring every ounce of her concentration not to try and exploit the gaps that her opponent left. At least the Dwarf was competent with his axe, but she had had years of practice against Braugr, she could read what this Dwarf was going to do almost before he knew it.

She forced herself to step forwards, giving Tyril an opening for an attack, bracing herself for the pain. The Dwarf caught her ankle with the haft of his axe, sending her tumbling to the ground, moving to stand over her with his axe raised. Her eyes widened as she saw the axe blade raised high over her neck, suddenly worried that the prince would be trying to make even more of a name for himself by killing the last Valkyrie. He lowered the axe slowly and used the blade to brush away the scarf covering her mouth and throat. Helania tensed for the blow as the deception was discovered, heard the intake of breath from the shocked prince.

She was amazed to hear his voice instead, a soft whisper, even though she had prepared herself for the grasp of empty death. "What is the meaning of this? Why have you taken Skjarla's place for this fight?" His axe was still raised, but no one except her could hear his words, and he was the only one who could see the colour of her skin.

The calmness of her voice surprised her more than anything, "Your father told Skjarla that she was to lose if the people outside your gates were not to be killed. She cannot be harmed if she wishes it, so to lose the fight I had to take her place." She left it hanging there, waiting patiently for the Dwarven prince to make a decision.

She was shocked at the speed of the blade hurtling down towards her throat, only to stop as it parted the outermost layer of skin. She fought against the urge to swallow, sure that it would drive the blade deeper into her neck. Tyril raised the blade to the crowd who roared as they saw the blood on the edge of the blade. He offered the prone Dokkalfar a hand, whispering as she got to her feet and replaced her scarf, "I swear I had no knowledge of this. I am not my Father, I still have my honour. No harm will come to your people, this I swear."

"Thanks," was all she could manage, somewhat lamely, her voice muffled by the scarf which was now getting damp with the blood seeping from her throat. The two of them walked out of the Blood Eye side by side, heading into the shadows of the tunnel, chased down there by the applause and cheers of the Dwarves and Dokkalfar of the crowd. Skjarla met Helania down in the preparation area, already tying a bandage around her throat to hide the lack of any wound. Tyril and the two Romans went on ahead to the palace while Skjarla and Helania stayed behind to change their clothes again.

As they pulled on their clothes Skjarla tried to break the silence, "You did well."

"What do you mean? I lost," grumbled Helania petulantly.

Skjarla growled, then softened her stance a little, "Look, you may have lost, but the manner in which you kept your calm is something most fighters can't do. I know that you want to be as good as you can, and to be able to control your emotions and be that clinical during a fight means that you're on your way to reaching your potential."

Helania rolled her eyes, "Fine, that may be the case and thanks for saying it, but you've never had to throw a fight before. You've never lost anything before, so you don't understand."

Before she knew what was happening she was pinned against the wall, a knife against her throat and the Valkyrie's furious face inches from hers. Spittle flecked her face as The Valkyrie roared at her, "How dare you say that. You, one of the Elder Peoples, are someone who should know what I have suffered better than anyone. I have lost everyone I ever held dear, my home, everything I knew and I have an eternity to live with that fact, and you dare say I know nothing of loss?"

Skjarla let a wide-eyed Helania slide to the ground, where she flopped in stunned silence. "Sorry," Skjarla said lamely, "Look, I'm sorry, you just hit a nerve. You'd have thought after four centuries it wouldn't be such a sore subject." Her sad chuckle tailed off and she turned away, clearly embarrassed by her outburst.

Helania was gingerly getting back to her feet, rubbing her throat. "No, I shouldn't have been so thick; it was a stupid thing to say."

Skjarla shook her head, still facing the dark stones of the wall rather than her friend. "Just leave it," She turned around and smiled sadly, "Come on, Turil should have opened the gates by now, let's go and see how Accipiteri and Braugr have fared."

Helania smiled, "Good idea, he looked to be in good shape from the top of the wall. I guess you'll be anxious to see Iskander?" There was a questioning glint in her eye and a mischievous grin flickered across her countenance. Skjarla responded with a snort of laughter as she headed out into the streets of Moonshadow Hold. Helania couldn't help but think how strange the Valkyrie was, one moment so normal, the next a raging killer, as if someone had thrown a spark into tinder dry wood.

The two of them did not head for the palace as was expected of them; Skjarla was expected to be there and be gracious in defeat but she had no desire to have Turil crowing in her ear for the next few hours. Instead they made their way to the courtyard just behind the gates. Turil had at least been good enough to act upon his promise and there were two carts of food waiting for the hungry refugees as they slowly streamed through the imposing archway. Accipiteri, his face sunken and worn by the travails of the journey was exhaustedly directing people into the Hold. They may have been camped outside the Hold for a few days, but the constant worry of attack had kept them all on edge, denying them the rest they needed. Skjarla's heart ached as she saw how few there were now, close to a third of their number looked to have died in the Ways.

A small part of her mind was grateful that it was mainly the old and the weak who had perished, but there were still some of the fighters she knew missing. Braugr was propped up against a wall, gently stropping his axe with a whetstone. He nodded to Helania when he saw her, but made no effort to join the two of them as they reached Accipiteri. Helania threw her arms around him and kissed him impulsively for just a fraction of a second before jerking her head away as if she had been stung. Skjarla watched with casual amusement as they both turned a violent shade of puce, the two of them pulled apart, before Helania began hesitantly, "It's good to see you in one piece."

"You too," was all that Accipiteri could muster as he stared at his feet.

Skjarla decided that bluntly changing the subject was the only option, "How was the journey Accipiteri? It looks like you had a far tougher time of this than we did."

He gave a dark smile, "I bet you've got some stories of your own to tell me at some stage, I can't imagine that you just spent," his eyes glazed over slightly as he tried to think. A shadow crossed his face, "How long has it been since we left you at Sundark Hold?"

"Six weeks and three days," came the response, concern in the voices of both women as they spoke together, "Don't you remember how long it took you?"

"No, you have no idea," his voice was strained, the pressures of the past six weeks building to a head, threatening to burst at this moment. He regained his composure as he continued, only the slightest tremor in his voice. "There was no day or night on those stony corridors, it may have been alright for you on a shorter trip, but weeks of being chased by Smaparmar, little sleep took its toll. I don't know how quickly you want to get out of this place, but I tell you this, if you try and leave in less than seven days then you'll be signing the death warrant of many of these people." There was a fire in his voice as he drew to a close, his eyes locked unwaveringly with Skjarla's and she was in no doubt how much this responsibility had grown on him. He clearly felt a duty to the people of Lonely Barrow, more so than before.

She put her hand on his arm, giving it a reassuring squeeze as she said, "Don't worry, we're in no rush. I can't say that I'll be overjoyed to have to spend more time here, but I'm sure that it'll make the Romans very happy." She looked around, a sense of alarm suddenly in her head, "Where's Braugr gone?" she asked nervously.

Helania's voice now sounded a little nervous, "I thought he was over there," she said pointing to the spot the Dwarf had been sitting in. "It's not safe for him here, Dwarves with the mark of the Shattered are pretty unpopular at the best of times. They're not technically outlaws, but people tend to turn a blind eye where they're concerned."

Accipiteri sighed softly, "Look, he can take care of himself, I've got enough to be dealing with at the moment, I'd be grateful if you both could stay and lend a hand."

Skjarla and Helania nodded once together, "Don't worry, we'll help out. Why don't you get some sleep? We can take care of distributing the food to everyone."

Accipiteri looked like he was going to argue for a moment, then nodded resignedly as he headed over to one of the piles of rough blankets, grabbing one and laying his head upon it in the first bit of space he found. Skjarla saw the looks that the people gave him as he passed; he was a rock to them, their hero who had led them over this difficult journey. Strangely there was no jealousy at being supplanted; she was glad that the people of Lonely Barrow had found the hero that they deserved.

She and Helania headed over to one of the carts and began handing out the dry loaves of flat bread and the other curious bits of Dwarven food which they had been sent. The guides who had been attached to the column were already making their way over to the palace to report, but one had come over to Helania before they had gone. "If it is alright with you, we will share the road a little longer," said the Dokkalfar who spoke for a small group of them, he had told her his name was Fjirsk. "I have long dreamed of seeing the sky, as our ancestors did. Stone willing I will see it on this adventure with you."

Helania wanted to tell him no, that this was no adventure but a simple struggle against insufferable hardships and horrendous odds, but she hadn't the heart. "Every blade we can gather is more than welcome," was all she could say as he retreated down the pathway, heading for his king in the palace.

The next two days were relatively peaceful, Skjarla and the others working to get the people of the column back into some shape where they could complete the next stage of their journey. Mercifully the journey from Moonshadow

Hold to the surface near the Black Mountains was only about twenty days in length. The only person who was conspicuously absent during this time was Braugr, of whom neither hide nor hair was seen.

When he finally surfaced it was to grab Helania as she walked the streets of the Hold. She felt relatively safe, as both kings Jori and Turil had made it clear that she was under their protection, so no one from Nightfast Hold would dare touch her. Braugr looked tired and dishevelled, but there was a feverish gleam of excitement in his eyes. Nervously she asked, "Braugr, are you all right?"

He gave her a toothy smile, one of the few genuine smiles she had ever seen from him. "More than all right, I have picked up the trail. I knew that Aetria had been sold to a merchant going to Ironstone Hold with instructions to sell her on once there, but I had never been able to find someone from Ironstone until now. They have people here for the tourney, but I can't talk to them." He sighed frustratedly, "You know how stuck up the people from there are, the worst is their Dokkalfar queen, but that's beside the point. They won't even acknowledge someone with these," He gestured to the marks on his face, "So girl, I have to ask you a favour. Talk to them, you know that slave Dwarves in the Holds are rare enough that she would be memorable." His eyes burned with passion and he squeezed her arm painfully, ignored by all of the people who passed the small alley he had dragged her into. "Do anything it takes, anything whatsoever."

With those last chilling words he disappeared back into the shadows of the alley between houses, leaving a stunned and slightly scared by the experience. After a moment she recovered herself and stepped out from the shadows into the red lit streets of the Hold, continuing past the squat, square red stone houses. She didn't like the way he had told her to anything necessary to get the information, she didn't like what he was suggesting. It was too close to what could have been her life for her to feel comfortable, and yet, she couldn't help but feel that she owed Braugr so much. What kind of person was she if she didn't use everything at her disposal to try to find her friend's daughter?

Her mind was still buzzing with this dilemma, stuck between wanting to do exactly as Braugr asked and wanting to preserve her sense of self worth. In the end, she decided that she would only resort to using her femininity as a last resort, praying that it wouldn't come to that. She would frankly rather beg Skjarla to threaten whoever she managed to find with knowledge of Aetria, than that, but hopefully it wouldn't come to that. The steps to the palace were behind her and as she entered the palace she was collared by Domitia, the Roman's face painted with various expensive powders and creams, rouge on her lips.

"Where have you been? You know that Jori has been looking for us. The first of the Royal Parties is leaving tomorrow, so Turil has ordered that the final feast will be held tonight. Like it or not you are part of Jori's retinue, so you need to be there." Domitia didn't understand why Helania was not that annoyed by this news, even seemed to be smiling at the prospect. She continued harshly, "Jori wants us ready in under an hour, so I suggest you call the servants to help you prepare for the feast."

Helania smiled at the Roman, "Thanks for letting me know," then she had a thought, catching the other woman's wrist before she could leave. She tried to sound nonchalant, "Have you met the Ironstone delegation? I've heard that they have more Dokkalfar in their armies, so they might offer me a safe route back to my people."

Surprisingly Domitia did not seem too suspicious, instead seemed delighted to show off the connections she had made during her time in Moonshadow Hold. She smiled warmly, "Why didn't you say something earlier, I'm only too happy to introduce you to King Caeled and his Queen Daena. They will of course be at the feast tonight, but if I am to introduce you to them then you must be polite and well presented." Her voice tailed off as she placed her hands on her hips and raked Helania with a pointed gaze.

Helania bit down on a combination of laughter and exasperation at the Roman's expression. As gaily as she could she replied, "Well, I'd better get ready then hadn't I." She smiled and headed back to her room, near choking on laughter.

She nearly fell over in shock when she reached her chambers. Glancing through the half open door she saw Skjarla adjusting the fit of an emerald green gown. She stopped in her tracks; it was such a shock to see Skjarla in anything other than her black armour, let alone a garment as figure hugging as this. Skjarla clearly had some kind of sixth sense, she spun on the spot, and seeing Helania peering through the half open doorway glowered at her.

Skjarla was bright red in the face, clearly irritated by all of this, and barked in response to Helania's shapely raised eyebrow. "Not a word."

Helania shook her head at the sight, her eyes rolling at Skjarla's murderous expression. "It doesn't look that bad."

Skjarla cast her gaze to the red stone of the ceiling, "I couldn't give a damn what it looks like, I can barely move in this bloody thing." It was true, the tight fitting fabric which stretched to well below her knees meant that her usually powerful stride was restricted to an unedifying mincing step. She smiled slightly, "Pass me one of those," she said, pointing at one of the small daggers hanging from Helania's hip.

Helania winced slightly at the idea of Skjarla applying the cold steel to the rich velvet and silk of the gown, but still handed over the blade. Skjarla bent down and sliced up the side of one leg, exposing a slash of pale skin beneath. She tried moving and seemed much happier, "Much better. If they've given you anything like this then I suggest you do the same," she said cheerfully, handing back the dagger.

Helania smiled and said coolly, "I'm alright, I'm trying to keep a low profile, not inspire a new fashion trend." She shook her head as she headed to her part of the room to change into the clothes she had been left. In fairness to Skjarla, her frame was slightly larger than that of average Dokkalfar, which was why she suspected the gown had been a little snug. She wondered what would have been laid out for her; on the previous occasions a gown of some form had been left out for her, and then disappeared the following day. For this final feast she had been left with a dark maroon coloured gown, not the mark of someone important. In the high society of the Old People, the brighter the colour the higher the status, so someone had chosen that colour as a deliberate slight.

'No matter,' she thought to herself, 'Appearing that I have low status in front of the Ironstone king and queen will be no bad thing.' Just as she tied the thin cord around her waist she heard a knock on the door. "Come in."

"Ready to go?" asked Skjarla. It never ceased to amaze Helania or any of their other companions how uncomfortable and out of her depth Skjarla felt in a formal setting.

"Yes" Helania paused for a moment, trying to keep her voice as level as possible, "Skjarla, why have you got your swords." Skjarla had crossed her two leather baldrics over the top of her green gown and had her swords strapped to her back.

Skjarla looked somewhat sheepish, "It didn't feel right going somewhere unarmed but I don't think even I can get away with carrying Dreyrispa." She gave a wolfish grin, "Plus, one of the bonuses of being a Valkyrie is that people don't make a fuss about what you do."

Helania shook her head slightly, "Come on, let's head down there. I can't imagine anything you do will shock them overly much."

As the two of them made their way down the passageways of the palace towards the great hall, Skjarla said quietly, "Thank you again for taking my place the other day. Whenever it gets to you, just think of how many lives you saved by doing it."

Helania pulled up short for a moment before asking, cold venom dripping from her voice, "Do you honestly think that makes me feel any better? Would anything I could say take away the knowledge that you lost on purpose were our roles reversed."

Skjarla smiled sadly, "No, it wouldn't, and you know it." There was nothing else to be said as they continued their way into the great hall in frosty silence.

The hall itself had been prepared magnificently for the occasion. Long tables groaned under the weight of food, and elaborate tapestries, shot through with silver and gold thread hung from the walls. Skjarla stopped before one particularly faded one, tears welling up in her eyes. It was an aged depiction of Valhalla, the wooden city seated at the base of Ygdrassil. The colours of the Bifrost almost seemed to erupt from the threads of the tapestry, and the leaves of the World Tree seemed to move in an ancient wind.

Turil came up beside her quietly, ignoring some of the other guests who bowed before their host. "I thought it would be something you'd want to see. You will be in one of the seats of honour at the high table with myself and my son, among other."

Skjarla could barely mumble, "As you wish my Lord," so entranced was she by the tapestry. She stood there in silence for as long as she could, waiting until every other member of that gathering had taken their seats, before numbly making her way to her own chair, just to the right of Tyril, who in turn sat at Turil's right hand. She tried to make conversation over the meal, as servants placed platters piled high with various cuts of meat before her, and regularly recharged the mead horn which was never far from her hand. Her mind though was still stuck in the morass of memories brought about by that one tapestry, fragments of a lifelong since past.

Over on the other end of the hall Helania was waiting patiently for the meal to finish. Once everyone was free to move around a bit more Domitia had promised to introduce her to Caeled, until then she was forced to wait. At least the food was good, and she doubted that there would be anything like this for the next stage of their journey, so she made the most of it while she could. The meal dragged on interminably, with speeches by each of the delegations praising the champions and the generosity of their host as well as congratulating Tyril on his coming of age. By the time the last of them had finished most of the city below them was long asleep, but the servants within the palace were wide awake, clearing the tables and shifting them to the sides of the room. Dozens of Dokkalfar servants began to prowl the room with jugs of strong honeyed mead in search of anyone who was not drunk yet.

She gently mingled through the crowd, trying to find the shimmering ocean blue of Domitia's gown, which she eventually spotted in a corner, in deep conversation with a pair of Dwarves. Her promise to Braugr ringing loudly in her mind, she sidled closer to Domitia and tapped her on the shoulder. The hubbub of the gathering meant that the only words she heard were Domitia saying, "I'll deal with my friend, we can continue this discussion later on." She looked annoyed as she spoke to Helania, her perfectly made-up eyes framed by arching eyebrows eloquently displayed her contempt at being interrupted. "Follow me, and remember to bow to the king and queen," she said sharply as she disappeared into the crowd.

They jostled their way through the press of people, the brightly coloured fabrics rippling around them like a storm of rainbows. Eventually they found the rulers of Ironstone Hold, surrounded by a coterie of fawning individuals.

Ironstone Hold was one of the most powerful holds thanks to its trade links with the surface; a large amount of goods from Taureum passed through their hands on their way to the other Holds. They nodded to Domitia as an equal when they noticed her; clearly the Roman had been making much of her status as the heir to the Imperial throne.

"My lord Caeled, My lady Daena, I am sorry to interrupt your conversation, but my friend here was desperate to meet you." She stepped to the side, allowing Helania a sight of arguably the two most powerful Dokkalfar in Midgard. Helania took in the two figures before her. Both had the usual lithe forms of the Dokkalfar, their faces chiselled into aloof expressions, haughty disdain bright in their eyes. The King's clothes were brightly coloured but strangely lacking in ornamentation, only a single ruby glistened against his throat. The Queen was spectacular in radiant white, emeralds and sapphires dripping from her sleeves and bodice, with what looked like diamonds woven into her ice white hair.

She was taken aback when Daena spoke to her, "You are the girl who ran away from Nightfast Hold correct?" There was no judgement in her curiously accented voice, reedier than that of the people of Nightfast Hold.

"I am, Milady," Helania said meekly, keeping her eyes on the floor, hoping for the opening she was looking for.

"Well, at least that shows you have a little spirit," the queen's eyes sparkled and her voice held some genuine mirth. Her husband merely grunted and Helania could not help but wonder who the true power on the throne was. Daena's tone became more businesslike, "I take it that there is a reason you asked your Roman friend to introduce you to us."

Helania recovered herself and dared to look the queen in the eye as she spoke. "My Lady, after my current service with the Valkyrie and her companions I will need some employment. I am not welcome in Nightfast Hold so I had hope to throw myself upon your mercy and request a place with your guards. Forgive me if I have been too bold." Out of the corner of her eye she could see the suspicious look on Domitia's face; she had never mentioned anything like this to the Roman.

Queen Daena looked at her for a long moment before glancing across to her husband who gave the minutest of shrugs, his shoulders barely moving. The Queen pursed her lips, seemingly in deep thought, "I will not guarantee you a position," She saw Helania's face fall, "But I will point you to the captain of our guards. If he thinks that you are worthy of a place then I will take his word for it." What the Queen failed to say was that once Helania swore an oath to Ironstone Hold then, if she was to remain true to her vows, she would have to obey orders. If she was at some point ordered to return to Nightfast, in whatever role was required of her, the she would be forced to obey or be put to death as an oath breaker. A useful bargaining chip if they ever had difficult dealings with the Lord of Nightfast Hold.

Helania smiled gratefully, "A thousand thanks my Lord and Lady, and I shall not let you down."

Daena pointed to a bored looking Dokkalfar leaning against a heavy tapestry on the far side of the room, his cold eyes constantly sweeping the chamber. "That is Captain Damraloth, go to him and tell him I sent you." With that their meeting seemed to be over and the Queen turned back to one of the group clustered around her. Domitia stayed at the side of the powerful Dokkalfar couple while Helania once more began to edge her way across the crowded room towards the distant figure of Captain Damraloth.

The Captain was wearing black, supposedly the mark of someone of the lowest status there, but on Damraloth it just gave him the look of a man who didn't give a damn. He was unarmed but still looked dangerous as she approached him. His eyes roved over her body, taking in the scars which danced across her exposed flesh, the white a jarring contrast to the black of her skin. She tried to ignore the lingering gaze on the curves of her body and instead tried to focus on him. His face was hard and weathered, he was old for one of her people, probably well past his two hundredth year, maybe past his two hundred and fiftieth.

Eventually, with a cold, almost toneless voice, "What do you want?"

"Your mistress sent me," she saw him flinch at the use of the word mistress; he stared at her intently before relaxing again. "I was hoping to join the Ironstone Guard in a few years, and she said to speak to you about it."

He looked at her for a long moment, "Well, you've clearly seen some combat, and if you've picked up some tricks from the Valkyrie then they'll serve you well. I've no desire to test you here; years from now may well see one or both of us dead." Helania made sure that she looked crestfallen, "However, given your record, if you appear the Ironstone Hold you'll get yourself a fair trial. The King is fond of his Dokkalfar guards, particularly ones as pretty as you."

The conversation seemed to be over but Helania lingered while Damraloth took a long swig from the battered horn in his right hand. She began nervously, "Look, there was something else I wanted to ask you, as a favour for a friend."

The Captain's expression took on an intrigued glint. "Oh, and what would that be?"

"About six years ago a Dwarven slave-girl would have been brought to Ironstone Hold. I want to know what happened to her once she arrived."

Damraloth smiled grimly, "I know the person you speak of, and I had to drag her back to her master once when she ran off into the Ways. Why do you want to know though, what interest could a Dokkalfar have in a Dwarven slave?"

There was no profit in lying to him now, "The friend who wants to know is the girl's father."

Damraloth gently closed his eyes and nodded, "Ah that makes sense. But I want something from this as well, an exchange if you will." Helania's heart was in her mouth and her palms were suddenly clammy as she thought her worst fears were about to be realised. She had to fight against the urge to shut her eyes tight as he opened his mouth, "A question for a question. I want to know why the Valkyrie threw the fight against Tyril the other day."

"What do you mean? She didn't throw the fight," Helania said as boldly as she could, but even to her own ears it sounded lame.

He snarled angrily, "Don't be ridiculous. Anyone who knows the point of a blade from the hilt could see that the Valkyrie threw the fight. No one who's been fighting for more than a year leaves themselves as open as that. Why did she do it?"

"Turil was holding the fate of our friends over her. If she didn't lose then he was going to have his troops drive the refugees back into the Ways with a hail of arrows."

Damraloth looked angry, "There is no honour in such behaviour. Turil let his greed get the better of him. Maybe the people of his Hold believe that their prince defeated a Valkyrie, but all of the monarchs know the fight was a sham. There is no shame in losing to one of the Old Gods."

Helania was getting a little annoyed now, "That may well be the case, but what about the girl?"

Damraloth grabbed a passing servant and had them fill his horn, almost to the brim. "She spent two years in service to a smith in Ironstone, an older Dwarf who needed help around the place. When he died his family had no need of her so she was sold on. Last I heard of her she was being taken to the port of Islen to be sold on there. That would have been close to three years ago."

Helania's eyes were wide. Islen was a port city on the western coast, at the boundary where the lands of the Haemocracy and the endless deserts of Vfar overlapped. As such it was a cosmopolitan city, a place where both cultures gathered to trade and send their goods on out to Leopolis and Taureum. The only bit of good fortune was that the place was run by the Haemocracy, who were particularly grubby when it came to taxes. As such there were records of every transaction going back years, all to make sure that the Haemocracy got its share of the profits.

"Then thank you captain, it looks like my friend's journey next takes him on to Islen. I'll leave you to your drink."

Damraloth did not say a word, did not even cast a glance at her as she faded back into the crowd. She saw Skjarla surrounded by several squawking courtiers, members of the various courts which had come to Moonshadow Hold. There was a temptation to go and rescue the increasingly furious Skjarla but Helania felt a duty to go and tell Braugr the good news, he was one step closer to finding his daughter. She slunk out of the high, vaulted arch of the entrance to the palace, slipping softly past the few guards standing stiffly to attention at the top of the stairs. The Dwarves and Dokkalfar were clearly tired by this time of the evening, leaning against their gaudily coloured spears, trying to take some of the weight of their heavy armour off their feet.

The tight fabric of the gown meant that she had to take the steps slowly; she was glad that it was the early hours of the morning and the streets were like a graveyard. As she hit the road at the base of the stairs she glanced behind her, not looking forward to the thought of making her way back up there later on. She made her way through the near deserted streets, passing only the occasionally drunk staggering his way home. Some glances lingered on her longer than she would have liked, but once they caught sight of her scars she was given a wide berth.

She reached the refugees quickly and began to make her way through the sprawl of sleeping bodies as she searched for Braugr. At least in this jungle of limbs he would be quite easy to spot as one of the only Dwarves in the group. Eventually she found him resting against one of the wagon wheels, fast asleep next to Accipiteri, almost as if the two of the had nodded off mid way through their conversation. She woke him gently with a soft shaking of his shoulder. Years at war meant that he flashed awake in an instant, his hand automatically reaching for the knife on his belt. The sleep swiftly slipped from his eyes as he realised who was waking him, indeed an almost boyish expression of hope lit his features.

"Have you found anything? Do you know where she is?" He grabbed her by the shoulders, staring intently at her, waiting to hang of the first syllable to escape her lips.

She nodded with a smile, "I've picked up the trail. She spent two years in Ironstone working for a smith." Her voice tailed of slightly and her smile faltered.

Braugr now looked worried, "And?"

Helania sighed and struggled to meet her friend's eye, "The smith died and she was sold on. The last that the guard of Ironstone knew was that close to three years ago she was sent to Islen to be sold."

Far from looking depressed Braugr seemed pleased by this news, "I'm closer than I was. Aetria I'm coming to find you," he said to no one in particular. He seemed to come back to the present, "Soon I'll have to make a little trip to Islen, maybe even now, before we head further south."

Shock and a degree of fear rippled through her voice, "You're thinking of leaving me, us, now?"

Braugr smiled thinly, a sad warmth on his face, "Can you begrudge me going to find my daughter? From trying to make up for my past mistakes? Plus girl, you're in good hands with these people here, they won't let any harm come to you."

"No Master Dwarf, we wouldn't, but I ask you to delay your journey." The two of them looked startled as Skjarla knelt down next to them so she could join their quiet conversation. "If we're going to get these people to Blackstone Castle and face whatever awaits us there then we need every blade we can get."

Braugr looked almost distraught, "But Skjarla she's my daughter," his voice pleading.

The Valkyrie's response was cold, "Braugr, even if you arrived there tomorrow, she still wouldn't be there, and she will have been sold somewhere else from Islen." Her tone softened, "Look, once the people are safely ensconced in the Black Mountains then you can go. If you want I will even travel to Islen with you." She looked him carefully in the eye, "Braugr, we need you on this journey."

The Dwarf licked his lips nervously, "Skjarla, I swore to follow you, but I also swore to find my daughter. I will follow you to Blackstone Castle, but in return I want your oath. I want you to swear to me that should I fall before I reach Islen then you will carry on my journey and find my daughter."

Now Skjarla looked a little nervous, someone who took their honour as seriously as she did did not make oaths lightly. Difficult as it was to predict the future she was now weighing up anything which could cause her to break her vow, but she couldn't think of anything other than death. "I will, while there is breath in my body, I swear to find your Aetria." They squeezed each other's hand, their gaze locked as they echoed the solemnity of the oath.

After a moment like that there was nothing else to be said, so Helania and Skjarla left Braugr to go back to sleep, if his excited mind would let him, and made their way back to the palace. As they walked Helania glanced at the Valkyrie striding so easily next to her, even though she reeked of mead she was steady as a rock.

"How did you manage to appear there?" Helania asked, partly to make conversation.

Skjarla shrugged her pale shoulders, "I saw you trying to sneak out of the palace and decided to see where you were going. Nothing more to it than that, following you was more interesting than listening to some minor lord droning on about nothing at all."

Then Helania made a small mistake, "Did you mean what you said to Braugr?"

"Every word," The Valkyrie came to a dead stop, her voice low and intense, "You should know by now that my word is everything to me, if I break it I am nothing."

The Dokkalfar tried to cover up her slip, "No, I meant about needing every blade you could get for the final push on to Blackstone Castle?"

Skjarla looked apologetic, an alien expression to her fine features, a look which sent a worm of guilt through Helania's insides. "Ah," she paused for a second, "Think about it, the only land route between the Svellvindr peninsula and the Deserts of Vfar runs through a pass blocked by the castle. There may be less trade these days by that route, but don't you imagine someone will have taken it upon themselves to prey upon merchant caravans?"

"I suppose they would have done. So you're expecting brigands to be waiting for us in the Black Mountains. Why does it matter if Braugr is there or not? Surely his absence wouldn't be too much of a difference against a few ragged brigands?"

Skjarla shook her head, they had reached the stairs of the palace and began to climb. Here the effects of alcohol were more noticeable on her, her breathing became laboured and she had to stop after a while. "Maybe not against the brigands, but the people who travel with us, need him for two reasons. First, he is turning a lot of them into fighters, something we're going to need to hold this new homeland of ours." They were both too intent on the conversation and too diverted by the alcohol to notice the cracks of light climb higher up Skjarla's arms, as if she had dipped them up to the elbows in a barrel of lightning. The spears of white were difficult to notice at the best of times against her pale skin. "Second, if everyone sees one of us, one of the people they look to for leadership, slinking away then they will lose hope. They will stop believing that we can get them to safety or protect them."

They were nearly at the top of the stairs and Helania was still amazed by the Valkyrie referring to it as their new homeland. "Skjarla, what will you do once these people have reached Blackstone Castle, keep protecting them forever?"

"No, much as they may have grown on me, we both know that keeping the Children away from the Fangs is far more important than anything else. I plan on …" She looked like she was going to say more, but they were approaching the guards and she did not want the existence of the Fang to get back to Turil. She changed the topic of conversation sharply, "Who was the Dokkalfar I saw you talking to this evening?"

"Why, jealous? That was a joke," she added hastily given the unpleasant expression which suddenly flashed across Skjarla's face, like a storm cloud across the horizon. "He's the Captain of the Ironstone Guards, he was the one who told me about what had happened to Aetria." Their conversation died as they passed between the guards and past the threshold of Turil's home.

They were safely inside the palace and made their way back to their chambers where Skjarla gratefully undid her swords from her back. Without the armour to distribute the weight more evenly the two baldrics had been digging deep into her shoulders for most of the evening. As she peeled of the clinging fabric of her gown she could see the ugly red lines branded into her skin, already starting to fade. It was a mercy to fall onto the bed, on the surface the dawn would be starting to break with pale fingers of light clawing at the horizon. Sleep washed over her quickly, the hum of intoxication gently buzzing in her ears as consciousness faded away from her.

Chapter 15

Three days after the Ironstone contingent had made their way off to the northwest, back to the chiselled granite walls of their Hold, the people of Lonely Barrow were loading up their carts. King Jori had already left with his household on the infernal Balfara, the noise of its clanking echoing down the carved stone of the Ways. They had been given generous stores of food; apparently they had Tyril to thank for that, clearly the Dwarven prince still felt guilty about the result of the Tournament. Braugr was still with them, in a bad mood and yelling at the people to hurry up with loading the carts, anxious to be off. He felt the sooner they reached the Black mountains the sooner he would be on his way to Islen.

Iskander had been going around the crowds of people and was now in deep conversation with an increasingly worried looking Skjarla. "There aren't a lot of professional soldiers left, but those few extra who escorted us through the Ways make a welcome addition. All in all there are about forty of us who have a lot of experience with various weapons."

Skjarla frowned, "That is a lot fewer than I would have liked, but I'd have thought that would have meant all of you made it through the Ways in one piece."

A sad, tight smile flittered across Iskander's angular face, "We both know that it's not the old who die, and it's the young and inexperienced."

Skjarla shook her head in sad agreement, "Too true old friend, but how many of the Lonely Company, as they like to call themselves, and are still standing?"

"Around one hundred and forty men and women. Some of the injured may return, but the nature of our last clash with the Smaparmar meant that we didn't exactly have a lot of time to stop and collect the wounded."

Even Skjarla shuddered at that thought, "I wouldn't want to be left alive at the hands of those foul creatures. I've heard they often make a meal of Dwarven flesh when they get their hands on it." A sickening image of bones being crunched between gnarled black teeth and flesh being stripped from still living bodies flashed through her mind. "I'm glad to have you with us Iskander, we'll have need of everyone's skills before this skald is over."

Iskander smiled, running his gnarled hand over his tightly tied back iron grey hair, "One last adventure with the greatest Reaver, who could turn that down?" He grinned irreverently, adding, "One last chance to convince you to share my bedroll."

She gave him a friendly shove, "Iskander, you always say that and you always end up disappointed, when are you going to give up and realise it won't happen."

A sly smile, "The day I get old." They both laughed at that, this man well into his fifties who refused to acknowledge the steady march of the years.

The other members of the column stopped to see why the two of them were laughing like maniacs, then shrugged and got back to what they were doing. Loading up the dried meats and cheeses alongside giant amphorae of water, many could be heard to remark that fresh air and fresh food were going to be a blessing when they reached the mountains. After long months of surviving off only dried foods Skjarla had to agree with them.

There was no fanfare as the column of refugees slipped into the unnatural brightness of the Ways. Many shuddered as they passed beneath the harsh white glow of those lights, the oppressive brightness bringing to the surface things best forgotten. They were accompanied down the ancient paving slabs of the Ways but the perpetual squealing of axles and the mournful sounds of the draught animals. Those who had already done a journey like this kept their hands on their swords, waiting for the first screeches of the Smaparmar.

Their guides from Sundark Hold had not travelled this way before, but they had been assured by soldiers from Nightfast Hold that this section of the Ways only lead up to the surface. Closer inspection of the walls showed that they were still made of rough sandstone, which meant they were still under the desert. It was strange to think that far above them were tribes of nomads eking out their existence around the few oases which dotted the endless expanse of the Vfar. They trekked on, Skjarla, Domitia, Metellus and Helania struggling under the constant glare which made sleep such a battle. The others had managed to prepare themselves for this ordeal, someone had had the bright idea of tying a length of cloth across the eyes when they stopped to sleep, and soon the rest of the column had copied them.

For the first few days, as they waited for an attack, the mood was subdued, but as the days drew on and no sign of anything monstrous was heard the mood became steadily lighter. The people tried to put behind them the memories of those who had fallen on the journey, close to seven hundred had died on the journey to Nightfast Hold. Those who survived had been hardened by their experience, many of them had a dull sheen on their eyes, the look of someone who believed that they would be trekking forever.

Accipiteri was working as hard as he could; he seemed to be everywhere trying to bolster people's spirits, giving encouragement where he could. It heartened Skjarla to see the rest of them following his lead, even the Romans helped where they could. When the journey had begun, thousands of miles away to the north, the Romans had very much been a group within a group but, partly because there were now so few of them, they had become part of the column.

The first part of lifting the darkness from the people came eleven days into their three week trek. The walls of the passages changed from the red sandstone, the colour of the setting sun, to the black rock which glittered in the light. The tiny crystals embedded in the pitch black stone seemed to glimmer and send a myriad of colours scudding across the ceiling, it was truly spectacular. Those youngest members of the column, around eight years old started to recover some of their childhood, playing and racing the length of the column. Often the delighted squeals of the children were pursued by the indignant bellows of the draught animals who disliked having small children darting beneath their bellies.

It saddened many people to hear this though. Most of the youngest children had perished on the journey between the Holds, unable to live with the punishing demands of the trek. Sigmund hoped that there would be new life again when they finally reached the castle. For the moment though, they were busy plodding along the Ways, but one day this seemingly endless trek would come to an end. In a way it was not something he was looking forward to, when they reached whatever was left of the castle he was expected to become a king. Not only would that, but everything he did when he had the Iron Crown upon his brow be measured against Sigurd, the founder of his dynasty. For all of the training and assistance that they gave him, his friends couldn't turn a man who barely a year ago was just a simple labourer into a king.

It was a thought that preyed on his mind constantly as he walked down the ways, feeling increasingly lonely in the crowd of people. His friends tried their best to console him, but only Domitia had any real chance of success, "Sigmund, I've told you before, being a ruler is not something which you can be trained for or choose to be, you're born with it in you. I know that if your ancestor was half the king the legends say then you have got everything you could possibly need inside you."

Sigmund gave a sad, hollow laugh, "That may be the case for someone like you, whose father is the emperor. Think about me though, this isn't my father or even my grandfather we're talking about, this is going back well over ten generations."

"Sigmund, the usurper would be a terrible emperor."

"By the usurper I assume you mean your half brother," he interrupted her.

"Of course I do," she snapped briefly, "but my point is that even though he's my father's son he is not fit to look upon the Imperial throne, let alone sit upon it."

Sigmund blew out a noisy breath and shook his head, "How is that helping your point?" His voice was full of frustration and anger, more at his situation than at her.

"What I am saying is that not everyone has it in them to be a ruler, but I think that you do." Her tone was sharp, angry at having to dig herself out of a hole.

Sigmund still wasn't satisfied, "Domitia, that may be the case, and it may be that leadership is in the blood. But listen, I still don't know what to do, how to write laws or pass down judgements. I don't even know how to lead men into battle, and these people deserve better than someone just using trial and error."

She smiled and squeezed his hand, "Well, I'll always be here to help if you want."

Sigmund dropped behind her, his mind whirring as he tried to work out what she had just said, what the true meaning of her words was.

***

There was something magical about it, the sight of motes of dust dancing through the air as the gentle breeze stirred them and they caught the sunlight spearing in through the mouth of the cave. The air had taken on a chill edge in the last few hours as the Ways had tilted gently upwards before vanishing altogether. They had sweated and grunted together for the last two hours as they heaved the heavy carts over the uneven ground which didn't look like it had seen human feet in decades. Sigmund had taken off his armoured breastplate to make it easier for him to throw his shoulder against the heavy oak frame of their cart, his legs pumping furiously to drive it over the rough ground.

As they reached the top he wished that he still had it on, the wind was whistling around the mountain from which they had just emerged, he could see it dragging plumes of snow from distant peaks. He stood there, on the gateway between the surface and the subterranean world from which they had just emerged, sweat running down his bare chest to collect against his armoured legs. The sun seemed watery down here, even though it shone off the thin layer of snow which dusted everything in sight. Iskander came and stood next to him, his thick, tattered Reaver cloak, so dark that it seemed to make a feast of the light, wrapped tightly around his shoulders.

"Quite the sight isn't it?" His voice was soft but full of awe.

Sigmund smiled, "Certainly makes a pleasant change from the monotony of the tunnels." He paused for a moment before continuing, his voice reverential, and "It feels strange to think that some of my ancestors might have stood and taken in this view."

They fell silent for a moment, waiting as the next cart, pulled by a sweating bullock and pushed by more sweating refugees, passed them by. The cheers as the people emerged from the Ways were truly heart warming, there was a sense that the many ordeals of their journey would finally be over.

Strangely Sigmund felt that Iskander would probably be one of the easiest people to talk to, he was so irreverent and yet so wise, he might be able to offer some useful advice. "Iskander, look, do you have any idea what is going to happen when we reach whatever is left of the castle."

Iskander smiled curiously, "You'll be proclaimed king of course, heir to the Iron Crown."

Sigmund sighed, "But why? Why must I be king? Surely Skjarla or Accipiteri or any of the rest of you would make better rulers than I would."

Iskander said as kindly as he could, "You may be right, but destiny is what it is and you've got to live with it. The reason you must be king is if we try to put anyone else on the throne then the tribes which once swore allegiance to Sigurd would probably take exception to that, it has to be you. As to whether someone would be a better king than you it is debateable. Maybe someone would make a better king than you, but the fact that you worry about failing makes you more likely to succeed. Trust me, the worst types of ruler are the ones who believe that just because they have some metal on their heads they are right and justified in everything they do." A dark shadow crossed his face, the normally affable mask suddenly and briefly becoming terrible to behold.

Sigmund wasn't completely satisfied, "But what makes you think that the other people from Lonely Barrow will accept me though? After all, they know that I am just a common day labourer, no royalty that is for certain sure."

Iskander tried to be kind but he wished that Sigmund would stop moping about it. For the past three weeks they had heard nothing but gripes from him and they were all getting increasingly fed up with it. Normally he was a nice enough man, but Sigmund was getting on everyone's nerves recently. "Look, you'll have all of us to back you, and you've fought side by side with the Lonely Company. They'll support you. I think that after all that you've done in the last few months to help lead the column the people will follow you, but if you don't think that's enough then nothing I can say will be." He stalked off, heading up to the front of the column where Skjarla was walking with their guides.

Sigmund still felt a niggle of doubt, but if Iskander felt like that then maybe there was some truth behind what everyone had been saying for the last few weeks. He jogged along the column, going to catch up with the cart he had lobbed his breastplate into. Effortlessly he scrambled into the bed of the cart and began shrugging the leather harness over his head and strapping the heavy plates of steel onto it. The pieces of the armour were certainly looking worse for wear, chips and dents scarred the surface and it had lost much of its sheen. He, and many of the others, were hoping that the Dokkalfar who came with them would have some of the skill at the forge that their people were so famous for.

The Dokkalfar with Skjarla were constantly glancing up at the sky, for Fjirsk, Torae and Tomani this was there first time not having hundreds of spans of stone above their heads. Helania and Braugr had tried to reassure them but the three of them could not comprehend the vast infinity of the sky. "Well Valkyrie, here are the Black mountains, as promised." Fjirsk spoke with a note of wonder in his voice at the sight of the towering black peaks clawing up into the sky, the pristine shards of snow clinging to the sides of the mountains.

"Don't look so worried, Fjirsk. If my memory serves me correctly then that mountain there in the distance ..." She pointed along the line of black crags stretching away to their left, "Is where we're heading for." There was a peak far away which seemed to be falling over, a gentle incline on one side which fell away in a sheer cliff from the peak. "Once we get there we are at the entrance to the pass straddled by Blackstone Castle."

Tomani pointed further to the left, into the small gaps between the peaks, "Skjarla, why do I get the feeling that that is not a normal thing for the sky to do?" She was pointing at a wall of cloud almost as black as the peaks of the mountains.

"No," was all Skjarla said before turning to the people behind her, "Hurry. Make for the nearest cliff, pass it back," she roared. There was no action as people looked at her in confusion, "Blizzard," she shouted at the top of her lungs, pointing to the rapidly advancing wall of cloud. That got some action from the carts behind them, oxen and bullocks bellowed as the drovers applied their whips and switches to their thick hides, eliciting as much speed as they could from the tired animals. That they had suffered under the grip of the occasional blizzard which had rolled down across the forest to Lonely Barrow meant that they had some idea of what to expect. The storm and the snow on the hills meant that it must be around Winters Eve time in this southern part of Midgard, but whether it was before or after no one knew. It meant that they had been on the road for close to a year and a half and had travelled nearly the entire length of Midgard.

They were still half a mile away from the ridge of peaks when the first snow began to fall. The flakes were large and fluffy, clinging to everything they touched until the hides of beast and men alike were clad in soft white robes of snow. The most startling effect was seen on the four Dokkalfar, whose black faces clashed violently with their now pristine white clothing. Skjarla stalked the winter wonderland in her black armour like some demon hidden within the cloud of snow.

There was no time to light fires to keep warm. All they could do was circle the carts against the side of the cliff and bring the animals inside the wooden circle. The frozen people of Lonely Barrow could only huddle together miserably underneath their threadbare cloaks as they clung to any shred of warmth they could. The wind whistled through the gaps in their protective wall of carts and whipped their cloths into a snapping storm of fabric. Time lost all meaning as people fought to keep the chattering of their teeth to a minimum and clung to one another as they protected the sparks of warm life within their bodies.

It was fortunate that the storm's ferocity and violence was matched only by its brevity. Even so, there was close to a foot of snow on the ground and a large drift had built up around their small fortress of carts. It took them the rest of the day to clear the earth enough to light a fire, made by dismantling one of their carts. Several people were still shivering uncontrollably and were placed closest to the fire. The dozen people from the edges of their circle who had perished at the hands of the murderous cold were dragged away from the rest of the column.

Skjarla accompanied them with the Reavers, "Help me strip the bodies."

"What?!" exclaimed the startled refugees who had volunteered to help bury the dead.

"Those people died of cold, we need all the clothes we can get to make sure that no one else dies for the same reason." She tried to sound reasonable but merely gave the impression she was grinding her teeth.

One of the party lent on his shovel, "It just doesn't seem right, leaving them in the earth with nothing on."

The Reavers had already moved forward, ready to start stripping the bodies but halted as Skjarla spoke again.

"Maybe, but nothing about dying of cold after you've survived this far is right. These people," she gestured to the row of blue corpses, "Don't care how they go into the earth, their suffering is over and it is our duty to minimise the suffering of our fellows." Her voice hardened, "That is why these bodies will be stripped, either by you or us I don't care, but there are living people who need those clothes."

The refugee looked like he was about to argue again, then thought better of it, bending his back to continue digging the shallow grave in the frozen earth. Elsewhere another group were performing a similar task, breaking up the frigid sods of earth as they dug the jack's trench. The Reavers bent to their task with cold, dispassionate determination, gently but determinedly removing the clothes from the corpses before bundling them up to distribute amongst those who were worst off. With one cart less to pull they took one of the bullocks away from the herd and slaughtered the beast. It wasn't much but it did at least supplement the dried food on which they had been feasting for months and the hot food did much to restore the mood around the camp.

The next day they pushed the earth in on top of the jack's trench and marched past the few sad mounds of earth which marked their fallen companions. Without another glance back they headed on towards the leaning peak in the distance. All of the land before them and the mountains to their left were covered in a thick blanket of snow, a white sheet spread over the surface of Midgard. As they sun made its slow, lonely journey across the pale blue sky the peak grew, until it stretched far over their heads, the sheer cliff face drinking in the light of the afternoon sun. Just beyond the towering walls of black stone there was a wide path, leading into the heart of the Black Mountains. It was wide enough for several carts abreast and seemed to climb for the next few miles. They marched with the fresh snowfall crunching underfoot and shards of light scattering from the pristine snow on mountains.

They made their way along it in cheerful chatter, the voices echoing back towards them from the mountains, although the snow did help to deaden the sound somewhat. Skjarla didn't mind the talking at the moment, it took a good week to traverse the Black Mountains, and Blackstone Castle was at the far end of the pass. When they got closer to the Keep then she would need quiet, whatever was waiting for them in whatever remained of the castle would be much easier to deal with if they could surprise it.

The air became cooler and thinner as they climbed higher into the pass, although the weather remained mercifully fine after the blizzard of the previous day. Looking back over their shoulders from the height of the pass they could all see the distant yellow smudge on the horizon which marked the edge of the great desert. The wind was whistling up the pass and swirling around the craggy peaks which flanked their passage, tossing swirling plumes of powdery snow into the air. It was strangely alien and yet wonderfully beautiful to behold. The last time that Skjarla had trudged this route it had been the height of summer and the breeze had been a blessing, but the mountains had seemed so harsh against the bright summer sun. Strangely she preferred it like this; it reminded her of winters spent away from Valhalla, riding across the snow covered ground of the old Midgard, seeking those worthy to dwell in the hallowed halls of Valhalla.

With all of the wood from the cart burnt the previous night they spent several cold nights in the pass, huddled into any crags and crannies which they could find as the wind howled mournfully. On the sixth night Skjarla called Iskander and Accipiteri to her and set off into the darkness, leaving Sigmund in charge with instructions to carry on along the pass when the dawn broke. There had been no snow in the last few days and the wind had scoured the black stone pass clear so that there would be no trace of their passing. Accipiteri had borrowed a cloak from one of the other Reavers so that his gilded but battered armour did not catch any of the moonlight.

It was to be a full moon that night, plenty of light for the three of them to cast their eyes over the defences. While Iskander had never assaulted a keep in his life they hoped that his eyes might spy some crevice in the land which they could exploit to approach the walls unseen should they need to. At first they thought that the fortress was abandoned, and indeed the outer area was, but the light of dozens of fires could be seen in the central two courtyards.

Blackstone Castle straddled the entire width of the pass; a great curtain wall on either side of the castle once forced all traffic through the gates and beneath the inner wall off to one side of the pass. Behind that inner wall was the brooding presence of the keep, towering into the night and built into a mountain. That mountain had been partly dug away, the stones which had made up its heart had been put to use in the once proud walls. All over though, there were signs of decay, towers had collapsed in the outer wall as the wooden skeletons within had rotted away, creating breaches in the wall. Similarly the inner wall was breached in two places, great mounds of rubble forming a ramp up into the centre of the fortress. The gates seemed to be scorched and battered, marks of a castle which had been fought over many times. Atop all of the stones was a dusting of snow which clung stubbornly to the rock, even as the whistling wind tried to dislodge it.

It saddened Skjarla to see this once great keep covered in weeds, small shrubs forcing their way in between the stones and breaking open cracks with their roots. The most interesting thing was that there was no light from the windows of the keep, which looked utterly deserted.

"We need to get closer and see what we're dealing with here," she whispered to her companions. She picked up

Dreyrispa, her gauntlet clacking as her fingers closed around the worn and well loved wood, while her companions got to their feet.

"Iskander, any ideas for a safe way into the castle?" Asked Accipiteri quietly.

Iskander was checking the thin blade at his hip and gently tugging his daggers from their sheaths, making sure that nothing would stop him if they had to cut their way out. "Climb in through that crumbling tower. It looks like there is still enough of a shell to it that we may be able to climb up the wall and see what is going on in the central courtyard."

Skjarla swore softly, "I'm guessing that means that you expect me to climb the tower seeing as I'm the lightest here."

Iskander gave a low chuckle, "You guessed it, gorgeous."

Keeping low to the ground they jogged along the path, feeling the shadow of the wall grow over them as they approached the ruined tower. The outer edge of the tower had given way, and had taken a section of wall with it, but there was still a shard of stonework stretching high above the rubble. Careful not to send a shower of stones down the makeshift ramp they clambered up the slope, the thin light of the moon showing them the way. Once they reached the bowels of the ruined tower, avoiding the spars of rotting wood which poked from beneath the rubble of the floors, Skjarla handed Dreyrispa to Iskander and took two daggers out of her baldric. These would be useful for jamming into cracks if there were no handholds.

Given the state of decay of the walls there were plenty of cracks for her to stick her feet into and even small shrubs growing out of the stonework that she had to navigate. The frozen stones and snow served to numb her fingers almost instantly but she doggedly kept climbing. Just as she reached the top of the wall, her muscles trembling from the exertion and her breath coming in deep gasps, she heard a thunder of wings and a cacophony of indignant squawking. She had disturbed a nesting raven that had made its home atop that precarious perch. Skjarla froze, waiting to hear the roars from inside the courtyard but there was nothing, and they clearly weren't expecting anything to happen that night.

Skjarla raised herself above the parapet, her eyes able to peer over the inner wall and get a glimpse of that was going on in the courtyard. Clearly there were some people camped against the inner wall, she could see the thin trails of smoke from their cooking fires climbing into the starry sky. Around the rest of the courtyard she could see bodies clustered around fires and there were a small collection of ramshackle huts built against the walls of the keep. Wary of being spotted, even though the occupants of Blackstone Castle seemed more intent on sheltering from the cold winters night by their fires than anything, Skjarla began her descent.

As she reached the bottom she peered into the centre of the castle through the four-span wide gap in the wall where the tumbling tower had taken some of the wall with it. She gathered her two companions close and whispered softly, "We need to take this breech. I would hazard close to one hundred people in the centre of the castle, if they bottle us up here then it is all over."

"Agreed," Accipiteri nodded severely, "How did the defences look for the inner wall?"

"One wide breach near us, about ten spans wide and a gentle slope up to it. The gates are lying on the ground in front of the gatehouse so once we're in then we can assault them on two fronts."

Iskander stroked his pointed chin, his hand grating against the grey stubble which was growing there. "How do you plan to take the outer wall then?"

Skjarla flashed her teeth in a lupine grin, "Simple, we hold it when they wake up. We're going to make our way back to the column and bring everyone who can bear arms back up here. It'll be close but we should be able to take the wall just as the dawn sun comes up."

Accipiteri nodded, "That would be best, I wouldn't want to have to try and take this breach, not when there is probably plenty of rubble on the walls for them to throw at everyone. We'd better hurry back to the others."

As quietly as they had come, the three shadows slunk back out into the pass, making their way towards the sleeping members of the refugee column. By the time they had reached the column the moon was already partly obscured by the peaks to the west, they did not have long. Messages were quickly passed along and people were shaken into wakefulness, groggily they strapped on whatever armour they had. Accipiteri and the others knew that they would have to use the more experienced and better armoured fighters as a fist with which to break this fortress open, otherwise the losses would be horrendous.

The stars were winking out one by one as the dawn crept onto the eastern edges of the sky when the Lonely Company finally set off. There were orders for absolute silence relayed the length of the column; surprise was going to be key here. As they crested the final rise in the pass, a little over a mile from the walls of Blackstone Castle they broke into an easy, loping run, quickly closing the distance to the walls. The dawn sun gave the Black Mountains golden halos of pale sunlight as the first rank of the assault column charged up the scree and rubble ramp and through the gap in the wall.

Shouts of alarm came from the inner wall as this sudden attack was noticed. All pretence of silence was abandoned as Accipiteri roared orders to the people around him. "Sigmund, you and the Romans take some men to the gate and go in through there." Sigmund nodded and grabbed the six remaining Legionaries, Metellus and five others, as well as their Dokkalfar guides and the first fifty men and women of the Lonely Company.

As he charged off to the gate, in the front rank next to Metellus, Accipiteri turned to Braugr, "Go with him, if he falls all is lost." The Dwarf charged off as fast as his short legs would carry him, they all knew that Sigmund's life was the most important thing they had to preserve, and he was their only claim to this place. "Skjarla, bring your Reavers, we're going to lead the assault over the top. Helania, use you bow and pick off anyone who shows their head over the top of the wall." The Dokkalfar nodded grimly and gracefully bent to string the thick limbs of her Whorl Root bow.

The rest of them set off up the stone ramp, only to be met at the top by a wall of steel. "On, on, drive them before you," roared Accipiteri, brandishing his broadsword. The current occupants of the castle were a rag-tag band, most were clad in old leathers, although there was some mail or scale armour between them. They brandished axes, spears or swords with their painted round shields, clearly people from the Svellvindr peninsula who had been driven north by something. The two lines collided with a fearful crash, the weight of numbers helping to push the defenders back from the crest of the rise.

With Accipiteri, Skjarla and Iskander at the tip of the spear they punched deep into the hastily arrayed shield-wall, a welter of blood and limbs covering them as the razor sharp steel claimed lives without mercy. From behind them they heard a scream followed by a sickening crunch as one of the defenders toppled off the battlements, run through by one of Helania's arrows.

Round in the darkness of the gateway Sigmund stepped back from the frontline, the dark, and rubble strewn corridor was only wide enough for four men at a time. He knew that the Roman line was the best chance for cutting a bloody passage through the darkness and crushing bodies. He set his shoulder to the man in front of him, and felt someone else behind his do the same, shoving the wall of red Roman shields forwards. Metellus and the other Romans held their gladii out in front of them, the blades flickering in between the gaps of the shields like snake tongues, the second rank plunging their blades into those unlucky enough to be trampled underfoot.

Steadily they drove them back into the courtyard, pushing them back away from the wall and up against the keep, leaving a trail of bodies, both friend and foe, behind them. The pressure on the two lines of fighters suddenly gave way as the defenders ran backwards. A roared order from one of them led to some angry looks amongst themselves, but they stopped. "Who comes to my castle?" called a voice from the crowd as a burly man complete with long plaited hair and a bright red beard pushed his way to the front.

Sigmund stepped out in front of the line of his fighters, all of whom were breathing heavily. It was a strange feeling, the eyes of everyone on him, but the knowledge that he could change nothing about his situation now, could not abdicate responsibility, and calmed him. "I ask you the same question? By right of blood this is my home."

There were some confused glances from the men behind him, but the leader of these brigands laughed scornfully, "You claim the blood of Sigurd Dragon slayer? What proof do you have?"

"I have this sword and this armour. Now, again, why are you in my keep?"

Before the giant bear of a man could answer Skjarla's voice rang out, she had stepped from the line and removed her helmet, letting the long raven-black hair spill out across her armoured shoulders. "You know who I am, or you will have heard tales of me. Take my word for it when I say that he is the heir to the Iron Crown."

There was a muttering from the crowd of cornered Vindrmen, as those who recognized Skjarla from their ancestor's tales told their companions who it was. The effect was magical, blades clattered to the ground and the cornered men bent the knee before Sigmund and Skjarla.

For a third time Sigmund asked, "Why are you here?"

The leader of these bandits spoke, staring at the ground, "We were driven from our lands at the end of the peninsula. The land sickened and died and we were forced to leave, chased by the servants of Wotan. None of the other tribes would take us in. Those of us who had fled rather than serve Wotan, who had been forced to leave our families behind, this was the only place we could find shelter. As you can see there is little food or shelter here, we were forced into banditry."

Sigmund made a decision, trying to keep the nerves out of his voice and sound like a king, "I'm going to offer you a choice. Serve me and help return this place to its former glory, regain your honour and become men once more or die here and now."

The leader of the bandits spoke again, "I will follow you, but I will not speak for my fellows."

One by one they all swore an oath to him, to become part of the Lonely Company and live like men again. Now came the real test, for Sigmund saw that the doors to the keep were still sealed and he had no idea how to open them. He walked between the kneeling ranks of the subdued bandits whose weapons were being collected by a few nervous looking lads from the Lonely Company. The door itself was a giant façade of ancient wood sheathed in thick bands of black steel. At the centre of the doors was a round object, part of a locking mechanism of some form, with a hole in the centre.

Sigmund ran his armoured hands across the ancient metal, covered with grey-green lichen. He had no idea what to do here, how the hell was he supposed to open the door to this fortress? His ancestor must have left him some way to get into the keep, although there was only one thing he carried which might work. He drew and reversed his sword, gripping the blade which still dripped with blood, feeling the edges biting gently into his fingers. He pushed the ornate pommel into the stone, a wave of relief washing over him as he heard the faintest click as the guards on the hilt kissed the steel lock and disappeared into the lichen.

He grimaced as he turned the blade, the razor sharp edge biting deep into his palms and fingers, he could feel the hot rush of blood as it seeped between his fingers. There was a soft grating noise as something began to shift within the keep, small puffs of dust appearing as the doors shifted an inch. He lent on the blade, gritting his teeth to stifle the scream as the blade slide along the length of his hand, the door sliding open enough for a small shaft of light to spear into the space. One more turn and he heard another soft click and the lock's grip on his sword, now shining crimson, released. He set his shoulder to the door and was rewarded with a deafening groan as tortured hinges, unused for nearly four centuries, shifted a little. Others came forward and helped him, throwing their weight against the cold steel of the door and sending the aged wood groaning across the stone flagged floor of the keep.

The hinges finally gave and the doors flew wide open, revealing the interior of a castle uninhabited since Sigurd's time. Cobwebs festooned every inch of the grand entrance hall and walls of dust were kicked up with every step they took. Sigmund stopped ten paces into the entrance hall and looked around, taking in the tall pillars, round and carved with all manner of beasts. At the end of the dusty room was a high throne, carved from the same black stone as the rest of the building, but inlaid with dusty gold and silver. Two smaller thrones flanked the main one, later Skjarla explained that the one of the left was for the queen while the king's advisor took the one on the right.

As Sigmund led the procession up the moth-eaten rug which covered the approach to the throne, a giant fireplace on either side of the approach, he caught sight of an object on the dust covered cushion. He mounted the steps of the dais to see the iron crown before him, although it was no longer the steely grey that Sigurd's crown had been famous for. Instead it was now a rough, reddish brown, with only the occasional grey of the original iron showing through. "A rusted crown for an age of decay, it seems apt doesn't it?" he said to no one in particular.

He was about to step forwards and pick up the crown when Skjarla stopped him. "No, wait for the rest of the column to arrive, everyone should see this and know that we have reached our destination."

He sighed, feeling very tired, "I suppose you're right." His vision was swimming somewhat when Helania stepped forward, in her hands she held some plain strips of cloth.

"You haven't bandaged your hands yet, let me do it," she said, gently taking his hands which were still dripping a steady stream of blood onto the dusty floor. He sat down on the dais, his face pale as he let Helania tightly wrap the coarse bandages around the deep cuts in his hands. Outside the wounded were being treated. About a dozen of the Lonely Company had died in the courtyard, once they had emerged from behind armoured heads of the columns and into the melee by the ruined gates. Sigmund got woozily to his feet, feeling that it was his duty to go and see the wounded outside. He could not describe it, but being here somehow gave him the feeling that he was meant to be here, and that he should try to be the king he would want to follow.

While he made his rounds of the wounded, helping tie bandages or just offering words of encouragement or comfort where they were needed Skjarla and Accipiteri made their way down the stairs at the back of the entrance hall. There was a far grander staircase leading up into the heights of the keep, but it was more likely that anything useful or valuable would be stored in the vaults below the castle.

"What are we looking for?" Asked Accipiteri, confused as to why this couldn't wait.

"Something which bares the mark of old Sigurd," Skjarla said, feeling along the walls for a torch she could try and light. Eventually she found one, thanks to the fact that it had been kept tinder dry for centuries meant that the oil soaked rags at the head of the torch lit at the first strike of flint. "I want someone from down in the plains beyond here to see it, I want to see if any will remember their allegiance to this castle, back in the days when Sigurd lived here."

"What makes you think that they will?"

"Nothing beyond the usual Vindrman curiosity and the hope that they remember the vows their forefathers made." Skjarla smiled, "I think they will come, by all accounts things aren't right on the Svellvindr peninsula. If they believe that there's a king here again that can protect them then they'll come."

"That makes sense," Accipiteri nodded, his lustrous armour seemed to take on a life of its own beneath the flickering orange glow of the torch. The walls down here were cleaner than those upstairs, no moisture in this part of the castle to feed the lichens which covered the stones elsewhere. "How do you know where you're going?"

"Accipiteri, you forget, I've been here before, lifetimes ago admittedly, but I've been this way before." She didn't turn as she spoke, continuing deeper down the spiral staircase into the bowels of the keep.

They reached the bottom of the stairs and were presented with an iron door, the key in the lock. "Guess that Sigurd must have been confident that no one would get past that outer lock." Accipiteri said mischievously pointing at the plain key.

Skjarla ignored him as she turned the key, the well-oiled lock giving a low click which echoed down the passageways. She and Accipiteri walked through the low stone arch, pushing the door out of the way as they headed into the vaults of Blackstone Castle.

Above their heads the carts of the refugee column had crested the rise, eliciting cheers of joy from the fighters in the courtyard and the distant crowd alike. Domitia had been leading the column at an even pace, worried about what they would find on arriving at the castle. The people had been restless; if the assault had failed then they would be forced to run, back towards the deserts behind them. There was almost no chance that they would live if they were driven into the wastelands at the northern edge of the Black Mountains.

There was a huge sigh of relief as they caught sight of the red and gold motifs emblazoned on the giant Roman shields, a sure sign that they were in control of the keep. They picked up speed, the people cheering like mad as they streamed down the hill, for the first time in over a year they had a home.

As they got inside the first wall, leaving the carts outside the ramp through the ruined tower as the gate was clogged with debris which would take days to clear; Domitia peered up at the top of the keep. She could see two tiny specs, figures in the distance, atop the flat black stone of the highest tower. Between them they seemed to be manhandling something up there, over the edge of the tower. As it fell the wind took it, lifting the length of fabric into the cold winter sky where it snapped in the breeze, anchored solidly to the stone of the keep.

The flag was as long as three men were tall, and nearly a span wide. On the rich blue cloth, the colour of the deepest ocean, were embroidered a pair of rearing stallions, every inch of their white hides picked out in spectacular detail. 'That flag must be the banner of Sigurd', was Domitia's conclusion although she had no idea why they had decided to fly it, surely it was better to create their own identity. Domitia also thought that advertising their presence was a mistake, just because the nearby tribes had once been loyal to Sigurd did not mean that they would now meekly follow Sigmund. It was more likely that they would try to take the Iron crown for themselves. She would have waited until the fortress was repaired, and then act from a position of strength, but there was nothing which could be done now.

She had fallen behind the main body of refugees as she stared up at the tower and now followed them into the castle. Greeted by scenes of jubilation as the tired, dishevelled and exhausted people of Lonely Barrow staggered the final yards of their journey she couldn't help but smile. These people had won her over with their unending fortitude and stoic bravery. Some unknown signal rippled through the crowd and they began to press into the dusty hall of the keep. The remnants of her guards found her and helped to forge a path through to the front of the crowd for her.

As she emerged from the sea of people she caught sight of her friends clustered around Sigmund, sat upon the throne. Skjarla stood before the crowd and a hallowed silence fell upon them, a collective intake of breath as she lifted the circlet of decaying metal above her head. "People of Blackstone Castle, welcome to your new home," There was a cheer at those words. "I present to you your king, Sigurd's heir, Sigmund Olafsson." She placed the rusted crown upon his brow, where it nearly fell down about his ears, but just managed to stay up. It would fit better once it was returned to its seat atop Sigurd's helm.

There was no cheering, the people were uncertain as to what they should do now. Sigmund got to his feet, taking in the cool gaze of his people. They were waiting to judge him as a king even though they all knew him as a man. "This place is steeped in history. The greatest king of our age once walked these halls, but we will add our own tale to his, for what we shall do here is something which will be inscribed on the very stones of this place for all eternity." He paused for a moment, "The most important thing we have now is a home, and I for one have no intention of losing our new land." This was met with cheers from the crowd, "For tonight we will all be in the courtyard, but over the next few days we will open the castle, mark out new buildings, we will rebuild this place and reclaim its glory from the rust and rot of time."

He sat back down slowly, signalling that his speech was at an end and the people filed out of the audience chamber, quietly talking among themselves. It would be hard to rebuild this place properly, but then they were no strangers to hardship. Sigmund gathered his council around him to begin issuing orders; it surprised all of them how much he seemed to have been possessed by the spirit of Sigurd.

"Accipiteri, I want you to supervise getting the carts through the wall and into the centre of the castle. Once they're there, Metellus, I want you to dismantle them and use the wood to erect some form of shelter. Fjirsk, I want you to head back to Nightfast hold," The Dokkalfar looked confused at this request and was about to say something but Sigmund ploughed on. "No one here has the skill to put the stones right, we need Dwarven masons, unless Braugr thinks he can direct things?" He turned to the lone Dwarven companion.

"Sorry, Lad, can't help you, I've never been one for working the stone."

"That's settled then, unless you think you need a companion or two for the road Fjirsk?"

The Dokkalfar shook his head with a grim smile, "I'll make the journey quicker on my own. It'll take some time though, I won't be back for close to two months, and that is if I can convince anyone to come with me."

Sigmund shrugged, "Well there's nothing else which can be done about it, and we need a mason. Domitia, you and Helania are to sort out food and try and get some people to get the cobwebs and dust out of here. Last but not least, Iskander, I want you and the other Reavers to supervise getting things out of the Vaults. Skjarla says there is quite the trove of useful things down there, things Sigurd thought he would need when he returned." He wasn't lying; Skjarla and Accipiteri hadn't found much in the way of gold but they had founds tonnes of steel, blades and armour all tightly wrapped in oiled cloths to prevent rust getting to them. That was a treasure worth having given the state of most of the arms and the lack of armour in the Lonely Company.

He had left Skjarla out for a reason. He wanted her to talk to the leader of the bandits about the situation on the Svellvindr peninsula and the presence of Skjarla would probably make that easier. The three of them stood around the throne once the others had gone, Sigmund was happy to let Skjarla do the talking for the moment; "Who is Wotan?"

The bandit, who had called himself Knut Halfdansson, looked nervous, as if the name itself carried a full power. "He is, or perhaps was, a Jarl right down on the stormy tip of the peninsula. About five years ago he started gathering people to his banner, and not a good kind of person either. Then the lands around his began to sicken and die, trees rotted and crops failed. Those Jarls who swore allegiance to Wotan saw their lands claimed, while those who failed to swear died at the hands of his followers. Every year the corruption spreads a little further." He licked his lips nervously and his eyes shifted twitchily, "Those of us who you found here, most of us were in the same situation, our

Jarls wanted to swear and we didn't, so we left. We didn't realise how nervous of Wotan the other clans are though, they wouldn't take us in."

Skjarla seemed interested in Wotan, "What do you know of this man Wotan, though, and what about his followers?"

"He was only a Jarl for a few months before the troubles started; he claimed the leadership by rite of combat. As for his followers, I've only heard tales and many of them seem beyond belief. They say that the men have regressed to beasts, their ferocity knows no bounds, but in his land they are normal and whole, it is said that their bodies change to reflect the corruption of the lands."

Skjarla shocked them both when she said, "Good."

Sigmund rounded on her, "Skjarla, how can a maniac whose very presence corrupts the land beneath his feet be a good thing."

She shrugged, "He creates fear. The Jarls up here will have heard the tales and be nervous. They will see the reappearance of Sigurd's banner as a sign that you have come to reclaim the lands of your ancestor from this Wotan and they will follow you. As far as you're concerned Wotan has made gathering Jarls to your banner that much easier."

Sigmund looked uneasy, "I'm not sure I like that way of looking at it."

"Well that is what you're going to have to learn to do, its politics, seeing advantage in everything you encounter." Skjarla sounded frustrated that Sigmund seemed so uncomfortable with his good fortune, she knew that if life handed you any advantage then you should grab it with both hands. There was a phrase she had heard in Leopolis, 'Don't look a gift horse in the mouth,' she wasn't sure where it came from originally but it seemed apt for this situation. She just hoped that Sigmund would grow quickly into the King the people needed.

Chapter 16

Over the next few days they began to put the fortress back into working order. A few of the carts were still in one piece. On the slopes of the mountains to the south there were thick forests of firs and the people of Lonely Barrow were quick to use their logging experience to harvest the lumber for use in the fortress. People went hunting among the long shadows and daggers of light which existed beneath the canopy, supplementing what remained of their dried grain with fresh meat. The pickings were slim on the ground but there were still some deer in the forest, as well as birds on the wing. They all hoped that the warmer weather of the spring would improve things, but for the moment they were careful to protect what remained of their stores of food.

The hunters reported seeing the occasional horseman ride to within sight of the keep, just close enough to be able to make out the details on the banner before riding away again. Soon the Jarls would be coming; their curiosity would drive them here. Metellus and Accipiteri had distributed armour and weapons to everyone and were now drilling them. There were some good-natured complaints, but on the whole the people were pleased to be armed as well as they were, in polished steel scale armour. They were worked until they were drenched with sweat every day, even with the cool winter wind to chill them. There had been no snow since that blizzard but the sky was an ominous grey, heralding more inclement weather.

The keep itself seemed to glow as life returned to it. More of the old hangings were removed from the vaults, their sheen of dust beaten off. It was a strange feeling, unearthing the belongings of a long dead king. Torae and Tomani had been kept very busy, the two of them had a rudimentary knowledge of forge-work, and had supervised the use of the smaller stones from the rubble to build a decent smithy. They had been making repairs from the moment that the fires had been made hot enough. Other people were busy clearing the rubble from the outer gate, hoping to remount them once the fortress was back in working order.

They had been in the castle for about ten days when the first messenger arrived. Most of the man's face was obscured by his helmet, although the thick black beard spilled from beneath it and rolled over his chainmail armour. Tied to the top of his spear was a length of white cloth and he was riding a shaggy horse, a big barrel chested animal with a reddish brown coat. He rode up to close to two hundred spans from the wall on the Svellvindr peninsula side of the castle and bellowed out to the walls, "Who flies the Dragonslayer's banner?"

Word was passed back by the people working on removing the weeds and shrubs from the stones of the wall to summon Sigmund. He and Skjarla came to the wall, the rest of their group starting to drift in the direction of the shouting match. "I am Sigmund, I have claimed the Iron crown by right of blood. I am of Sigurd's line." His voice was solemn as he intoned those words. "Who are you and who do you come to speak for?"

The lone rider called back, "I am Leif Ulricsson, here to speak on behalf of the assembly of Jarls. My Jarl, Olaf Ericsson, and his fellows wish to meet with the new

327

occupant of Blackstone Castle. Will you come and meet them?"

Sigmund was about to speak when Skjarla cut across him, "He will meet them, but they will come here, to the halls of the king with the Iron crown."

"Who are you to speak for your king, does he hide behind a woman for fear of the Jarls?" laughed Leif scornfully.

"I am Skjarla, last of the Aesir, and you will not mock me. You will return to your assembly and tell them my name and then I will guarantee their safety that will be enough for them." Skjarla's voice rumbling like the roll of thunder, echoed back from the hills. Those on the walls next to her could see her knuckles whiten as she gripped Dreyrispa, the Valkyrie was itching for a fight, and it was just something in her nature.

The emissary bowed his head, "I will tell the Jarls. If they agree to your terms they will come five days from now." With that simple message he turned his horse and kicked it into motion, an easy walk down the path towards the plains and forests to the south. The people of Blackstone Castle watched him go, until he had disappeared around the bend in the path and was obscured by the trees. It was clear that he was riding to the nearest village, visibly only as a few lonely towers of smoke listlessly climbing into the sky.

Sigmund spoke to Skjarla, "Can you go after him?"

She looked confused, her eyebrow arching delicately, "Why? I probably won't catch him before he reaches the village, he's mounted and I'll be on foot."

"That may be so but that village has something I need."

Now Skjarla was interested, "And what would that be?"

Sigmund smiled with a certain warmth, "Mead. We cannot welcome the Jarls here without it, especially if your legendary consumption is anything to go by. I want you to make your way to the village and arrange for them to bring us some mead when the Jarls come to us. I'd send someone else but I suspect you're the only one they'd listen to."

She shrugged, it wasn't the worst idea she'd ever heard, "Alright, I'll go now."

As she started to descend she heard another voice, "I'm coming too," she whipped round to see Helania checking the fletching on her arrows.

Skjarla said nothing, just nodded; after all it would be nice to have some company. The two of them walked out from the gateway as Sigmund stood alone atop the wall, watching them leave. In truth he was feeling more and more isolated as the days wore on, the number of people coming to him with complaints or for advice seemed to grow exponentially. Domitia had been a god send, helping him to organise his friends into taking some of the weight off his shoulders. Indeed she seemed to be taking the lion's share of the work and for that he was extremely grateful.

He sighed heavily, there was now even more work to be done. The keep had to be prepared to receive the Jarls and had to impress them. The Lonely Company would need to look the part as the Jarls would undoubtedly come with their own guards. Now that the Iron crown was back in play they would be looking for any sign of weakness. The walls were still gap-toothed, and would be for the next few weeks until Fjirsk returned with someone who knew how to work the stone properly. At least the two gateways had been cleared of rubble. Behind him at that moment a group of sweating, straining men and women were heaving at ropes and pulleys. They strained to pull the great gates back upright, ready to be re-seated on their hinges.

The lumber from the nearby woods was already being put to use building new houses and other buildings, the foundations of some in the ground already while others where just shallow trenches in the earth. To his surprise, and everyone else's, Knut and his men had been very helpful and loyal; Sigmund suspected that most of the Jarls in the area would not have been as forgiving as he was. He and his men had been instrumental in finding that most crucial of resources; water. The brigands had been collecting buckets from a stream which could be traced up to a small spring further up the mountain. With the opening of the keep though, they were able to channel the stream through some small pipes hidden in the stone down into the giant cisterns beneath the walls. It was a slow process but the water level was steadily climbing up the black walls of the giant stone wells.

He ran his hand through his hair; he was tired, worn out by the stresses of leading these people. The coming of the Jarls was just another struggle. He was being circled by hungry wolves sniffing for any hint of weakness. If he could not appear strong then his fledgling kingdom would be swept away like flotsam before the flood. Under the stern eyes of Metellus and Braugr the Lonely Company were growing into the armour that had been left beneath the keep. The problem was that the food supplies were dwindling, and with the Jarls coming they would need to slaughter another of the two remaining bullocks. Sigmund didn't want to kill the other oxen unless he had to; they were needed as the basis for a new herd.

Knut had been advocating that they should march out of the mountains and just take what they needed from the lands of the tribes below them, but Sigmund had quashed the idea. They didn't know how many warriors they'd be up against, they couldn't afford to antagonise the Jarls at the moment. More importantly, with the fortress still broken open, it would not be wise to risk conflict. He hoped that Skjarla was successful, if anyone was likely to garner a little respect from the fierce Vindrmen it was her.

***

Skjarla and Helania returned that night full of smiles. The Jarls had almost fallen down before the last remnant of their Gods and had fought to offer the most aid. She had secured promises for animals as well as mead, all of which would be delivered when the Jarls rode into Blackstone Castle. They had been curious as to why she followed another man, rather than claim the Iron Crown herself. Indeed, several of the Jarls suggested to her that if something happened to Sigmund they would support her if she chose to claim the throne. She had laughed and said no, she was not one to become trapped by a throne. The Jarls had all been intrigued by Helania, Dokkalfar were something of a rarity in those parts, although not completely unheard of.

On her return to the fortress she met with Sigmund and then went up to the top of the keep, climbing the endless spiral stair. Accipiteri had taken to spending a lot of time up here, alone in silent contemplation. She found him there again today, leaning against the black stone parapet, his eyes staring into the limitless expanse of the sky. All around them the black, craggy peaks, still with snow clinging to their rough exteriors, stabbed up into the cold air.

"Is everything alright?" She asked, coming to stand beside him, resting her arms on the stonework.

He smiled sadly, still looking out into the nothingness, "Just looking for a sign." He sighed at her questioning silence. "This was not my quest. We've brought these people safely to their new home and still I am earth bound. I guess I am looking for a sign from the Lady as to what I should do next."

It was an awkward gesture, but Skjarla put a consoling hand in his heavily muscled shoulder, "Maybe it means your quest is not yet over. The people here aren't safe yet, not with that Wotan making his way up the Svellvindr peninsula, or ..." she tailed off.

"Or what?" he asked slowly.

"Or, your quest was never to help these people; maybe your quest was to help me recover the Fangs?"

He looked at her carefully, weighing up her words, his mind comparing the two paths she had laid before him with the tenets of the Lady. Part of his mind was surprised that he had not been able to see these two quests before him, but he had been so caught up in still being without his wings that he had had little time for any other thoughts at all.

"I can't help but think that the Lady has saved the Fangs for you, they are your quest. Maybe saving the people of Svellvindr from Wotan's corruption will be enough to gain the notice of the Lady." He paused, shocked, "Does that mean you're leaving us?"

Skjarla shook her head with a smile, "Not for a while yet, I have no idea of where to look for the Fangs, and until I do then I might as well stay here." She chuckled, changing the subject "I think Sigmund might be in for a bit of a shock though."

"Why's that?"

"Most of the Jarls wanted to know whether or not Sigmund was spoken for," Accipiteri looked confused, "If he has a woman."

"Ah. Why would they want to know that?"

"Well, I suspect that many of them have daughters of one description or another, I'm sure that they'd all like to become the new King's father-in-law." She winked salaciously.

Accipiteri chuckled, "Have you told him yet, or did you save it for a surprise?"

Skjarla shook her head, "I'll tell him before they get here, don't want him getting too confused by all of these women coming at him at once." Accipiteri roared with laughter and it gladdened Skjarla to see her friend coming back to normal. He didn't like to admit it but the losses while he had been leading people through the Ways had hit him very hard, this was probably the first time he had laughed in nearly three months. She dropped her voice a little, more serious now, "I'm glad you're staying here, though. One of us needs to go after the Fangs, but this fledgling Kingdom will need a strong hand on it."

Accipiteri looked a little confused, "How do you mean it will need a strong hand on it?" His voice was slightly suspicious.

Skjarla stretched her arms upwards, feeling her back crack satisfyingly, "Sigmund may be king, but he is no general. Metellus is a good man, but he is too loyal to his mistress by far and we both know that Braugr won't be here for much longer. Sigmund will need you to lead his army, especially with Wotan growing to be a bigger threat."

"Yes Skjarla, but you can't guarantee that he'll want to put me in charge of his armies."

Skjarla's voice hardened, "We'll see about that." With that ominous pronouncement she left Accipiteri atop the tower, making her way back down the endless spiral staircase, through the black stonework.

By the time the Jarls were sighted the work inside the fortress had progressed well. Dozens of houses were completed by now and dozens more were half-finished. There was still plenty of space in the outer courtyard for the Jarls and the rest of the people who were still without houses to camp. There was quite a crush on the walls as people strained to see the slow procession of men and women walking up the hill towards the gate of Blackstone Castle. There were dozens of men on horseback, each surrounded by a sea of flapping banners in a riot of colours. Around each of the small pockets of horsemen was a steel ring of heavily armoured men, their wickedly sharp weapons glinting in the pale winter sunlight.

The column halted before the walls of the keep and began to spread out as the Jarls rode forward on their own. Thirteen horsemen reined in before the gate and one, a giant of a man with iron grey hair and an ancient sword strapped tightly to his hip, over his thick fur coat. "I am Jarl Magnus. Will you allow us entry into your hearth, with a promise of safety for us and our men?"

Sigmund's voice rang out across the open space before them, the first green of spring dusting the plains in the distance. "I swear on the Iron Crown to honour the Jarls in my home. I bid you welcome to Blackstone Castle." He called down behind the wall, "Open the gates." A dozen straining men set their backs to the heavy locking bar and heaved it out of its brackets. They then hauled the gates open, allowing the Jarls and their retinues to make their way inside the boundaries of the fortress. The people of Blackstone Castle couldn't help but notice that each of the Jarls seemed to have brought at least one young woman with them.

Men of the Lonely Company formed a wall of steel on either side of the path to the inner gate, allowing the Jarls to ride in between them. Metellus had had them polishing their armour since the dawn and they shone in the watery noon day sun. The Jarls stood in their groups, waiting for Sigmund to greet them; he had got down from the walls and made his way into the centre of the fortress as soon as he had given the order to open the gate. He stood before them in his ancestor's armour, the Iron Crown around his brow, the rust rubbing off onto his forehead and giving the pale skin a reddish tint.

"I welcome you, noble Jarls, to Blackstone Castle."

One by one the Jarls came to him and presented themselves and their daughters. They were the leaders of the tribes nearest to the Castle, but they promised that those further afield would bow before the Iron crown. Fear of Wotan meant that many of them saw the re-emergence of the Iron Crown as a sign. Sigmund was grateful for Skjarla's presence, she was a living legend among the people of the Svellvindr peninsula and her support seemed to count for a lot with the Jarls.

Nonetheless Jarl Magnus did speak for all of the Jarls when he said, "What proof do we have that you have the right to wear the band of iron upon your brow?"

There was an angry mutter from Sigmund's followers, they did not like to see one of their own questioned, but Sigmund held his hand up to still the noise. "A fair question. To open this keep, where the Iron Crown rested upon that throne there," he pointed to the throne at the end of the audience chamber behind him, "I had to unblock the sealed door. The only way to do that was with the hilt of my ancestor's blade, the very sword I carry now. Beyond that I have no proof of my blood, save for the word of the Aesir."

The Jarls muttered among themselves, discussing this, before Jarl Magnus spoke again, "That is sufficient for now. We have much to discuss with you, not least the continuation of Sigurd's bloodline." He roared with laughter and slapped Sigmund heartily on the back.

Sigmund managed to smile weakly, "Yes, but for the moment, there is food laid out for you, a true feast."

"It is no feast without mead," Magnus turned to some of his men, "Fetch the wagons, we will wet our throats with our new king." Everyone packed into the open space of the inner courtyard cheered at that. A few of the Jarl's guards made their way to the back of the group and began unloading barrels from the cart.

The smell wafting out of the door of the keep was spectacular, as below in the kitchens giant joints of meat turned slowly on the spit, their fat crackling as it dripped into the flames. Giant wooden trestles had been laid out in the colossal audience chamber and the looming hall was soon filled with happy chatter as the people began to eat and drink. There were just enough cups to go round, but people were forced to resort to eating from the points of their daggers. Cutlery had not been a priority when it came to getting the fortress up and running again.

The people packed into the great hall set to celebrating, drinking and carousing. The two groups of soldiers kept surreptitiously sizing one another up but there was no violence, Skjarla saw to that, drinking with everyone. Accipiteri tried to keep close to her, but many of the Jarls' daughters who had been brought to catch Sigmund's eye seemed to be more interested in him. Sigmund came close to him at one stage and whispered quietly in his ear, "I hope you're enjoying all of the attention, at least it means that they're not bothering me."

By the time that evening fell there were bodies of people snoring drunkenly against the walls while the others in the centre of the audience chamber kept drinking and eating. The feast dragged on into the night until a silence, punctuated only by the low, rumbling snores of the comatose guests was all that remained.

It was noon the following day before all of the Jarls were back on their feet, all congratulating Sigmund on the success of the previous evening. Without much fuss they all agreed to meet to discuss what their relationship with the Iron Crown should be. With that in mind they gathered around a table in the audience chamber and closed out everyone else. Sigmund had brought Skjarla, Accipiteri and Domitia in with him to advise him. The Jarls looked at him expectantly as he got to his feet, his stomach rebelling against the punishment he had inflicted on it the previous evening.

He rested his hands on the still green wood of the table and looked at each of the Jarls, representing the tribes nearest to him as he tried to decide how to approach this problem. "Jarls of Svellvindr, welcome to Blackstone Castle. Here is what I propose, once, your families and mine were bound by ties of loyalty, I wish to reinstate those. For a proportion of food from your lands, at least until we are able to harvest a crop from around here, and your loyalty, I propose to lead a campaign against the threat of Wotan. The other Jarls will join us, those nearest to Wotan's lands fear what will happen to their people."

One of the Jarls, Frigr the lucky, got to his feet. "King Sigmund, your people have told us that while you are a good leader for them, you were a common labourer. What do you know about leading men into battle?"

There was a low rumble of agreement around the table, "It is a fair point, and I agree that it would be a problem if I were to personally devise the plans and our strategy. I will not be doing this though; I intend to appoint Accipiteri as my war leader. He has more than enough knowledge and experience to make up for my lack thereof. Is that acceptable to you?"

Frigr remained on his feet, "Lady Valkyrie, will you vouch for this decision? If you will then I will accept him as commander of Sigmund's forces."

Skjarla clapped a hand on Accipiteri's shoulder, "You could do a lot worse than him. He will make a fine commander for your men."

Another Jarl addressed Accipiteri directly, "But do you lead in the proper, Vindrman way?"

"As much as is possible I lead from the front, but to say I will always be the first to strike the foe is a lie. If that is not enough for you then I am not your leader." Accipiteri looked the Jarl in the eye and his voice was level as he spoke.

"Well, you may not be a Vindrman but at least you're honest. We'll see how you do against Wotan, but my men and I'll be behind you." One by one the other Jarls got to their feet to offer their men to support Accipiteri.

Magnus waved his fellows to their seats, "Before we decide how best to fight this war, I want us all to agree that we'll support King Sigmund and help supply this fortress. Personally I won't do so without one further condition." He paused for a moment, looking around his fellows as he said, "The death of Sigurd led to years of strife and death as people fought to lead here. Without an heir there was no clear line of succession. I want Sigmund to chose a bride and marry her before I commit my men and my lands to his crown."

There was a muttering of agreement around the table, Sigmund paled visibly, this was not something he wanted or had planned for. Domitia jumped in to save him, "Noble Jarls, while Sigmund agrees that establishing a bloodline is vital for the new kingdom, you cannot expect him to decide who should be his bride right now."

"Why not? Surely we just line them up and he picks the one he likes the look of the best?" One of the Jarls demanded gruffly.

Before Domitia could open her mouth one of the other Jarls interjected angrily, "You'd like that wouldn't you Bragi, just because your daughter is famously the most beautiful woman on the Svellvindr peninsula."

Before the meeting could descend into a brawl, the Jarls all on their feet trying to shout each other down, Sigmund hammered his fist onto the table. When this failed he waved to the two men by the door who slammed their spears into the stone floor until the waves of echoing thunder quieted the Jarls.

"Jarls, I will not chose a bride on looks alone," Sigmund tried to keep a calm face, he had expected this. He had guessed that Jarls would be keen to be his father in law, that way if anything happened to him then they would become king or regent, an easy and elegant way for one of them to gain the Iron Crown. "I will make this concession, I will marry on Midsummer's eve. I suggest that you leave your daughters here and return before the day and I will have chosen my bride. I will need a woman who can help me to govern wisely, who can teach me the ways of the Svellvindr peninsula. I will learn to be the king your people deserve; I have the strong arm but not the knowledge of the local customs."

Though this would have sounded strange to the Jarl's ears they didn't care, all were too caught up in the feverish hope of becoming the father of the king. The Jarls of the Svellvindr peninsula were no strangers to intrigue; the murder of the king would not be too alien a concept to them.

He found his mind drifting as Domitia argued with the Jarls over the terms of their treaty, when they would send supplies and how much, and when they would plan their campaign against Wotan. He was more concerned with the thought of having to marry one of the Jarl's daughters. His eyes glazing over as he tried to think of a way out of this fix, but the truth was that without an heir or a marriage there was no alliance with the Jarls, and without the Jarls the fortress would wither and die.

The meeting drew to a close and the Jarls walked out of the room, still discussing the relative merits of the daughters they had brought with them. Sigmund sighed heavily and shook his head, he had never dreamed of being a king, and during the journey he had never expected it to turn out like this. Responsibility for all these people was a heavy burden which seemed only to grow, especially as the Jarls were to swear allegiance soon.

He got to his feet and climbed the stairs, going to his chambers, once the chambers of the greatest king the Vindrmen had ever known. Nailed to one wall and drawn in faded colours on the hide of a great deer was a map of Midgard. Highly detailed around the Svellvindr peninsula and becoming increasingly vague towards the west, where the lands of the Roman Empire and the Red Father were locked in constant battle. There was the small blob of the Island of Ryhm, the strategically unimportant lump of land in the Mare Interanum where the two great nations had been at war for nearly fifty years. Although either could bypass the island it had become a matter of pride that one of them took it in its entirety, so both sides poured men and resources into a battlefield not more than two thousand times the size of Lonely Barrow.

***

The next day the Jarls left for their own fiefdoms, leaving behind their daughters but taking with them Braugr. He had bartered a small amount of gold for a place on Jarl Knut's next dragon ship to Islen, a lucrative journey for the Vindrmen considering the demand for furs and whale oil in the Haemocracy and beyond.

The weak sun of spring shone down upon the courtyard for that forlorn scene, made even more so by the pitiful fluttering of the banners in the almost non-existent breeze. Helania was struggling the most; she had been so close to Braugr for years now, he had been a surrogate father to her. She knelt down in the dust of the courtyard as she wrapped her arms around him in a tight hug, ignoring the discomfort as the plates of his battered and scarred armour pressed into her skin.

He squeezed her affectionately, stepping back so he could see her and wipe a tear away from her eyes, "Shed no tears for me, lass, I go to find my daughter," his voice was choked with gruff emotion.

Skjarla spoke from beyond Helania's back, "That's no excuse not to come back to us with her, Braugr."

Although he looked at Helania his voice carried to everyone, "Just try and stop me, I'll be back with my daughter before you can realise how much better off you are without me." That raised a weak laugh from the crowd that had come to see one of their number off.

Slowly the group of friends said their goodbyes to the Dwarf, who smiled weakly throughout the experience while internally he chaffed to be off. In his mind the faster he left the faster he would find Aetria.

Before long the Jarls became restless, having long since said their own goodbyes to their daughters and to Sigmund, giving Braugr an excuse to curtail his own farewells. As the Jarls and their guards streamed through the great southern gate in the outer wall, those staying behind climbed to the stone platform atop the gatehouse. They stood there waving frantically as Braugr and the Vindrmen disappeared into the dark embrace of the forest.

As the vibrant banners of the Jarls disappeared from sight the crowd on the walls broke up and the people of Blackstone Castle returned to their daily duties. They were hungry again, and would be on half rations until the first shipment of the promised grain arrived. It led to a surly mood, without the pageantry of the visiting nobles the people had little to distract them from their grumbling bellies. Indeed, they had become used to eating properly for the week that the Jarls had been there, but this had drained their stores and now they felt the effects of this even more.

Over the next few days, for all the resentment that it generated, Sigmund insisted that the Jarl's daughters would be properly fed. It was this detail that stuck in people's minds, not the fact that Sigmund himself ate the same food as them. For a group of people who had spent so long as equals, sharing in the hardships of the road, to see one of their number treated differently was a hard thing to swallow.

The grumbling grew over the next few days, but it was replaced by cheers when a caravan bearing Jarl Knut's banner rumbled into view. Clearly the Jarl felt that the best way to make sure that his daughter was favoured by Sigmund was to be seen as responsible for the supplies of the fortress. His men had been sent with orders to ensure that she was seen helping to unload the food and to keep the other princesses away. Looking on as he warily watched the guards; Metellus had to admit that it was a clever ploy. It was a well known thing in Rome that the love of the people could be a powerful weapon if used correctly, and Knut clearly knew the way to their hearts was through their stomachs.

The greatest change in the minds of the people was seen when the Jarl's daughters turned out for weapons drill whenever they saw men and women training outside the keep. Back in Lonely Barrow, before all this chaos had started, the sight of a woman with a blade at her hip would have been beyond strange, completely unbelievable. Now though, it was not even worthy of a second glance, the people had learnt that those without weapons can still fall before them. He guessed as well that they had different ideas about a woman's place in this part of the world, and having seen Skjarla at work; he was in no doubt that women could be as deadly as their male counterparts.

With more food now in the fortress life became more normal, people still going out hunting to supplement the food the Jarls sent them, others working feverishly to clear the forest to the south. The newly cleared ground was planted with seeds in the hope that they would become self sufficient, or at least less reliant on the Jarls' caravans. The trees they felled were dragged agonisingly slowly up to the fortress where they were fashioned into the skeletons of new buildings, lanes and streets spreading out like arteries and veins through the fortress. Metellus and Accipiteri found themselves constantly having to shout down angry people as they tried to build haphazardly, buildings encroaching onto the main roads they had laid out. They knew that if the fortress were still to function properly then soldiers needed to be able to move quickly through the place.

Most of the buildings were going up on the southern edge of the outer courtyard, with others built against the walls of the inner courtyard, but there was still space for new arrivals. The walls were cleared of weeds and shrubs, and the rubble in the gaps was being cleared in preparation for the rebuilding effort. Domitia was a constant presence at Sigmund's side, offering advice and ultimately doing her best to make herself indispensable. Skjarla wondered if she was merely trying to shape the face of the fledgling fiefdom or whether the Roman was playing at some greater game. She kept her eye on her, but there was so much to do around the fortress that she couldn't spare herself the whole time. Instead she focused on getting the men and women under arms in a fit state to protect their new home against any threats.

Chapter 17

A month after the Jarls' visit Skjarla was on the north wall amid the pale dawn light, a fresh mist rolling down from the mountains to fill the valley of the pass. She had had trouble sleeping lately. The threat of the Fangs and the power they held hung over those all, she could not help but feel that she should be out there searching for them. She leant against the pitted black stones of the wall looking down at her hands. Skjarla Storm hands was the nickname she had been given by the people over the past few weeks, the lightning streaks of white against the black armour the inspiration.

Feelings of turmoil kept flooding through her head. Over the past month she had seen her friends grow closer together, particularly Helania and Accipiteri. Nothing definite had happened yet but they were growing closer, and Domitia was spending far more time with Sigmund, advising him on everything. Even Iskander had less time for her, the demands of organising the soldiers of the keep and acting as quartermaster for them kept him occupied for hours on end. She smiled at the thought of her rakish friend organising reports and preparing duty rosters. The truth of it had been that he was one of the few who could write properly, and so had got the post almost by default.

She was feeling her curse again. Seeing them all growing closer couldn't help but remind her of Heimdall and the fact that so many of her friends over the years were nothing but echoes within her memory. The thought of that happening filled her with sadness and reminded her that she should be on her way again; to see these friends grow old was something she would prefer to avoid.

The echoes of Heimdall seemed to weigh her down like an anchor attached to her heart. She still loved and adored the memory of him, yet she couldn't help but envy Accipiteri and Helania their romance. It was so alien compared to the explosive yet melancholic tumbles she had experienced over the past four centuries. She had found herself spending a lot more time with Metellus, the two of them drinking the hard spirit that the people had managed to distil from a small amount of grain that had been set aside.

He was in a similar mood to her, jealous of all the time which Sigmund was spending with Domitia even though he would never admit as such. That was part of why she was feeling so grey today, she had lain with Metellus the night before, safe in the knowledge that he would tell no one; he didn't want Domitia to find out. It had been a good evening, full of drunken vigour and passion, and Metellus had turned out to be a very attentive lover, focusing more on the pleasures of her body than his own. She had enjoyed the whole experience, but it been overshadowed by the fact that he was clearly imagining her as someone else, even as he thrust his body against hers. It was an alien feeling to her, feeling so soiled and used by someone so mortal, back in her Valkyrie days it would have been the other way round.

So it was that before the sun had dared show its head for the dawn, she had strapped on her armour and crept out of her chambers, leaving the softly snoring Roman behind as she made her way to the walls. She was distracted from her reverie by a flash from the mist further up the pass, coming over the rise. Her eyes were instantly peeled, trying to penetrate the fog, Dreyrispa gripped tightly in her gauntleted hand.

Seconds dragged on into minutes as she stood, motionless as a statue, peering into the gloom of the pre-dawn light. Silence reigned through the heavy white curtain which hung across the pass. Behind her there was silence as the people of Blackstone Castle slept silently in their beds. The shadows of the few men patrolling the inner wall prowled through the half light.

She was starting to doubt that she had seen anything when a small scatter of pebbles rolled out of the fog, followed by another flash of steel. Something was out there in the mist, and Skjarla doubted that whatever it was would be friendly. She stood, waiting to see what it was, wanting to know whether this was a threat or just a lost huntsman coming in.

Almost silently shapes began to materialise from the fog, the gently creak of leather and the soft jingle of mail reaching her ears. Her breath caught in her throat as she saw the giant bony crests emerging from the angular heads. There was no sound as they began to advance, the Children of the Dragon were communicating via their crests, flashes of colour giving orders silently. These Children were, for the most part, bigger and more imposing than the ones they had already encountered. She could see the cloud of fog running off their bodies like white water, falling away from them to cluster around their feet. They did not seem to be of this world as they advanced menacingly on the black granite walls.

As they marched on the breach in the walls Skjarla acted without thinking, using the only thing she could to warn the people behind her of the impending threat. She did something that she had never done before, reaching down to her hip and pulling the Gjallarhorn from its eternal place at her side. She placed her lips to the cold metal mouthpiece and blew with all the might and power she could muster.

The mournful, low note rolled out across the valley, echoing back from the mountains behind the Children to flood across the homes of Blackstone Castle. While people where leaping from their beds, wondering what had caused that noise, Skjarla was frozen in a moment. While everything around her seemed to move as if it was encased in ice she was staring at the most wondrous sight.

Floating before her eyes, stretching off into the mists, were the ethereal forms of the Aesir, glowing softly with an inner light. Tears sprang unbidden to her eyes as she took in the sight before her, Odin and all of the Gods before her, with the throng of Valkyries and Einherjar beyond them. She choked back a sob as she struggled to say, "Where are you?"

It seemed pathetic to her ear, but the All-father smiled gently to her, "We are nowhere, and yet everywhere. We are with you."

Heimdall spoke up as he saw her confusion, and the sound of his deep, melodic voice brought fresh floods of tears to her eyes. "You know we are gone Skjarla, but you are not alone. We are with you forever, so long as you breathe an echo of us lives on. So long as you still walk Midgard so do we."

There was a disorientating, rushing sensation as the mists closed around her. Suddenly it was only her and the watery figures of Heimdall and Odin left standing together. They were wrapped in the white cloak of the mists as they stood close to her, their soft glow seeming to make the swirling mists come to life. "Skjarla, you've got to stop thinking of what Hel did to you as a curse. You are the only reason we're still here. While some shard of the Aesir remains on the face of Midgard, enough people believe in us for us still to exist. We do not have the power of other gods, we are merely echoes, but without you we are dust.

Remember when I tell you that you are not alone." Odin gripped her shoulder tightly, his lone eye boring into hers as he tried to convince her of his message.

He held her for a moment before fading away, back into the mists, leaving her alone with Heimdall. She reached up and stroked his cheek, the silvery metal of her gauntlet disturbing the surface of the watery image. There were no words that could describe the feeling which flooded through her heart, all that there was was the moment, the feeling of being together after four centuries apart. He leant forward and kissed her forehead, stroking her hair softly, "Skjarla, I can't say how much I've missed you."

She swallowed hard, not trusting herself with words, just continuing to keep staring at him.

"Skjarla, I love you and I always will, but we are only echoes, and it does you no good to be chasing an echo until the end of time. Remember us but shed no tears for us, we died as we were destined to, and no one could escape that destiny, save you. We died as any good Norseman would have wished, and there are no regrets among us, you shouldn't have any either."

He started to fade slightly, "Wait, Where are you going?" Skjarla called out desperately.

His smile spoke volumes, all kinds of emotion carved into his strong features, sadness, joy, love and hope all were visible. "Where I've always been, in your heart and in your mind. We never left you and we never will, not until your dying day."

The mist suddenly seemed to close in around her, flowing into her and filling her with a sense of purpose and hope that she had not felt in centuries. She screamed suddenly as a burning sensation flooded through her limbs, the power flowing through her was incredible. As she came back to the present she heard a gentle pattering around her, like pebbles falling on the stones around her. As she glanced down she saw that scattered around her what looked like the remnants of burnt paper, scraps of blackened material.

She reached down to grab one to try to find out what it was, completely oblivious suddenly to the approaching reptilian Children. She nearly fell over in shock as she caught sight of her arm, gone were the silvery lightning bolt cracks, instead the armour was pure brilliant white. Her heart hammering she reattached the Gjallarhorn to her belt and reached down to grab her helmet. As she did so a curtain of blond hair fell across her vision. As much as she wanted to marvel in her restored appearance she had no time, the Children were barely fifty yards from the breach in the wall and there was the sound of commotion from within the fortress.

She sprinted along the wall, feeling the Gjallarhorn bouncing against her leg as she ran, heading for breach. There was no time for a careful descent; instead she half scrambled half fell down the stone wall. She landed heavily, feeling her left ankle give as her legs bent underneath her. As the Children closed down the last few yards she tested the joint, seeing how much weight she could put on it. She swore softly as she did so, able to rest the foot on the ground, but not able to support much weight at all.

A sudden mad urge to laugh shot through her. She couldn't run from here, and having finally found a reason to live she was likely to get what had been her fervent wish, death. Nonetheless she prepared herself for the fight, crouching low, most of her weight on the good leg and began to sway on the spot. The drums of war began to beat within her head; she could feel Dreyrispa thirsting for the blood of the foe. The Children started to stream up the bank to the breach, their breath hissing nastily and the clacking of their beaks rattling off the walls.

The first of them ran up to her and she cut the creature down, Dreyrispa shining through the air as it swung round and bit into the neck of the monster. Already she could hear the sounds of chaos behind her as Accipiteri and her friends organised the defenders but she didn't have time to think about that as the Children began to swamp her. She bit back another scream as she was forced to take a step back, putting her weight onto her bad ankle. This forced her off balance and a crude sword wielded by a muscular, scaled arm punched through her armour and into her shoulder.

She bellowed like a wounded animal as she struck down her attacker but dozens more were pouring through the breach. She swung Dreyrispa in wild arcs but she could not stop them all and the blows began to rain down upon her. Her armour was rent in half a dozen places and hot blood ran down her skin, mixing with the thick black blood of those she slew.

Her legs finally collapsed under her, her head ringing from the pounding blows to her helmet, and she tried to raise Dreyrispa on last time. Her vision blurred as she collapsed to the ground, but as she prepared for the coming oblivion she saw a streak of silver and gold as Accipiteri exploded into the ranks of the Children, his broadsword sending rivers of black blood flying through the air. She lost consciousness as the defenders pressed the Children of the Dragon back, away from her body.

"You men, get her to safety," Roared Accipiteri, viciously cleaving the skull of a heavily armoured Wyrmling. He was furious at himself for not having guards on the outer wall, someone who would have been able to support Skjarla in the fight. He couldn't help but admire the Valkyrie's suicidal bravery, throwing herself in front of the charging horde. There was no time to wonder how they got here, the only thing they could do was protect their new home. He was quietly impressed by the Svellvindr princesses, they had grabbed weapons and armour as soon as they heard the horn call and had been among the first people in the courtyard before the keep.

"Shields up, Shields up now. None of these bastards get through," Metellus's voice rang out from the lines, cajoling the Lonely Company into some semblance of order. Up on the wall, silhouetted against the dawn light Helania and two dozen archers could be seen making their way along the stone walkway. Iskander and the other Reavers were on the left edge of the line, helping to break up the charge before the Children hit the lines of defenders. One of them went down beneath the charge but there was no time to worry about that. Sigmund was at the centre of the line, the Iron Crown atop his helmeted head, Sigurd's banner next to him, and a rallying symbol for the defenders.

Accipiteri had never felt the burden of leadership so keenly. He didn't know if they could hold here, but if they fell back to the inner wall then they abandoned everything they had built in the courtyard. Worse still was that given the surprise nature of the attack he had no way of estimating the numbers arrayed against them? Even as he struck down another two Children, a broad swipe knocking them both to the ground he wondered at how they could have got here. They must have crossed the entire length of the Haemocracy before forging a passage through the burning sands of the Deserts of Vfar. He was reminded of what Skjarla had told him, that for them the search for the Fangs was not a duty but a physical need, they would never be complete until their master had been reformed.

The steel-clad defenders held resolutely in place as the sun peeked above the craggy black peaks, each locked in an endless series of personal duels. Glancing up to the wall Helania and her archers were engaged in a brutal struggle with some Children who had scaled the stone bulwark.

Accipiteri could feel the tide turning against them when he heard the low call of the Gjallarhorn again. He had no time to turn round but he heard the ragged cheer as the defenders caught sight of Skjarla, bandaged and battered but still standing defiantly beside the stallions of Sigurd's banner. Had he had time to turn he would have seen her, sword and shield in hand, bloody bandages poking through the gaps in her armour, pressing herself into the line. For someone so remote it was amazing what a talisman she was to then fighters, and seeing her in the line raised flagging spirits.

They fought with renewed vigour, fresh venom behind every strike of those two hundred blades, and they drove the Children back, reversing their earlier gains. Indeed, the Lonely Company fought with such fire and fury that the still limping Skjarla was left behind the advance. Still the Children would not give up in their fanatical pursuit of the Fang, and it was not until every last one of them had shed its black blood upon the earth that the defenders were able to stop.

Instantly most of them collapsed to the ground, sucking in great lungfulls of the crisp mountain air, heavy with the metallic taint of blood. Metellus swiftly cajoled some of them back to their feet and set them to work. Most of them were busy hauling the wounded clear of the mass of bodies, while others were given the grim task of cutting the throats of any of the Children still breathing. It was a bloody task and very quickly the men and women were covered from head to toe in black ichor, dripping from them like rock oil.

Skjarla limped back with the wounded, fresh blood seeping from soiled bandages, her ankle seemingly swollen to such an extent that her armoured boot was constricting it. In truth though, after the death of Appius there was no one who knew much of what to do for wounds beyond sewing them or tying them tightly with bandages.

Of the close to two hundred defenders there were one hundred and twenty four men and women either dead or wounded, and all of the rest carried minor scrapes. It broke Skjarla's heart to see Iskander in amongst the wounded, his face screwed up with pain as two men tried, as gently as they could, to splint his leg. Hobbling closer she could see that his knee was a swollen mess, crushed by one of the crude iron maces of the Children. He grimaced as they tugged the bandages tighter, "What a bloody awful way to go eh?" His usual mocking smile looked strained and sweat beaded on his brow.

Skjarla had been about to reply when Sigmund's voice broke over her, "You're not going anywhere. You're not going to die, and as far as I know you still have duties here in the Fortress." They saw Iskander sag slightly with relief.

"My thanks, Sire," and for one of the few times that Skjarla had heard his voice, he sounded sincere.

Sigmund helped Skjarla to an open space of floor where he left her in the care of one of the orderlies. He went among the people, offering words of encouragement, holding the hands of those whose wounds were too severe, talking to them softly as their life's blood flowed from their rent flesh. In that moment he became a king in the eyes of his people, a true leader who they would follow off the edge of Midgard.

***

Over the next fortnight life in the fortress returned to normal. The Children of the Dragon had been piled in a heap and burned beyond the fortress walls, an oily black column of smoke rising high into the sky. The dead from the fortress, sixty seven much mourned men and women were burnt in the central courtyard, the names of the dead roared to the sky. The wounded for the most part made a full recovery, though Iskander now walked with the aid of a crutch, the bones in his knee already fusing into an unsightly and unwieldy mass. Helania had a new scar, a white line carved into the black skin of her shoulder. She had been lucky that her collarbone had not broken under the force of the blow, but then, Dokkalfar steel was legendary.

Their resolute defence of the breach meant that there was very little damage to the buildings within the fortress so life was able to return to normal relatively quickly. The real consequence of the battle was that many more of the people turned out for the drill sessions. Most had no desire to fight in an army, but all now wanted the skill to defend their homes and Sigmund had no wish to deny them that. If anything it made him feel better about the coming war with Wotan, at least there would be some people able to defend the fortress while he was gone.

The problem was that there were now four hundred people training with blades, axes and anything else they could find. At least his ancestor had not left him short of arms but there was no way for the few leaders he had to effectively train all of the new recruits, some of whom he hoped would join the Lonely Company.

They were divided into several groups, the veterans spread around evenly and Sigmund and his friends helping to teach them. Many people were surprised by how much more companionable this new Skjarla was, leading them in drills and often helping and offering advice. She may be more approachable, but the people were still wary enough not to raise the subject of her changes, afraid of the answer they would get. Iskander seemed to be accepting his new role, helping with advice and becoming, to use a term common in the Haemocracy, the Seneschal of Blackstone Castle.

During a break in the training Helania had heard Accipiteri muttering to himself and once the crowd had dissipated she asked, "What were you doing during the funeral?"

Accipiteri smiled sheepishly, "I was commending the souls of the dead to the Goddess. They may not have followed her in life but they are worthy of a warm welcome into her halls."

Helania wasn't sure this was the right time, but her curiosity got the better of her, "Who exactly is this Goddess of yours? All you ever do is call her the Goddess, none of us know a thing about her."

Accipiteri smiled and his eyes took on a distant, faraway look. In truth he was glad that Helania asked about the Goddess, he wanted people to know about her but was never sure how to broach the subject. "She is the Lady of the Skies, mother of the Sun and Moon, bearer of the Winds. She is all that is good and she shines down on all of us, wishing we were all like her first born, the Sun." He saw Helania's puzzled glance, "The Sun is pure white light, and too many of us are like the Moon, reflections of that brilliance. She wishes that we become brilliant, glowing symbols of light in our own way."

Helania was slightly overawed by his fervour, unsure of what to say, so all she could manage was to laugh, "I think I, and the rest of my black skinned cousins may have difficulty becoming pillars of light." Accipiteri chuckled with her, but a shadow passed across his eyes as he did.

A week after the funeral for those who had given their lives something both momentous and amazing occurred. Skjarla, Sigmund and all the others ran to the wall after a shout of alarm and amazement from the men now stationed on watch there. Men and women grabbed their weapons in alarm, pressing up to the breach ready to defend their homes once more.

This was no invasion though, "What is it?" cried those below as the people on the wall let out a loud cheer. They had recognized the figure at the head of the column marching towards the fortress.

"Fjirsk, what's this with you?" bellowed Accipiteri cheerfully, but there was no cheerful response from the Dokkalfar. Instead he called his column to a halt and came forward with just one Dwarf, clad from head to toe in ominous black armour.

"Helania, Skjarla and Accipiteri, you're with me. Metellus, keep the Company ready in case something's wrong," Sigmund commanded, heading down the stairs with his small group of followers.

The Dwarf and Fjirsk had come to a halt fifty yards from the gateway, not wanting to stand in front of the breach in the walls.

Sigmund called out as he emerged from the shadowy maw of the gateway, his arrival precipitated by the clanking of chains as the portcullis was raised. "Who's that with you, Fjirsk? I asked you to find one Dwarf not an army." He smiled, but Fjirsk looked grim.

"I'll let him introduce himself, but you're not going to like the tidings he brings," Fjirsk looked pointedly at Skjarla as he spoke, his expression grim.

The Dwarf reached up and removed his black helm, the steel noticeably scarred and dented. The Dwarf had a severe face, dominated by a giant nose and a thick, black beard which had long since lost its lustre. Instead it was covered in dust and the grime of the road. His voice was tired and strained as he spoke, "I am Karst Sun hammer, and the people behind me," he pointed to the nervous crowd waiting at the crest of the pass, "Are all that remains of Sky's End."

Sigmund spoke quickly, "That sounds like a tale for later, what brings you to our door?"

Karst sucked in a nervous breath, "We were fleeing south, and in Sundark Hold and then again in Moonshadow Hold we heard of your column," he smiled at Skjarla, "The passage of a Valkyrie is something spoken of for a long time. The tale of what you planned to do and what had happened to your people seemed similar to ours. It seemed even more like destiny at Moonshadow Hold when Fjirsk was there saying that you needed Dwarven masons here.

We are here to become part of this Hold, we seek your protection, and in return we will swear fealty to you." Karst got down on one knee, kneeling before the man he hoped would be his new sovereign.

Sigmund got the Dwarf back to his feet, "We need more people here and there is no shortage of space. If you and your fellows will swear allegiance then I will protect all of you, see you fed and housed within these walls. How many people have you brought with you?"

Karst got back to his feet feeling relieved. Skjarla didn't say a word, but she and Helania both knew that for all of Karst's fine words they were his only option. Both knew that none of the Holds would have taken in refugees from the other kingdoms, the only options were surface cities and theirs would be preferable to semi slavery in the Haemocracy.

"Thank you. Truly, I thank you. There are nine hundred and eighty seven souls with me, seven hundred and thirty eight Dwarves and the rest Dokkalfar. We never had many of their kind in Sky's End."

Sigmund looked at a loss as to what to say next so Skjarla took over, "Get your people inside the walls. I'm not sure if we have buildings for them at the moment, but we should have the lumber for it soon. We'll have to hear what happened once they're inside, but get your people settled first. I assume you speak for them?"

"Yes, our entire royal family was killed defending the Hold, I was ordered to lead some men and what was left of our people to safety by our youngest prince." Karst looked ill at ease with the order; clearly leaving his home and his friends behind to die had not been easy for him. That was something which Skjarla could relate to; leaving behind all you'd known and everyone you'd ever loved was a crippling burden.

Karst jogged back up the gentle slope, his armoured plates clanking noisily as went to issue orders to the remnants of Sky's End. Fjirsk looked tired and worn out by the travails of his journey to and from Sundark Hold. His cloak was a worn rag and there were visible bags under his eyes.

Further up the pass the column of tired Dwarves and Dokkalfar began to make their way down the slope. They passed through the black gateway into the fortress, many of the people struggling under the weight of their burdens, carried on their backs the length of Midgard. Accipiteri felt a warm glow in his chest as he saw some of the defenders sheath their arms and help the newest refugees with their burdens, clearly remembering their own experiences. Maybe a third of the column was under arms, but from what Helania and Skjarla knew Sky's End had always been one of the most martial of Holds.

When the people of Sky's end were finally settled in to the space at the northern end of the outer courtyard Sigmund gathered his court so Karst could tell them what happened. The black armoured Dwarf stood at the centre of the great hall, explaining what had brought his people to the gates of the fortress. "For three days we felt the gentle tremors beneath the fortress, but on the fourth day they broke through the stone, bypassing the walls and emerging amongst the streets. Thousands of these lizard like creatures, covered in bony spines with these great crests killing anything that moved."

"The Children of the Dragon, Fafnir's children. We have had our share of unfortunate encounters with those monstrosities as well. Please, continue," interjected Accipiteri flushing slightly as he realised he probably shouldn't have spoken.

Karst looked visibly shaken by this, "You mean the legends are true? The Dragon really existed and those monsters are hunting for a way to bring their master back from the dead?"

"I'm afraid that it is all too true," Sigmund said as he lifted the Fang from beneath his armour to show Karst, "What happened then?"

"There was no reason to it; they were committed to senseless slaughter. Men, women and children, there was no mercy and there was no end to the sea of scaled bodies spilling from their new tunnel. For three days we fought, making them pay a heavy price in blood for every inch of ground they took, but always our numbers shrank before their seemingly endless might. At the end of the third day I was ordered to take enough men to protect all the surviving refugees and flee south while the rest of the Hold's forces bought us time to escape." Karst's tale came to an abrupt end, the thickset Dwarf was overcome with emotion, a feeling Sigmund could easily sympathise with.

"As I said earlier, you and your people are welcome in the fortress, provided you swear to follow my banner. If any among you has any skill with stone we would be most grateful for your help. As I am sure you could see, our walls are in dire need of repair."

Karst smiled grimly, "Sky's End was renowned for the quality of our stone. You'll have no complaints on that front. We will take our oath to you now if that suits you, sire."

"Come outside, we'll get this over and done with." Sigmund clearly did not sound comfortable about having yet more lives in his responsibility, but he could not turn them away. He could not live with himself if he did that. The small group made their way out of the black stone of the great hall, out onto the dust of the training yard where the nervous looking crowd of Dwarves and Dokkalfar stood. Many of them relaxed visibly when they saw Helania standing with the king, things must be different here for the elder races if one of them stood so close to the crown.

Karst's voice bellowed across the space, a voice used to giving orders and having them obeyed. "The King in the Iron Crown has agreed to take in all those who wish to join his kingdom. I for one do, but I will not force any of you, my brothers and sisters of the bloody road we have taken, to do so. Those who wish to stay here – kneel and swear allegiance to the Iron Crown."

With that he knelt down in the dust before Sigmund, and all of the grim looking refugees followed suit. The thought of swearing fealty to a Human lord might once have been abhorrent to them, but their circumstances were different now. They had only two things on their minds, safety and vengeance.

Sigmund spoke, his voice carrying across the crowd, both the refugees and the people of the fortress who had gathered to catch a glimpse of this strange spectacle. "People of Sky's End, will you swear to follow my orders and serve Blackstone Castle to the best of your abilities? If you will then I in turn swear to protect you and one day to lead you to vengeance against the Children of the Dragon who so cruelly robbed you of your homes and your loved ones. Will you serve?"

As one their voices rang out, "By Stone and Sky, by Blood and Steel, we will swear to follow the Iron Crown."

"Then rise, and together we shall build the greatest city on the face of Midgard." He helped Karst to his feet and the rest of the people from Sky's End followed suit, glancing nervously around them. Although they had not had much choice they had still committed their futures to an unknown power with the most solemn oath the people of Sky's End had.

Chapter 18

Domitia was woken by the squeaking of a door, not hers but either Sigmund's or Metellus's, it could only be one of those two as they were her only neighbours though others were further down the stone corridor. She waited in silence, the darkness wrapped around her like a blanket as she listened out for any sound. A moment later she heard the door squeak softly open again. Intrigued she got to her feet and shuffled to the door, trusting the white night dress to protect her dignity from any unwanted gazes.

Quietly she poked her head through the door and peered out into the corridor, lit by a few smouldering torches wedged into their brackets on the wall. She caught sight of Sigmund standing silently with his hands frustratedly on his hips, glowering at the door to his chambers.

"Psst," she hissed at him, trying not to wake the people around her.

Sigmund jumped out of his skin, looking around for the source of the noise while his hand shot to the hilt of his sword. He caught sight of Domitia's head poking out through her doorway and relaxed, "Oh, it's you. You didn't have to make me jump you know."

She smiled softly, "Sorry." She paused for a heartbeat, "Why are you standing outside your door? It must be gone midnight."

He walked closer to her so that they could talk in whispered tones, but before he could answer her she spoke again, "Come in, that way we won't disturb everyone else around here."

Sigmund looked nervous, "Are you sure, you must be shattered, I wouldn't want to keep you awake," he gabbled.

"I'm more worried about you waking up the others; I can't imagine that they'd be particularly happy." She raised her eyebrows as she looked at him with a coldly piercing gaze. He relented and let her lead him into her room.

He stepped inside the room, lit by the dim glow of a single candle, the furs on the bed crumpled in a pile. The walls were the plain black stone of everywhere else; the only concession to comfort was the threadbare rug on the floor. A battered wardrobe lent against one wall, the soft colours of the Roman princess's clothes just visible between the cracked doors.

Domitia sat down of the edge of the bed, the straw filled mattress rustling softly as it took her weight. Sigmund felt his breath catch as the heavy wool shift she was sleeping in shifted to reveal the creamy skin of her thigh. Unconsciously he shook his head, trying to dislodge the image from his mind. He lent against the wall, facing her as she spoke, "So what had you wandering the halls so late at night?"

Sigmund smiled and shook his head, "I had just finished planning the new granary with Accipiteri and was looking forward to some sleep, but when I opened my door I could see someone in my bed."

Domitia giggled prettily, "Who was it?"

"I didn't bother to check, it's not the first time one of the Jarls' daughters has tried to sneak herself into my bed." Silence hung heavy in the air for a moment, "I'd better get going, and I don't want to keep you up."

She smiled guilelessly at him, "Where will you go?"

Sigmund frowned with concentration, thinking hard for a moment, "I'm not sure, last time there was a cot free up in the watch-tower at the top of the keep. Now we've got more sentries though I might not have much luck there. I think I'll go and see if they've got a bed down at Journey's End," Journey's End was the inn Bran had opened in the fortress. Staggeringly, the portly innkeeper had survived the privations of the journey to resume his trade here in Blackstone Castle.

She smiled and shrugged, saying as casually as she could manage, "You could always stay here, the bed is big enough for us to be comfortable without being awkwardly close and I'm only too happy to help my king."

Sigmund went scarlet. "I couldn't do that." He realised what that must have sounded like and stammered hurriedly, "By which I mean I couldn't impose on you like that, not that I wouldn't be honoured to spend the night with you." He did a second double take as his brain caught up with his mouth, "I don't mean spend the night with you, I mean," he deflated as his shoulders slumped, "I hope you know what I mean."

In spite of herself she smiled at his discomfort, a soft chuckle tumbled forth from her lips. "I understand," she said as she lifted the thick bearskin and slid her legs underneath. She looked at Sigmund pointedly as he stood rooted to the spot, trying to make up his mind. She arched one flawless eyebrow and he moved. He stalked around the foot of the bed like some cornered animal before gingerly lifting the furs. She laughed, "I don't bite Sigmund," she paused for a moment before adding lasciviously, "Well, not that hard."

Sigmund felt his heart give the most terrible thump and Domitia's expression before she blew out the candle made him very grateful that his thick leather trousers hid the rush of blood to his groin. He could hear the blood pounding in his ears as they lay there in the darkness, silence stretching out between them. He felt her hand moving beneath the furs, seeking out his and giving his fingers an affectionate squeeze. He tried to sleep, but the incessant pumping of blood, laden with adrenaline meant that it was impossible.

After a few minutes he heard Domitia whisper softly, "Are you always this nervous close to women? I can practically feel it from here."

Sigmund had lain with a few girls back in Lonely Barrow, but no one as beautiful or as exotic as Domitia. He didn't trust himself to say anything, fearing his voice would betray him. He heard the gentle rustle of the furs next to him, unable to pick out any movement in the pitch black darkness of the room. The first he knew of what was going on was as Domitia's lips pressed themselves firmly yet tenderly against his, opening his mouth slightly as her tongue caressed his.

He felt a rush of desire, wrapping his arms around her slender shoulders he pulled her deeper into the kiss. She broke the kiss for a moment, moving herself so she was on top of him, feeling him relax beneath her as she came back to kiss him again. She waited until his hands had started to roam over her body, softly caressing her breasts through her night dress before trying to pull his own shirt over his head. The Fang was still nestled on his chest but she left it there, not wanting him distracted from what was going on.

Sigmund felt a voice, somewhere in the back of his mind whispering softly that this was wrong, but he didn't care, it felt so right. He felt it as she pulled off her night dress, his hands exploring every inch of her bare skin, his eyes still blinded by the darkness. He heard her soft moans as his fingers danced over her tingling skin. She moved off him so she could pull off his trousers and suddenly panic hit him.

Domitia felt his tension and whispered up to him, "Relax, my king." She heard him suck in a ragged breath as she bent her head low over his groin, focusing on him for a few moments. When she heard his breaths get shorter and more urgent she climbed atop him, placing his hands on her hips she slid him inside her. She pinned him to the bed by his shoulders as she writhed atop him, moving until she heard him give one final groan of pleasure and felt his whole body tense beneath her.

Effortlessly she slid off him, lying beside him with her head cushioned on his chest, listening to the thundering of his heart, like the sound of horses at full gallop. Eventually he managed a breathy, "That was amazing," even to his ear the words sounded awkward, a feeble way to express the feelings she had awoken within him. She responded by kissing him, this time just a chaste peck on the lips which left him wanting more.

He felt sleep begin to creep over him in the darkness and murmured idly, "Life would be so much easier if it was you I was marrying rather than one of the Jarls' daughters."

There was a pause and he fretted in the silence, terrified that he had offended her. "Why not?" came her coy reply, "Would it really be such a terrible thing? I mean would you rather be married to someone you barely know? A woman whose father will more than likely want you out of the way as soon as possible or to someone you've known for far longer?"

Sigmund was suddenly back awake, slightly scared by how quickly this conversation was moving, yet he couldn't but grudgingly admit that she had a point. "I suppose you're right. If I have to get married to someone then I'd rather it was a friend." He paused for a second, unable to read her expression in the darkness, "But are you seriously considering this?"

"Yes, and I think we should do it. I have found a new home here, a new life with your people and I don't want to lose that to some Vindrman Jarl. So yes, I think we should marry on the date you promised the Jarls."

Sigmund's mind swam, it was moving much faster than he had ever thought possible. So much of what she said was right, and it would seem so wrong to say no after what they had just shared. With a thundering heart and a mouth as dry as the deserts of Vfar he uttered a single word, "Yes."

"If you mean you think we should get married as well, you've done the right thing, Sigmund," she said joyfully, leaning in to give him one more passionate kiss before returning to her place, nestled into his side. The cloak of darkness hid the satisfied smile she wore, and the gleam of triumph in her eyes.

***

The news had gone around the fortress like wildfire, and the reactions were mixed to say the least. While many of the Jarl's daughters had been infuriated by Sigmund's decision the majority of the people had approved of him keeping the Jarls from having too much influence over them.

There were others, like Skjarla, who were deeply suspicious as to why Domitia had proposed this union, but they kept their doubts to themselves, waiting to see how events played out. There had never been a true spark of romance between the pair, but in their defence that wasn't easy amongst a crowd of refugees fleeing an implacable hunter. Only one person actually voiced their true feelings on the matter.

Metellus caught his mistress as she was entering her chambers, grabbing her wrist as she tried to avoid him, just as she had been doing all day. He gently but hurriedly pushed her into her chambers, closing the door softly behind them; he did not want to be overheard.

"Domina, why? What would your father say if he saw you prostituting yourself to this barbarian?"

She looked at him coldly, the reflected light of the smouldering torch gleaming in her eyes, setting them aflame like the fiery orb of the setting sun. Her face pale with fury she pried his fingers from around her wrist one by one. Her voice was cold as she locked eyes with him. "You forget your place Centurion," she put emphasis on using his rank instead of his name. Metellus flinched backwards as if struck.

Suddenly he felt rage and frustration welling up within him, "My place? Domina my place is where it has always been, at your side, protecting you and that is why I ask again, why this barbarian? I am trying to protect you from yourself and I have a right to know. Do you know how many times I have bled for you, how many times a part of me has died as I have watched the life flee from one of my men? And I have done all this without complaint, for you, surely that gives me the right to know your mind" He finished softly his eyes falling away from her as the fight seemed to flow out of him.

While she seethed internally at his effrontery Domitia knew that she could not afford to alienate her one true ally in this place, the one person she could trust absolutely. She knew how he felt about her, and as much as she disliked it she knew she had to use those feelings against him, to get her own way without having to issue orders.

She fiddled with one of cords which knotted about her waist with one hand, looking down demurely for a moment, letting the uncomfortable silence build, watching through her lashes as Metellus began to shift uncomfortably. Her voice was quiet forgiveness when it finally spilled forth from her lips, "You're right, you are my most faithful servant, my one advisor and as such you deserve an explanation."

She walked across the room and sat on the edge of the bed, the furs rustling slightly as they shifted beneath her, and gestured for Metellus to take the plain wooden chair against the wall. He walked stiffly across the room, unable to avoid the feeling that he had overstepped some invisible boundary, irreconcilably altered the bond between them. He heard every crash of his hobnailed sandals as he crossed the few paces of stone flagged floor to sit facing him mistress. His hands were suddenly twitchy, unsure of what to do with themselves. He felt like a badly behaved schoolboy.

"Metellus, you ask why I've done this, and the reason is simple. I need him to reclaim what is rightfully mine. If we return without an army at our backs we will be dead within minutes of setting foot on Roman soil. With these people to fight for us I can take my rightful place as Empress of Rome."

Metellus was more than a little unnerved by the fire burning in her eyes, the crazed obsession with the imperial throne. "But Domina, won't Sigmund become the Emperor? He will be your husband, which would put him on the Imperial throne by our laws."

She smiled a toothy smile, her face carved into a triumphant, malicious grin. She reached up with both hands and pushed her long hair behind her ears in a smooth, sinuous motion, "That is the beauty of it Metellus. The senate will refuse to recognize the marriage, they will not have a barbarian on the Imperial throne, plus each one of them will have his eye on marrying me and seating himself upon my throne," she scowled angrily, her features wrinkling with distaste as she did so. "Those old slugs would seek to supplant me, but I shall be in a position to take a Roman husband of my choosing. Someone who has served me loyally all through my exile." She left the unspoken promise hanging in the air between them, watching carefully as emotions warred within his breast.

Metellus's heart leapt at the thought of being with Domitia, and yet his stomach felt like it was falling down an endless well at the thought of becoming emperor. He knew that he would just be a puppet for her, but that didn't bother him. He had never wanted to be involved in politics, but if it meant that he could have her then he would willingly be her figurehead. Even though he had come to a conclusion he could not think of anything worth saying. Choking down the bile he felt at not expressing any true feelings he numbly intoned, "I serve and obey Domina. My apologies for the intrusion." With a wave of her hand she dismissed him, not even bothering to let her eyes follow him out of the room, she was too preoccupied with her success. She had shored up one wavering supporter and she was one step closer to being able to direct the fury of these barbarians against the usurper.

Chapter 19

Preparations for the coming wedding sent the fortress mad. They had two weeks to organise everything, although they were helped by Sigmund's insistence that it should not be too lavish, although the feast was still going to make the first one in Blackstone Castle look like a fast. Skjarla had been watching Domitia like a hawk since she had insisted on being married in the traditional Svellvindr fashion. For a woman who was Roman to her fingertips this seemed like a surprising concession and Skjarla was trying to work out what advantage Domitia gained from this.

From the women the Jarls had left behind to compete for Sigmund's affections, there was little in the way of disappointment. Most of them had only agreed to do so as a way of improving their family's standing. If they were honest with themselves, most of them would say that, while they liked and respected Sigmund for the good man he was, not one of them could honestly say that she loved him. Of the twelve, one of them spoke to Iskander, asking to be allowed to stay on in the fortress to fight.

Iskander had sucked air in through his teeth, buying himself precious seconds to corral his thoughts. Normally he would have had a quick retort and sly smile for her, but he felt less and less like his old self with every day that his knee continued to protest at the slightest hint of weight. The girl was just as he expected a Vindrman princess should be, fire in her icy blue eyes, straw-coloured hair spilling in a waterfall of gold down to her shoulders. She was tall and strong, but not heavily muscled; she had the heart of a fighter and the look of someone desperate for adventure.

He wasn't mistaken on that front; Myra knew that all that awaited her back in her father's longhouse was to be married off to one of his Huscarls. She had four older brothers, her father's bloodline was secure and all he was now interested in was getting a good bride price for her. She had avoided it so far, but her father had sworn that she would be married by her twentieth summer and this solstice would mark that awful day. The only way to avoid her fate was to be enlisted by the Iron Crown. She wasn't solely trying to avoid marriage though, she had always idolised the ancient tales of the Valkyries, the warrior maidens of the dead gods. Having seen Skjarla from a distance, and seen the women of the lonely company she was sure that she could be a success here, she just had convince the charming rogue before her.

"Look, Myra, I know you're a good fighter, I saw you rush out of the keep even before I was in the field." He saw her face light up and felt his heart sink further, "But, girl, you have to understand, in your case it is not just about being handy with a blade."

"Why not," she demanded fiercely, slamming her fist one the plain wooden table which separated them, "All those other women fight for you, why can't I?"

Iskander gently rubbed knee, feeling the puckered mass of barely healed scar tissue and the misshapen joint beneath it. He growled, more viciously than he would have liked, "It's more complicated than that, and you well know it. What will your father say when he finds out we have taken his only daughter into our army without even asking him?"

"Thanks for taking her off my hands, one less mouth to feed," she suggested with a smile in a reasonable impression of her father, the gruff Jarl Ragnar.

Iskander's mouth split in the first genuine smile he had managed in several weeks. "Be that as it may, I can't agree on my own," he held up his hand to forestall her quick retort, "But I will speak to the Sigmund. If he agrees then I see no reason why you can't stay on." His voice dropped to a more serious note, "However, if you do stay with us then know that you won't get any special treatment as the daughter of a Jarl, you'll just be another soldier."

It genuinely warmed his heart to see the smile that split her face, pure joy in her eyes as she, on impulse, lent across the table and kissed him on the cheek before almost dancing out of the room. In spite of himself he smiled affectionately at the figure retreating from the small rooms he occupied. He shook his head and muttered to himself, "She's far too young, even by your standards." Disgusted with his sudden attack of morality he went to go and find Skjarla, his wooden crutch echoing off the stone work with every step.

***

Accipiteri and Helania walked the newly restored section of wall hand in hand, the black stone in stark contrast to the pale blue of the mountain sky and the bright heat of the early summer sun. The work to the walls was still going on and had been much more extensive than they had originally thought. Karst and a dozen of his best masons from the small group of Sky's End refugees had toured the walls at length, proclaiming long stretches of wall not up to standard. At least they had not been up to Dwarven standards, but none of the humans or he himself had noticed anything wrong with the masonry.

"What do you think will happen after this wedding?" Helania asked, stopping to rest against the stone of the wall, peering out over the gently rolling, forested lands of the Vindrmen.

"There's a council of war planned for the day after the wedding, that's when we'll know for sure." Accipiteri stood beside her and slid his muscular arm around her thin shoulders, giving her a reassuring squeeze.

She turned to face him, looking up into his eyes, "Yes, but what do you think will happen? That was my question,"

He sighed and let go of her, a frustrated look on his face, "There can be no true war this year. We may raid Wotan's lands but too many of the Jarls' men will be busy taking in the harvest for a meaningful campaign, that will come next year. I suspect Skjarla will push for us to search for more of the Fangs, but she has to realise that unless we have somewhere safe to keep them then they may as well stay hidden. Also, I am going to send someone, or go myself, to the city of Taureum. We could do with hiring a mercenary company to bolster our numbers."

He turned back to her and smiled sadly, seeing she was concerned by the level of frustration in his voice, "It's nothing you've done, it's just that it means another year will pass before I have even the smallest hope of the Goddess granting me my wings."

He turned to continue their walk and almost didn't hear her whisper sadly, "At least one more year before you leave me."

He stopped as if struck, the realisation that she would be unable to follow him back to the Windswept Isle, his people were very suspicious of outsiders, especially Dokkalfar. Maybe there would be some way to change that; if the Goddess gave him wings then he may be able to convince his people to accept Helania.

He sighed, but couldn't bring himself to turn around and look at her as he said, "We'll make that leap when we get to that cliff." A favourite saying of his people but one which sounded hollow even to his ear in that moment.

***

The Jarls arrived the day before the wedding, coming in over the course of the day, accompanied only by small bands of their most loyal Huscarls. Sigmund made sure that he was there to greet each of them as they came into the newly restored fortress. He could see their eyes widen as they took in the strengthened and repaired walls. Although the outer wall at the far end of the fortress was still being worked on that section was hidden from view.

When Jarl Ragnar, the fourth to arrive, rode through the gates Sigmund waited for him to dismount and greeted him formally before drawing him aside for a moment. "Your daughter Myra, I wanted to speak to you about her."

Ragnar's eyes narrowed suspiciously, "Not been causing trouble has she?"

"No, nothing like that, Myra came to me asking to be allowed to stay here and be trained to fight in the Lonely Company. From what my quartermaster tells me she has no small amount of skill and could do well. I am inclined to grant her request, unless you have some objection."

The Jarl made a show of thinking hard about the request but secretly he was delighted. If his daughter remained at home then he would have to pay some expensive dowry for her, but this way she would be independent and no longer his problem. With a reluctant stroke of his thick red beard he told Sigmund, "If her heart is set on it then who am I to deny her happiness, but I want you to protect her as best you can, she is my flesh and blood." He offered his arm and Sigmund gripped his callused, scarred hand tightly as he shook it, noticing the dozen silver bands looped around the arm, warrior's rings.

Any further conversation they might have had was curtailed by a shout from the sentry, "Sig ..." the man caught himself before he finished the name. Domitia had instructed them that while the Jarls were around they were to address him formally; a subtle reminder to the Jarls that he was now their lord. "Sire, another banner has been sighted, it's Jarl Knut."

Sigmund was suddenly anxious again, he wanted news of Braugr, the last they had heard from the Dwarf had been his farewells as he stepped beyond the threshold of the fortress. He muttered a brief apology to Jarl Ragnar and dashed across the courtyard and up the stairs to the wall, his feet pounding against the black stones. From his vantage point he could see the rippling sea green of the banner, from this distance unable to pick out the three crossed swords on the Jarl's banner. Beneath the fluttering cloth he could pick out the Jarl, the only man mounted, surrounded by a dozen steel clad Huscarls. He waited as the column made its steady way up the gently sloping dust track to the fortress.

Impatiently he made the formal greetings as the Jarl reined in before the imposing ironclad gates, welcoming the man back to Blackstone Castle. The gates opened with barely a sigh on the freshly oiled hinges, the grease of bear fat having only been applied the day before. As Knut slipped from the saddle, landing with feline grace on the pressed earth beneath him, Sigmund came over to speak to him, only to see that he had been beaten to it by Helania.

"Jarl Knut, if I might have a moment of your time, do you know if my friend, the Dwarf, arrived safely in Islen?"

The Jarl smiled at her eagerness, nodding subtly to the Huscarls who had half drawn blades as she had rushed up to him. They carefully sheathed them while he spoke, "The dragon ship I sent had not returned when I left," he saw her face fall and continued, "but there is nothing strange in that, it is a long journey across the waves to the port of

Islen. What's more, I know that Leif Stemson is one of the finest helmsmen you could ask for, your friend will be fine." That seemed to end their conversation and Jarl swept off towards the keep, his steel scale armour glinting in the sun beneath the sea green cloak he wore.

Sigmund managed to catch her eye before she made her way back to the keep, and she gave him a small smile and nodded. It was enough for him to know that Braugr was still safe.

**

The day of the wedding was seemingly blessed by the heavens themselves. The dawn sun set the sky aflame, a good omen by Vindrman standards; they believed that it heralded coming war and riches. There was not a cloud in the sky as the sun burnt a glorious path across the pale blue infinity.

The audience chamber of the keep had been cleared, there was no need of seating as the Vindrman ceremony was simple and quick, designed to get people on to the feast as fast as possible. A riotous collection of banners hung down from the vaulted ceiling, reds, greens, blues and golds all mingling high above the multitudinous throng that had packed into the hall. Still more of the people stood outside, peering in through the high doors which had been jammed open for the day, allowing a cool summer's breeze to alleviate the stifling heat within the packed room.

Down the length of the central aisle stood men and women of the Lonely Company, their armour buffed to a mirror shine under the watchful eye of Iskander. Intermingled with them were a few of the Jarl's guards, each man and woman holding a sword ready to salute the married couple. The thrones atop the dais had been removed, replaced with a plain stone table, atop which sat a pair of plain golden bands, glowing softly in the sunlight pouring through the doorway. Around the edge of the Dais, looking out over the crowd were the Jarls, along with Helania, Iskander, Karst, Accipiteri and Skjarla. Two of the Jarls had been suspicious of sharing the space with two of the Elder races, but Skjarla had been able to convince them.

It was strange that most of the Vindrmen had no problem with the Elder races, but some of them still blamed their cowardice for the changes of Midgard. Most knew that Ragnarok was a matter of fate, whether or not the Dokkalfar and the Dwarves had shared the fate of their Ljosalfar cousins, the days of the Aesir had always been numbered.

There was a hush, quickly followed by a murmur of whispered conversations which built to a roar as Sigmund made his way up to the makeshift altar. Even Skjarla had to admit that he looked good. His ancestor's armour was polished so that it seemed to burn in the sunlight. Sigurd's blade hung from his hip, the razor sharp steel hidden beneath the soft leather of his scabbard. Out of the corner of his eye he saw the strained faces of some of the Jarls. They weren't as happy about this as they pretended to be, secretly they each wished that it was their daughter who was about to marry Sigmund.

As his feet took the heavy steps up onto the dais he heard Skjarla's voice whisper, "Are you sure that you want this? You don't have to marry her you know."

Carefully keeping his face serene he whispered back, "You know my deal with the Jarls, this is the only way to stop one of them from trying to kill me." He tried to look relaxed, but they could all see his hand locked tight around the hilt of Sigmund's sword.

Any retort Skjarla had was silenced by the fanfare of trumpets, their clarion call cutting through the burble of voices. As one the heads of the crowd turned to watch Domitia walk up the aisle towards her betrothed. Domitia looked radiant, her emerald green eyes acquiring a hitherto unseen depth against the white of her dress. The long flowing garment jarred with her face, tanned by the months of travelling and working in Blackstone Castle. She was accompanied down the aisle by Metellus and the last remaining Roman legionaries. Her guard of honour were similarly impressive, their giant shields proudly displaying the heraldry of Rome.

The small group marched down the carpeted aisle in a stately fashion, completely ignoring the guards on either side or the multitude of people surrounding them. As they reached the dais Domitia and Metellus climbed to stand beside Sigmund.

In solemn silence Sigmund drew his ancestor's blade and handed it to Domitia. The Vindrmen tradition said that she should hold it in trust for when their son came of age, but they had both agreed to return the blade after the ceremony. Domitia kissed the blade reverently before coughing softly, at which Metellus drew his own blade and offered it to Sigmund, a sign that he was now her protector rather than the centurion. A raucous cheer went up as Sigmund raised the blade to the crowd, before resting it on the stone altar with the rings.

Domitia moved first, picking the larger of the two golden bands and sliding it onto her new husband's finger, the ring resisting as she tried to force it over the larger joint. After a second it slid over the bone but she saw Sigmund wince as it did so. He then returned the favour, sliding the daintier of the two rings onto Domitia's soft hand.

She looked down at the ring, her face hidden from view for a moment as her long hair fell in a curtain around her countenance. In this brief moment of privacy she allowed herself a small, satisfied smile. The first stage of her plan to recover her empire was complete, soon she would have this naïve young man wrapped around her finger and she could point him and his armies at the traitor Tarpeus. Her head came back up; smiling radiantly for the crowd, hand in hand with her new husband, but beneath the mask the smile was altogether more sinister. It was a smile that promised blood, and tears, and betrayal.

Continued in Book II; Wings of Fire